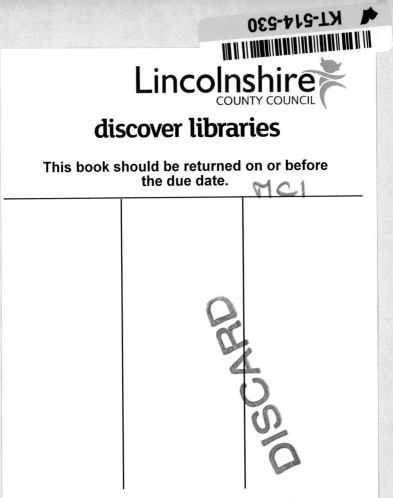

KT-514-530

Lincolnshire
COUNTY COUNCIL

discover libraries

This book should be returned on or before the due date.

MCI

author of The Night Sister

'What Remains of M~~e is a riveting, emotionally complex~~
thriller, filled with ch
grab your heart unti
This is Alison G

05126149

A. L. GAYLIN

A.L. Gaylin's first job was as a reporter for a celebrity tabloid, which sparked a lifelong interest in writing about people committing despicable acts. More than a decade later, she wrote and published her Edgar-nominated first novel, HIDE YOUR EYES. She's since published eight more books, including the USA Today and international bestselling Brenna Spector suspense series, which has been nominated for the Edgar, Anthony and Thriller awards and won the Shamus award. She lives in upstate New York with her husband, daughter, cat and dog.

Praise for **WHAT REMAINS OF ME**

'Label me a big fan.' Harlan Coben

An exceptional book by and exceptional writer. Gaylin is an expert at acute emotional observation combined with seamless plotting. I adored this book.' Alex Marwood

'What Remains of Me is an elegantly constructed thriller that earns every your-never-saw-it-coming turn. You'll stay up late to read it, then hound your friends to follow suit so you can stay up late to talk about it.' Laura Lippman

'Prepare to be blown away by this powerfully suspenseful and richly atmospheric novel.'
Jennifer McMahon, New York Times bestselling

it is a riveting, emotionally complex
characters who jump from the page and
until you reach the final, stunning twist.
Gaylin in top form.' Alafair Burke

A.L.GAYLIN

WHAT REMAINS OF ME

arrow books

1 3 5 7 9 10 8 6 4 2

Arrow Books
20 Vauxhall Bridge Road
London SW1V 2SA

Arrow is part of the Penguin Random House group of companies
whose addresses can be found at global.penguinrandomhouse.com

Penguin
Random House
UK

First published by William Morrow in 2016
(First published in Great Britain by Arrow in 2016)

http://www.penguinrandomhouse.com/

A CIP catalogue record for this book is available from the British Library

ISBN 9781784756185
ISBN 9781784756192 (export)

Printed and bound in Great Brtain by Clays Ltd, St Ives Plc

MIX
Paper from
responsible sources
FSC   FSC® C018179
www.fsc.org

Penguin Random House is committed to a
sustainable future for our business, our readers
and our planet. This book is made from Forest
Stewardship Council® certified paper.

FOR JAMES CONRAD, FOREVER MY "MAIN"

I would like more sisters, that the taking out of one,
might not leave such stillness.

—EMILY DICKINSON

At Carpentia Women's State Correctional Facility in Central California, the thermostat is always kept at a chilly 55 degrees. There's a practical psychology in this, one of the guards tells me. In cooler temperatures, prisoners are more alert and productive, more courteous too.

"The heat," the guard says, black velvet eyes belying his tall, muscular frame. "It does things to people."

In a way, Kelly Lund's story proves out the guard's point, for it was on June 28, 1980—the hottest night of the year—that Lund, then 17 and hopped up on a combination of marijuana and cocaine, walked into the Hollywood Hills mansion of Oscar-nominated director John McFadden and, in the midst of his own wrap party, shot him to death. Was it the heat, not the drugs, that drove this ordinary girl to enter a home filled with Tinseltown elite—with uber-cool rock stars and impossibly sleek models and the silver screen gods and goddesses whose glorious faces graced the pages of the movie magazines that lonely Kelly was known to have stashed under her bed?

Was it the 93-degree temperature—and perhaps the blinding rage it sparked—that propelled this Hollywood have-not past a glittering constellation of haves and into McFadden's opulent, Moroccan-themed living room where, finding him alone, she pumped three bullets into his chest and skull?

I consider that possibility now, as the guard leads me into Lund's cell—the tidy, dull square that has been her home for the past seven years. And as I reach the cell to find her sitting on her cot in her institutional orange, I decide, in my own way, to raise the issue.

"Kelly, do you ever miss the sun?"

She turns her gaze up to me, her gray eyes hard, dry as prison bars. In seven years, Kelly Lund hasn't aged a day. It's hard to imagine she ever will. Her skin is unlined, the whole of her as impervious to time as she is to all transformative emotions—shame, regret, caring. Guilt.

"The sun is still there," *she says.* "No reason to miss it."

"John McFadden isn't here anymore."

"That's right."

"Do you miss him?"

"I don't know."

"Do you feel bad about killing him?"

"It was meant to be."

"His death?"

"Yes."

"How do you know?"

"If it wasn't, someone would have noticed me before I made it into the den." *She pauses for a moment, deciding whether or not to go on. Weighing her options.* "I see myself," *she says, finally,* "as an agent of fate."

"Fate didn't murder John McFadden, Kelly. You did."

Lund's gaze drifts, and for a moment, she appears immersed in the dull gray wall of her cell, as though she sees something in it that exists in herself. "You have your belief system," *she tells me.* "I have mine."

On one level, it is probably a defense mechanism, Kelly Lund's complete lack of spark, of color. When she was just 15, her fraternal twin sister, Catherine, stole their mother's car, drove to Chantry Flats—a remote overlook in the San Gabriel Valley favored by lovers—and took her own life by flinging herself into the canyon. An aspiring actress, Catherine had been everything Kelly Lund was not—beautiful, vibrant, and with a natural charisma potent enough to gain her entry into Hollywood's young party circuit at the tender age of 14. But she was also troubled, vulnerable—the type of girl who felt everything a little too deeply—and who ultimately, tragically, let those feelings get the best of her.

Conversely, it may have been Kelly Lund's very blandness that kept her alive and afloat in the same tank of sharks that devoured her sister. The block of ice to Catherine's fast-burning flame, Kelly had few friends, and—outside of a brief and puzzling relationship with McFadden's son Vincent—lived a largely uneventful life before committing the brutal act that would gain her the fame her lovely twin died for lack of.

"I almost didn't go to the party, you know," she says to me now. "It was hot out and I wasn't feeling so great. But then, I changed my mind." Never before have I seen a face so utterly placid, a pair of eyes so still.

I can't help wondering what those eyes must have looked like through John McFadden's lens a week before his death, when on his son's insistence, he'd filmed Kelly Lund. "Would you still have killed John," I ask, "if he had been nice to you at the screen test?"

Lund smiles—the same smile she offered the world outside the L.A. courthouse the day of her sentencing. Not a smile at all, really. More a baring of the teeth. "How should I know?" she says.

The room grows even colder.

EXCERPTED FROM
*Mona Lisa: The True Story of
Hollywood Killer Kelly Lund*
by Sebastian Todd, 1989

CHAPTER 1

FEBRUARY 11, 1980

I t was when Kelly Lund's science teacher, Mr. Hansen, asked her the third question in a row that she wasn't able to answer—the one about mitochondria—that Bellamy Marshall passed her a note. Kelly said "um" and swallowed hard to get her dry mouth working when she felt the balled-up paper hit her in the leg. She didn't think *note* at first, though. She thought *spitball*.

Kelly got spitballed a lot. So often, in fact, that she'd once told her mom about it. "They throw spitballs at me," she'd said. "They laugh at my clothes because they're so cheap."

"Cheap?" Mom had said. "Your clothes cover you up where you should be covered, which is more than I can say about those other girls you go to school with. If you want to talk about *cheap*, Kelly. Those girls are what I call *cheap*."

Kelly had made a secret vow never to talk to her mom about school again.

So she didn't look at the note when it hit her leg. She ignored it, the way she ignored all the spitballs, the way she ignored so much of what happened to her, in school and elsewhere. *Ignore it and it will go away.* It worked for most things that hurt, if not all.

Mr. Hansen said the thing about mitochondria again, Kelly trying to hang on to the words, to mold them into something that made a little bit of sense. But she couldn't. She felt the sun pressing through the classroom windows and the itchiness of her cardigan sweater and the elastic of her peasant skirt cutting into skin—all of those things so much more real than the question.

Everyone was watching her. She felt that too.

"Miss Lund?" Mr. Hansen said.

Kelly gazed at the floor. Her eyelids fluttered. She felt herself starting to escape . . . "*Miss Lund*."

For a few seconds, or maybe it was more, Kelly slipped into a dream—an actual *dream* of being seven years old and with her sister again, of sitting cross-legged on their bedroom floor, of sitting knee to knee with Catherine, staring as hard as she could into Catherine's bottle green eyes.

"Whoever moves first, dies."

"But . . . but . . . I don't want to die, Catherine."

Catherine places a hand on hers. It is warm and dry and calming. "Don't be scared, Kelly. You know me. I always move first."

"Miss Lund! Am I keeping you awake?"

Kelly's eyes flipped open. She heard herself say, "No. I'm falling asleep just fine."

Oh no. . .

A strange silence fell over the room—an airless feeling. Mr. Hansen blinked, his jaw tightening. Kelly knew she was supposed to say "I'm sorry," and she started to, but before she could get the words out everyone started to laugh. It took Kelly a few moments to register that the kids were laughing *with* her, not *at* her. That never happened. Her heart beat faster. Her face warmed.

"Good one," said Pete Nichol behind her, Pete a champion spitball thrower who had never said anything directly to Kelly ever. Pete—tall and shining blond and rich too. The son of the producer of one of Kelly's favorite TV shows, swimmers' hair like white silk. Pete Nichol clapped Kelly on the back and Mr. Hansen said, "Miss Lund. You are on detention," and that made everyone laugh louder. Some even cheered.

Kelly turned and ventured a look back at the class and that's when she saw the balled-up piece of paper on the floor next to her leg—*not* a spitball—and when she glanced up and toward the next row over, Bellamy Marshall was gesturing at the paper, her silver bracelets jangling.

Read it, Bellamy mouthed.

Bellamy was new, the daughter of a famous actor named Sterling Marshall who'd been a big deal in the '50s and '60s and still kind of was. She'd started at Hollywood High after Christmas break, having been expelled from a fancy private school in Santa Monica for mysterious reasons. There was drama in that, high drama in the way Bellamy had shown up a week after school restarted, slipping into the back row of Mr. Hansen's class, the *very back row,* though Mr. Hansen had pointed at an empty seat in the front. Kelly had turned to look at this daring new girl in her bangle bracelets and designer jeans, her luxe leather jacket, Bellamy Marshall ignoring Mr. Hansen and breathing through frosty parted lips, like a movie heroine on the run.

Bellamy had smiled at Kelly and Kelly had smiled back, wanting to be her friend but a little sad for knowing that it wasn't possible. Not with this girl—this shining rich, leather jacketed girl who'd only smiled at Kelly because she didn't know any better . . .

That had been more than a month ago.

Once Mr. Hansen got everybody quiet, once he called on Phoebe Calloway in the front row and asked her the mitochondria question and Kelly felt reasonably invisible again, she kicked the piece of paper closer to her desk. She slipped it off the floor, unfolded it quietly.

PARTY AFTER SCHOOL. MY PLACE.

Kelly turned to Bellamy to make sure it wasn't a joke. She wore a different leather jacket today—a brown bomber. She probably had a closet full of them, all real leather.

Bellamy mouthed, *Well?* And then she winked at Kelly. She didn't look like someone who was joking.

Yes, Kelly nodded, amazed at this moment. Amazed at this day.

IT WASN'T REALLY A PARTY. JUST BELLAMY, KELLY, TWO BOYS FROM the soccer team, and a tall, skinny twenty-three-year-old guy named Len with a pencilly mustache and a sandwich bag full to bursting with what he called "Humbolt's finest." They met up in the school parking lot, Len shaking the Baggie at Bellamy and grinning.

The two boys piled into Len's black Trans Am, while Kelly rode with Bellamy in her red VW Rabbit. They drove in the opposite direction from where Kelly lived, sped across Sunset Boulevard and past Barney's Beanery, Bellamy swerving around slow drivers, sunglasses focused on the road, silver bangle bracelets slipping up and down her wrists as she steered. They drove up, up, up, into the hills, neither one of them talking, just listening to the radio, to The Knack's "Good Girls Don't"—a song Kelly had never liked, not until now.

Kelly had expected to be nervous when she got in the car, but Bellamy not talking to her felt like not getting called on in class. It put her at ease.

"Hand me my cigs, would you?" Bellamy said. "They're in my purse."

Kelly picked Bellamy's bag off the car floor—a Louis Vuitton. A lot of the girls at school had these. They called them "Louie Vouies" and treated them in such an offhand way, tossing them around like they were worth nothing, but Kelly knew better. Her mother had shown her one at I. Magnin once, tapping her nails on the price tag. "*Who would spend this kind of money?*" she had said. Kelly's mother worked at I. Magnin behind the makeup counter. But even with her discount, she never bought anything there for Kelly or for herself. "*It's obscene,*" she would say, about the prices, about the entire store. Kelly never replied. She found it beautiful.

"*Someday,*" Mom would say, "*I'll get us out of this town.*"

Carefully, Kelly unzipped the bag. She plucked out a box of Marlboro Reds—Mom's brand—and handed it to her.

"You can have one too," Bellamy said.

"Thanks."

Bellamy lit one off the car lighter, then slipped it to Kelly without looking at her. The gesture made her feel as though they'd known each other for years. Bellamy rolled the windows down and Kelly blew a cloud of smoke into the warming air.

"Len likes you," Bellamy said, "I can tell."

Kelly felt her cheeks redden. "How do you know him?"

She shrugged. "Just . . . around," she said. "He can be a jerk but he's always got good weed. And I love the smell of his car."

"Is he really twenty-three?"

"Yep."

"Wow."

Through the windshield, the Hollywood sign loomed before them, making Kelly think of Catherine. It always did—how she used to brag about their view of it to anyone who'd listen. "*You can see the* sign *from our apartment,*" she'd say, leaning on the word *sign* as though she were talking about the Empire State Building or the Eiffel Tower, when the truth was, the Hollywood sign had been an eyesore back then—full of holes, crumbling into the hills, the first and third *o*'s missing almost entirely.

"*Who* wants *to see it?*" Kelly would say to her. "*It's ugly.*"

"*No it isn't. It just needs fixing.*"

Two years ago, a whole bunch of rich movie stars and politicians had taken interest in the rotting sign and rebuilt it. Alice Cooper had even donated his first *o* to replace the more destroyed of the two and declared himself Alice Coper for the rest of the year—something Catherine would have found funny if she'd still been alive . . .

On the radio, The Knack was fading into Tom Petty—that song Kelly liked about a girl raised on promises. She took another drag off her Red and gazed out at Catherine's sign—sparkling white in the sun, the letters whole and welcoming. *Some things do wind up getting fixed.*

"You were killer today," Bellamy said.

"Huh?"

"In science! How did you get the balls to say that to Hansen?"

"Oh," Kelly said, remembering. "It uh . . . it just sort of came out, I guess."

" 'I'm falling asleep just fine . . .' " Bellamy said. "Man. That made my whole year. My whole *life.*"

Kelly took another drag off her cigarette, smiled a little. "I just had to say it," she said. "He was being so annoying."

Bellamy laughed—warm and contagious—and Kelly joined in. She tried to remember the last time she'd laughed at something that wasn't on TV. It had to be back when Catherine was still alive, when they were still little kids. "Hansen's face," Bellamy gasped. "He was clenching his teeth so tight, I thought his eyes were going to pop out!" And Kelly laughed some more, Tom Petty singing about his American Girl, the whole car full of music.

Finally, they caught their breath. Bellamy slowed down at a stoplight, braking smoothly. She was a good driver. Kelly couldn't drive at all. She'd signed up for Driver's Ed, but hadn't made it to most of the classes. What was the point? Mom would never let her use the car anyway.

"So," Bellamy said. "I guess they let you out early for a first offense?"

"Huh?"x

"You know. I expected you to be stuck in detention 'til sunset."

Kelly's mouth went dry. *Miss Lund. You are on detention.* Mr. Hansen had used those words. She'd never been on detention before, woodwork kid that she was—one out of a mismatched set, the quiet twin, the dull one. Beyond bad grades, she'd never gotten into any type of trouble before today, never acted up, barely spoke. But here, this, her very first time and she'd . . . *Mom will kill me.* She turned to Bellamy, cheeks burning. "I didn't go to detention," she said. "I never checked in."

Bellamy blinked her mascaraed eyes. "You're serious?"

"Yeah," she said. "I forgot."

She turned back to the road as the light changed to green, her face cracking into a bright grin. "I think I'm falling in love with you, Kelly Lund," she said.

Kelly grinned too. She couldn't help herself.

WHEN THEY GOT TO BELLAMY'S HOUSE, THE BOYS WERE ALREADY waiting out in front. "What's your name, sweetheart?" Len said. He kept smiling at Kelly, a slippery smile.

"Her name's Kelly, not Sweetheart," Bellamy said. "Try and keep from drooling."

One of the soccer boys said, "Who cares about names? Let's smoke."

Kelly was only half-listening. She couldn't stop gawking at Bellamy's house. It was huge—an adobe palace with a gleaming red tile roof, balconies all around. They'd driven through a gate to get here, up a long, palm-lined driveway that slithered up the side of Mount Lee, Kelly's ears clicking with each rising turn. It had made her heart pound, this drive, like traveling to another world.

And it *was* another world, wasn't it? The Bird Streets. That's what this area of the Hollywood Hills was called, the roads named for birds and perched so high, driving them felt almost like flying. Bellamy lived on Blue Jay Way. ("*Like the song*," Kelly had said back in the car. Bellamy had nodded. "*I hate the Beatles.*")

Bellamy's front door was made of polished, carved wood. A maid in a white uniform let them in and walked away quickly, eyes aimed at the floor. "Don't let my little brother come upstairs, Flora," Kelly said. But the maid didn't seem to hear her.

Kelly saw a pink marble staircase, a crystal chandelier, huge windows, at least two stories high, overlooking the canyon. She bit her lip. She kept her eyes down like the maid, because she couldn't look too hard at anything. She wanted to seem like someone who'd seen a place like this before.

Bellamy's room was at the end of a long, carpeted hall. And as they all walked in, the two boys laughing about something that happened at practice the other day, Bellamy asking Len to show her the bag again, Kelly used every muscle in her body to keep her jaw from flapping open.

There was a stereo with a tape deck and turntable, speakers tall as Kelly's chin. There was a big TV, a vanity table with a huge mirror, a walk-in closet, door ajar to reveal rows of clothes, grouped by color. There was a record collection that filled an entire wall, a red leather couch, a zebra print throw rug that may very well have been real zebra. And best of all there was a king-size bed with a white puffy satin spread and dozens of throw pillows—the type of thing a princess would sleep on, or a queen. There was a framed movie poster over it—*Saturday*

Night Fever. Kelly noticed a pen scrawl across John Travolta's pants leg, and moved closer to it. Travolta's autograph . . . with a note. *For Bellamy*, he'd written. *Best wishes*. Kelly stared at the looping script and had to touch it. She had to press her fingers to the glass, just to make sure it was real.

"I hate disco but I still think John's sexy," Bellamy said. "My dad knows him."

Kelly's hand flew back. She felt herself blushing.

Bellamy smiled at her. "I met him once."

"You did?"

"I wanted to touch that chin dimple so bad." She leaned in closer, dropped her voice to a whisper. "I wanted to put my tongue on it."

"Make it a fattie," said one of the soccer boys. He was talking to Len, who was sitting on the edge of Bellamy's princess bed, rolling a joint intently.

"If this were my room," Kelly said, "I'd never leave."

Len said, "Few hits of this, you might not be able to."

"You want to spend the night?" said Bellamy. "My parents are in Switzerland, so it's just me and the staff till Friday."

Kelly swallowed. She hadn't even called home, and she knew Mom wouldn't approve. "*Keep away from those Hollywood types*," Mom would always say—even though she'd sent her girls to Hollywood High, where the sports team was called the Sheiks after a movie character played by Rudolph Valentino. Nearly everyone at school was a Hollywood type in one way or another—what else would they be? Mom may as well have said to Kelly and Catherine, "*Don't make any friends*," Kelly following the rule, Catherine dying for breaking it. "My . . . my mom . . . I don't think she . . ."

"Hey, it's cool," Bellamy said. "Some other time, though, okay?"

"Yeah, I'd love to."

"Lotsa nice red veins in this stuff," Len was saying, the two boys oohing and aahing over it. They were both short and stocky with floppy hair and pink cheeks. Kelly didn't know either one of them, and they didn't seem like jocks at all. They reminded her more of two puppies from the same litter.

"Ladies first," said Len. He gave Kelly that slippery smile. Kelly nodded at Bellamy. "You can go first."

Bellamy plucked the joint away from Len. She put it to her lips and pulled off it deeply.

Len said, "Bet you wish that spliff was my Johnson." The soccer boys chuckled.

She pursed her lips to keep the hit down. "The spliff's bigger," she said finally, smoke curling out of her mouth.

Kelly laughed.

One of the soccer boys said, "Burn!"

"Baby," Len said. "You *know* that ain't true."

Bellamy rolled her eyes, though her cheeks flushed a little.

Kelly took a closer look at Len—the tight black T-shirt, the veiny arms, the thick belt buckle, shaped like a coiled rattlesnake. He seemed so old. She imagined Bellamy with him and the thought of it made her feel kind of strange, panicky . . .

"Earth to Kelly." Bellamy was holding the joint out to her.

"Sorry."

Kelly started to take it, when Bellamy pulled back. "Get out," she said—not to Kelly, to Kelly's left shoulder. When Kelly turned, she saw a skinny boy with Bellamy's same black eyes standing in the doorway.

"Hi," Kelly said.

The boy smiled at her. He wore a *Star Wars* T-shirt, spindly pale legs sticking out of white shorts. He couldn't have been more than ten.

"Don't say hi to him. He's Satan's spawn."

The boy blew a raspberry. One of the soccer boys laughed, and Bellamy got up from the bed in a rush. She slammed the door in his face. Locked it. When she turned around, her face was an angry pink. "My brother Shane." She said it to Kelly like a swear word. "I swear to God he won't leave me alone."

KELLY HAD TRIED POT ONCE, WITH CATHERINE. THEY'D BEEN THIRTEEN at the time and Catherine had brought it into their room along with their mom's pink lighter. Kelly had asked where she'd gotten the stuff, but Catherine had refused to tell her. "*Just try it,*" Catherine had said.

"*What if I freak out?*"

"*Would it kill you, Kelly? Would it kill you to freak out just one time in your entire life?*"

Kelly had inhaled too hard and coughed it all up and felt nothing.

This time, though, it had worked. At least Kelly thought it had. Her head felt soft and fuzzy, as though someone had rubbed lotion all over her brain. Bellamy had agreed to take the soccer boys home, seeing as they both lived nearby, and when Kelly had said good-bye to her, she'd seen her face in flashing frames.

Kelly had accepted a ride from Len—something she hadn't thought very much about until now, but as she slipped into the front seat of the Trans Am, that panicky feeling flooded through her again. She found herself focusing too hard on each movement. The click of the lock echoed in her ears and the leather seats squeaked and clawed at her. Kelly felt Len's syrupy gaze on her too, and when she turned a little, there was Len's face. Close. God, he was so old.

"Good stuff, huh?" His breath was hot and sticky. His eyes blurred into one.

"Really good."

Len's hand slipped up under her peasant skirt and rested on her thigh. Her whole leg stiffened. The car did smell good, she thought—like warm leather and pine.

He leaned in and kissed her, his mouth spongy and lax. His lips were too wet and the pencil mustache scratched at her nose. He thrust his tongue into her mouth and then just let it lay there on top of hers, slimy and sleeping.

My first kiss. She hadn't expected it to be like this. Catherine had once said her first kiss would feel like magic and she'd wanted to believe that. But then again, how was Kelly supposed to know what magic felt like? She closed her eyes, tried to relax. His mouth opened wider, so he was biting into her cheeks. What part of this was supposed to feel good? There had to be something. She tried running a hand through his greasy hair and he moaned, his wet lips vibrating.

The weed made Kelly nervous. It was getting hard to breathe, but she didn't want to pull away because she didn't want to have to look at Len. She didn't know what to say to him. *Thanks? That was interesting?*

At one point, back at the house when the boys were laughing about something, Bellamy had set her head on Kelly's shoulder. "*I knew we'd be friends,*" she had said. The memory of it relaxed her.

Len pulled away. Kelly's mouth still tasted of him, a sour taste. "Better get you home," he said. "Unless you want to stop somewhere first."

She didn't want to stop somewhere with him. But she didn't want to go home either. She heard herself say, "I don't care."

Len started up the car but kept his hand on her thigh. Kelly closed her eyes and leaned back, Bellamy's voice from this afternoon still in her head, making the hand feel lighter.

"*You're like me.*" Bellamy had said it into Kelly's ear, in a soft, pressing whisper she could feel more than hear. "*You have secrets.*"

CHAPTER 2

APRIL 21, 2010

Kelly gripped the wheel—one hand at ten o'clock, the other at two. She glanced into the rearview. No one behind her or next to her. No one on this entire stretch of the 10 sprawling east and into the desert, but still she clicked her blinker before switching lanes and checked the mirrors again—both of them, rearview and driver's side. She had to be safe. She couldn't break any rules.

She thought about turning the radio on, but decided not to. *What if it's on the news?* Instead she switched off the air conditioner, opened the window, and let the warm air wash in, feeling the roar of it, listening to the gallop of the wheels on the road. There was so much passion in driving alone at night. Kelly could always get lost in it, even now.

Kelly had learned to drive only five years ago, a month or two after her release, so it was still so new and exciting. Her husband had taught her over an eight-day period that must have felt very long to him, after business hours in the big empty lot outside the Costco in La Quinta.

He'd been so patient with her, never raising his voice— not even when she braked so hard the whole car convulsed and the backs of their skulls slammed into the headrests. "*Okay, we're definitely stopped,*" Kelly's husband had said, once they caught their breath. "*Next time, try to be a little less emphatic about it.*"

Kelly glanced at the clock on the dashboard. 2:47 A.M. *Please be sleeping,* she told him in her mind. *Please don't wake up and see that I'm gone.* Then she shut the drawer on her husband's face, his name. She locked him away.

One hour left. Just forty-five minutes more on the freeway and then ten or fifteen minutes on surface streets and then . . . She checked the rearview again. Peered hard into the glass and searched for headlights beside her, behind her, far back as she could see . . .

No one had followed her.

Kelly closed her eyes for a few seconds, breathed in and out. When she opened them again, she was thinking only of the drive—of the rush of air on her skin and her hands on the wheel and the vast, empty lane in front of the headlights, leading her into the darkness, bringing her home.

SHANE MARSHALL WAS UP AT SIX, AS HE ALMOST ALWAYS WAS THESE days, as he'd been for the past five years, every morning, up with the sun, up as soon as the pills wore off, watching his wife sleeping.

Shane brushed his hand against the side of her face, lightly so as not to wake her.

Twenty-five years of knowing her, fifteen years of marriage, five in the same house. The whole time, the same questions. The same wondering, and wanting to know her and not wanting to know. The same ache.

Kelly stirred. A lock of hair fell across her eyes, gold streaked with silver. Shane liked the way the soft morning sun made the silver hairs glisten. He put his camera up to his face. He wouldn't take the picture—that would be too invasive, wouldn't it? But he would watch her through the lens. He would take in her cream-colored skin and her round shoulders and her silence.

"I love you," he whispered.

She stretched, eyes shut tight, mouth curling into a smile, or maybe a grimace. He wasn't sure. She was so hard to read, his wife of fifteen years. *What's on your mind, Kelly Lund? Who is on your mind?*

He snapped a picture.

Kelly's eyelids fluttered.

"Good morning."

"Shane?"

"Expecting someone else?"

"Funny," she murmured. "What time is it? Six?"

"Catching the golden hour." He snapped another shot. The desert sunlight dappled her face. "Catching you."

"Shane," she said. "Please don't take my picture."

"I can't help it. You're beautiful."

She opened her eyes—those sad, opaque gray eyes. Shane was forever trying to see inside them, see through them and now . . . watching her eyes through the lens, he saw a coldness in them, something he didn't understand. Something new.

"Stop," she said, her face changing again, the eyes softening as though someone had dropped a veil over them. Why couldn't he figure her out?

He put the camera down.

"Did I sound harsh? Sorry. I'm just . . . God, I'm so tired."

Gently, Shane touched Kelly's face. "It's okay," he said. "I shouldn't have taken your picture."

She took his hand in hers, pressed her lips against his wrist. She held his palm to her smooth cheek, every part of her so soft—her skin, her mouth, like a silk scarf over a knife.

He wrapped his arms around her and held her to him, feeling her sweet breath at his chest, the filmy fabric of her camisole, inhaling the clean scent of her hair. He wanted more, even though he knew better. He kissed her neck.

"Shane," she said.

"I know."

"I'm sorry."

"I understand," he said, trying again. That was their life. Shane trying, Kelly pulling away. Kelly apologizing. Shane understanding.

God, he was so tired of understanding.

The phone rang. Shane started toward it, but then he realized it wasn't the bedroom phone ringing. It was the phone in the kitchen—his work line. At six? He rushed into the kitchen, plucked the receiver off the base. "Hollywood Photo Archives," he said.

"Shane."

How strange life could be. Just this morning, waking up, he'd thought about his sister for the first time in God knows how long. *Maybe Dad's right*, he had thought. *Maybe we should try and get along*. And now, here she was after five years of not speaking to each other, feeling the same way as Shane at the same time of morning? How was that possible?

"It's Bellamy," she said. "Are you alone?"

"I know who you are," he said. "Why would I be alone?"

"Oh God. I can't do this."

"Why are you calling me?"

There was a long pause on the other end of the line, Bellamy breathing in and out, loud enough for him to hear the breathing. Shane's jaw tightened. This was the Bellamy he knew, the Bellamy who loved her loaded silences, her mind games, the Bellamy he'd stopped speaking to for good reason. Was she drunk? High? Or was she tape-recording him for one of her projects?

"I'm hanging up now."

"No, wait," she said. "I'm sorry."

He swallowed. *Sorry.* "What is it?"

"Dad."

"Did he put you up to this call?"

"*What?* No. God, Shane. Oh my God I can't . . ." Her voice broke.

"Bellamy?"

"I can't say it."

More breathing. An awful feeling burned in the pit of Shane's stomach, rose up into his throat. A swelling dread. "What happened?"

"I can't."

His heart pounded. "Bellamy, please."

"Can't say it."

"*What happened to Dad?*"

"*Don't yell at me.*" She was crying now.

"*Tell me.*" He fought out the words, as though someone were strangling him. And when he looked up, he saw Kelly, standing at the far corner of the room.

"What?" Kelly said.

Shane shook his head hard, to shake his thoughts together and at the same time ward off Kelly, so he could be alone with them. He needed to be alone. *Go away.*

"What's going on?" Kelly said.

"*Go away!*"

Through the plastic earpiece, Bellamy was saying sorry again. Bellamy who never said sorry, Bellamy who never cried, breaking into sobs. Shane asked her no more because he knew. *Dad,* she'd said, the word crumbling to pieces. *Dad is dead.* "I'm sorry, Shane, oh Shane, I'm so, so sorry."

"SHOULD I COME WITH YOU?" KELLY ASKED, DURING THAT ONE BRIEF moment after Shane hung up, when she forgot who she was and what she'd done and saw only her husband, his loss.

"No, Kelly."

"Oh," she said, remembering. "Okay."

"I mean—"

"I get it."

Shane grabbed his denim jacket out of the coat closet. He opened the front door, and a warm breeze swept in, like breath. He turned and stood there for a while, facing her with the desert sun haloing all around him. "You'll come to the funeral, right?"

"Yes."

"You'll hold my hand."

"Yes."

"I love you," Shane said. His face was in the shadows, so Kelly couldn't quite see his eyes. She was glad for that.

"I love you too," she said.

AFTER SHANE LEFT, KELLY STARED AT THE CLOSED DOOR FOR A WHILE before walking back into the kitchen. She made a pot of coffee, toasted some bread—no sense in cooking a big breakfast if Shane wasn't going to be around. The whole time, she didn't think about Sterling Marshall. She didn't think about anything. She just listened for the birds.

The desert was so quiet, especially compared to Carpentia where there had been so much noise. All that shouting and clanging all night long, everything echoing—footsteps and singing and screams. Somebody would weep, it didn't matter how late at night it was or how far away the weeper was from Kelly's cell, the sound of it would travel. It would weave its way into her thoughts and wake her up if she'd been lucky enough to get to sleep at all. She used to wad up toilet paper, shove it in her ears, but that did no good. The sounds vibrated. She could feel them.

Here, though, in Joshua Tree, you had to strain to hear birds. Kelly leaned against the kitchen window. She put her ear to the glass as the coffee bubbled, listening for the *wow, wow* of the Gambel's Quail, the cry of the golden eagle, the death-rattle clacking of the roadrunner's beak.

When she'd first gotten out of Carpentia and she and Shane had moved here, Kelly had bought a guide and memorized all the desert species—their names, their field marks, their calls and nesting patterns. She'd put a few feeders outside to draw the braver ones closer, and now she wanted to hear more of them, the flap of their wings, the chirping and rustling as they landed and ate, and most of all, those subtle sounds she couldn't hear from indoors—the sounds they made leaving, knowing they'd come back.

IT WASN'T UNTIL KELLY HAD TAKEN HER COFFEE AND HER TOAST BACK to her workspace in the bedroom that she thought about her father-in-law again— and only then when she saw the news story on her home page.

Kelly's brain had a way of doing that. *Avoidance,* the shrink at Carpentia had called it, but she thought of it more as organizing her emotions. It was as though Kelly had a big file cabinet in her head and she could take her feelings and slide them into drawers and lock them up, deal with them later.

Problem was, lately, the drawers kept flying open.

Kelly stared at the picture: a dashing young Sterling Marshall, as he appeared in his Oscar-winning role in the 1950s war movie *Guns of Victory*. She clicked on the link and skimmed the article:

Movie legend Sterling Marshall is dead at the age of 79 of an apparent suicide . . .

Marshall had recently been diagnosed with cancer . . .

. . . though sources say he may have left behind a note, the contents of the alleged suicide note have not been revealed . . .

Suicide? A note?

Kelly's cell phone was on her bedside table—resting next to its charger, because she hadn't plugged it in last night. Kelly was always forgetting to charge her phone, forgetting so consistently that it almost felt intentional, almost as though she *had a need to see the phone die.* Shane had once said that to Kelly after failing to reach her one night. He'd apologized immediately—so obviously mortified over his own choice of words that it made Kelly's cheeks flush. "*I'm just not used to modern technology*," she had said.

The phone still had a few gasps in it. She plugged it into the charger, tapped in Shane's cell number. It rang a few times, then went to voice mail. "The news reports are saying suicide," she said into the phone. "They say your father had cancer. Did you know, Shane? Had he told you about it before? I wish I could help or . . . I don't know what I wish. I'm sorry. I hate to see you hurt." Kelly's voice sounded strange to her. Tinny and insincere. It didn't matter. She was speaking to no one, having ended the call before saying any of it. Kelly turned back to the computer.

The actor's daughter, Bellamy Marshall, 48, a multimedia artist who came to fame in the mid-'90s with a series of controversial painted photographs, accompanied by tape-recorded interviews . . .

Kelly stopped reading. Her gaze drifted back to the picture—the wavy dark hair and the cleft chin, the black eyes that were Shane's eyes and Bellamy's eyes—velvet-soft and fathomless . . .

Kelly shut her eyes, an old afternoon flooding her mind. A sunshiny, spring afternoon in 1980, when Sterling Marshall was only Bellamy's dad and his house was only Bellamy's house and Shane was nothing more than Bellamy's annoying little brother.

On this particular afternoon, Kelly had been curled up with Bellamy on her zebra print rug as they so often were back then, watching British music videos on Bellamy's enormous TV—first VCR Kelly had ever seen—a bag of Doritos nestled between them. They'd been stoned out of their minds, piling chips into their mouths and crunching away, their fingers stained that salty orange. Kelly could remember Mr. Marshall cracking the door and poking his handsome head into the room. *"Please turn the music down, girls."*

Without even thinking about it, Kelly had said, *"Okay, Dad."*

"Did you just call him Dad?" Bellamy had said. *"Oh my God, that's so cute!"*

Funny how close the past can feel—close enough to grab on to and let it pull you along. But once you reach out. Once you reach to touch it . . . She had loved him once. She'd envied Bellamy for having Sterling Marshall in her life, because compared to her own father he had seemed so strong. *"Okay, Dad,"* she had said. And maybe a part of her had said it on purpose. Wishful thinking, back then, back when she still thought wishfully . . .

Kelly exhaled in a rush, sweeping the memory away. For a few seconds, she allowed herself to recall the closer past, the previous night. And then came thoughts of other things that needed to be swept away, needed to be cleaned.

INSIDE KELLY'S CLOSET, ON THE FLOOR BEHIND THE TWO NEAT ROWS of shoes, lurked her clothes from last night—the jeans, the new Adidas sneakers, the soft, pale gray hoodie she'd bought at Target last fall. She thought about throwing them all out. Of burning them in the yard, maybe tossing them in the trunk of her car and driving 'til she could find an open gas station Dumpster.

But these were all favorite clothes, more noticeable in their absence—especially to Shane, observant photographer that he was. "*What happened to those jeans I love on you?*" he might say. Or, "*Didn't you just buy a new pair of running shoes?*"

Besides, the stains weren't that bad.

Kelly scooped the clothes up in her arms without looking at them, without seeing the rust-brown splotches on the sneaker soles, the hem of a pant leg, the edge of a pale gray sleeve. She brought them into the kitchen and dropped them in the washing machine—sneakers first, then hoodie, T-shirt, jeans, socks, followed by a cup of detergent, two cups of bleach. It almost felt like a ceremony. She worked the knobs on the machine, selecting Heavy Duty, selecting Hot Water, turning away as she did it. *Avoidance.*

It was a two-year-old stainless steel washing machine, sleek and efficient. And before Kelly returned to her workspace, she listened to it for a while. There was comfort in the whoosh of the water, the grind of the motor, the sounds the machine made, erasing Sterling Marshall's blood.

"It's over with," Kelly whispered. Then she went to work.

KELLY'S JOB ENABLED HER TO USE THE PART OF HER MIND SHE LIKED
using most. It was the same part she used when she drove—the part
that could escape her body, her life.

She flipped open her laptop and called up her latest photo, her work
in progress, a wholesome brunette she'd decided to call Danielle G.
"What's your story, Danielle G?" Kelly whispered, the way she always
did when she called up her photos.

For four years and counting, Kelly had worked for SaraBelle.com—
an online "no-strings-attached" dating service for married men and
women (mostly men) who were looking to cheat on their spouses. It
was her job to write what her bosses called "grabbers"—alluring female
profiles to accompany the models' photographs displayed prominently
on SaraBelle's home page. All of the grabbers were fake. Paying the
membership fee allowed you to click on them, which in turn would
unlock the actual site, where you could explore the real, more prosaic,
profiles and pictures.

Kelly's job may or may not have been legal. She hadn't asked. She
hadn't investigated. She didn't care.

A Hollywood Photo Archives client who happened to be a silent
partner in SaraBelle.com had recommended her at Shane's request.
After a brief phone conversation, the site's administrator had offered
Kelly what he called a "creative writing position." And she had said yes
immediately, no questions asked. Sitting at home, face hidden behind
a laptop screen, dreaming up "ideal women" all day long . . . There was
no job more suited to Kelly's needs or skill-set. The idea that Shane had
known that about her—that he'd been certain enough of her ability to
make things up to put her in contact with the powers that be—troubled

Kelly for reasons she couldn't quite put her finger on. But that didn't make her any less grateful.

Kelly had decided Danielle G should be thirty-two, the mother of a six-year-old son and married to a banker. Her hobbies: *Pilates, cooking, yoga, staying in shape.* (Redundant yes, but on this site, with these men for customers, you never could talk about your body too much.)

She opened up the field called *My Story,* started typing: *I always thought Bill was enough for me, but once our son Jack went off to preschool and I started spending long days at home alone, I was able to see everything that was missing from my life. More and more, marriage has seemed like a crutch—a convenience. There is such yearning within me—he doesn't see it but there is. Making love to Bill can't fill it. My fantasies and my romance books and even my vibrator can't fill it. It is a desire that overpowers. An endless, aching need.*

Kelly's hands jumped off of the keyboard. She blinked at the screen. *Where did that come from?* A line that had no place in a grabber. Too poetic. Too pretentious. But it was familiar. That sad kind of familiar that she couldn't get a handle on at first but once she did, once she knew . . . It was . . . Oh, it was . . .

An endless aching need.

A line from "The Rose." Bette Midler.

The doorbell rang. Kelly stood up, her heart still pounding, the song still in her head, that drawer flying open . . .

She headed out of her bedroom with her hands over her ears, as though the song were playing out loud and not in her head. "Stop," she whispered. "Stop it, stop it, stop it . . ."

It only subsided once she neared the front door. The bell rang again. Shane. It had to be. Probably forgot something. Or maybe . . . *Maybe he wants me to go to the house with him after all . . .*

She put her hand on the door but stopped when she saw the looming figure in the fogged glass beside it. Bigger and taller than her husband.

"Ms. Lund?" The voice at the door was deep and serious and not at all familiar.

"Yes?" She had to reply. He could see her through the fogged glass just as easily as she could see him.

"Would it be all right if I come in?" He pressed his badge up against the glass as the washing machine twisted into a new cycle. "I'm with the LAPD. Homicide."

CHAPTER 3

The drive from Joshua Tree to Hollywood took more than two hours, but Shane moved through it in a dream state, sliding up and down on-ramps, his hands numb on the steering wheel, the hot air from his Jeep's open window pushing in on him like breath.

Suicide. Bellamy hadn't said that on the phone. Shane had learned it from the radio: *Movie legend Sterling Marshall—who was suffering from pancreatic cancer—is dead of an apparent suicide. Details after the break.*

Shane hadn't waited for the break. He'd flipped off the radio, the word dialing through his head as he finally hit the Hollywood Freeway, maneuvering his Jeep through traffic that appeared to be out of central casting—the gleaming red Ferrari with its slick-haired driver, text-weaving in and out of the diamond lane; the big, dumb Dunkin' Donuts truck cutting him off, horn blaring aggressively; the douchebag Hummer clinging to his side and blasting hip-hop, bass amped up enough to inspire road rage. Or 'roid rage. Or both.

Suicide.

Who would have thought that Dad would commit suicide? Dad, who did all his own stunts, famously walking over hot coals to prepare for one film role, wrestling with a live alligator for another. Dad, who had been tortured as a POW in the Korean War. ("It ain't *Hogan's Heroes*," he used to tell Shane and Bellamy. But nothing more. "*You kids don't need to hear any more about it.*") Dad, who never even accepted Novocain at the dentist. Fearless, pain-taunting Sterling Marshall, killing himself over stage 2 cancer? It didn't make sense. Unless he had another reason.

Or unless it wasn't suicide after all.

Shane's cell phone rang. He glanced at the screen. *Kelly*, it said. He declined the call—a reflex, like killing a bug. "I'll call you later," he whispered, apologizing to no one. Apologizing for his thoughts.

Shane stared at the road and listened to the quiet roar of his tires on the macadam. He tried to clear his head, but Dad's voice still wormed in, Dad's voice over the phone two weeks ago, swearing his illness wasn't serious, that it was treatable, that he planned to fight it, just as he'd fought every bad thing in life and come out a winner. "*Stage two*," he'd said with a laugh. "*It's practically a baby.*"

Had he been acting? With Sterling Marshall, you never could tell. "*Don't listen to your mother, Shane. You know what a worrywart she is.*"

Same old Dad. That same sweetness about him, that same strength. Didn't matter what was going on. Dad made you feel like everything would be all right. "*Shane, can you do me a favor, though?*"

"*Sure.*"

"*Can you please give your sister another chance?*"

"*Dad . . .*"

"*I know, I know. But she means well. She loves you, son, whether or not she's able to say it.*"

First time Dad had mentioned Bellamy to Shane in years. Why? It wasn't like him to bring up painful topics . . . Had he brought Bellamy up out of emotional necessity? Was asking his kids to make peace a last request?

"A calming presence." Many years ago, someone had said that about his father—Shane couldn't remember who.

The voice had been deep. It was a man who had said it. "*Outside of Henry Fonda, your father has the most naturally calming presence of any actor I know.*" A kind voice, and so familiar. If Shane could place a name to it, maybe he could get this man to speak at the funeral . . .

"*You don't understand, Dad.*"

"*I just want my family to get along. It's the one thing that could . . .*"

He'd never finished the sentence.

Shane gritted his teeth. *Stop. Drive. Keep it together.* What else had he said, Dad's friend? If he really focused, Shane could almost hear the lilt in the voice, the smile in it. He had smiled, hadn't he?

"*You want to know a secret, kiddo?*"

"*Sure!*"

A car horn shrieked—the Ferrari. Shane had cut him off without realizing it. He sped up, but the Ferrari pulled up, kiss-close behind him.

"*Don't tell the gossip rags.*"

Shane pressed on the accelerator, but the Ferrari followed, riding the Jeep's bumper, flexing its speed. "*See, if anybody finds out, they'll get jealous, but the truth is, your father is the best actor I've ever worked with. I'm not kidding around.*" The voice shimmered in his mind now. More than thirty years later, but there was still no mistaking it. John's voice. John McFadden's voice.

The Ferrari flashed its brights.

"Asshole!" Shane yelled. But it came out a sob, and then more followed—wet, angry sobs that made it hard to breathe, to drive, to see the road.

"SUGAR PLEASE," SAID THE POLICE DETECTIVE. HE WAS PROBABLY TEN years younger than Kelly—big shouldered and ginger haired, complexion like strawberry ice cream sprinkled with cinnamon. He was too pink for Kelly, too soft. Of course he wanted sugar in his coffee. Probably liked it flavored too. Probably a big fan of hazelnut vanilla toasted caramel Cracker Jack crème brûlée.

Kelly filled a mug with coffee and set it down in front of the detective. She got the carton of sugar out of the pantry and poured some into a bowl. She placed the spoon on top and slid it across the kitchen table to him thinking, *Have at it.*

She couldn't remember his name. He'd introduced himself at the door, but everything he'd said after Detective and before LAPD Homicide had flown clear out of her head. Bruce or Brian or Barry . . . she thought it began with a *B. Brûlée.* First man she'd seen in a tie since . . . Well, probably since she last met with her parole officer. This detective's tie was gray, a spatter of red polka dots on it that made Kelly think of . . . Shane never wore ties.

He spooned in the sugar—two, three, four, five spoonfuls before Kelly's stomach went sour and she had to look away. As though on cue, the washing machine shifted cycles, thump-thump-thumping in time with her heart. "Thank you for letting me in," he said. "I know we usually call first, but I was in the area."

Thump, thump . . . "I don't have a lot of time."

"This won't take long," he said. "By the way, I'm sorry for your loss."

He scooped another heaping spoonful of sugar into his cup, which felt almost like an obscene gesture. (*How many was that? Nine? Ten?*) But he wasn't focused on the coffee. Scoop after scoop, his eyes stayed trained on her face. *Technique.* Everybody had a technique for talking to Kelly—journalists, psychiatrists, prison guards, cops. Especially cops. Especially sugar-spooning cops in spatter ties who couldn't stand anything bitter in their lives, not even coffee.

"Thank you," Kelly said. Was that the right response to say to someone being sorry for your loss? *Thank you for being sorry?* The washing machine thumped. Kelly wanted to throw something at it.

"You all right?" The detective said it in a probing way, made it sound like a trick question. All those years at Carpentia, Kelly had longed to speak to someone who didn't talk to her like this, who wasn't trying to pry something out of her brain with the penetrating gaze, the deliberate gesture, the expertly placed question designed to catch her off guard . . . The detective said, "You look pale. Like you didn't get a lot of sleep."

The washing machine made a socking sound, almost as though something alive were trapped inside, struggling to get out. Kelly's sneakers. Her bloodstained sneakers. "I slept fine," she said. "I'm good as can be expected. Under the circumstances."

"Doing some laundry?"

She didn't reply.

"You don't mind answering a few questions, Miss Lund?"

"Mrs. Marshall."

"Huh? Sorry, that machine of yours is kind of noisy."

"My name. It isn't Lund. It hasn't been for the last fifteen years. You can call me Mrs. Marshall."

"Fair enough." The detective blew on his coffee, took a tentative sip. "So, Mrs. Marshall," he said, "any reason why you aren't at your in-laws' house with your husband?"

"Only immediate family should be there."

"And you aren't?"

"Excuse me?"

"You've been married to his son for fifteen years. You'd think at that point, they'd have accepted you as one of their own." He swallowed more coffee, eyes fixed on her face as the thumping grew more insistent, the whole machine jumping with it, until it suddenly, mercifully eased into a lower cycle. "Are you sure you're all right?"

"I told you. I'm fine."

"Okay. When was the last time you spoke to Sterling Marshall?"

"I don't know."

"You ever text him? E-mail? Snail mail?"

"Not recently." In her mind, she saw Sterling Marshall's name in gold embossed letters on thick, creamy stationery. He'd written her in prison once, only once, a long time ago. She remembered his careful hand-writing and what he'd told her in the letter. Another drawer flew open . . .

"Did you speak to Mr. Marshall often? Did your husband?"

"Maybe."

"Can you give me more of an idea than 'maybe'?"

"You would have to ask my husband."

In the letter, Sterling Marshall had called John McFadden "a dear friend and one of the great directors of our time." Kelly remembered that phrase as though she were looking at it for the first time. *A dear friend.* Her stomach clenched up. He had talked about Kelly, how she hadn't "*been in control of her senses*" and so he understood. He knew she was sorry. But she wasn't sorry. She would never be sorry.

" . . . once a week? Twice a month? Or was it more like a holiday-type thing?"

The doctor at Carpentia has informed me of your very recent "news." Another line from that letter, still burned into Kelly's brain. The quotes around the word *news.* Want to demean something in one step? Put quotes around it.

"From what you knew of your father-in-law, would you say he had any enemies?"

I trust Shane doesn't know yet. I trust you'll do the right thing.

Kelly heard herself say, "Suicide."

The detective jumped a little. "Pardon?"

"The news reports. They said it was suicide."

"We haven't released any official comment to news outlets."

"What did he say?"

"Huh?"

"Sterling Marshall. What did he say in the note?"

He exhaled. "I'm not here to talk about what you read on the Web."

"Was there a note?"

"When was the last time you spoke to your father-in-law?"

"I told you. I don't know."

In the letter, Sterling Marshall had told Kelly that he'd helped Shane to start a photo archive business. He'd promised to keep supporting him, to make sure he's always taken care of, *but only if you do what needs to be done.* Underneath the table, Kelly's fists clenched up.

"Were you aware that Mr. Marshall owned a gun?"

She looked at him. "No."

"Did you ever see or hear about a gun when you visited him at his house?"

Kelly opened her mouth, closed it again.

"Maybe at a family get-together? Did he ever tell your husband about it?"

"About what?"

"Owning a gun," he said.

"Not that I know of."

"You're aware, aren't you, that your father-in-law was a pretty big antigun activist? You've heard of the John McFadden Fund."

The washing machine rumbled.

"I've heard," she said, "of the *John McFadden Fund.*" She made herself say the name clearly, deliberately. As though it had quotes around it. She met his gaze and saw something there, an uneasiness.

The detective cleared his throat. He slid back in his chair, which gave Kelly a type of sad satisfaction. *Good. Be uneasy.*

"Sterling Marshall was very close to the man you shot in the head."

She nodded at him. "Yep." He couldn't shake her. If the washing machine couldn't shake her, if the memory of that letter couldn't shake her, then nothing could, including him, especially him—Barry Brûlée or whatever his name was. He was made of cinnamon. She was made of rock.

"Would you say that you got along well with your father-in-law?"

"Sure."

"Really? Give me an idea of how close you were. Did you call him Sterling? Mr. Marshall? *Dad?*"

"This is how it's going to be, huh?"

"I'm asking pretty basic questions."

"Are you going to talk to my husband? Will you at least show *him* the suicide note?"

"Bellamy Marshall says that you and her father were not on the best of terms. Is she lying?" Kelly looked at him—the gold-spun eyebrows, the faerie green eyes. The pale pink hands, hovering over his mug.

He said, "Can I ask you something?"

"No."

"Did you ever feel like . . ."

"I said you can't ask me something."

"Did you ever feel like Sterling Marshall chose John McFadden over you?"

She stared at him. "I don't care if he did."

"Mr. Marshall gave an interview two days ago. In the *Times*. It was for the fifth anniversary of your release. I'm sure you read it. He said he still misses his old pal John. But he doesn't blame you, not anymore. You were just a kid after all. Raised by an uncaring, irresponsible mother. Tragically lost your twin just a few years before, and besides, you were on drugs. A teen addict. Didn't know right from wrong."

Kelly heard a noise outside the kitchen window—a swooping hiss. Turkey vulture. "He never said that about my mother."

"Where were you this morning, between the hours of midnight and three A.M.?"

"Here."

"You mean, in this house?"

"Yes."

"Can anyone verify your whereabouts? Your husband, maybe?"

She shut her eyes. Behind her lids she saw a fuse box—the same one she'd made up in her mind at seventeen when she'd stood outside the courthouse, surrounded by strangers, her whole future crashing in, turning to dust. Cameras flashing at her and men with mean voices shouting her name, but all she'd heard was the hum of that imaginary fuse box. All she'd seen were the two long rows of switches, shutting down one by one.

And she'd smiled.

"Mrs. Marshall," he said. "Were you at your father-in-law's last night?"

"You need to leave," she said. "You have no right to be here. You have no right to question me in my house, without a lawyer present."

The detective took a long drag off his supersweet coffee, then placed the cup back onto the saucer. The clink hurt Kelly's ears. The whole time, he never took his eyes off of hers, the green of them glittering with something . . . knowledge or hate. Or maybe it was both. That's what all this technique was, wasn't it? A combination of knowledge and hate, cooked up and heaped on you like teaspoons of sugar.

"We'll be in touch, Ms. Lund," he said.

AFTER HE LEFT, KELLY LOCKED THE DOOR. AND AS SHE TRANSFERRED her clothes and shoes into the dryer, she thought of Sterling Marshall's letter again—the only letter he'd ever written her, outside of the holiday cards addressed and signed by Mary, his wife. A letter sent to a prison fifteen years ago, when Kelly was thirty-two but still seventeen inside because prison locks you up in other ways, not just physically. And so, before starting to read Sterling Marshall's words, Kelly had spent a good amount of time marveling at the creamy paper, the glossy ink. She'd run her fingertips over the gold-embossed name and felt, for a time, special. A letter from *the* Sterling Marshall. Written in his own hand. To her.

She remembered how beautiful Sterling Marshall's signature had looked, even after she'd read the letter—a letter asking her to get rid of her baby and not to tell her husband about the pregnancy, ever.

She remembered what Sterling Marshall had written, just before signing it: *Family means everything to me.*

To this day, she still had no doubt he'd meant it.

CHAPTER 4

SHOTGUN WEDDING!
"MONA LISA" KILLER TIES THE KNOT
WITH MOVIE STAR'S SON

I now pronounce you man . . . and murderer?

In a top-secret ceremony behind the barbed wire gates of Carpentia Women's State Correctional Facility, Shane Marshall, 25, wed Kelly Michelle Lund, 32—the dead-eyed former teen drug addict currently serving 25 years to life for the brutal slaying of Oscar-nominated director John McFadden.

The son of movie legend Sterling Marshall, boyishly handsome Shane wore a charcoal gray suit and dark glasses as he entered the prison on May 15, his mother, Mary, at his side. "Shane's been visiting Kelly at least once a week for years," a prison insider tells the Enquirer. *"To say they're an odd couple would be a pretty big understatement!"*

Shane's mom was the only family member present at the wedding, which lasted 15 minutes and was performed by the prison chaplain. "My son is in love. I can't stand in the way of that," Mary said in a statement. But Shane's big sister Bellamy Marshall, 32, wasn't so accepting. "I wasn't invited to the wedding," said the art world superstar, whose chilling piece Mona Lisa *immortalized the coke-addled murderess at her sentencing. "I don't agree with or understand my brother's decision."*

Like it or not, though, the arty beauty may be an aunt soon! The Enquirer *has learned that Carpentia allows conjugal visits. And according to our prison source, sexy Shane wasted no time shacking up with his killer bride!*

National Enquirer
May 25, 1995

CHAPTER 5

FEBRUARY 12, 1980

Each sound echoed. The slamming of the Trans Am's door, Kelly's ragged breath, her footsteps, too heavy as she climbed the stairs to her third-floor apartment, her key sliding into the lock, turning.

Kelly hoped her mom was asleep, but that was a stupid thing to hope, especially once she'd opened the door and felt the blaze of the kitchen lights and heard the oldies station blasting and inhaled that piney, chemical smell.

Mom was cleaning.

"Is that you?" Mom's voice came from behind the high kitchen counter, singsongy like the voice on the tinny transistor radio. *In the jungle, the mighty jungle . . .*

"Hi, Mom." Kelly stepped around the counter. Mom was on her hands and knees, scrubbing. She leaned into it, working harder than was necessary, her whole body surging with each scrub-stroke like waves slapping the shore. "Where were you?" Mom said.

"Out?"

"Come on now, Kelly," Mom grunted, "be specific." Her breathing was sharp. Her fingers gripped the brush handle and Kelly couldn't help but stare at the knuckles, so white it looked like the bones were pushing through. "Who were you out with?"

Kelly's heart pounded. She'd worked this out in her mind when Len was driving her home, but back then she'd been higher than she was now.

"I was with a friend"—Kelly tried anyway—"from math class. We have a test coming up and we were studying late. I lost track of time."

"What's your friend's name?"

She swallowed. "Susie."

"Susie what?"

"Susie . . . Mitchell." Kelly gazed at the counter—Mom had bought a bunch of new bananas. They were splayed out in a bowl, nearly ripe but not quite, their skins that pretty pale green. Kelly liked them best that way. She liked that slight tartness, the whiteness of the fruit. Her stomach growled, and she wanted to take one, but she was afraid that if she did, Mom might make a fuss about her eating so late or worse yet, she'd know what she'd been doing. "*Do you have the munchies?*" Mom would say. She knew enough to say that, to use those words.

Scrub, scrub, scrub . . . "What do Susie's parents do?"

"Her dad is a doctor and her mom . . ." Kelly cleared her throat. "She's a nurse." Next to the bananas was a tin ashtray mounded with cigarettes. There had to be at least a pack's worth in there, and it had been empty this morning. It was hypocritical, Mom's habit displayed on the kitchen counter like a bouquet of flowers, Kelly using everything she had to hide one night.

One life-changing night . . .

"So if I called the school and asked for Susie Mitchell, daughter of Dr. and Mrs. Mitchell, they'd know who I was talking about?"

Kelly drew in a shaky breath. "You shouldn't smoke so much."

Scrub, scrub, scrub . . .

Kelly listened to the song. *Hush my darling. Don't fear my darling.* The antenna gleamed at her. She desperately wanted to go to her room.

"You didn't answer my question," Mom said.

Kelly looked down. Her skirt was inside out. Quickly, she shifted it so that the tag was in the back, crossed her arms over the waistband. "Sure," she tried, though she couldn't quite remember the question now.

The radio said, *a weem a woppa weem a woppa.* Mom's shoulders surged to the beat, her hair flopping. She wore faded jeans, an oversize, pale blue men's shirt that must've come from her most recent exboyfriend—a banker who, as it turned out, had both a wife and little kids. Kelly spotted a long sweat stain, running down the back.

Mom said, "I got a call from your school."

"Huh?"

Mom stopped scrubbing. She sat back on her heels and looked up at Kelly, a shiny lock of hair falling across her forehead. Her natural color was the same as Kelly's—"ash blond" she called it—but she dyed it a brighter shade to look good under the lights at I. Magnin. It reminded Kelly of a goldfish. It was the same color Catherine's had been. "It was the principal's office, Kelly. You had detention today and never showed up for it."

"Oh . . ."

Mom stared into her eyes, so sharp a stare that Kelly could feel it— as though she were trying to bash into her brain, read her thoughts . . . *Can she tell I've been smoking? Does she know about what I did with Len?*

"That's all you're going to say, Kelly? *Oh?*"

Kelly took a breath, wrapped her arms tighter around her waist. *Just sound normal.* "It was my science teacher." She said the words very carefully. "I didn't know the answer to a question. He got mad at me. He told me I was on detention but I thought . . . I thought he was just *saying* it. He's mean. He doesn't like me and . . ."

"They said he'd marked down that you were insubordinate."

"I wasn't, Mom," Kelly said. "I swear. He just . . . he doesn't like me."

Mom let out a heavy, rattling breath. "Go on to bed," she said quietly. "It's late." Kelly left the room, relief flooding all over her, through her. *I'm free.* She let her thoughts wander now because she could. She recalled what had happened in Len's Trans Am, all of it. She imagined herself on the phone with Bellamy, receiver pressed to her ear, her voice a thin whisper.

Guess what? I have another secret.

She wished she could call her. But it was 2:00 A.M., and she had school tomorrow and besides, the phone was in the kitchen. Right next to the bananas. Man, Kelly was hungry. Her stomach gnawed at her.

Kelly couldn't think of food anymore and so she made herself think of other things, of Len again, his bucket seats that reclined all the way back and how he'd said, "*Sorry,*" afterward. How he'd handed her a Kleenex, which was sort of gentlemanly in a way . . .

"Kelly," Mom called out. "Stop dawdling!"

"I'm not!"

Dawdling. What an old-lady word. Mom had an old-lady name too—Rose Lund. It didn't match her looks at all, but it suited her personality, especially in the past two years. She never laughed, hardly ever smiled when she wasn't with a boyfriend. And even with her boyfriends, Mom's smiles looked fake, like someone posing for a picture. She said things like "stop dawdling" and "don't you sass me, young lady" and spent her whole life working and cleaning and smoking, not enjoying any of it, dating boring men with boring jobs she thought could "get us out of Hollywood once and for all."

Mom hadn't always been this way. Kelly had dim memories from back when their dad still lived with them—one in particular, a chicken fight in some fancy pool, Catherine on Mom's shoulders, Kelly on their dad's. They must have been about six years old. Mom had been wearing a hot pink bikini and was laughing so hard, tears streamed down her cheeks. She may have been drunk, now that Kelly thought about it, but seeing her laugh like that . . . Mom had such a great laugh. They'd been at the home of a B movie producer—Kelly's dad was a stuntman, and Mom had worked as a makeup artist, so they used to get invited to a lot of these low-level Hollywood parties, their little family . . .

"Kelly Michelle Lund!"

"I'm getting ready for bed!"

"It doesn't sound like it!"

Kelly rolled her eyes. "Okay, okay." Passing Mom's room, Kelly noticed a big heart-shaped box on the nightstand. *Who's that from?* Her stomach gaped, begged. She could practically smell it. *Chocolate. Just one piece.*

Kelly heard the *weem a woppa* song ending, Casey Kasem's voice, murmuring something about a classic. Casey's voice reminded Kelly of her dad's, the gentleness of it. Outside of Catherine's funeral, where all he'd done was sob, Kelly hadn't heard Dad's voice since she was little, but still she remembered. At least she thought she did.

"We'll be right back," said Casey, and then some used-car ad came on, about fifty decibels louder than the show had been. Kelly slipped off her shoes, timed her footsteps on the soft carpet to land with each shouted word.

Catherine's framed picture sat on Mom's nightstand next to the chocolates. It wasn't normally there, the picture. It was usually on the TV in the den, and seeing it here, in Mom's room, made Kelly think back more than she wanted to.

Kelly looked into her sister's bottle green eyes as she slipped the lid off the box, took a piece from the edge—coconut, which her mom wouldn't miss. *Those eyes. They still laugh at you.*

Catherine had left them on Valentine's Day. Weird, that hadn't occurred to Kelly until now. The picture next to the bed. The chocolates. It had taken all that, just to remind her. But the truth was, it hadn't felt sudden. Years before she died, Catherine had begun leaving Kelly and Mom, a little at a time.

With Mom, it had started earlier, and it had been a lot more dramatic. Catherine yelled at her, called her a bitch. She slammed doors in Mom's face, mocked her "no Hollywood" rules, and made a big, spectacular show of pushing her away.

But she was sweeter about leaving Kelly. Instead of screaming at her, she eased out of her life in such a way, Kelly barely noticed it happening. First, she stopped watching *Happy Days* with Kelly at night, excusing herself to take phone calls in the kitchen and later heading out to, as Catherine put it, "destinations unknown." Instead of dragging Kelly along like she used to do when they were little and it was sleepovers and birthday parties she was going to, Catherine would leave on her own to meet her new and mysterious circle of friends, reporting back to Kelly when she returned and Mom was out of earshot. *"So this girl I met at the party? Her dad used to play drums for Jimi Hendrix!"*

"I kissed the most adorable guy. He's done commercials! You know that Tide one, where those kids roll down the hill and get grass stains . . ."

"Kelly, I can't believe you don't know who Jimi Hendrix was . . ."

"I'm going all the way. Don't tell Mom."

"I lost it, Kelly. For real. I bled and everything."

"The Whisky is amazing. You have to go there sometime. All these girls were doing poppers in the bathroom."

"I can't believe you don't know what poppers are . . ."

"I can't tell you who he is. He's . . . he's kind of famous. We haven't done it yet but we will. I can feel it."

Kelly loved these late-night talks, looked forward to them so much, she barely noticed that they were happening less and less, that Catherine was becoming weird and remote, claiming tiredness, slipping off to sleep, saying "tell you later. I promise." Later never came. Catherine was shedding Kelly, the same way you'd shed any bad habit, bit by bit by bit.

By the last few months of her life, Catherine had become a stranger. She'd grown lean and leggy and hard-eyed, while Kelly stayed a chubby kid. She started wearing lipstick you could only get in Europe that came in an elegant silver tube and was called *Rouge de la Bohème*. She took it with her everywhere, made a big show of applying it.

Mom didn't know what to make of her. "*Who are you, anyway?*" She said that to Catherine more and more.

Catherine hardly ever said a word to Kelly, sneaking in late without waking her, ditching her at the school bus with a quick wave good-bye. She would disappear for days at a time and return wearing brand-new clothes and once, a new necklace with a delicate, shimmering chain and gold, heart-shaped pendant that had two small diamonds at the bottom. "*Where did you get that?*" Mom had asked, between her teeth, eyes narrowing as Catherine just stood there, smirking at her. "*Answer me. Who gave that to you?*"

"*I think it's pretty,*" Kelly had tried. Neither one of them had paid any attention.

Kelly pined for Catherine. She started spying on her, following her down the street at a safe distance as she walked with her beautiful friends, strawberry blond hair swinging and gleaming. She strained to overhear Catherine's phone conversations, marveling at her coy laugh, her cagy, clever way with words.

She stayed up late, listening for Catherine's rides to drop her off outside their apartment. Sometimes it would be groups of girls, their laughter floating in the night air. Other times, Kelly would hear rustling and heavy breathing outside their front door and she'd know it was a boy.

Once, when Kelly was home from school sick and Mom was at work, she'd heard tires screech outside their window. Kelly had peeked around the curtains to see her sister hurrying away from the most beautiful car she'd ever seen—a shiny black Porsche, with tinted windows and mirrored hubcaps. Kelly had been so enthralled with the car that she hadn't even bothered to think about who Catherine had been storming away from until he got out of the driver's-side door and followed her a few steps. As Kelly watched, the Porsche's driver grabbed her sister's swinging arm, then spun her around, pushed her up against one of the palms that lined their street, and kissed her, hard. It looked strange and mean, as she'd never imagined a kiss could be.

As he headed back to his car, Kelly had been able to take a good, long look at him—mirrored aviator glasses to match the hubcaps, black T-shirt and sports jacket and slacks, not jeans. Very short hair, receding hairline. He wasn't a boy. He was a grown man, much older than Len. He was probably older than their father.

Kelly had hurried back into her bedroom and gotten into bed, closing her eyes and seeing it all again behind her lids—the beautiful car, the man with the aviator glasses. The way he'd grabbed at her sister.

"*You're here,*" Catherine had said. "*What are you doing here?*"

"*I'm sick.*"

"*Okay. Um . . . Hope you feel better.*"

It had made Kelly open her eyes—the crack in Catherine's voice. And then she'd looked at her face, the streaks of mascara down her cheeks. *You're crying,* she had wanted to say. *You never cry.*

"*Kelly?*"

"*Yeah?*"

"Do you remember Thumbelina?"

Kelly had nodded, remembering the doll they'd both begged for when they were little—tiny Thumbelina who could crawl and turn over and looked so real and cute on the TV ads. They'd pleaded with their parents for months—*Just one Thumbelina doll! We can share it!*—and finally their dad had relented. They'd torn open the box, only to find a cheap plastic thing with hollow eyes that whirred angrily when you pulled the string, flailing and falling on its side like something broken. The real Thumbelina had been nothing like the doll in the ad. She'd been scary, in fact, and while Kelly had been disappointed, Catherine had sobbed.

Cried real tears, just like now.

"We wanted that doll so bad," Kelly had tried.

Catherine had nodded slowly, touching the necklace, tapping a finger against the two small diamonds. *"We never should have opened the box."*

Valentine's Day couldn't have been more than two months later. Catherine had come home very late. Close to 3:00 A.M. Kelly had been sound asleep and she'd woken up to the front door slamming, a car roaring away.

"Where were you?" Mom had shouted.

And then Catherine had said it, in an awful, smirking tone that made Kelly pull the pillow over her head. *"I was with my Valentine."*

"Tell me his name."

"You don't get to ask me that."

"Catherine—"

"Get away from me!"

Mom had exploded. She'd called her all kinds of horrible names.

Kelly had gotten up. She'd left the bedroom she still supposedly shared with Catherine and padded into the hallway, just in time to see Mom slap Catherine hard across the face . . .

"*I'm sorry,*" Mom had sobbed, just after the slap. "*I'm sorry, baby. We can fix this. Let me help you fix it.*"

Catherine had spotted Kelly in the doorway and run for her, her whole cheek bright red. She'd thrown her arms around her, hugged her for the first time in so long. "*It's in the top dresser drawer,*" she had whispered in her ear. "*Keep it for me.*"

Before Mom could stop her, she'd grabbed the car keys off the hook by the door. She'd run out, starting up Mom's car and driving away—leggy, mature Catherine who had somehow learned how to drive. Mom had run out of the house, screaming after her own car before finally collapsing on the front step, Kelly staring at her, not knowing what to do.

"*Go back to your room,*" Mom had told Kelly. And so she had. She'd looked in the top dresser drawer and seen it there. The necklace.

ON THE KITCHEN RADIO NOW, THE ANNOUNCER INTONED, "loooooooowest prices evvvverrrrr" in a rumbling, movie demon voice, and Kelly tried to make those words drown out what was looping through her brain. *The car screech. Mom's sobs.* "*Don't leave me. Don't leave me.*"

It was easier to pretend Catherine was alive and in the room with her, sneaking candy, trying to put one over on Mom the way they used to before everything went sour.

In Kelly's shirt pocket was Len's phone number, written on the back of a Denny's matchbook. "*So you'll think of me when you light up,*" he had said.

"Did it count, Catherine?" Kelly whispered to the picture when the radio was at its loudest. "Tonight with Len? Can I call it my first time?"

Kelly popped the whole chocolate in her mouth, curling her tongue around it, closing her eyes for the sweet, rich taste.

She gagged. It was awful. Stale and nearly tasteless. Kelly spit it out into her hands, picked up another, tested it with her fingers. It felt like plastic—not even a hint of softness. *How old is this box of candy?*

"What is wrong with you, Mom?" she said, under her breath, then left the bedroom in a few long steps, grabbing her shoes on the way out, making it into her own room at last as an ad for some skin care cream blared. Softly, carefully, Kelly closed her door. She grabbed a tissue out of the box on her nightstand, wrapped the candy in it, a strange sadness flooding through her, the chalky taste lingering.

What is wrong with you, Mom?

She headed across the hall to the bathroom. "Rockin' Robin" tweetilee deeted out of the radio like drips of ice cold water.

"Kelly?"

"Just brushing my teeth!" Kelly brushed the awful taste out of her mouth, along with the questions floating around in her brain, the sadness. The past. Valentine's Day would be the two-year anniversary of Catherine's death and her mother was up all night scrubbing the kitchen floor, an ancient box of stale chocolates (*Who gave them to her?*) waiting on her nightstand. She brushed all of that away, too. And then she flushed the piece of candy down the toilet.

Once she was in her room again, Kelly checked the very back of her nightstand drawer—the place where she now kept the necklace. She changed into her pajamas and got into bed. A little bit of her high still lingered and she was glad for that. As she closed her eyes, she brought her thinking back to Len, how tightly he'd held on to her. She thought about Bellamy, her new friend, and what she'd say to her in science class tomorrow.

BELLAMY DIDN'T SHOW UP AT SCHOOL FOR THREE WHOLE DAYS. THE first day, Tuesday, Kelly could barely keep her eyes open from lack of sleep the night before. She spent most of the day in a haze but arrived early to science class and stood waiting at the new girl's empty desk, clutching the Denny's matchbook with Len's number on it—her new talisman. She stood there, waiting and waiting until Mr. Hansen came in and started writing on the board and Evan Mueller, who sat next to Bellamy, asked Kelly what the hell she was doing, all moony-eyed at Bellamy Marshall's desk like a groupie. "Are you a lezzie or what?" he said. Kelly didn't answer.

After school, she finally went to detention, which was held in the same room where she normally had study hall. There were three other kids in the room with her—a couple of punk rock boys with scary spiked Mohawks and dog collars and anarchy signs on their leather jackets, a girl in tight jeans and a tube top, chewing fruit gum Kelly could smell from three rows away. None of them paid attention to her and neither did Miss Rivers, the teacher in charge. And so the three hours went quickly. Kelly spent the whole time with her notebook open, writing long letters to Bellamy, asking her questions.

THE NEXT DAY OF BELLAMY'S ABSENCE, KELLY SNEAKED OVER TO THE administration office during lunch, the Denny's matchbook buttoned into the pocket of her denim jacket. She asked the receptionist, Mrs. Yanikian, if she could tell her where Bellamy Marshall's locker was.

"Why?"

"I'm in her science class."

"Yes. And?"

"And . . . we have a project. We need to work on it and I can't find her . . ."

Mrs. Yanikian glowered at her over the cat's-eye glasses she wore on a gold chain around her neck. The rhinestones at the edges twinkled.

"Can you tell me the locker number, please?"

The receptionist paged through a notebook on her desk, her manicured nails a deep bloodred, her copper hair molded into perfect waves. Mrs. Yanikian spent an awful lot of time dolling herself up, just to sit in this cage of an office all day long.

"Bellamy Marshall is absent today," she said. "But if you have a project together, you should already know where her locker is."

"I . . . forgot."

Mrs. Yanikian smiled at her with flat eyes. "Run along, Kelly," she said. "The bell is going to ring soon."

ON THE THIRD DAY, WHICH WAS VALENTINE'S DAY, KELLY SAT WORRYING through science, Bellamy's empty seat gaping at her back until finally she could no longer stand it. She raised her hand.

Mr. Hansen, who had been explaining something having to do with cell production, said, "Yes, Kelly?"

"Can I get a hall pass please?"

"Silly me. I thought you were going to contribute to class discussion."

A few kids snickered. Kelly took a breath. "I need to go to the bathroom."

More snickers. Mr. Hansen let out a heavy sigh and handed her a pass. It was everything Kelly could do not to leap out of the classroom, but she made herself take it slow. She made herself walk, not run, down the hall to the pay phone outside the nurse's office because running would get her stopped by a hall monitor or janitor. She knew this. It was the way life worked. Try to rush something, you get delayed. You break the rules, bad things happen.

Once she got to the pay phone, her heart starting pounding. In her mind, she told herself, *It will be fine.* Before she could think too long, she threw her quarter into the slot, plucked the Denny's matchbook out of the front pocket of her corduroys, and dialed Len's number.

It rang and rang and rang and rang.

Not home. She was about to hang up when, finally, a woman answered. Kelly's stomach dropped. "Who is this?"

"Who is *this?*"

She shut her eyes, felt her cheeks flushing. "Is Len there? Sorry. I'm just . . . I'm looking for my friend Bellamy and I don't have her number and so I'm wondering if maybe—"

"Len?"

"He's friends with my friend Bellamy and . . . uh . . ."

"Is Len your *boyfriend* or something?"

She cleared her throat. "I met him the other day. He gave me this number."

The woman started to laugh.

"He did. I swear."

"You sound young. How old are you, anyway? Twelve?"

Kelly exhaled hard. "No."

"Honey, trust me on this," the woman said. "Len does not want to see you."

"You don't know that. He gave me this number. He told me to call."

The woman laughed some more. "This number," she said, "is a pay phone."

Kelly's cheeks burned. She slammed down the receiver, her neck hot, her throat swelling, that awful tingle starting in her belly, coursing through her . . . same thing she had felt on her first day back at school two years ago, working the combination on her locker next to Catherine's empty one and knowing she had no one now. No sister to follow around. No chance of a friend.

Len had given her a made-up number.

She'd told him it was her first time. She hadn't planned to tell him that—she had wanted him to think it was no big deal, that she was like Bellamy. But the pot had felt like truth serum and his hands were crawling all over her and she'd wanted him to know. She'd wanted him to know how important this was and how, after it happened, she'd never be the same. He'd given her a Kleenex. He'd written down his number on the back of a matchbook and slipped it to her like a present. "*So you'll think of me when you light up.*"

Why bother lying like that? Why bother writing down a made-up phone number when she hadn't even asked? Was it some joke? Was all of it—Bellamy and her house and the pot and everything—was all of it a joke that Len had been in on?

"*Len likes you. I can tell.*"

Kelly felt that heat pressing up against the backs of her eyes. She knew she was going to cry. She couldn't be here any longer. Her legs moved beneath her, like they were a separate machine, coming to her rescue, propelling her down the halls and lurching her to safety.

"No running in the halls!" one of the janitors shouted. But Kelly pretended not to hear him. She didn't care about breaking rules anymore.

Before she could think very long about what she was doing, Kelly was out the front door of the school, and she was rushing down the steps, the sun too bright, the sidewalk hot beneath the wavy soles of her sandals.

It was an uncommonly warm day for this time of year . . . same as it had been two years ago, the stifling air from outside billowing into their house when Catherine opened the door for the last time. A blast of oven-heat in the middle of the night, just like Santa Ana season, even though it had only been February, the Santa Anas months away . . .

Or maybe that was just the way Kelly remembered it. Maybe it hadn't been warm out at all.

Kelly was on the sidewalk now. She heard someone making kissing noises at her out the window of a car, the blast of a horn. A girl on a Hollywood sidewalk never gets ignored, no matter how ignored she is everyplace else.

Kelly kept up a fast pace and forced her eyes down until she saw pink stars under her feet. Hollywood Boulevard. She'd taken a wrong turn somewhere, but it didn't matter. Her mother wasn't working today and the last thing she wanted to do was see Mom, with her questions and her disappointment and her sad, headachy eyes. So she couldn't go home either.

She couldn't go anywhere.

"You there," said a hoarse voice. Kelly turned and saw a shirtless man with a stained yellow beard, leaning against the window of a dirty magazine store, twitching. He was beyond broken—as though some huge monster had chewed him to bits and swallowed him and spit him back up again. "You'll die soon," he said.

Kelly's stomach dropped. She whirled away from him and stepped into the crosswalk. She heard the screech of wheels and froze and closed her eyes, not caring as much as she should have cared. Not caring at all.

But there was no impact. No crushing pain. Just Kelly's own name, yelled at her. She opened her eyes and saw the red VW rabbit, Bellamy behind the wheel, hair wild around her face, black-framed Ray-Bans guarding her eyes. "Are you deaf or what?" Bellamy said. "We've been chasing you for blocks. We were honking."

Kelly stared at Bellamy, then at the spiky-haired boy in the passenger seat.

"Well, don't just stand there, dummy," Bellamy said. "Get in the car."

"Where were you? It's been three days."

Bellamy sighed. "You go to school too much."

It wasn't until Kelly had squeezed into the tiny backseat and Bellamy had lit a cigarette and started driving again, flipping on a British bootleg tape of a band called Joy Division and telling Kelly, "You have to listen to this song, it is so *us*," that the boy introduced himself.

"I'm Vee," he said, deep blue eyes fixed on Kelly's face from the passenger-side mirror.

"Hi. I'm Kelly."

The song, Bellamy said, was called "She's Lost Control." For a while, Kelly and Vee listened to it in silence, both thinking about Bellamy saying *us*, both wondering which of them she'd meant to include.

CHAPTER 6

"Words can be bent to your will in a way that visual art cannot," says Bellamy Marshall, a smile curling her bright red lips. "In a way, all memoirists are fiction writers. But in visual art—in my art—all you have is the truth."

For the artist—who happens to be both the daughter of movie legend Sterling Marshall and a former classmate of convicted murderer Kelly Lund—the truth of her heady growing-up years in the early '80s is alternately ugly and beautiful. Her art installations encompass both qualities—most notably Mona Lisa, *which features a seven-foot-tall version of the iconic 1981 photograph taken of Lund outside the Los Angeles courthouse. Chilling in its own right, the photo takes on new meaning at this size, adorned with globs of gold and silver glitter and pink feathers—and accompanied, like all of Marshall's creations, by an arresting "soundtrack." In this case it's Lund herself, recorded during a prison phone conversation with Marshall several years ago and played in a continuous loop that grows more terrifying with each repetition. "I miss you," intones Lund's flat, childlike voice. "Why won't you visit?"*

"Mona Lisa *was utterly wrenching to create," says Marshall of the work, which derives its name from Lund's chilling facial expression in the photograph, dubbed "the Mona Lisa Death Smile" by noted crime writer Sebastian Todd. "It's gratifying for me that it has received such a strong response."*

*The central piece in Marshall's "Tales from Glamorland" exhibit—showing at LACMA from August 10–28—*Mona Lisa *captures both the seductive sheen of show business and the banality of sin. And it marks the striking 32-year-old's re-invention, from spoiled Hollywood socialite to a creator of art in her own right.*

It took a lot for Marshall to shake off the gloss of her father's legend. For a time, she even debated changing her last name, or dropping it altogether. But as she says now, it is her father's legend that shaped her—for better and for worse.

"I will always love Dad, but it was so difficult growing up in his shadow," muses Marshall, dragging a hand through her jet-black bob. "There were so many people who would do any-thing to get close to me. But it was never because of me. It was always Dad, always Sterling Marshall and the world I lived in because of him."

Was Kelly Lund one of those people?

It's a question that's presumably easy to answer. It was Lund's very brief friendship with a young Bellamy Marshall, after all, that allowed the killer's path to cross with that of doomed Oscar-nominated director John McFadden.

But rather than respond to the question quickly, Marshall ponders it in silence for quite some time. She adjusts her cat's-

eye glasses and takes another sip of coffee, her dark eyes seeking out some faraway spot on the café's cracked, adobe wall.

"She used to watch Dad's movies when she was a little girl," Marshall says, her voice quiet, almost wistful. "He was her mother's favorite."

FROM
"Art's Reluctant 'It' Girl"
Los Angeles Times Magazine
August 1, 1994

CHAPTER 7

APRIL 21, 2010

Shane found his way home without thinking about it. Strange, considering he had such a poor sense of direction, he practically needed the GPS to navigate his way from his and Kelly's place in Joshua Tree Highlands to "downtown" Joshua Tree—which was about five minutes away and all of two blocks.

But even stranger that he still thought of 2071 Blue Jay Way as "home."

It was a warm, dry day, that bright sun spilling in on him once he started climbing long, twisty Beachwood Drive and opened the windows. And in so many ways it was as if no time had passed.

Through his windshield, he could see the Hollywood sign—first time he'd seen the sign in daylight in half a decade, yet still it was the same, everything up here the same. Lurid red and pink bougainvillea climbing stucco walls, metal gates decked with security cameras, shielding infinity pools and tennis courts and Versailles-like landscaping that came at you in flash frames through thin breaks in the gates. You could only see them in full from above, the grounds of these palaces. But that sign, always that sign— the one view up here that wasn't in any way obstructed or guarded, that white sign sprawled out so obscenely at the top of Mount Lee, daring you to look anywhere else.

Shane made the turn onto Blue Jay Way, and immediately saw the vans lined up on the street. He couldn't tell how many were there, but as he drew closer, he saw they numbered half a dozen—one from Action News, one from TMZ, the others unmarked, probably freelance paparazzi. A helicopter buzzed overhead in a lazy circle, vulture analogy all too obvious.

Must be a slow news day. Dad hasn't made a movie in years.

Of course, celebrity suicides were always big news, weren't they? The phrase hung in his head. *Celebrity suicides.* He wished he hadn't thought of it. His throat clenched up again as he reached the gate, his thoughts going to Mom. Had she been the one to find him? Could she hear the buzz of the helicopter? *Is she all right? Can she think? Can she breathe?*

When he reached the gate that still shielded the mansion he grew up in and stopped the car, he heard their voices through his open window—the van occupants. The audience. "*You ask for an audience, you get one always, whether you want one or not,*" his dad used to say. "*They're always watching, son. You need to be more careful how you look.*" They were watching now. Watching and commenting like he was something on TV.

"Who is that in the Jeep?" one of them said. "Think it's the son," said another. Shane heard Kelly's name and his name and he pushed the button fast, shoving a memory out of his mind, a memory of Dad pushing the same button, Mom in the passenger seat, Shane and Bellamy in the back, young and small and forever safe . . .

One of the paps yelled, "*Shane! Over here!*"

"Who is here, please?" said a female voice from the other end of the intercom—a voice he'd never heard before.

He cleared his throat. "Shane Marshall."

"Did you see it coming, Shane?"

"Shane! Shane! What did the note say?"

What was wrong with these people? Did they honestly think he was going to answer? He started to say his name into the box again when the strange female voice said, "Come right in, Mr. Marshall," and the gate opened. Thank God.

"Shane, when was the last time your dad told you he loves you?"

He shut the window and pulled up and into his family's property, the gate closing around him like arms.

The driveway was long and steep, and as he took it toward the house, more memories pushed in on him until his head felt crowded—birthday parties, hide-and-seek, visits from all those tanned, sparkling people that were part of his parents' lives. Dad's life, actually. Actors, directors . . . Mom at the ready with her trays of finger sandwiches, mixing cocktails by the pool, sunglasses shielding her eyes so you never knew what she was thinking.

Shane swallowed hard.

It all looked so much the same—the manicured lawn, that embarrassing green, as though water were limitless in this town, his mother's bright rosebushes and hibiscus, the magnolia tree he used to climb to spy on Bellamy and her friends . . .

He tried to collect himself, to get his breathing back to normal. *All that paparazzi. Jesus. What a swarm.* Why hadn't Mom called the police on them? Why hadn't Bellamy?

When he reached the house, he saw three police cars parked alongside the house. *Is that normal for a suicide?* Shane thought, the word rattling him all over again. A thin woman in black jeans and a black T-shirt stood in front of the door. It took him a few seconds to recognize her as his sister.

How long had it been? Six, seven years. Not that long in the general scheme of things, but God she looked so different. So much thinner, paler, her lips meager without that poison-red lipstick, the dyed hair pulled back in a greasy ponytail, the jet-blackness of it so out of place now on this frail sketch of a woman—his sister, who hadn't aged so much as faded into something dull, something harmless.

I should have talked to Bellamy. At least I should have told Dad I was going to talk to her and forgive her, and maybe then . . .

Maybe we would never have argued. Maybe you'd still be alive.

Shane turned off the Jeep and climbed out. He went to his sister and hugged her, Bellamy so thin and brittle in his arms, leaning on him as though she'd become the baby, Shane the protector. *Bellamy, why did we waste so many years?* He knew the answer, of course. But it didn't feel important with her wet cheek against his neck, her bony body trembling against him. Bellamy, his only sister. Bellamy, who had lost her father too.

Shane stared at the police cars alongside his house, his home, and he started to cry again. Not just for Dad but for his sister, his family, his safe, happy youth. For everything he once had and no longer did.

"Why did he do it, Bella?" he said. "Why did Dad kill himself?"

Bellamy pulled back. Her hard eyes surprised him, as did her grip on his shoulders, so tight it hurt. "Let's go inside," she said.

SHANE FELT LIKE HE WAS STUCK IN A FEVER DREAM. THE HOUSE HE grew up in, crawling with police, yellow tape cordoning off the kitchen—and, Bellamy told him as he stood staring at it, coiling around the sliding doors he used to hang on as a kid, cordoning off his father's upstairs office too. "The scene of the crime," she told him. "That's what they're calling Dad's office, Shane."

"Is Dad still in there?"

"No," she said. "The medical examiner took . . . took him."

"They do that for suicides?" Shane said. Stupid thing to say. He didn't even know why he'd said it. It was as though his mouth was moving of its own accord, reality knocking into him like waves. His parents' home. The big window overlooking the canyon that he used to press his nose against, Flora complaining about the prints. And in it, in this place that used to be his whole world . . . Crime scene tape. Police uniforms brushing by, staticky radios. The click of cameras. White gloved hands . . . And then, his mother in a white silk robe on the red couch by the window, doubled over, collapsed . . .

"Mom." Shane moved toward her, Bellamy sticking close behind. "Mom."

Her head lifted, very slowly. She looked up at him, her mouth a trembling line, eyes like smashed glass. For a few seconds, it seemed as though she didn't recognize him. Then she whispered his name.

Shane tried to think of the last time he'd seen his mother—had to have been at least a year ago. He'd gone to one of her charity luncheons and she'd greeted him with a big smile, a hug. She never changed, Mom. Not before today. But now, it was as though someone had scooped all the life out of her. "You're here," she said.

Shane bent over, took her in his arms. She hung on him limply. She felt so frail, as though if he hugged her too hard, all her bones might crumble.

Mom had met Dad as a nineteen-year-old script girl. Married him three months later. She'd spent her entire adulthood as Mrs. Sterling Marshall and sure, they'd had their disagreements—Shane marrying Kelly being their biggest—but he had never seen two people more devoted to each other. "*I've had only one great love,*" Mom used to say. "*And I wound up marrying him.*"

"I'm so sorry, Mom."

"You poor boy," she whispered.

Shane pulled away. And only then did he notice Flora, the housekeeper. "There, there, Mary," Flora said. "There, there . . ."

"Shane, there's something you need to see," said Bellamy. A woman stood next to her—stern faced, in office camouflage: gray pantsuit, beige shirt, graying hair pulled back in beige clips. Shane blinked at her. *Is she what I need to see?* "This is Detective Braddock," Bellamy said.

The woman corrected her. "Brad-dock," she said, rhyming it with padlock.

"Uh, hello?"

"Come into the den, please, Mr. Marshall."

Braddock turned, headed toward the den without waiting to see if he was following. Bellamy took the crook of Shane's arm in both her hands, and led him.

"What about Mom?"

"She'll be fine out here with Flora," Bellamy said. "Right, Mom?"

They exchanged a look that Shane couldn't begin to understand. "What's going on?" he said. "What do I need to see? Is it the note?"

Bellamy sighed heavily.

"Is it Dad's note?"

"Come on, Shane," she said, making him feel five again, pulling him along as he turned, taking one last, long look at his crumpled mother.

"I'M GOING TO SHOW YOU SOMETHING," BRADDOCK SAID, AFTER Shane and Bellamy had sat down on the couch. There was an open laptop on the coffee table. She typed in a few commands and an image appeared on the screen—a figure in a gray hoodie slipping out of a door, getting into a midsize, silver car, then driving into the darkness.

She switched it off. The whole thing must have lasted at least five seconds.

"Well?" Bellamy said.

The detective shushed her. "Do you want to see it again?"

"See what?" Shane said.

She clicked at the laptop, and again he watched the image—the person, tallish, moving fast, flinging open the car's door, sliding in . . .

"What does that look like to you, Mr. Marshall," Braddock said.

"Ummm . . . Someone driving?"

Bellamy exhaled. "Jesus," she whispered.

Shane was starting to feel worried and adrift—the way he'd sometimes feel in dreams, when he was stuck in a play without knowing his lines, or at his old high school, taking a test in a language he'd never seen. "I . . . I don't know what's going on."

"What type of car does your wife drive, Mr. Marshall?"

"Excuse me?"

"We have her owning a 2009 Toyota Camry, is that correct?"

"Yes."

"Silver?"

"Yeah. So . . ."

"That car in the video. Does it look at all like hers?"

"I . . . I guess it kind of . . . Wait, what are you asking me here?"

"Does your wife own any hoodies, Mr. Marshall?"

He stared at her. "Everybody owns hoodies."

"I should be more specific, sorry. Does she own any pale gray hoodies, similar to the one worn by the person in the video?"

Shane swallowed hard. "What is this video?"

Bellamy started to answer, but the detective put a hand up. "It's footage from one of the security cameras at this house," Braddock said. "Taken this morning at two A.M.—your father's estimated time of death."

"Oh," he said.

"All other surveillance was shut down," Braddock said. "The security guard had left for the night, so the cameras were most likely turned off either by your father, or by this visitor."

"Oh . . ."

"Would you like to take another look at the video? We can plug the laptop into the big screen. Show it there."

He turned to the blank screen on the wall of his parents' den. State-of-the-art. Of course it was. In the eighteen years he'd lived here, the Marshall family had probably gone through twenty den TVs, switching up each time, and this one was trade-show material— a good eighty inches wide, slim as a credit card, a lustrous black pool of a screen. No doubt this piece of machinery was wonderful to watch his father's old movies on, but there was no doubt in his mind that, if even viewed on that screen, the surveillance video could only be what it was, which was crap. Shane had seen clearer, more discernable images in his dreams. "I don't know what good that would do." His voice shook a little. "I mean . . . I'm not even sure whether that person in the video is a man or a woman."

"Oh come *on!* " Bellamy stood up and whirled around and made for the window, the air filling with the scent of her—cigarettes, combined with a perfume smell, cliché-sweet and expensive, the kind you find samples of in fashion magazines. "That was her on the video, Shane," Bellamy said. "You know it was."

"Kelly?"

"No. Beyoncé. What is *wrong* with you?"

"It is five seconds of a person in a hoodie," he said. "It could just as easily be you, Bellamy."

"Are you fucking kidding me?"

"It could be anybody." He glared at Bellamy, memories tugging at

him. The walls of this room hadn't changed since he was a kid. No matter how many times the TV in here got upgraded, the walls stayed white, the framed photos—stills from Dad's movies, dozens of them—hung in the same positions they'd always been in . . . His gaze rested on the far left corner of the room, on the still from the movie he'd been thinking of: *Defiance*. There was rugged, western-style Dad, all beard scruff and blood spatter, aiming a pistol at the camera, his eyes glittering beacons in a dirty, chiseled face.

Defiance was Dad's one and only western. It had been shot in the mid-'70s, about an hour or two away from here in the middle of the blazing, dusty San Bernardino desert on a set so detailed, it felt like time travel.

Shane had been to the *Defiance* set many times as a little boy. He'd loved it there—the gleaming prop guns, the horses, the pretty, busty extras in off-the-shoulder peasant blouses, Dad dressed like a real sheriff with a white hat and badge, Dad sneaking Shane glazed doughnuts from crafts services, winking at Shane through fake blood.

But that one day . . . Man, it was amazing in how much detail Shane still remembered it. The grip of his mother's cold fingers as she squeezed his hand outside Dad's trailer, and her voice . . . the anger in it. "*You wait here, Shane. Mommy's going to see Daddy for a few minutes.*" She'd said it like a door slamming, and even though Shane hadn't understood why he couldn't at least sit in the trailer, why he couldn't play with that shiny badge while his parents talked—even then, at four or five years old, he'd known enough not to ask.

It was the only time he could ever recall seeing his mother that angry. And to this day, he'd never found out why. "You don't know everything about Dad," he said to Bellamy. "None of us really know each other."

Her lips went tight. She turned away.

"Mr. Marshall," Braddock said. "Did your wife leave home for any extended period last night?"

Shane closed his eyes. "No," he said, picturing her in his mind, Kelly drenched in morning light, stretching on the bed, her lovely back arching. Kelly's eyes had been closed for hours, Shane knew. There she was, brushing the sleep out of her eyes, opening them for his lens, the sad gray eyes, that strange coldness . . .

No. He had been wrong about that. Paranoid, but for other reasons. She'd been deep asleep. For hours. *And anyway, what were they suggesting? That Kelly had sneaked out of the house to watch Dad kill himself? Were they serious?*

Bellamy said, "You're lying for her."

"No, I'm not."

"Are you telling us everything, Mr. Marshall?"

Shane's eyes opened. "She got up at six," he said. "I woke her."

"Mr. Marshall. Do you and your wife sleep in separate bedrooms?"

A direct question. He couldn't lie to a direct question, asked by a cop. "Yes."

"Why?" Bellamy said.

He put his back to her. "Do you have any other questions, Detective?"

"Detective Braddock," Bellamy said, "Kelly Lund loves to take long drives at night."

"How do you know this?"

"She doesn't," Shane said. "She hasn't spoken to Kelly since she got out of prison. She's never been to our house. She has no idea—"

"*Mom told me.* She said you once complained about it." Bellamy looked at the detective. "She'd leave their house late at night and he'd ask where she was going and she'd say, 'Driving.' He didn't want to press her because he didn't want her to feel trapped. He wanted her to feel free. You know who Kelly Lund is, right? She's a convicted murderer."

Braddock was watching Shane's face in a way he didn't like. "I never said that to Mom," he said. It was true. He'd told his father.

Shane didn't want to talk about Kelly any more, didn't want to think about her. John McFadden had been the director on *Defiance*. And it was on that set, while his mother was in Dad's trailer venting her anger for whatever reason, that John had pulled Shane aside, telling him that Dad was the best actor he'd ever worked with. *Don't tell the gossip rags* . . . Bellamy had been on set that day too, ignoring Shane like she always did, running around with John McFadden's son, whom she called her "pretend brother." (Her "better brother," she used to call that kid, when she and Shane were alone and the grown-ups were out of earshot.)

Shane gritted his teeth. He'd taken a sleeping pill last night, just like he did on most nights. But it hadn't worked right away—he had a lot on his mind lately, thoughts he didn't want to look too hard at. Thoughts involving Kelly, her late-night drives, her secrets . . .

So he'd added a couple more pills. He'd taken five sleeping pills and passed out dead cold until the alarm had woken him. The Shane Marshall Ambien Coma, Kelly liked to call it. Kelly, who insisted on separate rooms because it was the only way she could sleep. In solitary. Kelly, who owned half a dozen hoodies. "I'm going to check on Mom."

"If you want justice for Dad," Bellamy said, "you'll tell the truth."

Shane stopped. *Enough*. "He committed suicide, Bellamy." He glared at the detective. "I want to see the note."

She blinked at him.

"I want to see the note, Detective. I want to read it and I want to grieve my father's death with my family in peace."

"I'm sorry, Mr. Marshall."

He exhaled. "No need. I understand. He was a famous man. People want answers, and believe me, so do I. Please show me the note."

The detective shook her head, her hair catching the light in a way that made him think again of Kelly this morning, silver hairs glistening among the gold, her face soft on the pillow, yet still that breach between them, that wall she put up . . . *I'm sorry, Shane. I can't.* How well can you know a woman who refuses to make love to you? Who hasn't let you in for close to fifteen years?

Did Dad ask Kelly to witness his suicide? Did he ask her to assist in it?

"Mr. Marshall," said Braddock, her eyes dull from forced sympathy. "I said I'm sorry because the reporters got it wrong."

"What?"

"This is an open murder investigation," she said. "There was no note."

CHAPTER 8

A bout half a mile up the mountain from Kelly and Shane's house, in a double-wide surrounded by an army of prickly pears he'd planted himself, lived their nearest neighbor, a chainsaw artist who went by the name of Rocky Three.

"Rocky Three?" Kelly had said five years ago, when Shane had pointed him out during their very first drive to the home he had bought for them. Kelly thinking she was hitting the ground running on her new life of freedom—starting fresh—when she'd spotted him out there among his prickly pears, a shirtless, sinewy, battered-looking bald man, deep green tattoos crawling all over his red-brown back, chainsawing the guts out of an enormous tree trunk, sawdust flying all around him.

"Yep, that's his name," Shane had replied. "Even says it on his mailbox."

"*Rocky III* was when the *Rocky* movies started getting bad," said Kelly. And then Rocky Three'd turned around and faced their car and she had locked eyes with him—bits of sharp blue in a sad, leathery, tattooed face, those bright eyes like something from another, better time of life. Kelly had waved at Rocky Three and he'd waved back. *I understand the name*, she had thought. *I understand him.*

"Keep away from him," Shane had said. "He's nuts, and probably dangerous."

"Our neighbor? But what if I need to borrow a cup of sugar?"

It had been a joke, but Shane hadn't laughed. "He hasn't lived here long. There are all kinds of rumors about him. Fortunately, he keeps to himself."

One week later when Shane was meeting with a client in their home, she'd excused herself, walked the three miles, knocked on his door.

Back then, she hadn't learned to drive yet. It was easier now.

Kelly pulled past the prickly pears and around the side of the double-wide and parked. His creations lined the back end of the trailer—an angry bear, a looming, sharp-fanged dragon, an angel with enormous beckoning wings and a skull for a face—Kelly's favorite. He'd named it for her.

All the chainsawed statues were at least ten feet tall, carved out of tree trunks salvaged from Northern California clear-cuts. Rocky had them delivered to his home. Far as Kelly could tell, he never sold these things—he carved them for company. Kelly gazed into the skull face of the angel. *Keep him safe.* A corny thought, but not a new one.

She felt someone watching her, and when she turned, she saw Rocky standing in the doorway. He wore white drawstring pants, his skin like burned, painted parchment, and he regarded her the way he always did, warm but exasperated, as though their meetings occurred on a regular schedule that he had to keep reminding her about.

A tattoo of a large green eye stared out of the hollow of his neck. It made Kelly's heart beat faster whenever she saw it. She had a theory as to the tattoo's meaning but she never mentioned it to Rocky, didn't want to, for fear he'd shoot it down. "Should I be sorry for your loss?" Rocky said.

Kelly nodded. "You saw the news."

"Yes."

"The police came to my house," Kelly said. "Well, one detective."

"Did he scare you?"

"Detectives don't scare me."

"I know. That was kind of a joke."

Rocky ushered her into the trailer. It was clean and spare and smelled of sawdust. A man like this, you'd expect him to live in a space as cluttered as his yard, his skin. But Rocky Three was the opposite of a hoarder. His walls were bare. He didn't even own a couch—just hard chairs, a bed that was barely softer, nothing that could collect dust.

There was a table in the kitchen area with a laptop on it, news headlines on the screen. Kelly saw a picture of Sterling Marshall. "I will miss him, you know," she said.

"You barely knew him."

"Doesn't matter." Kelly gave him a long look. "After all, I barely know you."

"That's not true."

Kelly sat down on one of the hard chairs, wanting to collapse. "Thank you for having me in."

He shook his head, eyes finding the bleached white floorboards. So clean, his home. So empty and perfect. "Your husband is with his family?"

"He's at his parents' house. He wasn't around when the detective questioned me."

"That's good, I guess." Rocky sighed. He went into the kitchen and drew a glass of water, placed it in Kelly's hand. His skin brushed against hers as he did, and she was grateful for that, the calluses on his fingers, the rough warmth of his skin, familiar as she wanted it to be. "He talked about things, that detective," she said quietly. "He asked me a lot of questions."

"It's what they pay him to do."

Kelly stared at him, but he wouldn't meet her gaze. "I don't know what to do, Rocky."

"Do the police think you killed Sterling Marshall?"

She gave him flat eyes. "What do you think?"

"I think maybe you did."

"Stop."

He shrugged his shoulders. The bottle green eye tattoo twitched with the gesture. "I saw a snake in the road the other morning. Made me think of you."

Kelly smiled a little. "Rattler?"

"No. Just a sweet little garter. I was walking up Old Woman Springs at sunrise and there was that little snake, slithering across the road, leisurely as you please."

"Old Woman Springs is a busy road," said Kelly. "The snake will get run over."

"That's what I thought. 'That snake is dead meat.' But still something is making it head that way, across a busy street, so slow and deliberate . . . You know? It's compelled to go where it shouldn't be going."

Kelly swallowed some of the water, cool and smooth in her throat. "And that reminded you of me. The snake."

"It reminded me of the situation. Our situation."

"Oh."

"All these years," he said. "All these years, you've been knocking on my door."

"Yes."

"And I open the door, every time you knock."

"So . . ."

"So, I can't figure it out, Kelly. Which of us is the pickup truck, speeding up Old Woman Springs at sixty miles an hour? And which of us is that dumb, slow-moving snake?"

Kelly stood up. Strange, Rocky was such a powerfully built man, it made sense he'd be very tall. Yet when Kelly was on her feet and facing him, she looked him directly in the eye. That never stopped surprising her, how evenly matched they were.

"I would have picked up that snake if I were you," she said, taking his calloused hand in hers, leading him to the bedroom. "I would have moved it out of the road."

"DOES YOUR WIFE'S JOB TAKE HER AWAY FROM THE HOUSE A LOT?" Detective Braddock asked. She sat across from Shane in the den, working her notepad. It no longer bothered him, the note-taking, nor did his sister's presence in the room with her perfume and her accusations. The room itself didn't even bother him. Nothing did—other than the obvious. He felt as though someone had kicked him in the gut an hour earlier and he still hadn't recovered from it.

What Shane wanted to know—what he needed to know—was what exactly Braddock had meant by "open murder investigation."

Shane's father had been shot in the center of the forehead, at very close range. Yet Shane had been the only one to mention suicide. There had been no note. He'd never known his father to be depressed. And what he had always known—well, since John McFadden's death anyway—was that Dad had hated guns.

Also, there was this, the one fact that stuck in his mind, the one he couldn't voice for fear that if he said it out loud, it might make more sense than he wanted it to: of the three shots that Shane's wife had fired into a defenseless John McFadden on June 28, 1980, the one that had killed him had been the one that had struck him in the center of the forehead, at close range.

"Kelly works from home," Shane said. His head felt numb and swimmy, the leather couch sticky against his back. He wanted an aspirin. A scotch. A handful of Ambien . . .

"Doing what?"

"Pardon?"

"You said your wife works out of the home. What does she do?"

"She's a writer."

Bellamy let out a noise of pure exasperation—half sigh, half scream. In the old days, the days before this past hour, Shane would have told her to shut up, get out of the room, at the very least, mind her own business. But again, things had changed.

"She writes profiles for a dating site," he said.

"Excuse me?"

"It doesn't sound like a thing. But it is."

The detective nodded, scribbling away. "Does she leave the home a lot? Go into Hollywood for her job?"

"I don't know."

"You don't?"

"She doesn't go anywhere for her job. She just makes up stories about pictures of soft porn models."

"But you don't know if she goes into Hollywood otherwise?"

"I . . . I like to give Kelly her space."

"So when she leaves the house, you don't ever find out where she's going?"

"If she's gone out for groceries," he said, "she comes back with groceries. But I don't ask ahead of time 'Are you going for groceries?'"

"My God," Bellamy whispered. "My God."

The detective said, "Let me ask you something, Mr. Marshall."

"Yes?"

"Have you ever spoken to your wife about the murder she committed?"

"Huh?"

"John McFadden. Have you ever—"

"Why does that matter?"

"Why do you *think* it matters?" Bellamy said, but the detective ignored her.

"I'm just wondering," she said, "what she thinks about it all now. If it haunts her at all, what she did to John McFadden. If she feels guilty, or if she thinks she was justified in some way and that your father's enduring respect for the man she killed . . . Well, I'm sure you saw what your father said just two days ago about Mr. McFadden, in the *Times*?"

"I don't know what Kelly thinks about." Shane's words hung in the air—the most honest words he'd spoken all day.

"Did you hear any noises last night?" Braddock was saying. "Possibly your wife leaving on one of her night drives?"

"I took sleeping pills last night. I was dead to the world."

There was a time in his life when Shane would have sworn up and down that he knew Kelly, knew her better than anyone—and weirdly, it had been when Kelly was in prison but before they got married, when she and Shane weren't allowed to touch each other but through that thick glass.

Back then, he would spend hours, days, writing letters to Kelly, most of those letters dozens of pages long, most of those pages answering the hundreds of questions Kelly would send him in her careful, looped handwriting, those questions so much more revealing than any statement could be. *What was the happiest day you ever had? Tell me everything you remember about it, in as much detail as you can. Do you ever feel like something is missing from your life—and if so, what? Can you please go outside and tell me what the sun feels like on the back of your neck, Shane? I really want to know what that feels like because today I'm not allowed out.*

What is it like to have a sister?

He wasn't sure whether it was Kelly's questions that had made him fall in love with her or her obvious joy at receiving his answers. But either way, she made Shane feel needed, which, as the youngest, weakest link in one of Hollywood's most shimmering families, was not something he felt very often.

I feel a connection with you, Shane. Do you feel it too? Sometimes, when I ask you questions, I already know what you're going to say. I can picture your response in my mind—the same words, even—and then you write those exact words and it's like we share one brain. Like we're two parts of something huge.

"Answer the detective, Shane," Bellamy said as Shane remembered his reply: *I feel it too. But what if this huge thing that the two of us are together is a bad thing—like Godzilla?*

Godzilla is good, Shane. He's just misunderstood because of the way he looks. (And by the way, I knew you would say that!)

Shane's gaze shifted to Braddock. "I'm sorry," he said. "Can you please repeat the question?"

She nodded. A lock of gunmetal hair fell across her eye. She pushed it behind an ear with a gesture that seemed half angry, as though her own hair were interfering with her investigation. "I had asked," Braddock said, "if there's anyone you know of who your wife *does* confide in."

"I don't think so."

"She isn't seeing a therapist?"

"No."

"Friends?"

"The only friend I can think of . . ." He couldn't finish the sentence without laughing, so he stopped.

"Excuse me?"

"Bellamy," he said. "Can you please go check on Mom?"

"I want to hear your answer."

"Mom's a mess. I'm worried about her. We can't just leave her out there with Flora."

"I'll check on her," she said, "after you say who Kelly's friend is."

"Fine." Shane exhaled. "It's you."

"What?"

"It's you," he repeated. "You're the only friend of Kelly's that I know of and you know what? I think that even after all these years and everything you've done to her . . . I think there's a part of her that still thinks of you that way. As her friend."

Bellamy, for once in her life, was at a loss for words. And for that, and that alone, Shane felt grateful.

He stood up, gazing down at his sister with a sense of power he knew was only temporary. "Pathetic, isn't it?" Shane said between his teeth, muscles tensing. He headed out of the room. "I'm going to go check on Mom." He said it without so much as turning around.

ROCKY'S SHEETS WERE CRISP AND COLD—SO UNLIKE KELLY'S OWN, which were made of a very thin, soft flannel. She didn't like thinking of home when she lay here, in his bed—and there really was no reason to. Her troubles with Shane—what the shrink at Carpentia had called *intimacy issues*—had been going on long before she'd ever laid eyes on Rocky Three. She told herself it was Sterling Marshall's threats, the fears they inspired, that kept her from getting physical with Shane. But in those very rare moments when she was honest with herself, she knew she could have gotten an IUD, knew she could have gotten her tubes tied if she'd wanted it that badly. It was something else . . .

She liked to think of Rocky, of *this,* as a recurring dream—something that existed on a different plane than her day-to-day life, something she couldn't be blamed for. A drawer that stayed shut.

Rocky seemed to feel the same way. He called them "meetings," their times together. He called it a "friendship," not an affair. And no matter how tender their meetings were, they never held each other after. They lay on their backs, the two of them, gazing at the bleached ceiling of Rocky's pristine bedroom, his hand covering hers in a way that felt more protective than affectionate—and all of it so right to Kelly, so familiar in that way she dared not voice. *Like years ago. Like going back in time.*

"I lied to you, Rocky," she said.

He turned. She felt his crystalline eyes on her, his face close to hers, the warmth of his breath. "About what?"

Kelly kept her eyes on the ceiling. "Earlier, when I said detectives don't scare me."

"They do?"

"That detective did. I didn't act like it, but he scared me a lot."

"Why?"

"What he could do to me," she said.

"What could he—"

"I don't want to go back to Carpentia. I mean it, Rocky. I'd rather die."

"Kelly."

"Yeah?"

"Look at me."

She turned to face him, this painted creature. The sheet had fallen from his chest, and she brushed her hand against him, traced the outline of the diamond-scaled fish that swam over his heart. They glistened silver—the scales. Something she'd never noticed. That was Rocky. His skin. Always something to discover in it.

"Look at me," he said again. "Look into my eyes."

She didn't want to. It always choked her up to look directly into his eyes. *Like going back in time.* But he'd asked and so she did—her gaze moving up from the eye on his throat, through those creeping vine tattoos crisscrossing his cheeks, curling around his thin, saintlike lips. So much pain he'd gone through, just to look different from the way he used to look, however that had been. She couldn't imagine him without the tattoos, though sometimes she wanted to . . .

"My eyes, Kelly." He said it just as she made it there, into that bright, sad blue.

"If I ask you a question, will you tell me the truth?"

"Yes," she whispered.

"Were you at Sterling Marshall's house last night?"

She swallowed hard. "Yes."

"Did you kill him?"

"Does it matter?" she said. "Would it matter to *them*?"

He brought his hand up to her cheek, brushed away a tear she hadn't realized was there. "I don't know," he said. "Probably not."

CHAPTER 9

hen Kelly Lund was found guilty of second-degree murder, Detective Barry Dupree was seven years old. Trials weren't televised back then, but there'd been courtroom sketches on the news. Barry had vague memories of those sketches on the TV screen in the kitchen, his parents pointing out all the movie stars testifying. He could recall how flat and dull they'd all looked to him, so much less colorful than the drawings in his comic books, or even real life.

But what Barry remembered most about the trial— what everybody remembered most—was that photograph of Kelly Lund standing outside the courthouse, just after she'd been sentenced.

What a photo. If Barry closed his eyes, he could still see it—the dead eyes, the shadows playing across that pretty but vacant face and the smile, *that smile.* The way it jumped out at you. The way it bit.

It had first appeared on the cover of the *Los Angeles Times,* and Barry's older brother Chris had grabbed it off the kitchen table when their parents weren't around. He'd made the photo dance in front of Barry's face, holding it so close he could smell the newsprint, Chris chanting at Barry in his cracking adolescent voice, *One, two, Kelly's coming for you. Three, four, better lock your door* . . .

At the time, Barry had no idea Chris had ripped that off from *A Nightmare on Elm Street,* but Kelly Lund's face haunted him in a way that Freddy Krueger never would.

He used to have nightmares—the teen killer, coming for him in the middle of the night with her pistol, shooting holes through his brain, slaughtering his family, her expression never changing. *The Mona Lisa Death Smile.* Man.

To Barry, to many who were children in L.A. in the early '80s he was sure, Kelly Lund was a bogeyman on a level with Richard "The Night Stalker" Ramirez or Charlie Manson. And even as Barry grew, even as he took boxing lessons and stood up to the bullies in school who called him Carrot Top and gave him wedgies on a daily basis, even as he graduated—sixty-five pounds bigger than when he entered high school and knowing full well he'd be a cop one day—even then, and even now, a grown man with a detective's shield and a black belt in mixed martial arts and a registered .40 caliber Glock in his shoulder holster (*Try and call me Carrot Top now, dickheads*) he couldn't shake the uneasiness he felt at the sound of her name.

Kelly Lund is coming for you!

Could you blame him? Could you blame anyone who had grown up with that photo emblazoned in his brain?

Lund had her champions, no question. She had her conspiracy theorists and her marshmallow-hearted movie stars and her knee-jerk feminist bloggers, writing letters to the parole board on this "poor girl's" behalf.

But Barry Dupree wasn't one of them. And when, five years after Kelly Lund's release, practically to the day, he and his partner had looked at surveillance video of a slim, hooded figure leaving the Marshalls' house, shortly after the approximate time of Sterling Marshall's death and getting into a car that resembled Kelly Lund's, it took every ounce of restraint not to yell "*I told you so.*"

Hadn't Marshall's wife, Mary, fought for Kelly Lund's release? Hadn't she been one of those misguided letter writers? He'd asked his partner, Louise Braddock, about that at the police building at five in the morning, right after they'd caught the case and they were sitting at their desks, speed-reading old newspaper articles, mainlining coffee, getting ready.

"If it wasn't for Mary Marshall's letters," he'd said, jittery from caffeine, "Kelly Lund might have never gotten paroled, and so she would never have killed Sterling Marshall. Am I right?"

But Louise had reacted the way she almost always did, which was to roll her eyes and tell him to calm the hell down. "Innocent until proven guilty, Barry," she'd said.

Sure you make it into Robbery-Homicide, but you get your mother for a partner.

The worst part of it was, Barry was somewhat indebted to Louise. She'd been in the prestigious division for more than ten years when he arrived six months ago from Monrovia, riding the coattails of a major bank robbery he'd caught simply because he'd forgotten his car keys at the station, and had gone back in to get them when the case had come in. It was a professional job—way too big for their understaffed division, yet working with him, the lieutenant at Robbery-Homicide had been impressed enough by Barry's thoroughness and dedication that he'd extended the invitation that he had always dreamed of. His big break . . . well, it *would* be his big break if they could find him a partner.

As luck would have it, Louise Braddock's partner had just retired and, given a choice between Barry and a douchebag named Cameron

Keogh who stunk as though he stewed in Axe spray six hours every night, she'd gone for the new guy. "Keep in mind, Cameron Keogh gives me migraines," Louise had said to Barry at the time and continued to say to him, any chance she got. "You were saved by the smell."

Whatever. Barry didn't care what Louise thought. He never cared what Louise thought any more than he cared what his own mother thought, and his mother had long ago made it clear that Barry should do his own thinking.

This morning they'd assigned two Robbery-Homicide teams to the Sterling Marshall murder—one to canvas the neighborhood, the other, Louise and himself, to speak to the surviving Marshalls. When Louise had pulled Barry aside when they were talking to Bellamy and told him she could handle the family questioning on her own, he hadn't put up a fight. "Fine," he said. "I'll go visit Kelly Lund." Louise had told him not to get "overexcited." Barry had done his best not to tell her to pound sand.

Like John McFadden, Sterling Marshall had been shot in the head—and with his own gun. Yes, the .22 had been registered to Sterling Marshall, outspoken antigun advocate. According to his wife, Mary, he had kept it in a locked desk drawer—never touched it. Sterling would have gotten rid of it, she had said, if it hadn't been a gift from a dear old friend: John McFadden.

Shot in the head with John McFadden's gun, days after talking to the Los Angeles Times *about John McFadden's murder. Days after the anniversary of his murderer's sentencing.* Did Kelly Michelle Lund need to draw them a map?

And so Barry had driven all the way to Joshua Tree. He'd taken his Chevy Cavalier through this alien land, the desert spring just beginning, weird flowers poking out of cactus limbs in shades of meat and blood and vein. He'd sped through a landscape straight out of the westerns he'd watched on TV as a kid—craggy red rocks, bilious sand clouds, and for-real tumbleweeds, angry, sharp-quilled plants that made you hurt just to look at them. A landscape that made you hear pistol fire.

He'd driven a series of dust-dry streets with "Springs" in their names—false advertising if ever there was—sun melting through his windshield at seven in the morning, Barry's mouth dry from it, air conditioner or not. Until finally he'd reached the driveway of a known killer, the bogeyman from his childhood nightmares. (*Bogeywoman? Why is there no such word?*) He'd crossed the threshold of the clean, craftsman house she now lived in. (Who would have expected Mexican tile in the kitchen? Who would have thought there'd be a gleaming stainless steel fridge or a line of oversize mason jars filled with colorful pastas?)

And he'd spoken to her. He'd sat across an expensively distressed kitchen table from Kelly Michelle Lund and he'd questioned her, face-to-face. Talk about "looking the devil in the eye."

When you're a detective, you learn to read gestures, expressions. Barry was especially good at it—so good, in fact, that he taught a USC extension course for screenwriters in interrogation techniques.

At this point in his career, Barry knew how to stay one step ahead of the average suspect, to decipher each blink and twitch and clearing of the throat. He knew the most common tells a suspect might be lying (looking up and to the left was a good one) and how to coax and bend a confession out of her using methods so subtle, she'd never know until it was too late.

But here's the thing: in order for an interview to go the way you want it, you need to be calm throughout—and that's easier said than done when your suspect happens to be the star of your childhood phobias, and she's standing over you with both fists clenched, asking you how you take your coffee.

Barry thought he'd done pretty well, considering. Lund had started off cocky, but he'd wound up rattling her so much she started yammering about lawyers.

And when he'd asked if she'd been home last night, she'd looked up and to the left . . .

Had she known how Barry had felt, though, sitting in her kitchen, breathing the same air as she did? If she'd known how he'd felt when, at one point, he'd caught a hint of it . . . *that smile* . . . Maybe she did know.

Maybe she knew everything.

Man, he had to get over it. He had to grow up once and for all and put these irrational fears behind him. Kelly Lund wasn't the first killer he'd shared breathing space with. For God's sake, he'd been in uniform ten years, a detective for more than five.

Beyond that, though, Barry needed to take into account the origin of his fears: his brother Chris—a pothead dentist on his third wife and counting who lived three blocks away from their parents, yet every single year was at least an hour late for Thanksgiving. It wasn't Kelly Lund who had tormented seven-year-old Barry and cursed him with nightmares, who'd sent that chill through his body at the sound of her name. It was Chris and his stupid Freddy Krueger song. Was Barry going to allow his jerk of a brother—his brother at *twelve*, no less—to mess with the most important investigation of his career?

"There is no way in hell I will let that happen." Barry said it out loud, which was a little troubling, seeing as he was washing his hands in the men's room and there were other guys in here.

"You say something?" somebody called out from one of the stalls.

Barry tried to sound genial. "Nope. Just clearing my throat."

"Sounded like talking."

Barry sighed. Six hours after his interview with Kelly Lund—six hours later, and still his mind was in this state. *Chris's fault.* "Nope."

He left fast. The guy in the stall was Hank Grayson, a senior detective whom Barry greatly admired—and who had been giving him odd looks all day, probing looks, as though Barry were an imposter. Hank, who had worked OJ, who had worked Phil Spector, who had been a Homicide detective back when Barry was still having Kelly Lund nightmares and wetting his bed.

Barry headed over to his desk—right next to Louise's, who had left for the day before he hit the can. Their two desks were interchangeable—devoid of personal touches, sleek and neat as though awaiting inspection. A few months ago, Robbery-Homicide had moved into this building—a soaring glass tower, built to replace the ailing Parker Center down the street, which had been condemned two years earlier after the most recent earthquake. And, much as he appreciated the classy new digs, Barry couldn't get himself to put down roots here. He had a strange feeling in this building sometimes, a lost feeling. He missed the crumbling Parker Center, where roaches sometimes skittered over your shoes and you tried not to think about the structural damage and the asbestos issues, and the detectives all sat facing each other, their desks arranged in a circle like covered wagons—a real team. He sometimes wondered if Louise felt that way too—if that was why she'd never broken out the framed pictures of her cat and her twin nephews and sat in her chair in that weird, tentative way. Not enough to ask her about it, though. Louise was never around when Barry had thoughts like this, which was probably a good thing.

He rubbed his eyes. Man, he was tired. He started to say his good-byes to the few remaining detectives when he felt a tap on his shoulder and heard someone say, "Hey."

Barry cringed. "Hey, Hank."

He braced himself for the concerned gaze, the pat on the shoulder, the "*You sure you can handle this case?*"

But none of that came. Instead, Hank Grayson said, "You want to grab a beer?"

"Well, actually I was just about to head home . . ." he started to say. But something in Hank's eyes stopped him.

"I have some information that might interest you."

"Information?"

Hank had a military background, and maintained that ramrod posture, even at his advanced age. A man of his size standing that straight was intimidating—no way around that. But the way he was looking at Barry—the way he leaned in close after glancing around the squad room—it made Barry feel privileged, as though Hank had chosen him first for his team. "Information," he said again, only quieter, between his teeth. "It's about the family of Sterling Marshall."

I LOVE MY HUSBAND, BUT I FEEL UNFILLED, KELLY TYPED. IT WAS THE last sentence of "Gina B," the twenty-fifth grabber she'd written since getting home—a high output, even for Kelly, who was one of SaraBelle .com's "top producers" according to "Joel," the site manager who e-mailed her models' photos, sometimes two dozen a day, and direct-deposited her biweekly checks from "Creative Choices, Inc."

Kelly was about to close the file and send it along when she saw her typo: *Unfilled*, instead of *unfulfilled*—which . . . *well, that actually works, doesn't it?* She smiled—first time she'd done so since driving back from Rocky's and opening the door to her empty house and checking all the voice mails to find nothing.

Unfilled. Why not? Gina B's needs are simple and physical. (An immature joke, sure, but what do you expect from someone who spent nine-tenths of her adulthood listening to the sophisticated wit of Carpentia guards?)

Kelly grouped the grabber with the others, sent the folder along to Joel, typo and all. "Done," she said. And then, only then, did she let herself feel the emptiness of her house, the crushing silence.

She had hoped Shane would call, but knowing where he was, who he was with, she didn't dare expect it. Instead, when she'd first gotten home she had locked the front door behind her and shut all the drawers in her mind, one by one—*Sterling Marshall, Shane, Bellamy. Rocky . . . All those years in Carpentia and those years before. Mom. Dad. Catherine. Everything that led up to today and today itself, all of it . . . Last night . . .* And she'd thrown herself into her job.

Despite Sterling Marshall being all over the news, "Joel" hadn't offered any words of condolence in his daily e-mail, which in a way was comforting. He hadn't even cut her any slack on the grabbers—sending her a record twenty-five model pics with a one-line note: *Finish today, please.*

She had. For hours now, Kelly had maintained focus, not looking up from her computer, hardly lifting her hands from the keyboard, until she'd cranked out the profiles of twenty-five fantasy females— names, workout regimes, dirty daydreams, secret kinks, clueless husbands . . . twenty-five carefully constructed sets of hidden, powerful longings that could only be filled by the right married man.

Unfilled. Is that just a weak way of saying empty?

Kelly clicked on her Internet icon. She hadn't checked her e-mail since downloading the grabber pictures, and it hit her that Shane may have written rather than called. Shane had never been much of an e-mailer, but today, at his old house and with his family listening in . . .

She saw Shane in her mind, Shane creaking open her bedroom door in the morning, the weight of him on the edge of her bed, peering at her from behind his camera with those soft black eyes.

Shane, always watching, snapping photographs of Kelly, of the sunrise, of *everything* just so he could hang on to it, keep it.

He'd said that once, after taking a picture of the two of them: *"If I could just keep this one moment . . ."* But still it all slipped away. He kept losing moments, losing people—both he and Kelly losing everything, everyone, losing parts of themselves so much faster than the rest of the world did, but trying so much harder to hold on.

Really, when Kelly thought about it, that was the main thing the two of them had in common, and she wished she could hold on to Shane tighter. Maybe she could, now that Sterling Marshall was gone. Maybe she could finally say yes to Shane without that awful feeling, that wall going up, parts of her shutting down, pulling away . . .

Kelly was older, yes, but she could still get pregnant. And she could keep the baby now. *Shane could keep the baby.* She closed her eyes for a few moments, tried to imagine what that might feel like . . . *Our baby.*

On Kelly's home page, a new Sterling Marshall headline. She clicked away from it fast and checked her e-mail, hoping to hear from Shane with crossed fingers and clenched fists. *Please write and we can start over . . .* But there was nothing. She clicked back on her home page and read the headline and her mouth went dry, heart beating harder as its meaning sunk in.

LAPD: STERLING MARSHALL WAS MURDERED

She clicked on the story. *"Numerous police sources reveal that, contrary to earlier reports, movie legend Sterling Marshall did not leave a note prior to his death of gunshot wounds last night . . ."*

Kelly stared at the sentence until the words started swimming . . . *did not leave a note.*

She glanced at the story again. *"We are treating Mr. Marshall's death as an ongoing murder investigation," the LAPD spokesperson said.*

If suspicions prove correct, it will not be the first time that brutal murder has crossed the path of the Oscar-winning actor. Marshall's son Shane is married to . . .

No note. Not a suicide. A murder investigation.

Kelly got up from the table—the kitchen table, where she'd taken her laptop so she could greet Shane as soon as he came home. Shane, who hadn't called, hadn't e-mailed. It was dark out, the only light in the room the glowing screen of the laptop. She walked over to the far wall and flicked the switch. With the room lit up she could practically see him planted there at the kitchen table, that big, pasty cop. Spooning sugar into his coffee as the washing machine clunked away. *"Where were you this morning, between the hours of midnight and three A.M.?"*

Kelly steadied herself against the kitchen counter. *He couldn't have known. He was just playing a hunch. If it was any more than that, he would have taken me in.*

Still, she couldn't get her hands to stop shaking, couldn't get that drawer to stay closed, the one that held last night—the blood pooling on the floor of his study, spattering the photograph of Mary on his desk, the coppery smell hanging in the air. His face, Shane's father's face, what remained of it . . .

And I kneeled next to him. I touched him.

The phone rang—not the kitchen phone, which was the business number for Shane's photo archive and not Kelly's cell phone either, but the one in her bedroom, the landline. The phone Shane always called because he knew enough not to bother with her cell.

Shane.

She sprinted down the hall to her bedroom, picked up the phone. "Oh God, I'm so glad it's you."

A woman's voice replied, a little garbled, reminding Kelly that she hadn't checked caller ID. "This is Officer Sullivan from the LAPD," she said.

No, please. Not yet. "Listen, I already spoke to one of your detectives this morning."

"I'm sorry," the officer said. "Am I speaking to Mrs. Shane Marshall?"

Kelly exhaled. She didn't want to reply. "Yes."

Sullivan had a slight southern accent. She was obviously young and with such a sweet voice for a police officer—not a touch of sarcasm to it. "I'm calling about your husband," she said. "He's been arrested."

arry slid into the seat across from Hank Grayson. "Haven't been here for a while," he said, making small talk, easing in.

"For good reason," Hank said.

They were in a downtown diner called Grady's—a former cop favorite that had, in the past few years, slid treacherously into hipster territory and landed with a splat. Grady's had been in a movie a few years back—Aranofsky, maybe . . . Wachowski, Polanski, Buttinsky . . . Barry didn't know from movie directors, but whatever his name was, an oh-so-cool Hollywood filmmaker had chosen to shoot scenes for some lame cop movie at Grady's, and that had been the downfall of this once nice, convenient place that served food and alcohol twenty-four hours.

These days, you couldn't go into Grady's without tripping over a flock of bearded numbnuts and their anorexic, tattooed girlfriends, snapping nicotine gum, gassing off about Jack Kerouac and cold-drip coffee.

Cops—real cops—only went to Grady's if they were desperate, which apparently was the case with Hank Grayson. He'd certainly gotten there fast enough.

When Barry showed up, in fact, Hank was already halfway through a beer—a Belgian brand, which surprised Barry a little. He'd figured him for a cheap-American-in-a-can kind of guy.

It made Barry feel a little better ordering a mocha cappuccino—something he'd sweated about on the way over. He knew he couldn't grab a beer with Hank—not without risking serious embarrassment. The ugly truth was, Barry couldn't hold his liquor. Never could. For all his purposefully gained bulk and martial arts training, when it came to drinking he was still the hundred-pound weakling he'd been back in ninth grade.

"You want nutmeg with that?" said the waitress, who wore a clingy retro uniform and looked very much like Snow White—only with gates in her ears, studs in both cheeks, and a tongue piercing that clicked when she said "nutmeg."

"Do you have chocolate syrup?" he said. "I'll take that if you do."

"You got it, Ace."

By the time Barry had figured out whether or not that was intended as an insult (it was) the waitress was long gone, and Hank was at the bottom of his Belgian beer and gazing dolefully at two mutton-chopped idiots at the next Formica table, rolling up the sleeves of their lumberjack shirts to compare tattoos. "There's nothing sadder," he said, "than a place that *was* good, *once*."

"Tell me about it," Barry said.

The waitress returned with Barry's mocha cappuccino and a full bottle of Hershey's Syrup. "Go crazy, Ace."

Hank watched her walk away. "Cute," he said. "If you like 'em perforated."

Barry poured syrup into his cappuccino, took a sip. He felt Hank's appraising gaze on him and said, "A beer would put me to sleep right now. I've been up since dawn with this Marshall thing."

"What do you got so far—I mean outside of ME and ballistics?"

"Surveillance video."

"Showing . . ."

"Kelly Lund."

"You sure?"

"Well . . ." *Innocent until proven guilty, Barry.* "Not completely."

"Did you talk to the family?"

Barry looked up from his mug, into eyes so sharp they made him jump a little. "You're talking uh . . . extended family? Because I personally paid a visit to Kelly Lund and . . ."

Hank put up a hand that looked exactly like Barry's dad's hand—big and powerful, with a wedding ring that seemed soldered on. "Barry," he said. "You've been a cop for how long?"

Barry blinked a few times. "About fifteen years."

"It's weird, isn't it? Working our job in Hollywood?"

"I guess."

"I mean, every city you work, there's gonna be people in power—the ones who can get away with things. But here, those people are movie stars."

"Get away with things?"

"I guess it's not so easy for 'em these days, with TMZ and whatnot." Hank smiled at him, but the smile didn't reach his eyes. "Stupid gossip Web sites have 'em all more scared than we ever did."

"Sorry, Hank. I don't think I understand."

The waitress was back again. "Can I get you another beer, sweetie?"

Hank nodded. Once she was gone, he leaned in close. "Back when I was in uniform, I must've gone four, five times to this one house on domestic disturbance calls," he said. "I'd get there, the guy would tell me nothing was wrong, just having a little spat. His wife would be there agreeing with him, her head bobbing away, but I'd see the blood on her, the bruises. Once he'd even knocked out a few teeth. And here's the thing. This guy was someone I idolized as a kid. It made me sick to my stomach, but he had the power, right? We never arrested him, kept it out of the papers . . . hell, I *still* can't even get myself to say his name out loud, and this had to be forty, forty-five years ago."

"Who was it?"

"Doesn't matter. I'm telling you this story to make a point. Back in the day, we saw all kinds of celebrity bad behavior—domestic assault, hard drugs you never even heard of, creepy sexual stuff . . . type of thing that'd put you off movies for the rest of your life . . . And seven, eight, nine times out of ten we'd turn our backs on it. Because they had the power."

Barry took another sip of his mochaccino, the foam tickling his upper lip. The waitress returned with another bottle of beer. Hank poured it into his mug and gulped at it for far longer than was necessary, and Barry felt as though they were reading from a script, Hank watching him over the rim of his mug with expectant eyes, waiting for him to say his line. "Hank?"

"Yeah?"

"You're telling me this because of Sterling Marshall, right?"

"You're a smart guy, Barry."

"Was he, uh . . . involved in anything you had to turn your back on?"

"No," he said quietly. "Not Marshall himself."

"Someone in his family."

Hank took another swallow of his beer. And, for the first time since he'd known him, Barry saw his shoulders slump a little. "Let me ask you something, Barry. That surveillance video. Have you seen it yet?"

"Not yet," he said. "Louise was the one who was at the family's house because I was interviewing Kelly Lund."

"What did she say about it?"

"Huh?"

"What did Louise tell you about the video?"

"It's . . . well, it's short, I guess. A tall woman in a hoodie is leaving the Marshalls' house."

"She said it's definitely a woman?"

Barry thought a minute. "I . . . I think so. And anyway, Bellamy Marshall told us it was."

"The loving sister."

"Excuse me?"

"How long was the video?"

"About five seconds."

"Five seconds. How do you know from five seconds of surveillance video if someone in a hoodie is a woman or a man or a fuckin' schnauzer?" Hank leaned in very close, his drill bit eyes trained on him.

Barry frowned at him.

"Think about it, Barry. The figure in the video. Getting into the silver car. Couldn't it have been a slightly built man?"

Seriously? "Hank."

"Yeah?"

"What did Shane Marshall do back then that would make him a more credible murder suspect than Kelly Michelle Lund?"

Barry's phone buzzed. He yanked it out of his pocket and looked at the screen. *Louise.* "Hey, listen can I call you back?"

"No need, Sport," she said. (Barry hated it when she called him Sport.) "Just look at the lead story on TMZ."

KELLY HUNG UP THE PHONE, HER HEAD THROBBING, UNASKED QUES-tions buzzing around inside it. Shane had been arrested for assault and drunk and disorderly conduct, Officer Sullivan had said. "Drunk?" Kelly had said.

"Under the influence."

Of what? Kelly hadn't asked.

Throughout the conversation with Sullivan, her mind and mouth had been out of synch, thoughts stalling and sputtering before she could voice them. *Assault.* Far as she knew, Shane had never been in a physical fight. And outside of his nightly Ambien comas, Kelly had never known him to be under the influence of anything . . .

She grabbed her car keys off the hook near the kitchen door and was reaching for the knob when she noticed the glowing light of her computer. Her heart pounded, body working on its own, sliding back into the kitchen chair. She called up TMZ. *They might not have the story yet, but let's just see . . . I need to see first. I need to know what I'm dealing with.*

Jesus. "They don't miss a beat, do they?" she whispered. Shane was the lead story. His mug shot filled half the screen, but the mug shot didn't look like Shane. It didn't look like anyone Kelly knew, didn't look like any human being so much as a fictional character, something TMZ had cobbled together in Photoshop to illustrate the headline . . .

STERLING MARSHALL'S SON GOES WACKO!

What a headline. What a way to describe Shane—who had just lost his father. To beat him up all over again with those harsh words, that burlesque font. *That picture.* Kelly stared at the purple swelling under the left eye, the cuts on the tear-streaked face, some of them still bleeding . . . It made her cringe, the idea of so many strangers gawking at Shane's tears, Shane's blood. Was there anything more invasive than that? Anything more awful?

Blood, pooling on the floor of his study, the awful slick feel of it, Sterling Marshall's blood . . .

Kelly shut her eyes. *Go away.*

She opened them again and skimmed the article, enough to find out that Shane had gotten into a "brawl" with a fellow customer at a strip club on Pico, and that he seemed "druggy" and "out of it."

She didn't need to know more.

She raced out the door, her bag slung over her shoulder, the slip of paper in her hand with the scrawled address of the police station, clutching it like a good luck charm. Once in her car, the address plugged into her GPS, her foot on the accelerator and the engine rumbling up through the wheel and into her hands, Kelly tried her hardest to think of nothing but driving, the feel of it.

For a time, she succeeded.

THE WHOLE RIDE OVER TO THE WEST HOLLYWOOD SHERIFF STATION, Barry Dupree had one thought in his mind: *What kind of a guy would marry Kelly Lund?* He'd gotten a pretty good answer out of Hank Grayson, who'd let him know over his second Belgian beer that in 1987 or thereabouts, sixteen-year-old Shane Marshall had consumed half a bottle of his father's best scotch along with several lines of crystal meth and proceeded to go ballistic on the family's longtime personal chef, wrestling him to the ground while slicing him up pretty good with a set of sewing shears.

But that had been a long time ago. By throwing piles of cash at both the chef and the housekeeper who had reported the incident, as well as glad-handing responding officers (including Grayson), checking his son into Betty Ford, and, most of all, by being the all-around, stand-up, Hollywood hero that he was, Sterling Marshall had managed to make the whole thing go away. Shane had grown up, gone to USC, started his own photo archive business, largely without incident—that is, until he said "I do" to the woman who murdered his father's closest friend.

What the hell was that about?

Barry didn't have a lot of experience with women. He'd had maybe three actual girlfriends in his life—one of whom he'd married and who was now bleeding him dry with alimony payments. These days, he preferred the company of *Penthouse* videos anyway. But he knew enough. He knew that crazy could be a turn-on, especially to a sheltered wannabe bad boy, yearning to piss off his legendary dad. But to *marry* crazy, to *stay* married to it for fifteen years . . . That, in Barry's opinion, took some serious whackadoodlery.

"How's his record?" Barry asked one of Shane Marshall's arresting officers, a husky guy by the name of Greg Herne with unusually rosy cheeks and a constant sweat-sheen on him, like his temperature was turned up too high.

"Pretty clean for a Hollywood type," Greg said. "Just a couple speeding tickets."

They were standing outside a holding cell—Barry, Greg, and Louise Braddock, who'd met him at the station. Inside the cell, Shane Marshall was passed out, snoring lightly. He was half-sitting on the bench, his body propped up against the wall at a weird angle that was bound to cramp him up in a bad way once he regained consciousness. Louise and Barry had hoped to question him and, being one of Barry's sort-of gym buddies, Greg had said, "No problem." But clearly Shane Marshall was no good to anybody right now.

"No drug arrests?" Louise said. "DUIs?"

"Well, he is a Betty Ford grad," Barry said.

Louise frowned. "And you know this how?"

"Hank Grayson told me."

"He *did*?"

Barry smiled a little inside. (*That's right. Hank Grayson and I are pals now. We go out for beers together. Chew on that for a while.*) But he kept his expression neutral—watched Shane Marshall's chest rising and falling, the snore whistling out of him. Such a harmless-looking guy, really. Small, slightly built . . . Not the type you'd expect to beat the crap out of somebody in a strip club. Hank Grayson was convinced Shane Marshall had a dark side—a "Mr. Hyde" that jumped out and bit whenever he fell off the wagon. But Barry wasn't so sure. You had to look at the big picture here. The guy's father had just been shot to death. Grief did strange things to people.

Louise said, "What was he on tonight? TMZ said he was druggy."

"Ambien." Greg gestured at Marshall, his sweaty hand flying into Barry's line of vision. "We spoke to his mom. I guess when he was back at her house earlier today, he stole a whole bunch from her bottle."

Louise's voice pitched up an octave. "*Seriously?*"

Barry turned, looked at her. "Ambien doesn't make everybody fall asleep," he said. "Some people get mean on it. Some can black out and do things they don't remember—eating, having sex, driving even . . ."

"I know that, Barry."

"So why the shock?"

"Because earlier today, I talked to a friend at the Joshua Tree police department. A little more than a week ago, Shane Marshall was taken in for trespassing on someone's property. He was wandering around this guy's yard at three in the morning, trying to look through his windows."

Barry turned to Greg. "Why wasn't it on his record?"

"The guy didn't want to press charges," Louise said. "Mainly because Marshall truly had no idea what he was doing. He was acting hypnotized—possessed even, my friend said." Louise looked at Greg, then Barry. She held his gaze. "Turned out he was having a bad reaction to Ambien."

Barry looked at her. "So . . ."

"He woke up in the police station two hours later. Didn't remember a thing. He'd blacked out everything—including the drive to the neighbor's house." Louise started to thumb through her notebook.

"Jeez," Greg said.

"This morning, when I spoke to Shane Marshall, he told me he had taken sleeping pills last night," she said, reading her notes. Barry glanced over her shoulder. He'd never known anyone with such perfect handwriting. "He said he wouldn't have heard his wife coming or going because, and I quote, 'I was dead to the world.'"

Barry shook his head. "You honestly think he could have taken Ambien last night and blacked out not only *a two-hour drive* to his parents' house—but getting his father's gun out of a locked drawer, killing him with it . . ."

Louise stared at him. "I think he could *claim* that's what happened."

"You're kidding me," he said. "Right?"

"Do I look like I'm kidding?" She blinked at him, pursed her lips even thinner than they were to begin with.

"Louise," Barry said. "You never look like you're kidding. Your face doesn't go that way."

"One week ago, he blacks out on Ambien, wanders around some random neighbor's property long enough for the guy to notice, call the cops . . ."

"Wait. You think he was *setting the stage*? Like this is part of some *grand plan*?"

"I don't *think* or know anything. It's a possibility," she said. "At this point, anything is a possibility."

Inside the cell, Shane Marshall stirred in his sleep. "No," he said. "No, no. Get off of me."

Greg wiped his sweaty forehead with the back of his hand. "You guys are freaking me out."

Barry looked at Louise. "Was his wife told about this, uh, altercation in Joshua Tree?"

She shook her head. "He was mortified. Begged those cops not to tell."

"And they listened?"

"They know him there. Everybody knows him. He's a nice guy, my friend said, and kind of a local celebrity because of his dad. So they went along with it. Never called his wife."

Barry nodded. "Who was the neighbor?" he said. "Was he a friend of Marshall's too?"

"*Get off of me!*"

Louise shook her head. "Some local weirdo," she said. "Chainsaw artist. Goes by the name of Rocky Three."

KELLY SCREECHED HER CAR TO THE CURB ON SEWARD, JUST AROUND the corner from the Hollywood Police Station. By now, more than two hours had passed since TMZ had broken the news, and it showed in the vans outside the station, the bank of paparazzi clustered on either side of the front door, as though Shane's arrest were some kind of red carpet event.

She got out of the car, slammed the door shut, and took a few deep breaths. "Collect yourself," she whispered—same thing the shrink at Carpentia had said to her the one time she'd ever cried in therapy. She'd been talking about her dad. Her poor dad, who had never hurt anyone other than himself and, when she thought about it, was not unlike Shane . . .

"*Collect yourself please, Kelly,*" the shrink had said. As though bits of her had fallen off and would blow away if she didn't gather them up fast.

Did Shane know about last night? Was that what had sent him over the edge? She wanted to tell him what had happened, but how could she? She tried rehearsing it in her mind as she headed up Wilcox and waited to cross at the light. She tried several ways to phrase the story, but every version fell flat.

She wouldn't even be able to tell Shane how she'd been able to sleep last night, because the truth was this: sleeping had been easy. The hard thing had been waking up.

Kelly was nearing the police station now. Some of the paparazzi caught sight of her. She noticed them turning toward her and put her head down. As she approached the front of the building, she heard one of them say, "Is she anybody?" And then a mumble—Kelly couldn't discern the answer, but she suspected it was "no." For a teenage killer, aging was the ultimate disguise, and Kelly Michelle Lund was now forty-seven, not seventeen. She was grateful for that as she passed the group of them, muttering and shouting and pushing at each other, saying Shane's name, Sterling's name . . . growing restless and vicious like the pack they were.

"Wait, wait, wait," said one of them, a woman. "I think she might be the wife."

Kelly sped up her pace, pretending not to hear. *Just get to the door. Open it. Ask for Officer Sullivan. Don't turn around. Keep your head down.*

"You mean the murderer?" said another, this one male.

Almost there. Kelly's foot was on the first front step when she heard, "Kelly. How *are* you?" She froze. She recognized the voice—deep and gravelly and unfortunately one of a kind, each word laced with a British-by-way-of-Massachusetts lockjaw. Intimidating to Kelly when she was just a kid, but so ridiculous now—so ringingly, pathetically phony. Kelly's head jerked up at the sound of it.

And there he was. Sebastian Todd. ("*Call me ST, Kelly. All my friends do.*") Since she'd last seen him, Todd had replaced his wire-rimmed granny glasses with squared-off tortoiseshell frames. His swoop of snow white hair had been shaved all the way down, so that in the light it looked like glitter sprinkled over his head. But he was still 100 percent ST, still wearing one of his signature cream-colored suits, slumped shoulders straining against the expensive fabric, his posture reminding Kelly—as it had when she'd met him—of a cartoon vulture, grinning from a tree branch.

He'd been talking to a woman with gunmetal gray hair and another man, whom, after a few seconds, Kelly recalled as the detective from this morning. The sugar lover. *Of course they're hanging out together. Why wouldn't they be?*

Kelly said, "I'm doing peachy, ST." And then she put on the smile for him. *The Mona Lisa Death Smile*, as he'd named it himself. Flat eyes, mouth stretching. She hadn't realized what she'd been doing back when he'd named it. She'd been a young girl, scared out of her mind, imagining a fuse box, escaping . . . But after Kelly had read his first essay about her in the *Los Angeles Times*, after she'd seen that phrase spelled out on the page, *Mona Lisa Death Smile* . . . Well, she'd kind of liked it. During her first few days in, she'd spent hours practicing it in front of the mirror. Tilting the chin, narrowing the eyes just so . . . The reward had come the first time she'd tried it out on Javerbaum, the biggest, meanest guard at Carpentia. "*Answer me when I talk to you,*" Officer Javerbaum had said. And Kelly had smiled that smile at the bitch and watched her face change, watched her crumble . . . The detective was looking at her the same way Javerbaum had, which made her smile for real.

Todd shook his head mournfully. She could practically hear the clucking of his tongue.

The only one unmoved was the gray-haired woman, who strode toward Kelly, hand outstretched. "Kelly," she said. "I'd like to ask you some questions about your husband." The woman pressed a business card into her hand.

"My husband?" she said.

Behind her back, shouts echoed.

"Have you talked to Shane, Kelly?"

"What drugs was he on?"

"Did you kill Sterling Marshall, Kelly? Is that why Shane went nuts? Because you killed his dad?"

"*Kelly! Over here!*"

Kelly's head went down again. She looked at the business card in her hand. LOUISE BRADDOCK: LAPD ROBBERY/HOMICIDE.

She nearly laughed. "About my husband, huh?"

Kelly heard the click, beep, and whir of their cameras at her back, her name shouted louder and louder. She brushed Louise Braddock aside, pushed open the door, and yanked it closed behind her. "Free at last," she whispered. The irony wasn't lost.

COMPARATIVELY, THE INSIDE OF THE STATION HOUSE WAS QUIET AND, despite the fluorescent lights and the sickly yellow walls, soothing.

The air conditioner was on full blast. It froze the sweat on the back of Kelly's neck, snaked under the neck of her T-shirt. She shuddered as she made her way to the front desk, where a ruddy-faced and sweaty young male cop stood talking to an equally young policewoman, blond hair pulled back into a ponytail. "I'm telling you, it can happen," the sweaty one was saying. "Just because a drug is supposed to work a certain way, doesn't mean it'll work that way on everybody. Body chemistry is a strange thing."

"Come on, Greg. It's a sleeping pill."

"You come on. Big Pharma's obviously got you brainwashed."

"Excuse me," Kelly said. "I'm here for Shane Marshall."

The sweaty one abruptly stopped talking. The blonde trained her clear blue eyes on her. "Mrs. Marshall?"

"Yes."

"I'm Officer Sullivan. We spoke earlier . . ." Kelly caught that hint of a southern accent.

"Yes?"

"Listen, ma'am. I'm sorry you had to come all the way out here."

Kelly frowned. "Huh? It isn't a problem."

"No," she said. "No, that's not what I meant."

"Excuse me?"

"What I mean to say, ma'am, is that Mr. Marshall's already left."

"What? But I'm—"

"He left with his sister. She posted bail, and we let them out the back, to avoid the reporters." She took a step forward, gave Kelly a pained smile. "I'm so sorry. I tried calling, but it went straight to voice mail."

Kelly grabbed her phone out of her bag and pushed at it. The battery was dead. She'd never plugged it into her car charger, never even plugged it in at home, when she'd gotten back from Rocky's. *Almost as though you have a need to see it die . . .* "Don't worry about it," she mumbled, heading out the front door before Sullivan could reply.

That press murmur again, tugging at her: *"Kelly!" "Where's Shane?" "Are they keeping him, Kelly?"*

"Did he help you kill Sterling?"

At least he'd been able to sneak out the back, keep them all waiting out here for no reason. Kelly hoped they'd stay all night. She glanced over at Todd. "Something wrong, Kelly?" he said in his ridiculous accent.

Oh, how she wanted to slap him.

He took a few steps toward Kelly. Her cue. *One foot in front of the other, fast as possible, starting now.* She hightailed it, running into a broad shoulder as she passed: the sugar-spooning detective on his way into the station, his partner the business card giver at his side . . . *Dupree. Barry Dupree.* How odd, for her to remember his name now. "Sorry," Dupree said.

Sorry?

"Kelly, can I ask you what kind of mood your husband was in last night?" It was the business card giver talking.

"No," said Kelly. "You can't."

Barry Dupree stifled a smile.

More and more, this night was feeling like a bad dream, one she knew she'd had before and would hate herself for having again, were it ever to do her a favor and prove itself a dream and end.

She ran past the shouting paparazzi, across the street against the light, horns blaring at her, bringing back memories that she pushed away, pushed them hard, fast as they came. *Stop thinking. Charge your phone. Check it to see if Shane called, and then drive away.* Kelly heard her name again, footsteps behind her.

"*Leave me alone!*" It came out a scream and her voice sounded foreign, unhinged.

Once she made it around the corner, Kelly peered down the street. Her car was about half a block away, license plate glaring back at her from under a streetlight. The street was a residential one—unassuming duplexes, a squat, three-story apartment building she hadn't noticed during the rush to the station, but, as she now saw, much like the place where she and her mom and Catherine used to live. "*Mama, look! Kelly and I can see the sign from our bedroom window!*"

Most of the windows were dark, the sidewalk empty. She hurled herself at her car, breathing heavily, her sneakers slamming into the concrete. Once she reached her Camry, she shoved her key in the door and flung it open. She stuck the key in the ignition and plugged her dead phone into the charger, waited just long enough to be able to turn it on. She'd received a text. Just one, from Shane. It was only one line long.

I NEED SOME TIME AWAY FROM YOU.

"What?" she whispered. "Why?"

"Why?" She said it again. Such a dumb question. There were so many reasons why Shane would need time away from her, with last night at the top of the list, Rocky a close second, and what followed nearly endless. So many wrong things Kelly had done and kept stashed away from her husband of fifteen years, hoping he'd never find out, believing that her secrets might outlive them both.

"*What you don't know can't hurt you.*" Kelly's mother used to say that. Kelly's mother, who had driven Catherine out of the house and to her death with her rage and then Kelly, two years later, to a different type of death . . .

Kelly thought about calling Shane. She imagined herself tracking him down at Bellamy's house and banging on the door, demanding to see him. But then she looked at the text again. The words he'd chosen. Not just *time away*, but *time away from you.*

Another one. Gone.

She started up the car, so lost in her thoughts she didn't feel anyone approaching, didn't notice the passenger door opening until it slammed. She turned fast to see Sebastian Todd, vulture-slumped in the passenger seat as though this were a planned meeting.

"What are you doing here?" Kelly said.

"Apologizing."

Kelly stared at him, barely noticing the paparazzi rounding the corner and making for her car. "*Apologizing?*" She pulled away from the curb but kept her eyes fixed on his face. "For what?"

Sebastian Todd gave her a weak smile that had nothing to do with anything that was going on around them. "I know you didn't kill John McFadden."

CHAPTER 11

STERLING MARSHALL'S SON GOES WACKO AT A STRIP CLUB!

Less than 24 hours after his movie star father's brutal and mysterious shooting death, Sterling Marshall's son Shane went completely CRAY CRAY at Teaserz on Pico, terrifying the dancers and leaving fellow patron Cary Wurst with a broken jaw and black eye. "I've never seen anything like it," Cary's friend Dave Farnsworth told TMZ. "The dude was like a wild animal!"

Farnsworth told us that Shane Marshall, 40, arrived at the club alone and blotto. "He was hammered on something," said one of the club's dancers, who goes by the name of Bliss. "Definitely he has anger issues and was looking to pound somebody to a pulp!" Other patrons told TMZ that Shane's eyes were half closed, and his head was "lolling," in a really drugged-out way. "Looked like meth to me," said another eyewitness, who thinks it also could have been bath salts. Whatever Marshall was on, it wasn't pretty. After leaping onstage and mauling a dancer as she tried to perform, Marshall was approached by Cary Wurst, who politely told him to keep his hands off the girls. "Shane Marshall made this growling sound, like an animal," Bliss said. "Then he dove on poor Cary—he just started tearing him apart."

The scariest part was, Marshall spoke to Wurst throughout the entire, vicious attack. "You could only make out a little of it but it was weird," said Wurst's friend Dave. "A bunch of times, I heard him say, 'Kelly.'"

Marshall's wife, convicted murderer Kelly Michelle Lund, could not be reached for comment. But regardless of what he was saying to his victim about his wife, Marshall clearly wasn't behaving like a loving, loyal husband on the night of his father's shooting death.

"It would almost be sad," Dave Farnsworth continued, "if that guy hadn't broken Cary's jaw and nearly killed him!" Cary Wurst—a 35-year-old accountant from Arcadia—is currently being treated for his injuries at Cedars-Sinai hospital.

Added another witness, "Murderer or not, I feel sorry for Shane Marshall's wife. That guy is a hot mess and a ticking time bomb for sure!" Took the words right outta our mouths . . .

UPDATE: Shane Marshall has been arrested for assault and drunk and disorderly conduct. He has been released on bail—TMZ will provide additional updates as they happen. A spokesperson for the LAPD says Shane Marshall's blood has been tested. Toxicology results will be available in two weeks. The investigation continues into Sterling Marshall's death. When contacted by TMZ, Kelly Michelle Lund hung up on our reporter.

Lead story, TMZ
Morning of April 22, 2010

CHAPTER 12

FEBRUARY 14, 1980

They just drove, Kelly, Bellamy, and Vee. Drove with no destination, no plan of action other than escape. Windows down, cigarettes lit, Bellamy's music blasting—Joy Division, Bauhaus, Siouxsie and the Banshees. British bands Kelly had never heard of until Bellamy announced them but still felt as though she knew in a way, those melodies so sad and haunting, those singers, all of them with voices like ghosts. Kelly leaned against the locked door, her hair blowing out the open window, warm air all over her, warm smoke in her throat, easing past her lips, warming them too.

Before long, the earlier part of the day—that awful phone call at school, that woman laughing at her when she'd asked for Len, not to mention Len himself, his fake phone number—all of it slipped away like a passing thought that hadn't been important to begin with.

Vee's full name was Vincent Vales. He was just sixteen but had already passed the GED. He was a professional actor and lived in his own apartment like a grown man. The apartment was on Gower, near the studios, and it had been built as a place to house starlets back in the 1940s. "It looks sorta like the Sleeping Beauty castle at Disneyland,"

Bellamy said. "Only a lot smaller." Bellamy was the one who told Kelly all about Vee. Vee didn't seem like much of a talker. But that was okay, since Kelly wasn't much of a talker either.

"You want to know how Vee and I met?" Bellamy said as she pulled into the Mobil self-serve station on Robertson and Sunset and turned the car off, Siouxsie's ghost voice going silent.

"Yeah." Kelly imagined the two of them shopping side by side at Fiorucci, slam dancing at The Whisky, sipping champagne with Jack Nicholson on a Mulholland Drive balcony, making out . . .

Bellamy turned off the car. "He was in a movie with my dad."

"Which one?" Kelly said.

"Would you know it?" Bellamy said. "It's a western." She turned around in the seat to face her, Kelly's blurred reflection swimming in her Ray-Bans. "Oh no, wait. Let me guess. Your mom would, right, because she's seen all his movies? She's a big fan?"

"Umm . . ."

"Everybody's mom lusts after my dad. It's kind of gross."

"Actually," Kelly said, "my mom lusts after bankers."

Bellamy tilted her head to the side and regarded Kelly for several seconds, as though she were trying to figure out whether or not she was joking. "Good for her," she said finally. "Movie actors are dicks."

"Hey," Vee said.

"Present company bla bla bla."

As Bellamy got out of the car, Kelly looked down at her hands. *What would Mom say if she knew I was here right now, ditching school with a movie actor and Sterling Marshall's daughter?* She didn't want to know, didn't even want to think about it.

Bellamy started pumping gas and Vee turned around in his seat—the first time she'd seen his face head-on, not in a mirror. He was startlingly handsome—shiny black hair, full lips, eyes blue as gas flames set against caramel-tan skin. He almost didn't seem real—more a piece of art than a person. Kelly forgot whatever it was she'd been thinking about, and just stared at him. Against her will, her face stretched into a goofy smile.

"*Defiance*," he said.

"Huh?"

"*Defiance* was the movie I was in with Bellamy's dad. I was just eleven years old. I played Sterling's son, and I was killed in the first act."

She forced herself to stop smiling. "Was that hard," she said, "pretending to die?"

"Nah, I just had to lie there." He grinned. His teeth were pearly. "During most of the takes, I fell asleep."

Kelly laughed.

"Anyway, Bellamy would come to the set—she was there a lot. She was the only other kid my age, and so we got to be friends. Since I was playing her dad's son, she started calling me her 'pretend brother.' The director would let us sit in his folding chair. John McFadden. Ever hear of him?"

Kelly shook her head.

"He's kind of well known." He didn't say it in a mean or snooty way. Just like someone making conversation.

"Pretend brother," she said. "That's cute."

He shrugged. "That's Bellamy. She's still my pretend sister, I guess. When you're not in school, it's harder to find friends, so the few you have wind up being pretty important."

They're just friends. Kelly's heart leaped a little, surprising and embarrassing her at the same time. She felt her cheeks flushing and hoped he didn't notice. Why did her face keep doing things she didn't want it to do? "Do you have any real sisters?"

"Nope. I'm an only child."

"Me too."

Vee's smile faded, and he looked at her, really *looked* at her, those gas flame eyes lasering into hers. "But not always. Right?"

"No," she said slowly. "Not always."

"I'm so sorry."

"How do you know?"

"I knew Cat. She was your twin sister, right?"

Kelly squinted at him, thinking about all the times she'd spied on Catherine, all the boys she'd seen her with. She'd never seen Vee. She would have remembered Vee. "Wow . . ."

"She used to talk about you," he said.

"She did?"

"She always said you were a better person than her—the good twin," he said. "It stuck in my mind because, you know . . . Cat was a really good person herself."

"Wow," Kelly said again. Such a dumb thing to say. It made her sound like some spaced-out fan, but she couldn't help it.

Not many people at school had known Catherine—mainly because she'd barely gone to school. She'd wanted to be an actress, a *real* one, she used to say, and only life can teach you that. Not school, not books. *Living life up to its bendy edge, pressing against that edge, hard as you can . . .*

So the people from school who came out from under rocks in the weeks after her body was found, the kids who talked loudly in the hallways, bragging that they'd known "that dead freshman"—those kids called Catherine lots of things, but "good" was never one of them.

It was as though she'd become something else in death—"the wild girl," "the slut," "that chick who partied way too hard"—a character in everyone else's story, reduced to just a few, wrong words. Because they *didn't* know her, not really. She may have been going through a wild phase, sure, but more than that Catherine was good. She always had been.

"She was just two minutes older than me, but it always felt like a lot more," Kelly said. "You know . . . she taught me how to swim."

Bellamy was in the kiosk now, paying. Vee glanced at her as she settled up. "I bet you taught her a lot too," he said. "You just didn't know it."

Wow . . . Kelly stopped herself from saying it out loud again as Bellamy swung open the car door, bangle bracelets jangling as though to announce her presence. "Why the long faces? Jeez, I leave you two alone for five minutes."

Kelly forced a smile. "Yeah, well."

"What did I miss?"

"Acting," Vee said. "We were talking about acting. And how you used to call me your pretend brother."

"Can you blame me? You're a hell of a lot more fun than my *real* brother." Her gaze settled on Kelly. "That doesn't explain why you both look like your dog just died."

"Wellll," Kelly said slowly, drawing the word out.

"Yeah?"

"Vee knew my sister."

Bellamy's face went still. "Oh," she said. "Oh Kelly." Bellamy opened the car door and leaned into the back, where she was sitting. Kelly wasn't sure what she was going to do at first, but she pulled her close and hugged her with a strength that surprised her. "I'm so sorry."

Tentatively, Kelly hugged her back. "I . . . Um . . . I didn't . . ."

"I knew her," she said. "Not well but . . . Everybody knew her. She went to the parties."

"I introduced you guys," Vee said.

"Right." Bellamy pulled away. She looked at Kelly. "I didn't know whether or not to bring it up."

"It's okay," she said. "It was a long time ago." It wasn't. It had only been two years, but neither of them pointed that out.

Bellamy tilted her head again, watching her, Kelly wishing she'd take her sunglasses off until finally, she broke into a smile. "Hey, you know what, if you want to act, Vee can get you a screen test."

Kelly swallowed. She had never thought about acting before, not even once. Catherine had been the actress, while Kelly had been the . . . what had she been? The actress's sister. "I don't know if I'm movie material," she said quietly.

"Are you kidding? You're a babe!"

Kelly blushed—her face betraying her again.

"You are," Vee said. Her cheeks burned purple now. Her heart thrummed.

Vee said, "I can get you a screen test with John."

"John?"

"John McFadden. The director I was telling you about."

"You know him that well?"

"Yep."

Bellamy slipped back into the front seat, sighing dramatically. "He's Vee's *dad*."

"Oh," Kelly said. She looked at Vee, who had turned around again. He was sitting perfectly still, the tips of his ears a deep red.

"His last name's different because of nepotism," Bellamy was saying as she started up the car. "He wants to make it on his *own*. Of course, he doesn't mind his big shot daddy casting him in his pictures. And paying his rent."

"Whatever, Bellamy."

"Oh come on. I'm just kidding around." She ran a hand through his glossy hair.

"Cut it out."

Bellamy cast a quick glance at Kelly. "Let's not fight in front of the children."

Vee said, "Just. Drive."

Bellamy screeched away from the pump. Siouxsie began moaning again, but Vee switched it off. "I'm sick of this black-shroud shit."

"I thought you liked it."

"I like Jack Daniel's too. But if I drank it all day, I'd puke." He slipped another cassette in the deck, all horns and fun, the singer shouting, *One step beyond . . .*

"Madness," said Bellamy.

It took Kelly a little while to realize that Madness was the name of the band on the tape, but she didn't let on. "I like Madness," she said.

Vee smiled at her in the rearview. "Me too."

And then Bellamy was pulling up to a red light, calling a Chinese Fire Drill, Vee and Kelly throwing their doors open in unison and jumping out into the street, horns blaring at them from all around, the singer shouting it again: *One . . . step . . . beyond!*

"Oh my God, you guys!" Kelly shouted, but she got out too. The three of them circled the red Rabbit once, twice, three times as more horns joined in, people calling them stupid kids, yelling cuss words at them.

"One more time!" Bellamy screamed.

Off they went. Kelly laughed until her sides ached. *I'm with friends,* she thought. And a part of Kelly, a tiny spark of her, felt like Catherine was watching them, watching them and smiling.

"THIS ONE'S CALLED PASSIONFRUIT SHIMMER," MOM SAID. "YOU JUST want to put the slightest hint of it on your cheekbones. Any more than that, it looks trashy."

Mom dusted Kelly's cheeks with a soft brush, her breath tickling her skin. She'd gotten a new line in today—the spring line already, even though it was just mid-February—and Mom always liked to practice with a new line before trying it out on the paying customers.

"Want to be my guinea pig?" Mom had said to Kelly when she'd slipped through the door at the normal time—four o'clock, just like every other day when she went to all her classes and took the bus. Mom had a tone to her, an urgency. Though that could have just been the way she was interpreting Mom, the way Kelly was thinking, the state she was in.

Everything felt urgent.

At any rate, yes was the only possible answer to the guinea pig question, and normally, Kelly loved it when Mom made her over— Mom so caring with her steady, cool hands, the authority in her voice as she explained each step. The attention she paid her, as though Kelly were a piece of art she was creating.

Mom was very good at makeup. She studied faces hard before she chose her shades, and she could turn anyone into a beauty, even Kelly. "Like a princess," she would say after her makeovers were complete, both of them gazing at Kelly's face in the mirror—eyes bright, cheek-bones defined, lips just the right shade. Kelly would look at herself and the way her mother was looking at her, and she would feel transformed.

Today, though. Today, Kelly already felt beautiful. Walking through the door, still in the final, glittering lap of her very first cocaine high, Kelly had replayed the car ride in her mind—a ride that had stretched all the way to Venice Beach and back with so much laughter, so much confession, so many secrets, presented like gifts. "*I've never told anyone this before, Kelly. You're just so easy to talk to . . .*"

Kelly in the backseat, Vee and Bellamy in the front, turning to her. Friends. "*We're the Three Musketeers,*" Bellamy had said, "*or maybe Charlie's Angels.*"

They'd parked in Venice Beach in a spot where the ocean stretched out before them, the sun low in the sky, so many people walking by, shirtless and on roller skates, in patched cutoffs and bikinis, beach tanned and sunburned and heroin pale—all of them beautiful and ugly at the same time. That was when Bellamy had slipped the mirror and the folded-up piece of paper from her purse, Vee rolling up a twenty, Bellamy shaking the white powder onto the mirror, cutting it into lines. Listening to the ritual click of the blade against the glass, Kelly had felt the strangest, most powerful longing—a need for a feeling she'd never known.

And then the relief—oh, the medicinal drip down the back of her throat, the numbness of her gums, the way her nerves came alive in an instant. And Vee, how he had looked at her. "*The first time is always the best*," he had said.

Like all expensive things, cocaine was better even than Kelly had imagined. It made her feel so much—the tingling of her pores, the sparkling of her eyes. Yes, Kelly could actually *feel her eyes sparkling*.

"Mom," Kelly said.

"Sssh. Stay still. I have to do your lips."

"No, wait a second."

Mom heaved out a sigh. "What?"

Kelly cleared her throat. "Have you ever heard of a director called John McFadden?"

She cleared her throat. "Yes, Kelly. Everyone's heard of him."

"Catherine was friends with John McFadden's son."

It was the cocaine talking. Kelly wouldn't have said it normally. Not on the anniversary of Catherine's death, what with how Mom felt about Hollywood people and Catherine's old friends and even the sound of Catherine's name. Every time you said her dead daughter's name out loud, it killed Mom a little. Kelly could see it in the way she was looking at her now, with those bruisey eyes she always got when someone hurt her, a look on her face like she was recovering from a punch. I'm sorry, Kelly wanted to say. But the words wouldn't come out. She wasn't sorry. She was tired of living by Mom's rules, tired of missing Catherine in silence and alone.

Mom said, "How do you know that?"

"I talked to some people from school."

"I don't want you talking to those people."

"What people?"

"The ones who . . . the people who would *know that* about your sister."

Kelly wanted to ask her what she meant by that, but of course she knew. The People Catherine Met at Parties. Catherine always used to claim that their mother was jealous of all the parties she went to—and of Catherine herself, young and connected as she was, just fifteen years old but on the fringes of the New Hollywood, *this close* to being a star . . . Kelly didn't believe it back then. Mom always said she was just trying to protect her, "*to save you from yourself*," as she used to say. "*Those people are like the movies they make—best viewed from a distance.*" And that had made sense to Kelly. It had made sense up until the beginning of this week. But it didn't anymore. Kelly heard Catherine's voice in her mind, the voice becoming her own. *How could you of all people tell me who to spend my time with? You who couldn't even make it in the movies as a makeup artist. You who . . .*

" . . . got knocked up by a lousy stuntman."

"*What?*" said Kelly's mother.

She hadn't even realized she'd said it out loud. But the coke made her brave, and reckless with the truth. "That's the closest you'll ever get to being a star. Getting knocked up by a stuntman."

The lip brush dropped out of her mother's hand, clattered on the floor. Kelly stared at it—the mother-of-pearl handle, delicate and wand-like. Her mother's brush. She'd never noticed before how pretty it was. Some things you only notice when they fall to the ground.

"Who have you been talking to?"

Kelly knew she should stop now. She'd gone too far already, but she couldn't help it. There had been so much confessing this afternoon, so much truth. "*Sometimes, I think my mom would have been happier if Catherine and I had both died. It's like . . . she has this grief and guilt. But since I'm still around, she can't get lost in it. It's like the worst of both worlds.*"

"People," Kelly tried. "Just—"

"Which people?"

She looked at her mother—and the pained, bruisey eyes. "Sterling Marshall's daughter."

Mom backed up a few more steps. Her lip trembled. Kelly could actually see it trembling, and when she spoke, her voice shook too. "I don't want you spending time with that girl."

"What? Why?"

"I don't need to give you reasons."

"I'm seventeen years old, not three!"

"Did you hear what I said?"

"You don't want me to have friends."

"That isn't true." She took a breath. Closed her eyes for a moment. "What about Susie?"

"Who?"

"Susie Mitchell. The doctor's daughter."

Jesus. "Mom," she said.

"I know what's best for you."

"You don't," she said, anger rising. "You don't know anything."

"*Do you want to end up like your sister?*"

"*Yes!*"

"Go to your room."

Kelly stood up, every muscle in her body tensed, her blood rushing hot. She was taller than her mother by a few inches now, and for the first time, she felt it.

"Catherine isn't dead because of Hollywood," she said. "She isn't dead because of the parties she went to or the friends she had, and she definitely isn't dead because of Sterling Marshall or his daughter."

"Don't say another word."

Kelly stared her down, the words coming before she could stop them, before she wanted to stop them. "Catherine is dead because of you."

"How could you say that?"

"If you hadn't hit her, she would have stayed home. She never would have gone off to Chantry Flats. She never would have been so angry and hurt and horrible-feeling that she jumped into the canyon."

Mom said nothing. Her lip trembled.

"You killed her," Kelly said.

Mom's eyes narrowed. She spoke so quietly, it was nearly a whisper. "Pack your things."

"What?"

"Pack your things."

Kelly's mother crossed her arms over her chest. Kelly's palms began to sweat, the back of her neck. Sweat trickled down her ribs and the cocaine high drained out of her along with it, her shirt damp and clinging. She felt cold. "I'm sorry," she whispered.

"Pack your things."

Kelly couldn't argue. She couldn't speak. She went into her room and grabbed a suitcase out of her closet and pulled what few clothes she had off her hangers, out of her drawers. Her hands wouldn't stop shaking.

Once she packed it all, she slipped to the floor and reached under her bed, where she kept her stash of "trashy" magazines—*Tiger Beat, Teen, Rona Barrett's Hollywood*. She threw those in too.

Kelly pulled herself up off the floor. "This can't be happening," she whispered, still shaking. For a few seconds, she felt as though someone was watching her. But when she whirled around hoping for her mother, she saw no one. Kelly was alone. Her cheeks burned. Her mouth was dry. She caught a glimpse of herself in the mirror—half made-over, half not. Pale, chapped lips, cheeks smeared with Passionfruit Shimmer. She felt lost.

As she passed her mother's room, Kelly saw the framed picture of Catherine still on her nightstand, placed next to the heart-shaped box filled with stale, old candy. A coil of anger sprung out inside her. Without even thinking about it, she swiped up the box and the photo, shoved them into her suitcase, snapped it shut. *She'll miss these,* she thought. Then she went back into her room and opened her nightstand drawer, took out Catherine's necklace, and for the first time, put it on. She stared at her reflection, the delicate chain at her throat, the two diamonds glistening . . . *Do I dare?* She remembered the way her mother had looked at it when Catherine had first worn it home. *Where did you get that? Answer me!*

She undid the clasp, put the necklace into her shirt pocket.

When Kelly reached the living room, her mother was sitting on the couch, her head bowed.

She tried again. "I'm really sorry."

"Are you still going to be friends with her?"

"Bellamy Marshall?"

"Yes."

Kelly said, "She's the only friend I have at school."

She stood up, faced her. Mom's hands were dropped to her sides now, and she looked softer now, less angry. "You're high, aren't you?" she said. "Coked up."

Kelly shook her head. "Not now, Mom. Not anymore."

"It doesn't matter." Mom handed her a thick wad of twenty-dollar bills, then a slip of paper with an address written on it.

Kelly couldn't speak. She thought of all the things Mom used to say about Catherine when they would fight. *You're not a star. You're not an actress. You're a party girl. Party girls are like party favors. They get used up and thrown out.* And in the end, that's all Catherine had turned out to be. A used-up, thrown-out party favor. A dead party girl at the bottom of a canyon.

Do you want to end up like your sister?

"I called you a cab while you were packing," Mom said. "Should only cost about fifteen dollars."

Kelly swallowed hard. A tear trickled down her cheek. "Mom, please."

"You can come back," she said, "if you promise never to speak to Bellamy Marshall again."

Kelly stared at her. Tried it again. "She's my only friend."

"Good-bye, Kelly."

"I can't stop talking to her. You can't make me. This isn't fair."

"You'll be fine."

She grasped the paper in her hands, throat tightening, tears coming. "Whose address is this?"

Mom smiled a little—a thin smile that didn't reach her eyes—and then the cab pulled up outside their building, its horn tooting. "It's your father's," she said.

CHAPTER 13

APRIL 22, 2010

"T ell me about those last four months before John McFadden's death," Sebastian Todd said, once Kelly had swung the car onto the 10 without signaling, leaving the paparazzi vans behind. "The time you spent living with your dad."

Kelly said nothing. She'd kept silent ever since he'd barged into her car. "I know you didn't kill John McFadden," he'd said, and she hadn't offered so much as a "hmm," instead allowing the self-described "literary journalist" to stare intently at the side of her face, nodding his head slowly as she drove, holding his trademarked pregnant pause all the way to its breaking point.

This was one thing Sebastian Todd had never gotten about Kelly. Unlike most other interview subjects, she had no need to fill conversational pauses. Kelly was fine with silence. She always had been.

Funny he hadn't remembered that. Sebastian Todd was very proud of his interviewing skills, Kelly knew. In the preface to one of his books—she couldn't remember which one—he'd compared them to the skills of a big game hunter. (*Know your prey. Know their weaknesses and their strengths. Find the perfect ammunition and use it.*)

Of course, that was a load of crap. Todd had no need for interviewing skills as his "groundbreaking" prison talk with Kelly—the one printed in his Pulitzer Prize–nominated book, *Mona Lisa*—was described by the author himself as "creative nonfiction," which as it turned out was a fancy way to say "almost completely made up."

She'd never said any of those things he claimed she did in the interview, never said John McFadden's death was "meant to be." Never said anything about a belief system and certainly never called herself "an agent of fate."

In fact, Kelly couldn't recall saying much of anything at all to Sebastian Todd, this "important journalist" she'd never heard of and who wore a white suit to a woman's prison—a white suit and matching hair, like the Man from Glad. She still remembered thinking, *I'm supposed to trust this guy?*

Kelly had been between lawyers at the time, no parents around to advise her, Dad half fallen apart already, Mom dropped off the face of the earth. Todd had written her a few letters that had read to her as fawning, almost psycho. Kelly hadn't wanted to talk to him at all, but the warden had made it sound like a requirement.

"*Why did you kill John McFadden?*" he'd asked Kelly back then, after being ushered into her cell, after some inane foreplay about the weather, Todd telling her how bright and sunny it was outside, as though Carpentia didn't have a yard. ("*I go outside every day,*" she'd said, confused.) And then, boom, the $64,000 Question, her first name at the end, just to make it personal. "*Why did you kill John McFadden, Kelly?*"

He'd tried the pregnant pause with her back then too. Kelly had stared Todd in the eyes until he blinked, until he cleared his throat. And then she'd looked at the guard and said, "*I don't want to do this anymore.*"

Really, you'd think he would have remembered that.

"What was your father like during those months?" Todd was saying now, filling the silence yet again. "When you lived with him? Was he functioning then at all?"

"Functioning?"

"Yes. When he was questioned during your trial, your father said—"

"You know what I'd like, ST?"

Another pause. "I think I do."

"Really?"

"Yes. You'd like your story told. The true story."

"Nope," she said. "What I'd like is to throw you out of this car."

"You don't mean that."

"Oh, I do. I'd like to reach over and open your door and push you out and over the side of this overpass. You're not buckled in, so it would be easy."

"Look," he said. "I know we haven't always seen eye to eye. I know you didn't appreciate the facts I brought out in my book."

"*Facts?* You put words in my mouth."

He shook his head. "I put voice to your thoughts."

"Jesus."

"I know I hurt you."

"You're overestimating your importance in my life." Kelly sped up the car, switched lanes. She heard the click of his seat belt and, in spite of everything, smiled a little. *Scared him.*

"Kelly, please," Todd said. "Try and answer my questions."

"Why would I want to do that?"

"Because I can clear your name. People won't be so quick to judge you over Sterling Marshall if they realize they've been wrong all along about John McFadden."

"I don't have time for this."

"Your dad was addicted to painkillers, wasn't he? All those injuries he incurred as a stuntman. He was either in constant pain or dosed on pills. He could barely get through the day, even back then."

"So?"

"So the movie he sustained so many of those injuries on. The one where he was burned . . ."

"It was some horror movie. I don't know the name."

"It was called *The Demon Pit.*"

"Never heard of it."

"Very few people have. It was a B movie, put out by an Italian producer. It never saw the light of day, really."

"Thanks for the cinema lesson. Now where can I drop you?"

"*The Demon Pit* was John McFadden's first film."

Kelly gripped the wheel. *Why didn't Dad ever tell me that? Why didn't anybody . . .* "So what?"

"McFadden never compensated him."

"You think my father suddenly killed John McFadden and pinned it on me. Because of a twenty-year-old workman's comp issue."

He took another long, pregnant pause. Kelly let it sit there. "It isn't me who's saying it," he said.

Kelly turned to him. There was an off-ramp coming up, and she veered onto it, pulled to the side of the road, screeched onto a residential street, and stopped the car. She had no idea where they were. Didn't care. "Have you been talking to my father?"

He smiled a little. "Relax."

"Don't you dare tell me that."

"Kelly," he said. "I highly suggest you watch the movie. I think I can track down a copy for you, e-mail you a downloadable link. Go to the 1:23 mark. Easy to remember. One, two—"

"Listen," Kelly said. "My father isn't in his right mind. And if you've been agitating him I swear to God—"

"Hold up, hold up."

"I'll kill you. And I don't give a damn how that sounds. It's on the record. I *will kill you.*"

Todd put up both hands, spread his fingers. "I haven't been speaking to your father," he said.

"So you're just full of crap then?"

His mouth twitched a little, his hands still up, as though Kelly were holding him hostage when really, it was starting to feel like the other way around. "I've been talking to the movie's makeup artist."

Kelly's breath caught. "What?"

"The makeup artist on *The Demon Pit,*" he said. "Surely you know how your parents met. The makeup artist was your mother."

Kelly turned to him. She couldn't speak.

"Your mom looks great, by the way," he said, grinning at his prey, triumphant. "You two should really get back in touch."

HE MADE GOOD ON HIS WORD, KELLY THOUGHT, BECAUSE WHEN SHE arrived at her dark, empty house two hours after dropping Sebastian Todd back at his car, there was an e-mail from SToryteller@aol.com in her in-box—a download of *The Demon Pit.* It was the only e-mail she'd received, and when she checked both voice mails, they were empty too. Well, the Hollywood Photo Archives voice mail was full of calls from reporters, but nothing from Shane. No message at all.

"What did I do to lose you?" She said it aloud in the dark empty kitchen as she turned the light on, and then her gaze landed on the dryer. She thought of the clothes inside, the bloodstains scrubbed and bleached away as though they'd never been there. *It isn't what you* do *that makes you lose people,* she reminded herself. *It's what they* think *you've done.*

She clicked on the link. While it downloaded, she went to the refrigerator, pulled out a can of beer, and popped the top. She let the cool bitter liquid ease down her throat and felt the way she always did when she drank alcohol after being deprived of it for the better part of twenty-five years. Free. And slightly queasy.

The download was complete by the time the can was empty. She moved back to the computer, and clicked on it. When the black rectangle appeared, she hit the full screen icon, then "play."

The opening credits popped up immediately, artlessly—lurid, dripping red, floating over the terrified face of a voluptuous young woman, bound, gagged, and blindfolded.

THE DEMON PIT
A JOHN MCFADDEN FILM

Kelly stared at the name, JOHN MCFADDEN, at the bleeding letters. She remembered how much she'd liked him at one point in her life, how much she'd envied Vee for having a man like him for a father—clean and clear-eyed and responsible. *The way a father should be,* she'd thought, back before she found out who John McFadden really was.

And here, her parents had met on the set of a McFadden film . . . *Yet another thing my mother never told me.*

Kelly tried to push the thought of her from her mind—Rose Lund, or whatever she was calling herself these days, behind the walls of that place she lived in . . . Commune? Cult? It was somewhere *simple and safe* and it was a *place to start over,* Rose had said in a letter sent to Kelly twenty-seven years ago. And she had called it *Home.*

I love you, Kelly. I'm doing the best thing for us both. Don't think of me as leaving. Think of me as going Home.

For a moment, Kelly let herself try to imagine what her mother must look like now: Sebastian Todd had said she had white hair and full, rosy cheeks and it was hard to picture her with any of those things. The Rose Lund she knew had been sinewy and strawberry blond, expertly made up for the bright lights of I. Magnin, ten years younger than Kelly was now . . .

Please don't leave me, Mom, Kelly had written back, her heart beating so hard her handwriting jittered on the page. *I don't have anybody else.* She had never received a response.

She's alive. Kelly had always assumed she was. But assuming and knowing were two different things. "*She has been living in the same place all these years,*" Sebastian Todd had said. "*Would you like to know where?*"

"*Absolutely not.*"

Kelly focused on the screen, where names of actors she'd never heard of scrolled by, a shadow falling over the face of the blindfolded woman, her back arching in that type of ecstatic terror that doesn't exist in real life, only in bad movies—more a pose than an emotion. Some of the buttons on her shirt popped open.

God, Kelly didn't know how much more of this crap she could take. *Go to the 1:23 mark. Easy to remember. One, two . . .*

She moved the cursor to the forward button on-screen as a claw ripped the young woman's blindfold off. A large tribal tattoo had been drawn between her terrified eyes—a big reveal of an elaborate, bloodred pentagram adorned with stars, ancient letters. The painstaking work of Kelly's mother, the makeup artist . . .

The woman's lips quivered around the gag. She shrieked as the demon pulled her shirt open to show the whole of a black lace bra, eyes going huge as its claws slit her throat . . .

Kelly froze. The demon was leering at the camera now and so she scrolled back several seconds—not to see the bloody B movie actress, but to reread the final credit, rolling up the screen.

Kelly shook her head. He had funded the film. "You gave John McFadden his start." She said it to the screen. To the dead Sterling Marshall. To the darkness. Then she scrolled up to the 1:23 mark. Watched her father burn.

SEBASTIAN HAD CALLED HER ROSE LUND IN HIS FIRST NOTE. ROSE Lund—a name she hadn't used in nearly thirty years. It had made her stop breathing for a few seconds—her old, sad name written out in swirling, unfamiliar handwriting on a hot pink envelope and then again on the note inside.

Her name was Ruth Freed now. She'd chosen it herself thirty years ago when she'd given up her meager worldly goods and her far more significant worldly mistakes and moved in with Zeke and the group. Everyone here in the compound chose new names upon arrival—a decision both practical and symbolic—and the former Rose Lund hadn't taken that choice lightly. She'd taken it somewhat dismally, in fact. How was she supposed to choose a name for herself when all the choices she had made in her life had been so consistently wrong?

"*Try finding something from Shakespeare, or the Bible.*" That advice had come from Zeke, full name Ezekiel, who had clearly gone the latter route. And so Ruth had done the same, pouring over Bible passages until she found Ruth—lost and childless and longing for redemption. Perfect. The Freed part had literally come with the territory. It was Ezekiel's last name too—the last name of everyone who lived here in the compound, its meaning obvious and true.

Yet when she'd seen *Rose Lund* written out like that, Ruth had felt . . . nostalgic was the wrong word. She didn't want the name back any more than she wanted the life it came with. But there was something else she did want to the point of longing. It became tangible only when she read the note, the part of it that said, *I know you love your daughter*.

It had been six months ago, early evening just after supper. On cleanup duty that night, Ruth had been stacking plates. Jeremiah, who'd been on guard duty, had raced into the canteen, such a tense look on his face that Ruth had thought it was the cops again. "Is there a former Rose Lund here?" Jeremiah had said, because no one here knew each other's former identities. No one wanted to. That was the point.

Ruth had raised her hand shakily. Jeremiah had given her the note, explaining that the man who had left it for her was outside the gate, waiting. She'd read the letter in the cactus garden, Zeke at her side.

"*Old friend?*" Zeke had asked.

"*Complete stranger. But he knows one of my daughters. He wants to meet me. Should I?*"

"*You're asking me. But you know the answer.*"

Ruth had left the cactus garden and stepped outside the gate for the first time in years to meet with the stranger, Sebastian Todd.

At first sight, she'd been impressed by him, intimidated almost—this elegant, bald man from the outside world, a Pulitzer Prize–nominated journalist dressed all in white who claimed not only to know Kelly, but to have written a book about her. ("*I can send you a copy,*" he had said. "*But you might not like it.*")

He had then given Ruth two pieces of information: (1) Kelly had been out of jail for nearly five years. (2) She was now married to Shane Marshall.

Ruth had crumbled at the name. Sterling Marshall's son. Bellamy Marshall's brother, and now Kelly's husband? It wasn't possible. None of this was possible. She'd managed to keep the past at arm's length for so long, but listening to this man speak, she'd felt it caving in on her, crushing her. She'd accused Sebastian Todd of lying because Sebastian Todd lying had been her only hope. She had told him to leave and never come back, but still the damage had been done.

One week after Sebastian Todd's first visit, Zeke had woken up drenched in sweat, his lips blue, his body shaking uncontrollably. He'd used the emergency phone to call an ambulance, coming back from town days later with a diagnosis he refused to talk about.

Ruth knew logically that Sebastian Todd's visit wasn't connected to Zeke's illness, but a part of her—the same part that knew she was to blame for both her daughters' fates—felt otherwise. Ever since her conversation with that white-clad harbinger of bad news, Zeke had been getting sicker and sicker, wasting away as he was now in his cabin, lying flat on his back on his thin, sweat-soaked futon, all the covers kicked off and Ruth at his side, spooning him lukewarm chicken broth, the only thing he was able to keep down these days.

Deep in that same dark recess of her brain, Ruth now had a strange knowledge that Sebastian Todd was back, the light knock on Zeke's door confirming it—that and Demetrius's voice. "Ruth? You in there?"

"Yes."

Demetrius poked his head in—such a handsome young head it was, blond curls and full cherubic lips and crystal-blue eyes. Zeke's eyes. His mother, Ophelia, had left the compound three years ago. But unlike Ruth, Ophelia had left behind a child who was strong, mature, and confident, with a father capable of raising him. Demetrius was eighteen now, the same age Kelly had been when she was found guilty of second-degree murder. It broke her heart to look at him, how grown-up he was.

He held out a hot pink envelope. "There's . . . uh . . . a man in a white suit outside the gate?"

Her stomach clenched up. "I don't want to see him."

"Are you sure?" Zeke said it, his voice so soft and weak. "Don't you want to read the note? It seems like it would be a good idea, doesn't it?"

Ruth sighed. She couldn't say no to Zeke. She lived to keep him calm and happy, and turning down one of his suggestions felt like the opposite. She said nothing, just held out her hand. Demetrius padded over to her and gave her the note. He was a foot taller than Ruth, but still a little boy to her. She'd helped toilet train him after all. She still baked him cookies—double chocolate chip were his favorite. There had been a time when he was around five or six—a good eight months to a year in there—he'd insisted on calling her Nana. That had been the happiest time in her life. "Thanks, Deedee," she said—his childhood nickname. He smiled. She wished she could hold him close, turn him back into a little boy, keep him that way forever.

Before he turned to leave, Demetrius moved to his father's bedside and kissed Zeke's forehead very lightly.

"I love you," Zeke whispered.

But Demetrius was already out, cabin door closed softly behind him.

"He's a good young man," Ruth said. "You should be proud."

Zeke closed his eyes. "Read the note," he said.

She did. It was just one line: *Kelly is in danger*.

RUTH MET SEBASTIAN OUTSIDE THE GATE AGAIN. SHE DIDN'T FEEL right about inviting him inside, not because she didn't trust him (though she didn't). The real reason was, she was afraid of the effect he might have on some of the children, the ones who were born here and had grown up knowing only clumsily sewn clothes and hand-me-downs. And looking at him now, leaning against his money-green Bentley, fine white suit glowing in the moonlight, she knew her instincts had been right. Sebastian held out his hand to shake hers and she noticed the watch—bulky and futuristic. Probably a Rolex—or whatever the equivalent was these days in the outside world. Back when she was Rose Lund, Ruth would have pined for this man.

"Thank you for seeing me," he said. "I know we didn't part on the best of terms."

He wore sleek-looking glasses and had an intense, purposeful gaze she knew better than to meet. "You didn't leave me much choice in the note." It was a clear, starry night, and a windy one. Cool air crept under Ruth's flannel shirt, ruffled her hair. She shivered. "What's happened to Kelly?"

"Sterling Marshall."

That name. She shut her eyes tight. "What about him?"

"He's dead."

"What?"

"He was shot to death. Two bullets to the chest, one to the head. Just like John McFadden. The police suspect Kelly."

Ruth's knees buckled. She collapsed to the ground, legs slipping out from under her, earth crashing into the side of her face, her hip, the palms of her hands.

"Oh my God . . . Ruth," Sebastian said, crouching down beside her. "Can you hear me?"

She hadn't passed out. It wasn't that—it was her body giving out on her, surrendering as though her muscles, her bones and cells could no longer take being a part of her. *Sterling shot to death. Kelly suspected.* "It's my fault," Ruth whispered.

"What? No," he said. "Of course it isn't your fault." He put his arms around her, lifted her to her feet. He brushed the hair out of her face. His hands were soft and he wore an expensive cologne—first time in so long that she'd been close to a man who didn't smell of sweat and home-made soap, and again, it took her where she didn't want to go . . . "It is."

"Listen." He grabbed her by the shoulders. "Listen to me."

Kelly. The name filled her thoughts, a thick weight in her heart. "She killed Sterling Marshall."

He shook his head. "She didn't. I would bet my life on it," he said. "And I honestly don't think she killed John McFadden, either."

Ruth let herself meet his gaze. In the moonlight, his eyes were an odd shade of yellow-green, like a cat's. "You're serious," she said.

He nodded. "I spoke to your ex-husband."

"Jimmy?" She nearly collapsed again. "Jimmy's still alive?"

"He's in a rest home and he's . . . well, he's all right," he said, looking at the ground. "He told me all about *The Demon Pit,* how McFadden was responsible for his injuries. He said McFadden deserved to die and that he had killed him."

Ruth crossed her arms over her chest, hugging herself against the cold, against her thoughts. *The Demon Pit.* God, that awful movie. The memories it dug up . . .

" . . . saw the film myself," Sebastian was saying now. "The scene where that poor man burns is horrifying. And he was never compensated. Not a dime. I'd have done it too. I'd have killed John McFadden in a heartbeat."

"Have you seen her?" She swallowed hard. "Have you spoken to my daughter?"

"Yes. Right before I came here."

"How is Kelly?" she said.

"She didn't want to talk about McFadden or her father." He looked at Ruth. "And I should tell you that I lied to her. I said you were the one who told me about *The Demon Pit.*" He cleared his throat. "I'm sorry but if I hadn't, she would have thrown me out of a moving vehicle."

She drew a deep breath. In the distance, she heard a coyote, the howl so much like crying. "I just want to know how Kelly is. Is she healthy? Happy? I mean, aside from—"

"Rose," he said. "I don't think she has any idea how much danger she is in."

"But . . . You said she didn't kill Sterling."

"It doesn't matter. She's a murderer. She'll always be a murderer, and as long as that's true, she will always be the bad guy."

"They can't arrest her based on opinions."

"Whether or not she's arrested, a good man has been killed. A movie hero. And there are many who hate her for it." He took a step closer, put a hand on her shoulder. "She's in danger."

"What can I do?"

"You can help me," he said. "Help me rewrite her story."

Ruth leaned back against the Bentley and gazed up. Amazing how many stars you could see out here in the desert, the sky crowded with them like rhinestones on a black velvet shawl, every night so beautiful it bordered on gaudy. To this day, it was hard for Ruth to wrap her mind around the fact that at this moment, this very same sky was starless in Hollywood, rendered a dull purple from bright lights and automobile emissions. Those same stars that took Ruth's breath away now had always been out there. But to Rose Lund they hadn't existed.

"They threw rocks at my apartment," she said.

"What?"

"After Kelly was arrested, they threw rocks through my windows. They called me a bitch, a bad mother." Her voice was soft, sad. Not her own.

"Who?"

"I didn't know them. It didn't matter. Whoever they were, they were right."

A tear ran down her cheek, warm and shameful.

Sebastian brushed it away. "Will you help me?"

"I'm a bad person."

He turned her face to his, cupped her chin in his hand very gently, as though she were something small and fragile and clean.

"I can't . . ."

Sebastian put a finger to his lips. He shook his head slowly. "Nobody's bad forever, Mrs. Lund," he said. "Not unless they want to be."

KELLY REPLAYED THE SCENE AGAIN. THE LEADING MAN, BLANDLY handsome, pushing the evil demon into the fiery pit. The quick cutaway and then back to the demon writhing, Kelly's father writhing in his demon suit, throwing his head back, pulling at his scaly skin . . . an audible scream and still the camera had kept rolling, the leading man backing away, his uncertainty so obvious, so real . . . *John McFadden's camera keeps rolling as Jimmy Lund burns.*

Kelly wiped a tear from her eye. "*To my father, there are two types of people in the world—those who matter to his story and those who don't.*" Vee had told her that once. She couldn't remember why he'd said it, but it was probably the truest thing he'd ever told her. "*My dad can tell a good story. For some reason, he thinks that makes him a good person.*"

In a rare moment of non-self-absorption, Kelly's mother had once told her that before his injuries, Jimmy had been something of a jock. Quite an adventurer too, as one might expect from a professional stuntman—the type who sought out what they used to call "natural highs." "*I could watch him surf forever,*" she had said. "*There was no wave too powerful for that man, and the way he'd hold his arms out, Kelly. My God. He was magnificent.*"

Jimmy was in an assisted living facility on Hollywood and Highland. Kelly had visited him there once, just once. The week she'd gotten out of prison. His mind was gone. Dementia, brought on by pernicious anemia, made worse by years of malnourishment and drugs. He shared a room with another old man who kept shouting at odd intervals. But Jimmy didn't seem to mind—ever his easygoing self, even in the throes of confusion. He was painfully thin with bashed-in cheeks. His skin was crinkled and spotted and his sparse white hair stuck out at odd angles, like bits of frayed cotton. But his smile was the same. And that sameness—that one thing remaining of the Jimmy she had known—that smile was so much more heartbreaking than all the changes had been. "You've always been a pal to me, Sondra," he had told Kelly. Confusing her with Sondra Locke. She'd never gone back. She called to check in on him every week. She spoke to the nurses. But she couldn't see that smile again. Couldn't bear it.

Kelly put her head down on the kitchen table, tried to close that file drawer, the one that held her father, the same one that now held John McFadden and the stories he told. But the drawer stayed open, glared at her. She banged her head against the table just once, the sound of it breaking the silence, the pain echoing.

Kelly headed for the refrigerator, grabbed another beer. With Shane, she often used to joke that she'd "filled up her chemical dance card," meaning she'd done enough mind-altering substances in her teens to last a lifetime. But while that was true, she needed something right now. Something stronger than beer to smooth things over, to put it all in soft focus.

Beer would have to do. She cracked open the can, downed it in three gulps before it hit her that she was drinking alone. All alone. Shane was gone. Acting out in strip clubs. Staying with his sister. Shane and his father, both gone within a day . . .

The kitchen phone rang. She picked it up fast, said it without thinking. "Shane?"

"Kelly?"

"Yes . . ."

"I'm with TMZ and first of all, I just want to say, I am *so totally sorry for your loss*—"

Kelly cut off the call, heart pounding, hands shaking. She clicked on caller ID and scrolled back through recent calls, all those calls from the *Los Angeles Times* and AMI magazines and every Hollywood blog on the Internet, every one of those bastards who'd left messages on the voice mail, laced with fake politeness, falling all over each other to reach her, to reach Shane, begging to let them tell the story.

There are two types of people in the world . . .

She scrolled through all of them until finally, nearly last on the list, she found Bellamy's call from this morning and hit redial. It was well past midnight, but she didn't care. Time didn't matter.

Ever the night owl, Bellamy picked up after one ring. "He doesn't want to talk to you," she said. And Kelly closed her eyes, tears seeping out the corners. Her voice sounded so much the same. They could have been kids, for that was the last time they'd spoken. *Could have been kids, arguing over a boy . . .*

"I don't understand what is going on." It wasn't what Kelly had planned to say, the last thing she'd ever imagined herself telling Bellamy, in all the angry daydreams she'd had over the years. But in her daydreams, in life, Kelly had never felt this way—helpless, as though the whole world had been pulled out from under her. She hadn't felt this way in thirty years.

"You don't know what's going on?" Bellamy said. "You're a psychopath. You're evil. And finally Shane knows it."

Kelly took a breath, tried to steady herself. "I need to talk to Shane."

Bellamy sighed—a long whoosh that hurt Kelly's ear. "You can't. He's passed out."

Kelly closed her eyes. "Bellamy, I'm sorry."

"You killed my father. You killed his best friend and then you killed him and all you can say is—"

"I meant I'm sorry about Shane."

Bellamy gasped. "I let you into my life. I let you into my life and you . . . you just . . . you destroyed it. From the inside out."

Kelly gritted her teeth. She clenched her fists. "Bullshit. You destroyed me. You made me into something I'm not. You know damn well what John McFadden was."

"I do know what he was," she said, quietly. "He was my father's best friend."

Kelly was shaking now, her whole body trembling, a white-hot burn in her brain, drawers flying open and clattering, breaking. Outside, she heard a clap of thunder, then the gush of sudden rain, the sky opening up as it hardly ever did here, the sky sobbing.

"I thought you were my friend," she said into the phone. "The only friend I ever had. You didn't testify, but that was okay. I understood. I missed you so much, Bellamy, and you never called. I wrote you letters and you never answered and when you finally did . . . When you finally called . . . God, that one day you called me and asked me how I was and I thought my heart would burst. You really did care. I missed you. I needed you—and you got me to say that. You got me to cry and tell you I missed you. But you did it so you could . . . make it into art. Do you remember what you said to me, Bellamy? Do you remember what you said during that five-minute phone call when I was in prison? After I told you I missed you?"

The rain drummed on the roof.

"You said you loved me, Bellamy."

No response. Kelly listened to the rain until it eased to a dull patter. It took her several seconds to realize Bellamy had hung up a while ago, that she'd poured out her soul to a dead line. "At least she wasn't taping me," Kelly whispered, her voice choked. Broken.

She started to cry—for Shane and for her parents, for Sterling Marshall and for Catherine, for the friends she used to think she had, for all the things she used to believe. She cried for everything she'd lost with John McFadden's death—and for those few small things that still remained.

She cried like she never had, not since she was a child, wailing loud, since no one could hear her, the one good thing about being completely alone.

When she finally calmed down enough to wipe the tears from her face, to slow her breathing back to normal, Kelly realized that the rain had stopped. She touched the kitchen window, moonlight soaking in, making the drops glisten. *When was the last time it rained here?* Kelly couldn't remember. She couldn't get herself to believe it would ever rain here again.

Kelly heard a pounding on the front door. Her gaze shot to the clock over the stove. 12:55 A.M. Shane was passed out, according to Bellamy. Who else would be knocking? She thought of the reporters on her voice mail, the detective this morning, all the people out there who had hated her in the past, probably hated her still and all the more now, what with Sterling Marshall, with what they all would soon believe . . .

Shaking, she went for the wooden block at the end of the counter, yanked out the butcher knife. She moved to the door, pressed her face against the glass . . .

It was hard to see through, but she saw his shape. The moon backlit him like a movie villain. But even by moonlight, even through fogged glass she could see his face, his tattoos. She dropped the knife and threw open the door.

"Rocky," she said, falling on him, burying her face in his neck, breathing him in like a memory.

CHAPTER 14

In many ways, McFadden is cut from the same cloth as Stanley Kubrick and Hal Ashby—that rare brand of director who breathes, eats, and sleeps his work. "I approach a film contract in the same way you'd approach a marriage contract," he says. "I will only sign if I'm completely in love with the project, and throughout its duration, I will give it my all." McFadden smiles, warm brown eyes crinkling at the corners. "I'm as faithful as they come."

McFadden's all-consuming devotion to his craft has meant sacrificing other aspects of his life. His one and only marriage, to model Leilani Valle in his early twenties, proved briefer than some of his film projects, lasting barely two years. "It's amazing she put up with me for as long as she did." He laughs. "But I don't regret my time with Leilani. It helped me to grow in significant ways." Most significant of all, the short union produced Vincent, 14, who—in a McFadden family version of a father-son fishing trip—appeared in Dad's film Defiance *as an eleven-year-old. "It brought us closer." McFadden smiles. "The work always does."*

And the work always takes precedence. Though McFadden's circle of industry friends includes legendary bad boys Jack Nicholson and Robert Evans, the handsome 38-year-old is largely absent from the Hollywood party scene. Squeaky clean (especially by Tinseltown standards) McFadden doesn't smoke, rarely drinks—and hardly ever even goes out on dates. "Johnny is a bit of a monk," jokes his close friend, legendary actor Sterling Marshall. "I keep saying to him, 'Why let those good looks go to waste?' But he won't listen to me. All he wants to do is, 'create.'"

It makes McFadden about as rare in the New Hollywood as Brylcreem, undershirts, or "saving it for marriage." But with his eyes firmly on the prize, he doesn't mind. "I may be boring, but I know what I want out of life," laughs the director, whose easygoing charm, coupled with intense attention to detail has brought out stunning turns from such greats as Marshall, Nicholson, and Henry Fonda. "I want to tell stories," he says. "Nothing more, nothing less."

FROM
"John McFadden: Portrait of an Artist"
People
April 15, 1978

CHAPTER 15

APRIL 14, 1980

What's that?" Bellamy said.

"It's a sandwich," said Kelly. "I think."

Bellamy laughed, but Kelly felt kind of bad about it. Her dad tried so hard.

They were sitting on the zebra rug in Bellamy's bedroom, just as they did most days when they were supposed to be at school, getting stoned, Kelly unwrapping her lunch, the two of them mining it for anything edible.

Kelly's dad, whose name was Jimmy Lund, got up in the morning and packed her lunch every day. He did this no matter how strung out he was feeling, no matter how sick. Kelly hadn't been speaking to Jimmy that much lately—they passed each other in the hallway, ate dinner mostly in silence. When she'd first moved into his apartment, he warned her that sometimes it hurt him to talk. "*It's not you, it's me,*" he'd said. And this was one of those times. But whether or not they were engaged in regular conversation, she could always tell how bad off Jimmy was from one day to the next by the quality of the lunch. She looked at the sandwich—a curling piece of American cheese between two Wonder Bread heels. *Pretty bad,* she thought.

"Anything else in there?" said Bellamy.

Kelly pulled out a small bag of Lays potato chips that looked like it had been run over by a truck.

Bellamy sighed. "You know what? I'm going to brave the kitchen." She handed Kelly the joint. "Want any more?"

Kelly took a long hit, held it in like she knew how to do now, easing it out through parted lips so that it rose up and into her nose like vapor. *French style,* Bellamy called it. She closed her eyes and soon she felt smooth, elastic. She was good at getting stoned.

This morning, after making Kelly's lunch, Jimmy had stood over the kitchen sink with the hot water running for a good ten, fifteen minutes, the whole room filling with steam. Dishes had been piling up in the sink for a few days now, and so Kelly had assumed he was finally washing them. *Maybe he's feeling a little better,* she had thought. But then she'd looked at him, really looked at her dad standing there, so perfectly still, his body tilted at that strange angle, and it hit her: He'd nodded off.

Kelly had turned off the water and left him there, sleeping on his feet. She'd headed straight out the door, to Bellamy's waiting car. *Why wake him,* she'd reasoned. But maybe she should have.

In some ways, Kelly's dad was exactly how she'd expected he'd be, but in others he was surprising. She'd expected druggy. Her mother had told her long ago that after being severely burned as a stuntman on a low-budget horror movie, Jimmy had gotten hooked on booze and pain pills in order to keep working. "*Your father numbs himself with a regular diet of Percocet and Jack,*" she'd said.

So that wasn't a surprise—the sleepiness, the confusion, the nods and the sweats and the crying bouts in the middle of the night when the pills wore off and Kelly should have been asleep. All of that, she'd expected.

When she'd shown up at his door, in fact, she'd figured she had maybe fifty-fifty odds of his being awake enough to answer it. She'd knocked tentatively, her heart beating fast, her face still sticky from the tears she'd cried in the cab.

She'd thought about knocking harder, but then he'd answered it—this skinny guy with big, swimmy eyes like fried eggs. He was smaller than she'd remembered. But then again, she was bigger than she'd been the last time she'd seen him.

"*Hi. I'm . . . Um . . .*"

His eyes had lit up right away. He'd thrown his arms around her. "*I know who you are!*" He had clapped her on the back with a strength she hadn't expected and asked after her mother ("*Is Rosie okay?*"). He'd carried her bag into his house and boiled water for tea and said, "*I can't believe it! My little girl!*" over and over, like he'd won the lottery. That was what had surprised her about Jimmy.

Kelly looked at the clock on Bellamy's nightstand, still thinking about Jimmy at the sink. It was around ten-thirty. It had happened three hours ago. She'd never seen him nod off on his feet before and for a moment, she thought maybe she should ask Bellamy to drive her home, just to check on him. But when she tried to stand up, the room swirled. She couldn't go anywhere, not like this.

She caught a glimpse of herself in the vanity mirror—the dark circles under her eyes, the sloppy platinum blond streak that Bellamy had put in her hair a week ago . . . She wore a T-shirt of Bellamy's too—skimpy and sleeveless, an unflattering shade of green and a size too small. Bellamy had told her it looked cute, but in Kelly's opinion, the shirt seemed angry to be on her.

She had to fix herself. She didn't want anyone to see her like this—especially Bellamy's parents, who might come home any minute. She'd only seen them once, when Bellamy had asked her to stay for dinner, but they'd both made her so uncomfortable, the sheen on them, the perfection. Mrs. Marshall with her perfect haircut and her pearls and her voice that never rose above a polite whisper. And Mr. Marshall . . . Sterling Marshall, like he'd been peeled off an old movie still, *the* Sterling Marshall sitting across the table from her . . . She didn't think he liked her very much.

Kelly had longed to say something witty to the Marshalls, something that might make them smile. But she may as well have been in one of her classes, shyness overtaking her, words darting out of her grasp, the blood rushing in her ears as she felt every bead of sweat on her body, the way her clothes bit into her and her hair hung lank down the sides of her face . . . It had been all she could do to give them "yes" and "no" answers to their questions, all she could do to pass the peas without spilling them everywhere. And Bellamy's little brother hadn't helped either, the way he kept staring at her. There was something wrong with that kid.

Bellamy had to have some lip gloss, blush, something. Kelly pulled open one of her vanity table drawers, started rummaging around inside. She found a few lighters, some perfume, a set of pens. You'd think Bellamy's drawers would be perfectly organized, but they were actually all over the place. The next drawer was more promising—nail polish, mascara, a few blushes. She chose one—a nice coral. She brushed it onto her cheeks, examining herself in the mirror. *Just the slightest hint. Any more than that, it looks tacky . . .*

Kelly heard footsteps landing on the staircase and threw the blush back in the drawer. She was about to slam it shut when she noticed something, wedged up against the back corner—a Baggie. Kelly slipped it out of the drawer—she couldn't help herself. If there was one thing the past two months with Bellamy and Vee had taught her, it was that good things came in Baggies.

This one held a single razor blade. Nothing else. It looked rusty, but when Kelly held it up to the light, she saw that the blade was crusted with . . . *blood?*

"What are you doing?" Bellamy was standing in the doorway, a bag of Cheetos in one hand, videotape in the other.

"I'm sorry. I was looking for blush."

Bellamy's face flushed. But what could she say? She couldn't get angry at Kelly. She had to understand, didn't she? A few days earlier, Bellamy's little brother Shane had some friends over, and since Jimmy was off at a shoot anyway, they'd driven over to her place to escape the noise. At one point, Kelly had gone to the bathroom and returned to find Bellamy rooting through her dresser. She'd glanced up at her and grinned as though she'd every right. "*Checking for secrets,*" she had said.

"Can you put it back, please?" Bellamy said.

Kelly stared at her, the Baggie dangling, a million questions running through her mind. But the look in Bellamy's eyes shut her up. She put the Baggie back in. She closed the drawer. *Nobody's perfect. Everybody's got a drawer somewhere, with something hidden in it.*

"Checking for secrets?" she tried.

Bellamy smiled—a forced smile, that didn't reach her eyes. "Guess you found one."

Kelly felt as though something had shattered, but she wasn't exactly sure what the shattered thing was. "I'm really sorry."

Bellamy moved closer. "I haven't done it for a long time."

"Done what?"

Bellamy dropped the video and the Cheetos on her bed and kneeled down next to Kelly. She pushed her silver bangle bracelets back and showed Kelly the inside of her wrist. There were six even slashes on it—healed over but still visible. "See how faint they are?"

Kelly gaped at them. She didn't know what to say.

"You have to promise me something," Bellamy said, that look in her eyes fading, confidence coming back.

"Anything."

"Never talk about this again."

She replied quickly. "Okay."

"Don't tell anybody—especially Vee."

"I promise," she said, wondering, *Why Vee?* But saying nothing. Bellamy looked at her for a long time. Her eyes were pinkish, but Kelly wasn't sure whether it was emotion or just pot. They were both stoned, after all.

"I'll never talk about it."

Bellamy kissed her—so lightly and gently, their lips barely touching, that it was nearly as though it hadn't happened at all. "We're sisters now," she said. "We keep each other's secrets."

"GO GET THE BUTTER." BELLAMY SAID IT IN MARLON BRANDO'S RASPY old man voice—a perfect imitation. Had to be the tenth time she'd done it since the movie ended—*Last Tango in Paris*, a real X-rated movie that Bellamy had stolen from her parents' private screening room while Kelly was rooting through her drawers. They'd watched it on Bellamy's VCR, Kelly nervous the entire time that Sterling Marshall might show up and catch them. Nervous, and also queasy. She hadn't thought an X-rated movie could be that gross and depressing. And Marlon Brando . . . what did that young girl see in him, all flabby and wheezy and . . .

"*Maria Schneider was just two years older than us when she made that movie,*" Bellamy had told her as the credits rolled. Something Kelly, especially stoned Kelly, hadn't needed to know.

"I'd better sneak that movie back," Bellamy was saying now. "I'm scared Flora saw me swipe it. She was vacuuming in my dad's study."

Bellamy slipped out of the room. Kelly crumpled up the Cheetos bag and threw it in Bellamy's trash. Her buzz was wearing off. She thought of Jimmy again, Jimmy this morning, standing by the sink, and made for the phone by Bellamy's bed. She had her dad's number memorized now, and so she dialed it, listened to it ring once, twice, three times.

"Hello?" It was Jimmy's voice.

Relief washed through her. *He's alive. He's answering the phone.* She was going to just hang up, but that felt mean to her, confused as Jimmy was. He said it again. "Hello? Is anybody there?"

"Hi."

"Kelly? Are you okay?"

"I'm . . . I'm fine."

"Are you calling from school?"

"Yeah. I'm . . . uh . . . I just had lunch and I just . . ."

"Yeah?"

"I wanted to thank you," she said, "for making my lunch every day."

There was a long pause on the other end of the line. "You're welcome, Kelly."

"Bye, Dad." It wasn't until Kelly hung up that she realized what she'd called him. *Dad.* She'd been calling him Jimmy since she moved in.

"Go get the buttuh."

Bellamy was back. Kelly turned toward her, standing in the doorway. "Stop saying that!" she said, before she realized Bellamy wasn't alone.

"Look who the cat dragged in." She took a step to the side, turned out her arms like a *Price Is Right* model.

"Hi, Kelly," said Vee, the game show prize.

He wore tight jeans, a black T-shirt, a glossy leather jacket that matched his black hair. His smile was kind and his eyes glowed the warmest blue she'd ever seen.

"What are you girls doing out of school?" He said it deep and mock-angry. Kelly laughed, a lightness coming over her. Vee always had that effect on her, and not because he was stone-cold mint or even because he was nice. It was more in the way he looked at her. She'd still yet to meet Vee's dad, the director, but she figured that was where he got it from. Someone who looked at you in that way . . . Someone who could make you *feel* like that could convince you to do anything in front of a camera. Anything.

"Vee," Kelly said, "let's all, like . . . I don't know."

"Took the words right out of my mouth," said Bellamy.

Vee smiled, in that slow sly way of his that promised things. "You ready for an adventure?"

"Yes."

"Duh," Bellamy said.

"Well, good," he said. "Because I brought something."

"You did?" Kelly and Bellamy said it together as he reached for his jacket pocket, both excited for the Baggie to come out, aching to sample whatever pill, plant, or powder that Vee had brought with him this time.

But it wasn't a Baggie. It was a gun. Vee held it out to them like an offering, on careful, plattered hands.

"Holy shit," said Bellamy.

"Where did you get it?"

He grinned at Kelly. "It's my dad's. He collects them."

Kelly's eyes felt dry and salty—she'd forgotten to blink. "Did he give it to you?"

Vee just laughed.

She wanted to say something more. "Why?" or "Come on." Or "Are you kidding?" But Bellamy beat her to the punch, clapping her hands together, jumping up and down like a kid. "What are we waiting for?" she said. "Let's try it out!"

THEY TOOK THE GUN AND GOT IN VEE'S CAR, HIS DAD'S JAGUAR. IT was a deep sapphire blue, with cream leather seats that were better than anything Kelly had ever known. She wound up in front, Bellamy slipping into the back. "You haven't lived until you've rode shotgun in the Jag," she said.

And she was right. Before Vee even started up the car, Kelly knew from the way the seat held her, that leather against the back of her neck and knees, so impossibly soft. *The things rich people have in their lives. The things they live with, every day.*

Vee's arm brushed Kelly's knee as he placed the gun in the glove compartment and shut it. "This is gonna be fun," he said. He flipped the air conditioner on and passed a joint around and when he started up the car, she felt happy, teary happy. Happy beyond words.

"Mariposa?" Bellamy said.

Vee nodded.

Kelly said, "Are you guys speaking Spanish?"

"It's where we're going."

"Mariposa is a tiny little town," Vee said. "It's way inland near Death Valley . . . I like to go there sometimes."

"It's where his dad shot that movie, *Defiance*," Bellamy said. "I think Vee likes going there because he feels like a little kid again, right?"

He shook his head. "I like going there," he said, "because nobody else goes there."

Kelly relaxed into the bucket seat's embrace. Hard to believe that someone with Vee's life would want to escape to a place where there were no other people, or that someone with Bellamy's life would nod at him in such an understanding way, as though she had a life like Kelly's, one that it made sense to escape.

It made her think of something Catherine once said: "*Not everything happens for a reason. But the important things do.*" She couldn't remember exactly when Catherine had said it, but it had been during those last few months before she died. At the time, she'd had no idea what her sister was talking about.

Maybe Catherine was talking about this, Kelly thought. *Maybe she meant meeting people like these.*

THE RIDE TOOK A LITTLE OVER TWO HOURS. THEY LISTENED TO THE radio—KROQ—until it started to crackle and fade, and then they spoke to each other in hushed library tones, all of them aware of the gun in the glove compartment, deferring to it as though it were another passenger.

"My dad owns this property," Vee said as they drove through an open gate and down an unpaved road, dust clouds billowing around them. "He bought it when we shot the film and said he was going to build on it. But he's never done a thing with it. I think he forgot he bought it."

"A whole tract of land?" Kelly said. It was a large tract too. Kelly felt like the road they were on stretched out at least a mile. "How could he forget that?"

Vee shrugged. "My dad forgets things pretty easily."

"Your mom, for instance," Bellamy said.

He nodded, but he didn't look at her.

The road turned into a driveway, and Vee stopped at the end of it. There was no house here—no structures. Just a large swath of red-brown dirt with a few palm trees growing out of it, some scraggly cactuses and a stream. The sun beat down on them as they got out of the Jaguar—a shock to the system after the air-conditioning.

"I'm going to go stretch my legs," Bellamy said, and she took off, jogging toward the stream.

It was strange here in Mariposa. Vee had said it meant "butterfly" in Spanish and it really did feel like a cocoon—so weirdly quiet, the silence roaring in your ears. Kelly gazed at the red-tinged sand, the meager stream coursing along without a sound.

"There's fish in there," said Vee. He'd been watching her.

He leaned back into the Jag, flipped open the glove compartment, and removed the gun. "Can you hold it a sec?" he said to Kelly. "Don't worry. It isn't loaded yet."

Kelly exhaled. "Wish I knew that in the car."

"Why?"

"Loaded guns scare me," she said. "I was afraid you'd hit a bump and it would just . . . go off in there."

Vee smiled. "It doesn't work that way."

Kelly held out her hands. Vee placed the gun in them. The weapon was much heavier than it had looked. Warmed by the sun, it felt like an iron on Kelly's opened palms. She wanted to spread her hands out wider because she was scared she'd drop it. *Get control.* She wrapped her hands around the grip, avoiding the trigger at first. But then she pressed it. Couldn't help herself. Even though the gun wasn't loaded, pressing the trigger made her weak in the knees. Kelly pointed the barrel at the ground. The weight of it took her arms straight down and she felt stronger.

Slowly she raised it, aimed the barrel at the horizon, and stared down the length of her arms, the heavy metal thing an extension of her, power coursing out of it and back, into her hands, wrists, through the muscles in her outstretched, straining arms, into her heart.

Vee was standing close. She could feel his gaze on the side of her face, his breath tickling her ear as he spoke. "Who would you want to use it on?"

"Evan Mueller."

"Who?"

"This jerk from my science class. He calls me names. He throws spitballs."

Vee snorted. "Spitballs," he said. "Waste of a bullet."

"No, Vee. He's mean."

"A loser who throws spitballs at girls isn't even worth thinking about. Tell him to go fuck himself. Save the bullet for someone who's *important*."

"I can't . . . I can't just tell him to go fuck himself."

"Why not?"

"He's popular. He has friends."

"You have *better* friends."

Kelly smiled. She never wanted to leave this spot. Never wanted to lower the gun, which was a new drug in a way, the best kind of drug, like cocaine only stronger. "I feel like a different person."

"What kind of person?"

She turned to him. Looked straight into his beautiful, dangerous blue eyes and, for the first time, didn't blush. "Perfect."

His cheeks flushed, the tables turned, Vee the one blushing. "What makes you think you aren't perfect already?"

For a few moments, the slice of air between their two faces seemed to hum. Kelly still staring into Vee's eyes, aware of her outstretched arms, the gun in her hands feeding her, making her strong. *Kiss him. Kiss him now or it will never happen . . .*

Vee said, "Where did Bellamy go?"

Kelly's shoulders relaxed. That had been the last thing she'd expected him to say. She lowered the gun, the spell broken. Had it all been in her imagination? Had that hum been completely one-sided, Vee's flushed skin the result of desert heat? Kelly nearly asked—that was how close she still felt to him. But then he pointed to the stream, to Bellamy beside it, sitting on the dirt with her back to them. She looked small and fragile, curled up like a pill bug with her knees drawn up to her chin.

For a few seconds, Kelly was mad at Bellamy. *She's doing it on purpose. She wrecked the moment, just so she could be the center of attention.* But she felt guilty for the thought as soon as it formed and took it all back once they got closer. Kelly saw Bellamy swatting at her eyes. *Crying?*

"What's wrong with her?" Kelly whispered.

"Who knows?"

"Did I say something I shouldn't have?"

He shook his head. "She always gets like this when we come here to Mariposa."

"Like what?"

"Weird."

She looked at him.

"Maybe she'll talk to you," he said.

Kelly jogged up to Bellamy. She knelt down beside her and said her name. She put her hand on her shoulder, said her name again, but Bellamy wouldn't look at her. "Please tell me what's wrong."

"Nothing," she whispered. "I . . . I think I'm dehydrated or something."

"Do you want to drink from the stream?"

She shook her head and took a deep, rattling breath.

"You sure you're all right?"

She wiped her nose with the back of her hand and looked up at her. "I swear. I'm fine. I just . . . there's something about this place. The quiet, maybe. It gets to me."

Kelly pretended not to notice the blotchy skin, the red eyes. "Okay," she said. "You want me to leave you alone?"

"No."

"Okay."

"Kelly?"

"Yeah?"

"You ever wish you were a little kid again? Like . . . too little to understand how the world works?"

She turned to her, Bellamy's face fading into Catherine's face, Catherine's seven-year-old face, crying over Thumbelina. "All the time," Kelly said.

"I think that's part of why I hate Shane so much. He climbs trees. He plays with toy soldiers. He trusts our parents. He doesn't get life at all."

"You don't trust your parents?"

"I don't trust anybody, Kelly. Except you."

A warm breeze brushed against them. Kelly glanced at Vee, leaning against his father's sapphire blue Jaguar—a silhouette in the distance.

Click.

Kelly turned back to Bellamy, the gun in her hands, barrel pointed at the stream. "Vee better have brought bullets," she said.

Kelly nodded, marveling at Bellamy, the way she'd aimed and shot without hesitating, without asking first whether or not the gun had been loaded.

VEE LOADED THE GUN AS BELLAMY REAPPLIED HER MAKEUP, USING the Jag's window as a mirror.

She spun around. "How do I look?" she asked, adjusting the straps on her bright yellow tank top, tucking a lock of raven hair behind an ear.

"Beautiful," Kelly said. She meant it.

With a type of reverence, Vee placed the loaded gun on top of the car, backed away from it slowly. He turned to Bellamy. "You okay?"

"I'm always okay, Vee. You know that."

"Good," he said. He was leaning back into the Jag now, opening the glove compartment. "Because I've got a surprise."

"Another surprise?"

"Yep." He produced a Baggie and held it up, sunlight glinting off of it. Bellamy and Kelly moved closer. The Baggie contained three tiny white squares that looked like miniature postage stamps.

"Glory be," said Bellamy.

Kelly said, "What are they?"

"Tabs," Vee said.

"Huh?"

"Acid."

Kelly took a few steps back, her heart fluttering. "Doesn't that last like twelve hours?"

"Give or take."

There was a story going around—girl who went on an acid trip and never came back. Sixteen, and in a nursing home, shaking and drooling like a sick old woman. Probably wasn't true. None of these stories that went around were, but still. Still. *Where do the stories come from if they aren't at least a little bit true?* "We . . . uh . . . we have a loaded gun."

"Oh don't be such a worrywart." Bellamy grinned. "You've got to live life up to its bendy edge, press up against that edge, hard as you can."

Kelly's heart dropped. "How . . . Where did you hear that?"

"What?"

"That," Kelly said, breath catching, Catherine's voice in her mind saying those exact words. Catherine, who, during the final months of her life had said them so often they'd become part of her personality, Kelly never asking where those words had come from because at that point, Catherine probably wouldn't have answered anyway. "Where did you get that saying?"

She grinned. "It's a line from one of my dad's movies."

Kelly shot a glance at Vee, who seemed immersed in the Baggie, the white squares inside. "Cool line," she said.

Bellamy closed her eyes. "Live a little, Kelly," she said in a soft, singsongy voice. "Press up against that bendy edge." She opened her mouth, stuck her tongue out flat.

Kelly watched as Vee placed one of the white squares on her tongue, Bellamy smiling around it, teeth white as the square, her earlier tears gone, brushed away like dust.

"You won't feel it for a little while, but when you do, *whoa*." He placed a tab on his own tongue and Kelly felt panicky, as though she was blocks away from the bus stop, watching a bus pull up, knowing it was the last one of the day and if she didn't run to catch it, if she didn't jump on now . . . Kelly closed her eyes, opened her mouth. "I'm ready," she said.

CHAPTER 16

Two 17-year-old girls and one boy, 16, were arrested at 10:00 P.M. on April 14 and charged with drunk and disorderly conduct and destruction of public property. The three youths had been caught shooting up a Dumpster with a .22 caliber semiautomatic pistol outside the Mobil Station on Euclid. The three were released on $3,000 bail, posted by the boy's father, the legal owner of the gun.

Police Blotter
Mariposa News
April 15, 1980

CHAPTER 17

Sometime during the ride home, inanimate objects stopped breathing. Kelly couldn't say it out loud, not with her dad driving, air conditioner on high so he could stay awake. But she felt deeply relieved, scared as she had been for so many hours watching everything around her expand and pull back and puff out again—the wheels on the Jag, the haloed streetlamps, the holding cell bars, Bellamy's Louis Vuitton bag. From the time she'd peaked (that's what Vee had said. "*You're peaking.*") it had been as though every still, dead thing in the world had come alive and gone after her, all of them breathing, watching, closing in . . .

The Dumpster had shivered and bled and the sound of the shot had shattered her ears, her shoulder sockets jamming, her whole body thrown back . . . Shooting a gun on acid. Who'd thought that would be a good idea? It had been awful, like living out a nightmare. "*Like Vietnam,*" Bellamy had said, cackling like a maniac. "*Like* The Deer Hunter . . ."

"Can you put on the radio?" Jimmy said. First time he'd spoken a word since he'd picked Kelly up at the Mariposa Sheriff's Department more than an hour ago, walking out

into the surprisingly cold night to his beat-up Buick Regal in the parking lot, Kelly trailing behind him, rubbing her arms to keep warm
while trying to ignore the slithering and hissing of the white lines on
the asphalt.

Kelly switched on the radio. Jimmy's car only had AM and it was
turned to a country station. Kelly hated the song—some female singer
whining about the days turning into years, her guitar making that
awful country-guitar sound, like an old woman sighing. She started to
switch the station—a survival move—but Jimmy held his hand up.
"Leave it," he said. "Please."

She watched Jimmy's profile—the rugged face, still handsome despite all the wear and tear he'd put himself through, maybe even because of it. Ever since she'd moved in with him, she couldn't stop
looking at her father—spying on him at odd moments when she didn't
think he'd notice, searching hard for features similar to her own. In
profile, he looked like a tough guy. A hero or a villain, depending on if
he smiled. Then, of course, he'd turn and look at you with those sad,
fried-egg eyes of his and he'd just be Jimmy again. Poor old Jimmy.
Kelly looked nothing like him.

He mouthed the words with the singer, his eyes watering a little.
Kelly couldn't tell whether it was the crappy song doing it to him or his
constant physical pain or Kelly herself—the situation she'd put him in.
"I'm sorry," she said.

"Hey. Who am I to tell you what to do?" He said it very quietly.

Kelly stared out the window.

"What do you think the population of that Mariposa is? Twenty?
Twenty-five?"

She smiled a little.

"The sheriff and the deputy were definitely related."

"Yeah," she said. "I thought so too." It was a lie. The only time she'd gotten a good look at the sheriff and the deputy, she had to turn away fast because they'd both grown fangs and pig snouts. But she wasn't going to say that to Jimmy.

"Coming down now?"

She nodded. "I'm really sorry."

Jimmy shook his head. "I get it," he said. "Guns are fun. My dad used to have this .22 caliber revolver. A Colt. We'd take it out to the desert, shoot cans . . ." His voice trailed off, the thread gone. "She kills me."

"Who?"

He nodded at the radio. "Barbara Mandrell. That voice . . . Like she's telling you all her secrets." He ran a hand across his face, brought it back to the wheel. "You don't have to worry," he said. "I didn't tell your mom."

"Okay." Kelly turned to her window, pressed her forehead against the cool glass. In a weird way, she'd wished Jimmy had told Mom. Not so much about what she had done, but who she'd done it with: The People Catherine Met at Parties. That's the part that would hurt her and she wanted Mom to hurt.

Jimmy had been shuffling around in the kitchen, making Kelly's lunch this morning, when the phone had rung. Kelly had picked it up and, when she heard her mother's voice, her heart had leapt. It had been the first time Mom had called her since she'd moved in with Jimmy. *She misses me,* Kelly had thought. *She's sorry for kicking me out.* But Mom hadn't said anything like that. "*I know you stole some things from me. I know you stole my Valentine heart.*"

"*What?*"

"*You can keep the picture of your sister. But I want my Valentine heart back.*"

"*Are you . . . are you serious? It's been two months.*"

"You didn't throw it out, did you?"

"The candy is old. It's disgusting. It was stale two months ago."

"Kelly. This is important."

Kelly had wanted to hurl the phone across the room. *"I did. I threw out your stupid Valentine heart,"* Kelly had said. *"I ate all the stale, rock-hard chocolate candy from whatever rich old married boyfriend gave you that. And then I barfed it up and threw the box into the garbage."* Then she'd slammed down the receiver.

"Bitch," she whispered.

"Huh?" said Jimmy, who had been talking to her.

"Nothing. What were you saying?"

"I was saying that I heard he put up your bail."

"He?"

"John McFadden."

"Yeah, I guess." Kelly had met him briefly when the three of them had been released, Mr. McFadden introducing himself, asking if she already had a ride, kind and calm and responsible, the way a dad should be. His eyes had been alert, the whites pure. Clearly, he'd never touched a pill in his life. Probably didn't even drink.

"I could have paid," Jimmy said. "Or worked it out with a bonds-man."

Kelly took a breath, that word swirling in her newly clear head. *Bondsman.* She'd been arrested. She'd spent three hours in a holding cell for women with Bellamy and some crazy prostitute, both of them laughing their heads off over nothing while Kelly tried not to scream about everything coming alive, and now she had a criminal record. That part was real. "Jimmy?"

"Yeah?"

"Will I have to . . . like . . . go to trial?"

"Not if John McFadden can help it."

She looked at him. "Do you know John McFadden?"

"I worked on a few of his films back in the old days," he said. "I wasn't in the union yet and he was cheap as all get-out. Still is, I'm sure."

"But . . . how would he make it so I don't go to trial?"

"People like McFadden can make things go away." He said it in as certain a way as Kelly had ever heard him say anything. She didn't want to ask why, or how he knew. She wasn't sure she cared. "That's good," she said.

He stared straight out through the windshield, didn't look at her. "It can be," he said. "Sometimes."

KELLY WAS ASLEEP, COUNTRY MUSIC PLAYING IN HER DREAMS, WHEN the car jerked to the right, jolting her into the passenger-side door. Her head smacked the window. "You okay?" Jimmy said it loudly, over a blaring truck horn.

"What happened?"

"I nodded off for a few seconds."

"Oh my God."

"It's late."

Kelly touched her fastened seat belt, her breath quick and shallow. "It's late," he said again, hands trembling on the wheel.

"Okay." Kelly rubbed her eyes. "That's okay." She looked at the clock on the dashboard. It *was* late—close to 2:00 A.M. on a school night. And, seeing the way she'd spent her supposed school day, there was no way she'd get away with ditching again tomorrow. She thought of Mr. Hansen's science class, Mrs. Parks's homeroom. She thought of the smirking cheerleaders with their swishy ponytails, the strong, jocky boys with their ski tans and varsity jackets, legs spread wide in their seats. All of them seemed like characters from a dream she'd had a long time ago, less real even than breathing cell bars or parking lines turned to snakes.

Their off-ramp was coming up. Jimmy flicked on his blinker and swung the car into the right lane. "I wish you wouldn't hang around with those kids," he said.

Kelly sighed. "You sound like Mom."

"Yeah, well. She has reasons."

"Everybody has *reasons*," Kelly said. "Mass murderers have *reasons*."

The rest of the way home, Jimmy didn't speak a word. The country station had long ago faded out, but he kept it on, the car filling with the crackle of static. Kelly's head throbbed—a souvenir of her acid trip—and she was so thirsty, her tongue swollen from it. Too thirsty to ask questions. She closed her eyes.

IT TOOK FOREVER TO GET FROM THE OFF-RAMP TO PICO AND, ONCE
Jimmy turned on it, even longer to get home, which was half a duplex with a crispy brown lawn, a roof of crumbling Spanish tile, and plastic flowers in the window box courtesy of the old lady owner who lived in the other, bigger half.

Jimmy pulled into the driveway. He undid his seat belt and winced. He was always wincing. He wore a plaid shirt under his beige vinyl jacket, and as he eased out of the seat, the shirt collar slipped open a little and Kelly saw the scars on his chest. *War wounds,* he called them. Even though he'd gotten them on some cheap horror movie.

"Take a picture—it lasts longer," Jimmy said, and she realized she'd been staring. He gave her a play punch on the chin.

Kelly's head was still throbbing from thirst, her mouth so dry she could barely form words. She tried to smile. "You're a good dad," she said, which was kind of a lie. But like most lies, it seemed like the right thing to say.

"That kid—John McFadden's son. I introduced him to your sister."

She looked at him. "You did?"

"How old was she when she decided she wanted to be famous—thirteen? Fourteen?"

Kelly closed her eyes, tilted her aching head back on the seat rest. "I thought she always wanted to be famous."

"Yeah," he said. "Anyway, she was about that age. I was working on some horror movie on the same lot as McFadden . . . He was shooting a miniseries, I think. Catherine got wind of it. Showed up on my doorstep one day out of nowhere. I hadn't seen her in years and I was so happy. See, I *wanted* to be a good dad, Kelly. I've always wanted that, more than anything."

"You are, Jimmy. I told you . . ."

"She begged me to take her to the set. And Vincent . . . Vee, whatever you guys call him. He had a small part in the miniseries. He and your sister hit it off. Started spending lots of time together."

Kelly opened her eyes. Jimmy wasn't looking at her. He was gazing out the windshield, sad eyes aimed up at the starless sky above their roof. "I let them spend time together," he said. "I'm not a good dad."

"What do you mean?"

"If it wasn't for me introducing Catherine to Vincent and his father, she never would have gotten in with that fast Hollywood crowd."

Kelly put a hand on his shoulder.

"If I wasn't so permissive about that stuff, your mother wouldn't be so mad at me. She'd let me see you guys more often—not just when you run away."

There was a light on inside their house and Kelly's eyes throbbed from looking at it. There were so many things she wanted to say, but she couldn't get them out. It was hard, arranging her thoughts into words when she felt like this. "Vee is a really nice person," she said.

"I don't know about that."

"And also." She took a breath. "I didn't run away. Mom kicked me out. She gave me your address." She put a hand on Jimmy's shoulder. "She sent me to you."

He turned, looked at her. "She did?"

"Yep," she said. "Can we go inside now, Dad? I'm really tired."

His smile came back. "Oh yeah, right. School day tomorrow." He said it as though she'd never been arrested. As though it wasn't two in the morning and he was picking her up from band practice or track and field, rather than a police station two hours away. "Do you have a lot of homework?"

Kelly sighed. "I'll be okay."

He groaned his way out of the car. Kelly followed him up the sidewalk, watched him open the door.

Once they were inside, he hurled himself onto the couch and collapsed. Kelly hurried into the kitchen, poured a glass of water and gulped the whole thing down, the crippling headache finally starting to fade. From the other room, she heard her father's moans, and so she put some ice in the glass along with a few fingers of Jack Daniel's and grabbed the half-empty bottle of pills off the counter, where he had left them. When she got back into the living room, his eyes were closed, his head thrown back. She placed the glass in one hand, bottle in the other. She grabbed the maroon plaid comforter off the couch and draped it over him. "Thanks, kiddo," he whispered.

She kissed him on the cheek, walked back to her room.

IN KELLY'S DREAM, HER MOTHER CAME AT HER WITH A MEAT CLEAVER. "Give it back!" Mom shrieked. "It's mine!" Once she got closer, Kelly saw that it wasn't Mom at all but some kind of monster-movie version of her, with snakes for hair, sharpened teeth, and pinwheeling red eyes. "*Give it back or I will kill you!*"

Kelly stared at her, this creature she'd never known to be her mother but who had apparently been her mother all along, making meals for Kelly and Catherine, driving them to their old school, taking care of them when they got sick and giving them makeovers and cooking popcorn for them on top of the stove in the silver-foil container, the most delicious popcorn she'd ever had, Mom and Kelly and Catherine shoving buttery handfuls into their mouths as they watched the Academy Awards . . .

She'd always been like this, a monster, even though Kelly was just seeing it now—bloodred eyes shining, the cleaver swinging.

Kelly said, "You killed her. You killed Catherine."

"Give it back! *Give the heart back!*"

Monster-Mom slashed at her with the cleaver. The blade connected with Kelly's chest and she couldn't breathe she couldn't . . .

Kelly gasped herself awake, panting in Jimmy's tiny spare bedroom, sweat pouring down the back of her neck, her hand to her own throat, trembling all over. *What a dream,* she thought. *What an awful dream.*

Kelly glanced at the dresser—at the bright numbers on the digital clock. 4:32 A.M. A countdown. She tried closing her eyes, but she couldn't go back to sleep. Not now, not yet.

She switched on the lamp next to her bed, crept over to the small closet in the corner of the room, and slid the door open. At the bottom of the closet, she'd stashed her empty suitcase. But it wasn't empty, not really. She unzipped it, removed the framed picture of Catherine and then, the heart. She hadn't even looked at it since arriving here at Jimmy's, but she noticed now how frayed the red ribbon was at the front, how faded the fabric.

Who had given this to her mother? Why had she kept it so long?

From the living room, Kelly could hear Jimmy snoring. He'd never made it to the bedroom, but that was okay. He was a very heavy sleeper.

Kelly headed into the kitchen, anger pulsing through her, Mom's phone call echoing in her mind and that dream . . . that dream. *A monster all along* . . . She dropped the Valentine heart in the sink, opened it, and turned the hot water on full blast until the box started to fall apart, the stale chocolates destroyed, the entire sink filling with steaming water, drowning it. When she turned the water off, the box was in pieces, the chocolates floating. Ruined forever. A pang of guilt tugged at her—*Why had Mom kept this box for so long?* But she brushed it away. She wasn't Mom. Not anymore. She didn't deserve Kelly's guilt—not even a pang of it.

Kelly drained the sink. She scooped the chocolates out and dumped them in the trash can underneath, along with the remnants of the box, tied off the trash bag, sneaked out the front door and tossed it in the Dumpster around the side of the house. Sometimes, it was good having a dad who was such a sound sleeper.

When she slipped back inside, Kelly found herself remembering a time when she and Catherine had been around eleven, left alone by Mom for a few hours in the afternoon, feeling like grown-ups. Kelly had immediately turned on the TV. Flipped the channel to *All My Children*—a show she used to love, mainly because Mom had said it was too mature for a girl her age.

Catherine, meanwhile, had gone snooping in their mother's closet and, as usual, she'd been the one to make the day's big discovery. "*Kelly!*" Her sister had shrieked her name so loud, she'd thought something awful had happened. But when Kelly had rushed into the room, she had found Catherine on the floor, an open cardboard box in front of her. Kelly had asked what was in it, but her sister had been struck silent. All she could do was point at it.

In the box was a stack of black-and-white postcards showing the same young woman in four different outfits: a bikini, a nurse's uniform, a spangled, strapless evening dress, and a sexy farm girl outfit, complete with pitchfork. In the corner of the cards was the phone number of a talent agent and the name of the busty blond actress in the photos: Rainy Daye. It had taken Kelly a lot longer than Catherine to recognize Rainy Daye as Mom.

"*Wow,*" Kelly had said. "*It's like we never really knew her.*"

"*You know what, Kelly? I don't think anybody really knows each other.*"

"*Except you and me, right?*"

"*Except you and me.*"

Kelly opened the nightstand drawer and reached in, to the very back until she could feel the delicate chain of Catherine's necklace. Watching herself in the mirror, she carefully slipped the chain around her neck and fastened it. The golden heart glittered at her throat, the chain resting against her neck. It made her feel beautiful. Kelly would never take the necklace off. She would wear it forever, Catherine's secret. She would keep it with her always.

Kelly touched the two small diamonds at the base of the heart. She stared into the mirror, smiled at the girl she was turning into.

KELLY MADE IT THROUGH THE FIRST HALF OF THE DAY, BARELY. THE low point was Miss Collins's English class, when she fell asleep at her desk in the middle of a pop quiz. Miss Collins, a skinny, pursed-lipped woman whom Bellamy claimed was still a virgin at thirty-five ("*I can tell these things. Trust me.*"), had been so annoyed with Kelly she hadn't woken her. As a result, she'd awakened with a snort in the middle of the next class's pop quiz, enduring their laughter as well as that of her following class, American history, when she'd walked in bleary-eyed and twenty minutes late.

It was all she could do to make it through to Mr. Hansen's science class—and for that, thankfully, she was awake and on time. Bellamy showed up a few minutes after her, hair and eyes shiny as ever, notebook clutched to an electric blue V-neck sweater Kelly had borrowed from her once—a Dior. She looked happy and rested, as though she'd been able to squeeze in a spa visit between the fourteen-hour-long acid trip and school starting this morning.

"Long time no see, Miss Marshall," said Mr. Hansen, who had greeted the just-as-long-absent Kelly with a curt nod.

"Yes, Mr. Hansen, it certainly has been a while." Bellamy said it so sweetly, without a tinge of sarcasm in her voice as she headed to her desk, handing Kelly a folded-up piece of notebook paper as she passed. A few of the boys in the back row snickered, but Mr. Hansen just stared after her, his face reddening slightly, powerless to speak. How could he, after all? She hadn't said anything wrong.

Kelly touched the heart pendant at her neck, Catherine's necklace, which, in a way, made up for the rest of what she was wearing—the tired flannel shirt, the green corduroy pants from JCPenney that Mom had bought her a year ago, when she was three inches shorter and at least a size smaller. No, the necklace fit. It always would. It wasn't Catherine's secret anymore. It was hers now, and to touch it reminded her of the changes in her life. Big changes. Wonderful ones.

Something hit her in the back of the head. Spitball. Kelly heard them laughing behind her, Pete Nichol, Randy Butler . . . Evan Mueller, barking like a dog. Her face reddened, Vee's voice in her head. *Tell him to go fuck himself.* It drowned out the other voice, the tiny, timid voice that always told her to pretend it's not happening, ignore it and it will go away. *Ignore them.* But she couldn't. Mr. Hansen scribbled on the chalk board, oblivious as he wanted to be, oblivious as he always was to the pain of students he didn't care about. The invisible ones in cheap clothes who didn't get good grades, whose parents weren't rich. The ones, like Kelly, who didn't matter.

The chalk knocked and squeaked against the blackboard. Another spitball hit Kelly on the arm. She spun around, glancing quickly at Bellamy, busying herself with her notebook and then at Evan Mueller. She stared him down.

Slowly, he brought his index and middle finger up to his mouth and stuck his tongue through the crook between them, his eyes half closed, his face lewd and ugly. Kelly's stomach clenched up.

"Freak," he whispered.

She said, "Go fuck yourself."

The boys stopped snickering. Bellamy's eyes widened. Her hand flew up to her mouth.

"What did you just say?" Mr. Hansen said.

And she turned to him—that look in his eyes, a mixture of anger and shock, something else mixed in too. Was it fear? She could hear the rest of the class, whispering to each other, Phoebe Calloway in the front row saying, "Uh-oh . . ."

"They threw spitballs at me." Kelly's voice was quiet, calm. "So I told them to go fuck themselves."

Silence settled in fast—like someone throwing a towel over a birdcage. For a long moment, everything froze. Time stopped. The air in the room turned thick and still.

"Go to the principal's office," Hansen said.

"Okay." Kelly slipped the note from Bellamy into her pants pocket and stood up. She dared to look at the row behind her as she did—at those boys staring up at her with shocked, unblinking eyes and then, at Bellamy.

Bellamy smiled. *Way to go,* she mouthed.

Kelly walked out of the classroom, her back straight. A different person. *Perfect.* As she walked down the hall to the principal's office, she removed the note from her pocket, read:

JAILBIRD PARTY TONIGHT AT VEE'S.
BE THERE.

"WELL," JIMMY SAID AS HE PUT ON HIS BLINKER AND TURNED UP their street, "I guess you've got a few days off from school."

First thing he'd said to Kelly since he'd picked her up at the principal's office. She wished he'd said something different: *It wasn't your fault. All you did was fight back, for once.* Something like that. "I didn't do anything wrong," she said. "I didn't deserve to be suspended."

He shrugged. "Principal said you swore at some boys in the middle of science class."

She started to say something, then stopped. She looked at her dad's bowed shoulders, his scarred hands on the wheel. He got beat up for a living—threw himself off of buildings and set himself on fire, did whatever directors told him to do, no matter how much it hurt or how long the pain lasted, just so some stupid actors could look brave. Jimmy didn't fight back. Not ever. How was he supposed to understand? She remembered the hush that had fallen over the classroom as she walked out, the way Bellamy had smiled at her, the way she'd *understood.* And tonight, a party. A *Jailbird Party.* Kelly was going. She'd sneak out of the house if she had to. She'd wait 'til he was passed out, and then she'd hitch a ride . . .

"I've got a shoot tonight." Jimmy said it like he'd been reading her mind.

"Huh?"

"Low-budget piece of crap, which means there won't be too many retakes. But I probably won't be home 'til tomorrow morning." He gave her an awkward smile. "No parties at the house."

"Is it okay if I spend the night at a friend's?"

Jimmy sighed. "Tonight?"

"I . . . um . . . I get kind of scared staying home alone."

He looked at her for a few seconds. "You need a ride there?"

"No. She can pick me up. But . . . Uh . . . I may need cab fare for the morning."

"Sure."

Kelly bit her lip to keep from smiling.

He pulled into the driveway, turned off the car. "Kelly?"

"Yeah?"

"You're just going to spend the night with one girlfriend, right?"

"Huh?"

He turned to her, watched her face in such a way it forced her to look up and meet his gaze. "No more messing around with McFadden's kid," he said. "No more trouble. Promise?" It was as though all his features were sinking, the watery eyes sadder than ever.

"I promise." Kelly said it in a tone to match the look in his eyes. "I won't mess up again."

He kept watching her, his face changing, Kelly hoping harder and harder for him to look away, for the lie to take.

I blew it. He doesn't believe me. "You . . . uh . . . you okay?"

"You're wearing it," he said.

"Huh?"

He pointed at the necklace. "I . . . I thought it was gone."

Kelly exhaled. "No, Catherine gave it to me."

"She tell you where she got it?"

Kelly shook her head.

Jimmy's face relaxed. He started to roll up his car window. "I had a hell of a time getting the jeweler to put those two diamonds on there. He thought it looked better with just one and he was kind of a picky bastard."

She stared at him. "It's from you?"

He stopped. Looked at her. "Had it made special. A diamond for each of my little gems. I picked them out and everything. See? That one on the right is just a little bit bigger. That's you."

Kelly blinked a few times. Said it again. "You were the one who gave Catherine that necklace."

"Not just Catherine. Both of you girls. I'd have given you two necklaces, but I couldn't afford it, so I did the next best thing."

"She never told me. She . . . she acted like it was some big secret."

"I don't know why she'd do that."

Kelly sighed. "Me neither."

"Catherine stayed with me for a few days after one of her fights with your mother. Do you remember that?"

"She disappeared a lot. Never told us where she was going."

"Well, one time she came here. I bought her that necklace. Gave it to her in exchange for a promise that she'd give your mother another chance. I told her to share it with you."

Kelly shook her head. "I don't know why she never told me. I wouldn't have made her share the necklace if she didn't want to."

"Well," he said. "Your mother never liked me buying things for you kids. She thought you'd get spoiled."

Kelly rolled her eyes. That was Mom, all right.

"At any rate, I'm glad you're wearing it, Kelly," he said. "I'm glad Catherine gave it to you."

"Me too." She smiled at him. Jimmy. Dad. *I'm only lying for your own good.*

Jimmy opened his car door, started to get out. "Listen, when you go to your girlfriend's tonight, make sure and get the homework assignments from her," he said, over his shoulder. An afterthought. "Suspended doesn't mean you're out of school forever."

BELLAMY WAS RIGHT ABOUT VEE'S BUILDING. IT DID LOOK LIKE THE Sleeping Beauty Castle at Disneyland. What she hadn't mentioned, though, was that Vee lived in a tower. His apartment was one big, perfectly round room, with a minikitchen on the end near the door and a huge curved window on the other, a bathroom off to the side of it. His only furniture, if you could call it that, was a mattress, its far end shoved up against the window. He'd covered it with a tie-dyed sheet to make it look like something to sit on, but when Kelly arrived, nervous and winded after climbing the seven flights of stairs, there were about fifteen people in the room and they were all standing.

She scanned the crowd. She couldn't find anyone she recognized from school, which was more good than bad, but still it made her feel paralyzed. She stood in the doorway for a long time gaping at the group of strangers—girls in tight jeans, sleeveless T-shirts and chains or sheer halter tops showing tanned shoulders, their hair loose and shining or in perfect asymmetrical bobs, guys in ripped T-shirts with punk band logos on them, hair spiked up sharp or half shaved off, slippery bangs falling over kohl-lined eyes, cheekbones jutting, each stunning face like something off an album cover. Nobody looked familiar. Kelly wondered if maybe she'd gotten the apartment number wrong, but then Bellamy flung herself out of the bathroom, Vee trailing behind her. Kelly's shoulders relaxed. She was able to move again.

"Kelly!" Vee said it first, then Bellamy, both rushing to her. A few of the guests turned and looked at the three of them—one a skinny girl of about thirteen with copper hair and wide, startled eyes. The girl looked familiar—so much so that Kelly smiled at her, started to wave . . . But then she realized she knew her from a Peter Paul Mounds commercial and dropped her hand, the girl's startled eyes narrowing at her in . . . what? Disgust? Confusion? Kelly didn't care. She tried not to, anyway.

Bellamy was throwing her arms around her and Vee was saying, "We were scared you wouldn't show," and Kelly felt instantly, happily, at home. "I like your skirt," Bellamy said as she pulled away. Same peasant skirt Kelly had worn when she'd first gone to Bellamy's house, that strange day and night with Len . . . How far Kelly had come since then. Though, when she thought about it, she wasn't sure whether she'd come up or down. "I got suspended," she said.

Bellamy clapped her on the back. "Good job! I knew you would!" She steered her around a group of boys, into the kitchen, the boys looking them up and down as they passed. "Hi, Beautiful," said one boy to Bellamy. He was a ringer for Robby Benson. In fact, for all Kelly knew it could have actually *been* Robby Benson, but Bellamy ignored him anyway, rolling her eyes at Kelly for emphasis, making Kelly love her even more. "That's a gorgeous necklace," she said.

Kelly smiled. "Thanks."

Vee handed Kelly a Styrofoam cup full of champagne. "If you're suspended it means you don't have to go to school tomorrow."

"I never want to go to school again." Kelly took a sip. The bubbles tickled her nose, exploded on her tongue. She had never tasted anything like it and it wasn't as though she'd never had a drink before. It reminded her more of cocaine or solid gold jewelry or the seats in Vee's Jag or one of Bellamy's leather jackets against her skin—more a feeling than a taste. The gun in her hands. It made her heart soar.

"Dom Pérignon," Vee said.

She took another long sip. "I love it."

"We've got something even better," Bellamy said, "but we can't take you into the bathroom now because Vee's dad is watching."

"His dad?"

Bellamy gestured at the startle-eyed Mounds girl near the window. Kelly took a closer look at the group she was talking to—two women and three men, all of them adults, all stunningly beautiful. The oldest, Bellamy told her, was John McFadden. He wore tailored dark pants, a pale blue button-down shirt that picked up the color of his eyes—the same color as Vee's, noticeable even from twenty feet away. His arm rested at the waist of the woman standing next to him—tall and tanned in a short macramé dress with full lips and golden hair like Julie Christie's. But his eyes were focused on Kelly in a who-are-you-supposed-to-be way, a way that made her feel as though she didn't deserve to be friends with his son. She put the cup of champagne down on the counter and stared down at her sandals, her confidence floating away. "Who are those people your dad is with?"

"They're all from the movie he's shooting now," Vee said. "It's called *Resistance*."

Bellamy said, "You recognize Cynthia Jones, right?"

"Who?"

"The chick standing next to him. Totally famous model? She's on the cover of *Cosmo* this month?"

Kelly shrugged. "The only one I recognize is the kid from the Mounds commercial."

Bellamy laughed. "You are like the best person I've ever met."

Kelly flushed a little.

"The only way he let me have this party was if he came and, like, chaperoned," Vee was saying. "I'm incredibly sorry about that, but that's the way he is. And I don't have too much bargaining power after Mariposa."

Kelly thought it seemed pretty reasonable, considering what they'd all put him through the previous night. But she stayed quiet about it. And within moments, Vee's dad was in the kitchen with them, sticking out his hand. "We didn't meet properly." He smiled, his face instantly turning less angry and severe. Up close, he looked almost exactly like his son—a carbon copy, only with thinning hair and laugh lines. She shook his hand. "I'm Kelly," she said. "I'm uh . . . I'm really sorry."

"It's entirely Vincent's fault," he said.

Bellamy laughed.

"Thanks a lot, Dad."

"Honestly, I'm a real believer in learning from your mistakes. And what is being sixteen about, other than completely screwing up time and time again?" He gave Vee a look. "Vincent certainly lives by that credo."

"Okay, okay."

"Well, I'm seventeen and I've definitely learned my lesson." Bellamy's voice was shaky. Speedy. Her pupils were dilated and her eyes were opened much too wide. Kelly hoped John McFadden didn't notice. Her mother surely would have.

"I certainly hope so," McFadden said. "I'm getting older, son. I have a busy life and I don't need this kind of stress."

Bellamy laughed, which wasn't the appropriate response at all. Kelly felt like she should deflect attention, but as it turned out she didn't need to. John McFadden's eyes remained on her. "Vincent tells me you're interested in a screen test," he said.

She frowned. "Huh?" And then she remembered. Two months ago, in Bellamy's car, they'd been talking about acting . . . So strange the things you say, the things you agree to, when you're trying to get someone to like you back.

"Dad," Vee said, "Kelly is Cat Lund's twin sister."

"Who?" McFadden said.

"Cat Lund," he said. "You've got to remember. I introduced you."

He shook his head. "Sorry." He gave Kelly a wink. "I'll have my girl call you," he said. "We'll set something up."

McFadden went back to his sparkling group, and they absorbed him, Cynthia Jones snaking a tanned arm around his waist, resting her golden head on his shoulder.

"Did I sound weird?" Bellamy said.

"Not really," Kelly lied, her eyes on Vee's, the hurt in them. "So," she said. "I guess I'm going to have a screen test."

"I can't believe he doesn't even remember her," Vee said, very quietly.

Kelly took another long sip of champagne, but it didn't give her the same feeling. The taste was familiar now, dull almost. She thought about how thrilling it had been to head up Bellamy's driveway for the first time, or that first moment when Vee had turned and looked into her eyes and she'd seen the whole of his face. There was comfort in getting used to wonderful things. But there was sadness in it too. "Your dad probably meets a lot of people," she tried.

"You could have refreshed his memory," Bellamy said. "Like . . . you know . . . tell him how Cat and Kelly's dad is a stuntman."

"Jimmy did say that he's worked with your dad before," Kelly tried.

"He should remember Cat because of *me*," he said. "Not her dad." He swallowed hard. "Sorry, Kelly." He went back into the bathroom. Kelly looked at Bellamy.

She shrugged. "I have no idea," she said. "But I'll tell you one thing. Just between us."

"Yeah?"

Her eyelids fluttered, her voice dropping to a whisper. "I shouldn't say this, because he's my dad's best friend and I love Vee so much . . ."

Kelly was starting to get impatient. "*What?*"

"John McFadden is . . . kind of weird."

"What do you mean?"

Her gaze darted to McFadden's group, then back to Kelly. "Nothing," she said. "Forget I said that. I'm just . . . you know."

"Okay."

"Paranoid."

"Right."

"Anyway, that's great you're getting a screen test. I forgot you wanted to act."

She was speaking very quickly, reminding Kelly how wired she was. Had to be the cocaine—or whatever speedy drug she and Vee had done in the bathroom. But still Kelly felt as though a curtain had been pulled back, but just for a few seconds—not long enough for her to make out what was behind it.

She touched the diamonds on her sister's heart necklace—a new habit. It felt almost as though she was talking to Catherine and also, it stopped her from saying things she shouldn't. Now, for instance. Kelly was thinking about John McFadden—how the whole time he was talking to the three of them, she was the only one he'd looked at—not the daughter of one of his prized actors; not even his own son. Kelly Lund, the daughter of a stuntman, the sister of a girl he claimed not to remember. She was the one who had captured his complete attention. Maybe it was because he'd never met her before and he wanted a good look at the girl who had been arrested with his son. But even if that was the case, it didn't explain why, during the entire conversation, he hadn't looked once at her face. He'd been looking at her necklace.

She had wanted to say something to Bellamy about that. But touching the diamonds kept her quiet. And what she was feeling was something she couldn't quite put into words. Something that was probably best kept to herself.

THE GUESTS MOVED IN AND OUT, MUSIC BLASTING—MADNESS, THE
Specials, X-Ray Spex, Gang of Four. Bellamy and Vee shouted the band names into Kelly's ears as she drank and smoked, the beats blurring into one another, guests singing along and dancing and shouting to be heard.

Vee kept refilling Kelly's champagne glass and sneaking lines with her and Bellamy in the bathroom, her heart racing and slowing, meeting people whose names she would instantly forget. It went on and on—a loop of color and sound and touch, peaks and plateaus—until finally they were the only three people in the room, lying on the mattress next to the big window smoking Bellamy's Marlboro Reds, the neon sign from the hotel across the street making everything in the room glow sunrise-pink.

Kelly was good at smoking now, just like she was good at getting high. She could French inhale in a way that Vee once told her was sexy, and she could light a match with one hand, just by squeezing the matchbook together. She could blow smoke rings too, and that's what she was doing now, creating a whole series of perfect, slender rings that Bellamy kept piercing and breaking, one by one.

"Why do you keep doing that?" Kelly said.

"So they don't die virgins."

Kelly pulled up onto her elbows. She arched her back and let her head drop and exhaled a cloud at the wall behind them. "I'm a dragon," she said.

"I love you," said Bellamy.

Kelly smiled. She wished Vee had said it though. Vee, so strangely quiet for the last she-didn't-know-how-long.

"Lucky cigarette!" Bellamy was down to the bottom of her pack, to the last cigarette, turned upside down for good luck. "Light it for me, we can both make a wish." She put it between her lips, and Kelly got out her matchbook, lighting a match with one hand. Kelly glanced at Vee to see if he'd been watching, but his eyes were closed. Passed out, probably. As she held the match up to Bellamy's cigarette, she closed her eyes and listened to his breathing and wished hard for something she couldn't put words to.

When she opened her eyes, Bellamy was still wishing. Kelly watched her as she took a hit off her lucky cigarette, watched her mouth the words to her wish, eyes shut so tight she was grimacing. So funny how hopeful she was. Worldly, cynical Bellamy Marshall, taking her cigarette wish so seriously. Kelly put a hand over hers. "I love you too," she said.

Bellamy exhaled, smoke billowing out of her lips. She opened her eyes and grinned at Kelly.

"Got my wish," Bellamy said.

FIFTEEN MINUTES, MAYBE HALF AN HOUR LATER—IT WAS HARD TO figure time—the cocaine had worn off, leaving Kelly drained and floaty from the champagne, sleep closing in on her. On her left, Bellamy was dead to the world, snoring lightly, while Vee was as silent as ever.

Kelly closed her eyes and basked in the darkness, let her muscles sink into the mattress. She was almost gone when she heard Vee speaking, his voice barely above a whisper. She hadn't even known he was awake. "She thought she could do anything," he said.

"Who?" Kelly said.

"Cat," he said. "Your sister."

"Oh."

"She said she'd changed her face and body, just by thinking hard about what she really wanted to look like. She was a good actress just because that's what she wanted to be. She never took lessons because she didn't need to. And also, she said she'd willed all of her friends into her life. Including me. She used the power of her mind."

Kelly opened her eyes. "Really?"

"I know it sounds weird."

"Not really," she said. "I mean, it sounds like Catherine. 'Not everything happens for a reason . . .'"

"'But the important things do.'"

"Yes," Kelly said. "Wow. She said that to you too."

He took a deep breath, let it out slowly. "She thought that if she tried hard enough, she could learn how to fly."

She turned on her side and watched him, his face bathed in pink light. He stared up at the ceiling. His eyes glistened.

"Do you think that's what happened, Kelly? Do you think she was trying to fly and that's how she wound up at the bottom of the canyon?"

She moved closer. She saw tears on his face.

"Vee?"

"Yeah?"

"How well did you know my sister?"

"I think . . ." he said. "I think I loved her."

Kelly put her arms around him, emotions coursing through her—confusion and longing and hurt—Vee's and her own. *I wish you would have told me that earlier,* she wanted to say. *I thought you and me,* she wanted to say. *You know. You and me . . .* But she didn't. She couldn't.

He wrapped his arms around her waist and buried his head in her neck and started to cry, softly at first, then harder, his body shaking. She pulled him closer and kissed his head, his tearstained face. "It's okay," she whispered. "It's okay."

She wanted to feel sorry for herself. For the feelings she'd had for Vee, those wasted feelings. But instead she found herself thinking about the boys who used to drop Catherine at home late at night, the sleazy, stoned-looking ones she'd sometimes see her with on the street, their arms around her, hands jammed into her jeans pockets. She thought about the older man in the Porsche with the aviator glasses and she held Vee tighter, poor Vee, who had so much more to feel sorry for. Kelly held Vee until she felt his pain as her own, until her shirt was wet with tears and there was nothing left inside him.

KELLY WOKE UP ALONE. IT TOOK HER SEVERAL PANICKY SECONDS TO figure out where she was, to piece together the evening and the morning, and even then there were big gaps. She checked her watch, 7:00 A.M. She smelled coffee and stood up and, to her immense relief, saw Bellamy and Vee in the kitchen, mugs in their hands.

"'Bout time," said Bellamy. "Some of us have to go to school today, you know."

Vee said, "My dad is going to give you guys a ride home."

"Your dad?"

"He has a place upstairs. He stayed there last night."

Kelly studied his face. She had a flash of holding him last night, of feeling his tears, though she couldn't remember why exactly. That champagne. All those drugs . . .

"I don't have my car," Bellamy was saying. "I've been driving since I was fourteen, my parents are suddenly all weird about me behind the wheel. They made me take a cab."

"Getting arrested might have something to do with that," Vee said, and as though on cue, the front door opened, John McFadden unlocking it with his own key.

"So much for privacy," Bellamy muttered.

McFadden said, "You ready?"

"See you guys," Vee said. He gave Bellamy a quick hug and then

Kelly, hanging on a few seconds longer . . . She felt his lips against her neck. His breath in her ear. "I love you," he whispered.

Do you remember?

Bellamy and Kelly followed McFadden out to his car—a cream-colored BMW with tan leather seats. On their way there, Bellamy gave Kelly a nudge, gestured up at the top window—John McFadden's apartment. A female figure moved behind the thin draperies. "How much you want to bet that's Cynthia," she whispered, though to Kelly the figure looked smaller than Cynthia. Flatter chested. Of course, it was hard to tell, looking up from the street, and for all she knew, Cynthia Jones had been wearing some padding under last night's macramé.

Kelly smiled. "We could totally call *Rona Barrett's Hollywood.*"

"My dad would kill me." Bellamy slipped into the backseat and asked to be dropped off first so she could make it to school on time. John McFadden turned the radio to KROQ. Frazer Smith's show was on, and for the whole ride to Bellamy's, The Fraze's crazed voice filled the car, neither girl saying a word. Kelly had never seen Bellamy this quiet before. She remembered what Bellamy had said at the start of the party. "*John McFadden is kind of weird.*" She still didn't know what that meant . . . or if it even meant anything. Sometimes, Bellamy just said things just for the sake of saying them.

McFadden was tapping his hands on the wheel to the Dead Kennedys song The Fraze was playing when he arrived at Bellamy's gate. He said his name into the box and pulled up the driveway. A man was heading toward their car from the front door, dressed completely in tennis whites. When he got closer, Kelly saw that it was Sterling. "Kids give you any trouble, John?" he said.

"Nah, it was a tame party. Everybody completely well behaved—as well they should be."

"I'll call you," Bellamy told Kelly. She gave Vee's dad a quick wave. "Bye, Mr. McFadden." She joined her father, who put an arm around her shoulder.

"Hello, Kelly," said Sterling Marshall. It warmed Kelly a little, hearing him say her name.

"Hi."

"Don't let her get into any trouble," John McFadden said to Sterling Marshall. "Or I guess I should say, any *more* trouble, right, Bellamy?" He smiled. Bellamy didn't smile back.

ONCE THEY WERE NEARING KELLY'S HOME, MCFADDEN SWITCHED OFF the radio and spoke to her for the first time. "You're Jimmy Lund's daughter!" He sounded shocked and kind of thrilled with himself, as though he'd just remembered the name of a song he'd been trying to think of for days.

"Um . . . Yes."

He sighed heavily. "No wonder Vincent was so annoyed with me for not remembering your sister."

"That's okay."

"No, it isn't," he said. "Jimmy's worked on a few of my films. He's a good man. How's he holding up?"

She forced a smile. "Good," she said. "He's um . . . he's doing well."

He pulled to a stop in front of Jimmy's house. Kelly grabbed her overnight bag, started to open the door. "Listen," he said. "I'm really sorry for your loss."

"Thank you."

"Please give your dad my best." He smiled—a good, kind smile. Vee's smile. *Nothing weird about him.*

"Okay," Kelly said. "Thanks for the ride."

Jimmy's car still wasn't in the driveway, which was good news. She didn't need to lie or hide her hungover eyes or do anything, other than go to sleep. As she unlocked the front door and let herself in, Kelly allowed herself to think about her upcoming screen test, how maybe it wouldn't be so bad after all, and Vee's dad would put her in a movie and she'd be rich and famous and never have to go to school again. She could even support Jimmy so he could retire.

What do you think of that, Catherine? I'm going to be an actress, just like you wanted to be. Kelly brought her hand to her throat to touch the two diamonds. But she felt nothing, only skin.

The necklace was gone.

CHAPTER 18

She is the anti-Suzy Chapstick. The dark side of the bright-eyed, sparkly girls on the cover of Seventeen *magazine. In her smile outside the courthouse reside the dream-free lives of our youth, raised on a steady diet of soulless pop music and cinematic ultraviolence, on assaultive TV advertising fueled by fathomless, limitless greed.*

It has been said that certain faces reflect the times we live in, and in her case—in her smile—that rings particularly true. Of all the smiles that have captured our consciousness through the ages—those described in books, flickering on celluloid, beaming out of glossy color photographs and glowing on the painter's canvas—hers is the first Death Smile. As we wade warily into the penultimate decade of the twentieth century, hers is the Smile for Our Times—a baring of teeth, as chilling and inevitable as a mushroom cloud.

You can look away from her—and look away you will—but those dead eyes will follow you. You will never forget.

Kelly Michelle Lund is our Mona Lisa. We brought her on ourselves.

EXCERPTED FROM
"A Smile for the Ages" by Sebastian Todd
Los Angeles Times Op Ed
March 3, 1981

CHAPTER 19

APRIL 23, 2010

e deserved to die," Rocky said, close to an hour after arriving at Kelly's house, as they lay on their backs in her bed, breathing together.

The start of sunrise poked through the filmy draperies—cloth she had chosen herself because it was the furthest thing from prison bars she could find. *"They won't block out the sun,"* Shane had said, when she'd first brought the draperies home and hung them. *"The sunrise will wake you up."*

She'd smiled. *"You act like that's a bad thing."*

That had been before she'd met Rocky, when she'd just seen him working in his yard. But once her gaze traveled from the draperies to his face—to those blue eyes shining out from painted vines, she felt as though she'd known him longer and better than anyone, Shane included. Shane especially.

She knew, for instance, that when Rocky had said "He deserved to die," he hadn't meant Sterling Marshall. He'd meant John McFadden. "How do you know he deserved it?" she said.

"I know *you.*"

"And?"

"If you killed him, you had reasons."

"Everybody has reasons," Kelly said. "Mass murderers have reasons." She stared up at her ceiling, the long crack in it, listening to his breathing. "Thank you, though."

"For what?"

"Assuming the best of me?"

Out of the corner of her eye, she saw him smile.

"Your trial was a total farce," he said.

"You followed it?"

"Yes."

"When it was going on?"

He nodded and her heart leaped, just a little. Rocky had never spoken about his past. And the idea that he'd followed her trial, that he knew who she was before she'd knocked on his door, that he'd cared about what happened to her . . . *He deserved to die.* He'd sounded so certain when he said it, hadn't he? Almost as though he'd known it for a fact . . .

Almost as though he'd been there.

The trial had been a farce—Rocky was right about that. Kelly's lawyer Ilene Cutler had opted not to put her on the stand. "*You seem older than you are, and not in a good way*" was how it had been explained by Cutler—a Big Deal Hollywood Defense Attorney somehow retained by Kelly's mother (in exchange for what? free makeovers?). Instead of focusing on guilt or innocence, Cutler had strived to portray Kelly as a poor, messed-up teen who was out of her element—making a big deal of all the drugs she'd done before the *Resistance* cast party and the fact that it hadn't been Kelly's gun; it had belonged to John McFadden, swiped by "aspiring actress" Kelly from his private collection that very same night. "*She thought maybe she could scare him into casting her,*" Cutler had said—an out-and-out lie. "*That's how misguided this poor, drugged-out girl was on that fateful, record-hot night.*"

Cutler had called it a "crime of passion," though in private, she'd made it known that she'd seen no passion in Kelly—only "smugness" as she put it. "*You're an actress,*" she had said to Kelly, who again was most assuredly not. "*Try to at least act remorseful.*"

She'd made Kelly wear barrettes in her hair. Ballet flats, high collars, and no makeup, not even lip gloss. It was supposed to make her look young and innocent, but, as Kelly had tried to tell Ilene, it actually made her look bitter, as though she'd missed out on a lot of fun and wanted revenge.

Ilene had gone for involuntary manslaughter, but the jury had convicted Kelly of second-degree murder and she'd been sentenced to twenty-five years to life. "*I told you not to act smug,*" Ilene had said, after the verdict—the last thing she'd ever said to her.

Kelly said, "My lawyer didn't like me very much."

"That's no excuse," he said, "for making you dress like a nun with a grudge."

She ran her hand softly over the side of his face. "Nun with a grudge." She smiled. "That's pretty good." A faint stubble pierced his warm skin, five o'clock shadow making thorns on the vines. "Where did you come from, Rocky?"

"Up the hill."

"That's not what I meant."

He moved on top of her, stroked her hair. "Do you really want to know?"

She started to say yes, then stopped. His eyes were calm. She couldn't figure out what was going on behind them. "Maybe," she said.

"Ask me when you're sure." He eased off of her, and she reached for him.

"Rocky."

"Yes?"

"Don't leave me."

"I have to," he said. "Your husband might come home, and even if he doesn't, the press are bound to show up here soon. All those phone calls . . ."

"No, no. I know you have to go back to your house," she said. "Just . . . please . . ." She took a breath, steadied herself. "Don't leave my life."

"What makes you think I'd do that?"

"Everybody else does."

"I'm not everybody else," he said. "Neither one of us is—which, when you think about it, is pretty much our whole problem."

He slipped out of bed and started pulling on his clothes. Kelly remembered going to Rocky's house for the first time—on a whim, but such a planned, premeditated whim, waiting until Shane and his client were deep in conversation, slipping out for a "little walk" she'd been debating in her mind for days. She remembered how fast she'd walked those three miles, the way her heart had pounded, the tugging doubts. But when she'd knocked on the door and Rocky had answered it, a calm had come over her as though, for the first time in her life, she was where she belonged. "*I know you*," she had said. No, that was wrong. She hadn't said it. She'd only thought it.

It was the eyes. The only part of Rocky that hadn't been tattooed, and she knew them. At least she thought she did. *Vee's eyes*. For five years, she'd wanted to ask, "*Are you Vincent Vales?*" But she hadn't been able to bring herself to say the words. If he said yes—or if he said no—where would that leave them?

Rocky said, "That lawyer. The one who didn't like you."

"Yes?"

"Did you tell her that you killed John McFadden?"

Kelly nodded.

"Did you tell her why?"

"No."

"Why not?"

"She said it didn't matter," she said. "Reasons don't matter. Facts don't even matter. What matters is what they think of you—the press, the jurors, the general public. Everything depends on what story they want to buy."

"She wasn't wrong."

Kelly's gaze traced the pale blue seahorse on his back, its long tail coiling around his spine. "No," she said. "Fashion choices aside, Ilene wasn't wrong about anything."

Rocky said something she could barely hear. He was still facing away, speaking more to the lamp than to her and in such a soft voice it was as though he was alone in the room.

"What did you say?"

"Nothing," he said.

But it hadn't been nothing. Kelly could have sworn he said, "*I should have testified.*"

"Is that you, Vee?" she whispered.

He turned. "What?"

"Nothing."

He kissed her gently—a good-bye kiss. Heat flooded through her, tears in her eyes and that feeling—the sweet pain of his leaving. Had she ever felt this way with Shane? With anybody?

"You're my only friend, you know," he said.

Rocky yanked on his white T-shirt, stepped into his flip-flops. As he pulled on his windbreaker, she stared into the green eye on his neck—the same bottle green her sister's eyes had been. "Rocky," she said quietly.

"Yes?"

"Sterling Marshall deserved to die too."

He stopped. Looked at her, the expression on his face mirroring hers—shock. She hadn't expected to say that. She'd never even known she felt that way, not until the words had come out of her mouth.

Rocky said, "I saw that interview he gave the *Times* a few days ago."

Kelly shook her head. "It isn't the interview."

"Then what? Why?"

She wanted to tell him so much, needed to. She took his hands in hers, and he didn't move closer or pull away. He just stood there, watching her face, waiting. "I got pregnant from a conjugal visit." She looked down at their clasped hands. "One of three times Shane and I ever . . ."

"Three times?"

"Yes. All right around when we got married."

"Okay."

"Shane never knew I'd gotten pregnant, but Sterling did. The prison doctor called him—nobody keeps secrets from Sterling Marshall. He threatened to cut us off, and I didn't want to hurt Shane. Not because of the money. He wouldn't have cared about losing the money. But he loved his dad so much. I didn't even want to think about what would happen to Shane if Sterling stopped talking to him."

"So you ended the pregnancy."

"Ended everything. My feelings for Shane. Any romantic feelings . . . I can't . . . I can't *be with him* anymore. I keep thinking things will change, but there's this barrier. It never feels right. He's patient. He thinks prison did it to me, but it wasn't prison. It was his father. Him too, in so much as he's his father's son and I can't ever forget that."

"I understand," he said quietly.

She stared into Rocky's eyes. He did understand. She knew that. Rocky always told her the truth, and it went both ways. She couldn't lie to him, even if she wanted to. "I didn't kill Sterling Marshall," she said. "I went to his house, but he was dead when I got there."

"Why did you go to his house?"

She swallowed hard. "Because," she said quietly, "he asked me to come."

"Why?"

"I don't know."

Rocky pulled the windbreaker hood over his shorn, painted head. "I wish I could save you, Kelly."

"From what?"

"Other people's opinions."

He slipped out of her room without waiting for a response. Kelly listened to his footsteps on her walkway, the opening and slamming of his pickup truck door, the rev of the engine, tires crushing gravel.

She got out of bed, moved over to her dresser, and cracked the top drawer. She didn't open this drawer, not usually. It was for keepsakes, and it didn't hold much: a few beaded clutch purses that used to belong to Jimmy's mother, a bag full of beach rocks from a trip with Shane to Big Sur, a framed photograph of Catherine she'd stolen from her mother, back when she'd moved out of her house, four months before the murder. But what she was looking for was at the bottom of the drawer, slid under the clutch bags where no one would find it. A postcard. She hadn't looked at it since she'd first put it in the drawer— hadn't wanted to, though she thought of it, often.

"Where did you come from, Rocky?" she whispered.

"*Ask me when you're sure,*" he had said.

Kelly felt for the postcard and pulled it out. She read the faded postmark: May 30, 1982. Los Angeles, California. And then the note. Just one word:

Someday.

It had been addressed to her in prison and it hadn't been signed. She ran her fingers over the pen indents. That handwriting. Those clean, block letters. She'd always been so sure who had sent it. But was that just because she'd *wanted* to be sure? Kelly had hardly ever seen Vee's handwriting, yet she'd convinced herself of it anyway, kept the postcard with her at all times, under her pillow in prison and then in this drawer. She'd received so many postcards and letters when she was in jail—hate mail and love notes, questionnaires from journalists and missives from public advocates and conspiracy theorist nutjobs, not to mention all those wonderful letters from Shane. Yet this one-word postcard had been the only piece of prison mail she'd kept after her release.

Vee.

Vincent Vales had left Kelly's life the night of the murder—not just her life, but everyone's. Back then, you could disappear without technology betraying you, and so that's what he had done. Even Sebastian Todd had been unable to find him. Sebastian Todd, who had apparently managed to track down Kelly's cult-member mother.

She'd admired Vee for being able to do that—to fly away like one of her desert birds, without ever migrating back. At just sixteen years old, he'd taken a leap that had lasted decades. But that hadn't stopped Kelly from seeing him everywhere—in the crowds at televised sporting events, in Carpentia's visiting room, in the backgrounds of photographs in glossy magazines . . . and up the hill from her new home, sawing those creations in his yard.

Kelly gazed at the postcard, at those hopeful block letters, written when both of them were still children: *Someday.* She turned it over and looked at the picture on the back: a flowering cactus. The desert spring. The caption beneath: VISIT JOSHUA TREE, CALIFORNIA!

You're my only friend.

Six months before her release, she'd told Shane she wanted to live here. She hadn't told him why, but deep down, her request had been based on the belief that one day, *someday,* the three of them could be friends again—Vee and Bellamy and herself, Shane serving to bridge the divide, the diaspora reunited. Happily ever after. That's the type of thing you think about when you are in prison for that many years, the imagination being a powerful salve, the fact remaining: you're only as sure of anything as you want yourself to be.

She slid the postcard under the beaded bags, shut the drawer. She grabbed her robe off the hook by her bedroom door and pulled it on, glancing at the clock by her bedside: 6:00 A.M. Twenty-four hours ago, she'd woken up to her husband taking her picture. God, things knew how to change.

RUTH WATCHED ZEKE SLEEPING FOR QUITE A WHILE BEFORE SHE TRIED to wake him. She'd been doing this often—sneaking into his room to watch the steady rise and fall of his frail chest, to listen to him breathing. She used to do the same thing with the girls when they were babies, but now more than then she feared the spaces between breaths.

Ruth crouched down next to Zeke's futon and took his hand in her own. He'd always had strong, graceful hands, but the one in hers felt clammy and weak, the spark that was Zeke already fading. Three days ago, he had asked her to shave off his beard, complaining of its heaviness, its itchiness. Ruth had brought a tub of warmed, soapy water and a straight razor into his cabin and gone to work, marveling at the face as it revealed itself. In twenty-seven years, she'd never seen him clean-shaven and she'd never expected those cheekbones, that chin . . . "*Why would you want to cover up a handsome kisser like that?*" Ruth had said, trying to keep things light.

He'd given her a smile—sweet but full of pain. "*It's a face only a mother could love.*"

When Ruth had first met Zeke, he'd been a boy. Twenty-one at the most. She'd been sitting in a coffee shop near her old apartment—unemployed, close to broke. She'd lost her job at I. Magnin eight months earlier and hadn't even the slightest chance at new work since. She was infamous, after all. The bad mother of a bad girl. But every morning, she'd put on full makeup and a nice outfit. She'd go to this coffee shop two blocks from her home, and sit there for hours, reading the want ads over one cup of coffee with bottomless refills. Taking advantage of the owners' generosity. Acting as though she had somewhere to be.

He'd slipped into the seat across from her, this brash boy in a flannel shirt, his heavy black beard reminding her of a character from the Bible. "*Mrs. Lund,*" he had said. "*I've been looking for you.*"

Ruth—then Rose—had glanced up from her newspaper, expecting another scum-of-the-earth supermarket tabloid reporter. But then she'd locked eyes with this young stranger, and her whole world had changed. Zeke's eyes were the kindest she'd ever seen.

"*How would you like to go somewhere where you'll never hurt anyone again?*"

Looking back, it had sounded a bit like a death threat. But it had turned out to be the opposite—a lifeline. A place to start over. Zeke had a piece of land, and he'd made it into a type of failures' utopia—a self-sustaining farm in the middle of nowhere. "*It's for people like me, who have made mistakes they don't want to repeat,*" he had said. "*People who are better off set apart from the rest of the world.*"

"*Like prison?*" she'd asked.

"*A little. But you only stay as long as you like.*"

Orange and lime trees, a vegetable garden, a chicken coop and five cows, a generator, indoor plumbing, a small library, and thanks to the efforts of some of the newer, more tech-savvy recruits, an old computer in the canteen with pirated Internet . . . Zeke's compound had everything anyone could ask for. And until now, Ruth had had no desire to leave it. While other residents had come and gone, she remained constant in her belief that the outside world—Kelly especially—was better off without her.

But then she'd spoken to Sebastian Todd. *I need you,* he had said. *Kelly needs you.* And she'd believed him. Despite all those awful, untrue things he'd written about Kelly in the past, in the newspaper and book excerpts she'd found while searching the Internet after he left; despite the fact that when she'd asked how he had tracked her down here in the first place, he'd tried to make her believe she'd told him herself (*"Don't you remember the letter you sent me?"* As though she were some senile old woman who sent letters in her sleep). Despite all of his lies, Ruth had believed him, which she hoped hadn't been the biggest mistake of her life.

She placed a hand on Zeke's smooth face, felt his eyelids flutter open. "What did he say?"

"What?"

"Sebastian Todd. What did he say? How is your daughter?"

"She's all right."

"Switch on the light," Zeke said. "I need to see your face."

"Why?"

"Because you've never been able to look me in the eye and lie to me."

She removed a wooden match from the box on Zeke's nightstand, lit the three candles in their slate holder. They were beautiful candles—the color of fresh cream and with a heady vanilla scent. Demetrius had made them—he was wonderful at crafts.

"Now," Zeke said, face flickering in the candlelight. "Look into my eyes and tell me your daughter is all right."

On the wall behind him, a print was tacked—a portrait of the biblical Ezekiel, the lifelong exile, son of Buzi, whose name meant "contempt."

Underneath the portrait, the meaning of the Ezekiel's name: *May God Strengthen Him.* Ruth read the line and prayed it at the same time.

"I'm waiting," he said.

"I can't," Ruth said slowly. "My daughter's in trouble." She cleared her throat. "Sebastian Todd told me. There's been another shooting."

His eyes opened wider. "Who was shot?"

She tried to say the name, but choked on it. "Kelly's father-in-law."

He let out a long, shaking breath. "And you know for sure Sebastian Todd was telling the truth."

She nodded. "I went into the canteen. I read the news on the Internet. People think she did it. The comments on the news stories—"

"*People* are the reason why we never leave this place." He struggled up to sitting. It took him two tries. "Well, hardly ever," he said softly. "Has she been arrested?"

"It looks like she's about to be. I don't know what to do. Kelly's an adult now. She might very well get the death penalty."

Zeke stared at her. "She won't."

"You don't know that."

"Listen," he said. "I've got some money saved up. A lot of money. We can hire her a great lawyer . . ."

"*I did that thirty years ago,*" Ruth said, her voice louder, shriller than she wanted it to be. "I used every penny of my savings and hired Kelly the best lawyer in the business and look where it got her!"

"I'm sorry."

She shook her head. "No, I'm sorry. I don't want to hurt you, Zeke. You don't deserve that."

He collapsed back onto the futon, pain twisting his handsome features.

"Can I get you anything?" she said. "Glass of water? Something to eat?"

Zeke shook his head. "Ruth."

"Yes."

"What can we do for Kelly?"

She couldn't meet his gaze. Even by candlelight, she could see the illness in his eyes, the whites a dull yellow. Hodgkin's lymphoma. Stage 4. He'd never told her about it. "Just a temporary bug," he kept saying. "Nothing they can do for me at the hospital." But at some point, he'd looked it up on the computer: *Hodgkin's lymphoma. Stage 4. Survival chances without treatment.* She'd seen it tonight in the search history. And looking it up herself, she'd learned that it would have been treatable even six months ago, when Zeke had gone to the hospital in an ambulance and come home armed with a battery of lies.

Why the lies, Zeke? Why wouldn't you want to save yourself? Do you want to escape the world so badly that even this place is too much for you?

He struggled up to sitting again and strained to hug Ruth, for she'd been crying without realizing it. Crying for him.

She pulled away. "I gave Sebastian Todd an interview," she said.

Zeke nodded.

"I didn't say a word about you or any of the other residents. He promised not to reveal the location of the compound. He just wants to paint Kelly in a different light. Show the world she's human."

"Do you think it will help?"

She sat down on the smooth wooden floor. Her eyes were hot from tears. She looked at Zeke in the bed and tried to imagine what she would think if she were seeing him for the first time—the frail arms, the sunken cheeks, the skin, so pale it was nearly translucent—the illness devouring the man. "I do think it will help," she said.

Slowly, he shook his head, his face as sad as she'd ever seen it. "No you don't."

She thought of Zeke as a boy again—that strange bearded boy with the kind eyes. "*I'll help you,*" he had said. "*We can help each other.*"

Ruth had left the café with him. Headed out to his van without hesitation and driven with him to the compound without even stopping home to pack bags. She'd never looked back. Not once.

"Zeke," she told the pale shadow on the bed. "You saved my life. I want you to know that." She made sure to look into his eyes when she said it.

"Vice versa, Ruth," he said, his voice barely a whisper. "Vice versa."

CHAPTER 20

Kelly stared into Shane's empty bedroom. "We don't know each other anymore," she said.

She thought about all the letters she used to write him when she was in prison. All those questions she asked him, each one answered so carefully. Had they ever spoken to each other aloud with the same abandon as in their writing—or had they been strangers throughout their marriage, ever since her pregnancy, that first secret Kelly had decided to keep from him?

Time for another letter.

Her laptop was still on the kitchen table, screen still frozen on *The Demon Pit. Just send him an e-mail.* She ejected the DVD, then clicked on the Internet icon. She was about to open up her e-mail, but her fingers froze on the keyboard.

Kelly's thirty-year-old mug shot stared back at her from her home page, alongside a photograph of the medical examiner's van, leaving yesterday morning through the gates of the Marshalls' home on Blue Jay Way. She read the headline:

TWO MURDERS: EERIE SIMILARITIES

She clicked on the article, forced herself to skim through. No new information, yet so many phrases that jumped out and slapped her: *As Marshall's family members gathered at his home, Lund was nowhere to be seen . . . Shane Marshall is now living separately from his wife . . . None of the Marshall family is talking to reporters, but sources close to the Hollywood dynasty say there is no love lost between them and Lund, an "odd duck" who largely keeps to herself and makes a living by working in some capacity for notorious "cheaters' Web site" SaraBelle.com . . . Spotted leaving the West Hollywood precinct, where her husband had been held following his emotional breakdown at Teaserz, Lund appeared to show no emotion . . . "Kelly never really got along with anyone in the family," says a source close to the Marshalls, who wishes to remain anonymous. "Shane distanced himself from them during his marriage, but now, they're so happy to have him back in the fold."*

Kelly looked bad on paper. She always had—though in the past, she'd at least had youth on her side. But that wasn't what bothered her. Of everything inferred by the Web news piece, what hurt her most was one phrase: *a source close to the Marshalls, who wishes to remain anonymous.*

"Why do you hate me so much, Bellamy?" Kelly whispered. "What did I ever do to you?"

She thought about Shane, passed out in his sister's spare bedroom, location unknown. She thought of the text he'd sent her: I NEED SOME TIME AWAY FROM YOU. It didn't sound like Shane—at least not the Shane she thought she knew. Had Bellamy sent it? Had she stolen the phone when Shane was safely passed out and typed out the words she'd always wished he would say? It made sense. Bellamy had always been her father's daughter, after all . . .

And Shane was weak—weaker than anyone knew him to be. A few weeks ago, he'd been out with his camera and Kelly had gone into his room to borrow a pen. In his nightstand drawer, she'd found easily thirty empty bottles of Ambien—so many bottles above and beyond his regular prescription, no doubt to be disposed of when the time was right.

She hadn't said a word to him about it. In fact, she'd forced it out of her mind. What right did she have to confront Shane, after all? What were a few extra pills anyway, compared to the pregnancy, compared to Rocky? *You have your secrets,* she had told herself. *Let Shane have his.* But where had that gotten her? Where had it gotten them both? If she had spoken to him about it, he might not have taken whatever he had taken back at his parents' house, trying to drown his grief. He wouldn't have gotten himself arrested and he wouldn't have wound up at his sister's. He could have come home. They could have told each other everything.

"*Secrets can kill you.*" Kelly's dad used to say that when he was nodding off, but he'd never explained what he meant, so it had come across as babbling. "*They gnaw at your insides. You try and kill 'em with booze, but that's just like watering plants, kiddo. The secret grows bigger and stronger inside you. Gets to feeling sometimes like it can burst right through your skin. Like it can eat you alive . . .*"

She'd never asked Jimmy what secrets were killing him back then and now they were all gone, her father's secrets scrambled with everything else in his brain—mashed together with fantasies and memories and lies.

Kelly clicked out of the article, opened her e-mail, and typed Shane's address into the box. She wrote quickly:

> Shane, we need to talk. If you are going to leave me,
> I can't stop you. But first, please, let's tell the truth. Let's
> share all the secrets we've been keeping from each other

*and end things clean, so we both know who exactly it is
that we're leaving.*

With love,
K

She took a deep breath. But before she hit "send," she stopped herself. If Bellamy was screening Shane's calls and possibly sending his texts, odds were she was also checking his e-mail. And even if she wasn't, did Kelly really want to put these feelings into writing? You put anything out there—your words, your tears (or lack of them), your face, bending into a nervous smile—it's all there for public consumption. And make no mistake: it *will* be consumed and digested and spit back out as something it never was. And then there's nothing you can do but live with it. Become it. Your one-word responses become evidence of cold-bloodedness. Your shabby clothes become a sign of disrespect. Your facial tic becomes The Mona Lisa Death Smile.

What was it that Ilene Cutler had said? *The world's a stage, Little Miss, but very few of us get to write our own roles.* Ilene Cutler, right about everything.

Kelly deleted the e-mail. The best solution, the only solution, was to speak to Shane in person. In his own words, he could explain to Kelly why he'd gone to a strip club and beaten up a stranger while saying her name. He could tell her about his pill addiction—when it had started, why—and let her know why he was leaving her. In turn, she could tell him about her late-night drives, about her terminated pregnancy, about Rocky . . . And she could open up that final drawer in her mind for him, the one she'd locked tight two mornings ago when she'd pulled into her driveway with dawn close to breaking, the sleeve of her favorite gray hoodie spattered with Sterling Marshall's blood . . .

Moments later, Kelly was standing at the sink with the water running, breathing hard, that locked drawer opening. The night of April 21 sprung to life in her mind, starting with the midnight drive up Outpost Road—a short solo run to clear her head before sleep, the radio on and that song playing, making her feel seventeen again. Bette Midler. "The Rose." Bette had been singing about an endless aching need when Kelly's cell phone had started ringing—ringing past midnight. She hadn't recognized the number on the screen. And she never would have answered if the song hadn't brought back memories, if it hadn't made her feel so stupidly, stubbornly hopeful.

More hopeful still when she heard Sterling Marshall's voice. "*Are you alone?*"

"*Yes, Mr. Marshall.*"

"*Call me Dad,*" he had said. "*Call me Dad, Kelly,*" and "*Please don't tell Shane. We need to talk. I need to see you.*" And then, "*Kelly, my girl, I have cancer. I'm dying.*" A triple blow. Who wouldn't have gone to Sterling Marshall after that? How could anyone resist that kind voice? *Call me Dad . . . My girl . . .*

And so Kelly had gone. Instead of turning around and heading home, she'd swung onto 62 and flown toward Hollywood at eighty-five miles per hour. "*I'll be there,*" she'd said into her phone. Like an idiot. Like a child.

When she arrived, the gate had been open. She'd driven through and parked in the Marshalls' driveway and rung the front doorbell and when no one had answered she'd opened it herself. Like someone dumb and trusting. She'd run up the stairs to his office—weird how it all felt to her, as though no time had passed, as though Kelly really were the same person she'd been thirty years ago, before McFadden, before prison. She'd half-expected Bellamy to greet her as she passed the den, seventeen-year-old Bellamy, shaking a bag of magic mushrooms, her smile lighting up the room, the street, all of Hollywood and beyond . . . "'Bout time you showed up, Kelly . . . Let's have a 'no-day.'"

Kelly had run up the stairs, feet clomping like a kid, "The Rose" still playing in her head along with Bellamy's voice, her best friend's voice . . . "Check it. I got some of my mom's pills too. I think they're downers. Wanna try?" The whole house had been silent, Mary Marshall passed out in her room no doubt, the servants sleeping, everyone asleep save for Sterling Marshall and whatever he had to say to her . . . An apology? After all these years?

She'd thrown open the door to her father-in-law's office, thinking, I'm here, Dad. God, that really had been what she was thinking. All is forgiven. I'm home.

And then the smell had hit her, that awful smell, coppery and intimate. Blood. Bits of bone on the polished wood floor, his face destroyed. A gun next to his hand and she'd knelt down, she'd touched him.

Had it all been a setup? Had he called her with a plan? I'm dying of cancer, Kelly. I'm killing myself and leaving no note and you, you, my girl . . . You will take the rap. My son will be rid of you at long last.

She'd pulled up her hoodie. She'd run out the back door. But did that matter? Did any of it matter—a convicted killer, leaving a dead man's house at 2:00 A.M.?

Kelly's car in his driveway. Her number in his phone. All that blood. Her footprints in it. Her fingerprints on him, two days after he'd given an interview to the Los Angeles Times on the fifth anniversary of Kelly's release, reminding the world of her role: Hollywood havenot. Drugged-out wild child. Murderer.

"He even gave me a motive," she whispered, her voice hollow in her ears, doomed.

ONCE SHE WAS IN SHANE'S ROOM, KELLY TRIED TO IGNORE THE VIN-
tage movie poster over the bed (*Sterling Marshall shines on in GUNS OF VICTORY!*). She headed for the desk in the corner of the room and turned on his computer. Shane's bedroom doubled as his office. (With clients, he called it the "guest room." Yet another secret in their lives.) And so it was very neat—pristine, save for the empty pill bottles stashed away in the nightstand drawer—the computer ringing in such a clean, professional way as she switched it on and clicked on the icon marked "address book." She searched for Bellamy's name, found it. But there was no address listed; no e-mail, even. Just a home phone.

Without thinking much about it, Kelly clicked on Shane's Internet icon and opened his e-mail. In the five years she'd lived with him, she'd never once used his computer without him in the room, let alone opened his e-mail. But after scrolling through to find only client correspondence and, later, queries from the press, she switched screens to Google. She had never before checked his search history.

But she did now, moving from step to intrusive step as though by reflex, as though Shane had forfeited his right to privacy by turning into someone she needed to figure out.

A sound just outside the house snapped her out of it. A car horn honking, out on the road, and when she listened more carefully, voices. *People out there.* Shame filled her, an awful cold feeling, as though whoever was outside had actually *seen* Kelly at Shane's computer. She shut it off—but not before she noticed something strange on her husband's search history. In the midst of searches for porn and photo processing centers and generic Ambien, one name had jumped out at her. And judging from its placement, the search had taken place within the last week or two.

Shane had googled Artist + Rocky Three.

Kelly swallowed hard. She left Shane's bedroom quickly and headed back to the kitchen. Outside, she heard tires skidding to a halt. A door slamming. A man's voice saying, "Dude, this is our space."

"What, you reserved it?" another, deeper voice laughed.

"What the hell . . ." Kelly cracked the front door.

"Kelly!" a woman's voice yelled.

She opened the door a little wider and found herself staring at a small cluster of news vans parked just across the street.

"Kelly, have you spoken to your husband?"

"Do you know who killed Sterling Marshall?"

"Does Shane have substance abuse issues?"

She sighed. Slammed the door. "No, maybe, and yes," she said quietly.

Amazing. Her address wasn't listed. And, except for meetings with his most trusted clients, Shane did most all of his photo archive business remotely. Yet still the press had found her.

The press could find anybody . . .

Kelly backed away from the door, an idea closing in on her. She grabbed her purse off the table, opened her wallet, pulled out Sebastian Todd's business card. She tapped the gold-embossed number into her phone.

"You're a mind reader," Todd said by way of answering. "I was just about to call you. What did you think of *The Demon*—"

"I'll give you an interview."

"Wow that's . . . impulsive of you."

"An exclusive. When the time is right. I'll talk about my parents. John McFadden. Anything you want."

"To what do I owe this—"

"I just want one thing in return."

He cleared his throat. "I don't pay."

"I don't want money."

"I'm married." Sebastian Todd laughed. Kelly didn't.

She took a deep breath, let it out slowly. "The only thing I want," she said, "is Bellamy Marshall's home address."

"THIS IS GOING ON TOO LONG," MARY MARSHALL SAID. **"I NEED TO** plan the funeral."

Barry Dupree coughed and got an elbow in the ribs from Louise Braddock. He frowned at her. *What?* He hadn't meant anything by the cough. It was just a cough. What kind of an asshole did Braddock think he was?

"Mrs. Marshall," Braddock said. "I understand your frustration. But as I said before, the medical examiner will be releasing your husband's body very soon."

"I need to contact his relatives. He has relatives all over the country. He comes from a big family. How will they be able to get out here if I don't know when the funeral will be?"

She said it to Barry, not Louise, but they were both used to that. Most older ladies preferred Barry's company to that of his partner— either because he was a guy and therefore more trustworthy to them or because Louise was about as welcoming and warm as the iceberg that sank the *Titanic* or both. Probably both.

Louise held Sterling Marshall's appointment book in her lap, and she kept tapping on it—an almost hostile gesture, somehow made worse by the fact that she was wearing evidence gloves.

Barry said, "Can I get you a glass of water, Mrs. Marshall?"

She shook her head. Pointed at Louise Braddock. "She isn't listening to me."

"We're both listening, ma'am," Barry said. But he couldn't return her gaze. It was the look in her eyes—*this-can't-be-happening* to the hundredth power. He'd seen it before on people like her—attractive, wealthy, basically happy people who'd lived a certain number of years and thought they could make it all the way to the finish line without the world falling in on them. What could you say to that look—*Life sucks? Shit happens? Sorry you had to live so long?*

Making matters worse was the pharmaceutical influence. By her own admission, Mary Marshall had been zonked out on sleeping pills when the shots had woken her. She was half groggy when she found her husband's body, and had tried to numb the initial horror with a handful of Xanax (she couldn't remember how many), then a few Klonopin parsed out by her well-meaning daughter when the Xanax-calm started to loosen its grip.

As a result, the shock was settling in little by little as the drugs wore off. One minute, she'd be perfectly lucid, answering questions, asking them . . . and then reality would hit her and she'd get that look in her eyes and she'd shatter. She'd go either comatose or combative—and at the moment she was definitely combative. "You can't just hijack my husband's body," she said.

"No one is taking Mr. Marshall's body for any longer than it needs to be taken. You must try to be patient," said Louise, ever the diplomat, talking to Mary Marshall like she'd been complaining about her dry cleaning not being ready. Barry couldn't believe Louise had given him shit for coughing. Did she ever even listen to herself?

"When was the last time your son spoke to your husband?" Louise said.

"My *son*? Why are you asking about my *son*?"

"He took a whole bunch of your pills, ma'am."

"I know that."

"A dangerous amount."

"He is grieving, Detective Braddock. We're all grieving. Do you know how that feels?"

"They didn't see each other much, though, did they?"

She looked at Barry again, for such a drawn-out moment that he felt obliged to nod. "My son and my husband spoke on the phone every week," she said. "They were close."

"When was the last time you and your husband had dinner with your son and his wife."

"We don't do that."

"When was the last time the two of them just got together to play golf? Shoot the breeze?"

"I don't know."

"So would you classify Shane and Sterling's relationship as strained?"

"No," she said. "No, they loved each other very much."

Louise opened the appointment book. "When was the last time Mr. Marshall spoke on the phone to Shane?"

She exhaled. "Just this past Sunday."

"What did they talk about?"

"Sterling told Shane about his cancer diagnosis. My daughter, Bellamy, had already known for weeks."

"Were you in the room during the phone call?"

"No."

"How did your husband seem after he hung up with your son?"

"He seemed the way he always seemed," she said. "Why are you asking me about Shane?"

"Did your son know that Sterling had made an appointment with his lawyer for this coming Monday?"

"What?"

"It's in his book." She tapped at the open page. "Did you know about it?"

She shook her head.

"When did he last speak to your son again?"

"Sunday."

"He made the appointment on Monday, for one week later."

"So what?"

"Is there anything your son could have said to him during that conversation that would make him call his lawyer?"

"What are you hinting at, Detective?"

"Louise," said Barry.

"Did they fight at all? Did your husband mention anything about changing his will?"

"What are you trying to say about my son?"

"Louise, it stands to reason that he would want to get his papers in order." He gave Mary Marshall a sad smile that he hoped would appease her. "I mean, in his condition."

"Yes," Mary said, the tension draining out of her. "Yes, that's true." So often, Louise and Barry played good cop/bad cop. But it was very rarely intentional.

"I'm going to check in with the rest of the crew." Louise got up from the couch, leaving the two of them, taking the appointment book with her.

It was probably the kindest thing she could have done under the circumstances, but that didn't make it any less uncomfortable for Barry. "We called your daughter a little while ago, ma'am," he said. "She said she would be here soon."

"With Shane?"

"I'm not sure."

Mary gave him a weak smile, which crumbled fast. "I hope he's all right."

A few tears trickled down her cheek. She wiped them away with a handkerchief she'd tucked into the sleeve of her silk blouse, plucked a gold compact out of her handbag, and applied red lipstick. "Do I look okay?" she said. "I don't want to scare my son again."

"Again?"

"I think one of the things that upset him yesterday . . ." She cleared her throat. "I think I frightened him with the way I looked."

"You look great, Mrs. Marshall," he said.

"You've got to act and dress as though you always have an audience," she said. "Sterling used to say that." She let out a long sigh that became a sob. "Hell of a curtain call he's taking."

Mary Marshall cried quietly into her handkerchief. Barry waited for the crying to subside. He wanted to pat her on the back but resisted the urge. Even in his mind, that felt awkward.

Finally, when she calmed, he cleared his throat, turned the page in his notebook. "Can you tell me a little bit about Mr. Marshall's schedule on April twenty-first?" Barry already knew about Sterling Marshall's schedule that day—at least he knew what he'd planned to do from the appointment book Louise had been tapping to death at the start of this interview. The uniforms going through Sterling Marshall's office had found the book straight off, and it had told them more by far than any witness interview. Turned out Marshall didn't have a personal assistant, and while he did have a computer that had since been taken into possession, he preferred scheduling on paper, as anybody would expect from a seventy-nine-year-old movie star with a drawer full of fancy pens.

"I'm not asking you for specific times or anything," he said. "Just what you might remember him doing."

She dragged the handkerchief across her eyes. "I wasn't home the whole day," she said. "I . . . I had tennis and errands."

"I understand. If you can just think back, though. Did he do anything out of the usual? Was he behaving strangely at all?"

"He had a doctor's appointment."

Barry nodded. He'd seen that in the book. "What kind of doctor?"

"His oncologist."

"Routine, or . . ."

"Nothing was routine. He'd just been diagnosed a few weeks ago with pancreatic cancer." She got up from the couch, moved over to the window.

"Yes. Of course," he said. "I guess what I'm saying is, how was he handling it?"

"Handling it?"

"His diagnosis. On that day. Was he acting strangely?"

"Detective Dupree. I have a question for you."

"Okay . . ."

"How do you suppose Kelly Lund got into our house?" She said it flatly, matter-of-factly, and she didn't turn around. She stayed facing the window, the sun on her silver hair, her posture rigid as a ballet dancer's.

He stared at her back, not sure what she was asking. "We don't know who that was leaving the . . ."

She turned and faced him. "It was Kelly Lund. I know it was."

"All I can tell you," he said, "is there were no signs of a break-in."

"It was the maid's day off. The cook only rarely stays nights and didn't last night. He and I were in the house alone." She stared at him, eyes hurt and blazing. "And I was asleep."

He took a breath, said it calm as he could. She was trying to put words in his mouth, and he couldn't let her do that. "You're saying," he said, "that whoever this on the surveillance video is . . ."

"Kelly Lund."

"Fine," he said. "You're saying your husband must have let her into the house."

She nodded vigorously.

"So . . ."

"So, if that's the case," she said, taking a few steps toward him, the hurt in her eyes turning fierce. "If Sterling allowed Kelly Lund to come into this house, then yes. My husband was behaving very, very strangely."

There was a soft knock on the closed door. Barry cracked it, saw Braddock's face.

"I need to talk to you," she said.

"Seriously?"

She didn't even bother nodding.

Mary Marshall was back on the couch now, her head in her hands.

"Excuse me, ma'am," he said.

She didn't look up.

Once he'd closed the door behind him and was out in the great room, Braddock pulled him aside to one of the enormous windows behind the pink marble staircase, overlooking the canyon. Every once in a while, it would hit him how incredible this house was—probably the ritziest crime scene he'd ever set foot in, and with such perfect air-conditioning. He'd wonder if Mary planned to unload it fast and take the hit, or wait at least three years so her Realtor wouldn't be obligated to tell prospective buyers what had happened in the study. He'd go back and forth over what he would do in her position and then he'd feel bad for it—what an obnoxious train of thought to be having at a murder house.

A uniform stood beside Braddock—a tiny young girl who looked far too happy, given the situation. He half-expected her to start jumping up and down.

Louise said, "Get anything?"

He hoped the uniform hadn't smiled like this around Mary Marshall. "Not really." He gestured at the much-too-young officer, that face she was making—like somebody had just given her backstage passes to a One Direction concert. "Looks like she does, though."

"This is officer Nutley. She's on the team that's been going through everything in Sterling Marshall's office." Louise handed Barry a pair of evidence-handling gloves. "She did indeed get something."

The smile erupted, taking over the kid's entire face. Nutley going nuts, as it were. She held out a burner phone.

Barry put the evidence gloves on and took it from her—a basic flip phone. Didn't even have a display screen. It was still on, battery charged.

"It was at the bottom of the trash can," Nutley said proudly.

Barry stared at it. He flipped it open.

"It's on," she said. "It was on when I found it."

"You always jump to conclusions, Barry," Louise said.

Barry looked at her.

"With this case, you were all ready to tie Kelly Lund to the crime, relying on your intuition like you always do. And you remember what I told you yesterday morning?"

"Innocent until proven guilty."

"That's right. And of course I still hold by it. But, Barry . . ."

"Yeah?"

"That intuition of yours. It isn't always wrong."

"What are you talking about?"

"Hit redial."

Barry put the phone on speaker, pressed the redial button on Sterling Marshall's burner, and connected with the dead man's most recent call—very recent, considering that the phone had been on when it was found and still held a charge.

It went straight to voice mail. Kelly Lund's voice mail.

BELLAMY MARSHALL LIVED CLOSER THAN KELLY MIGHT HAVE IMAGINED— in Irvine of all places. Sebastian Todd had explained to Kelly that Bellamy had done an artist-in-residence year at the college several years ago and had liked the town so much she'd stayed on, long after the one class she'd taught had graduated and moved away.

But knowing this did nothing to ease Kelly's shock when she saw Rancho Escondido, which was the name of the sprawling, sterile-looking condo complex where Bellamy now lived. When they were kids, Bellamy used to call them "space fillers," complexes like this, every house exactly the same, manicured lawns, carefully trimmed topiaries doled out equitably, two to each lot, shining Spanish tile roofs and faux adobe, each house exactly the same as the next, the whole lot looking as though it had gone up overnight. There were hundreds of these in Southern California, particularly the more recently developed areas in Orange County. But never once in thirty years had Kelly expected ultrahip, march-to-her-own-beat Bellamy to live in one.

Bellamy's street was called Vista Verde. Kelly had to look carefully for the address; even her GPS had trouble discerning which of the houses was hers—but then she saw it in one of the driveways: a deep green Jeep Cherokee. She pulled up behind it and saw the license plate, Shane's license plate, the Hollywood Photo Archives bumper sticker— a marketing idea of his from three years ago, as though seeing a sticker in traffic would lead anyone to make a decision regarding vintage movie photos. It got Kelly choked up—the simple sight of her husband's car. It made her wonder if maybe this was a bad idea, coming to Bellamy's house now, with her feelings still so raw.

Of course, she didn't have the luxury of waiting, not the way things were going, with her prints all over Sterling Marshall's study and the press already connecting the dots.

Kelly got out of her car and headed up the path to the front door. A single sprinkler halfheartedly spritzed Bellamy's square of a lawn, a FOR SALE sign positioned up front, the two regulation topiaries flanking it like backup dancers. *Okay, so she doesn't love it here after all.* Kelly reached the front door and pushed the bell without taking a breath, giving herself no time to think about reconsidering.

No answer. She pushed it again. Pressed her ear to the door, but heard no movement. She tried the big, faux-antique knocker, then balled her hand into a fist and pummeled the door with the side of it.

Still nothing. Were they both still asleep? Gone to comfort their mother? Passed out indefinitely? Or were they hiding?

Kelly walked around the side of the house, rapped on one of the windows. "Shane," she said. "Shane? Bellamy?"

"Excuse me?"

Kelly turned to see a tiny, white-haired woman of about eighty. She wore a velour tracksuit, JUICY COUTURE spelled out across her chest in tiny pink rhinestones. "Hello," Kelly tried.

The woman said, "Are you the Realtor?"

Kelly looked at the dark house, then at the woman. Instinct took over. She nodded slowly.

"I'm Connie, the next door neighbor."

Kelly swallowed. "I . . . I was supposed to meet Miss Marshall," she said.

Connie smiled. "I know," she said. "She had to leave, though. I'm sure she told you . . ."

"Yes," Kelly said, her voice growing stronger, her back straighter as the lie sunk in. "Such a terrible thing."

Connie shook her head slowly, clicking her tongue. "Her father was one of my favorites," she said.

"Mine too."

"Anyway, she asked me to give you the key. No sense in your coming all the way here for nothing." She reached into her hoodie pocket, pulled out an envelope, and handed it to her. "Hope you get a bite."

Kelly forced a smile. "Thank you," she said. "Her brother left with her?"

"Huh?" she said. "Oh, you mean the young man? She never introduced me." Connie leaned in, gave her a wink. "Tell you the truth, she and I don't talk much. We move in different circles, I guess."

"Yep," Kelly said. "She and I do too."

Weird thing for a Realtor to say, but luckily Connie didn't seem to notice. She went around the front of the house, opened the door on a living room—hardwood floors, flat-screen TV, overstuffed leather couch, piled with Navaho print pillows. All of it tasteful, more elegant than the house's exterior—save for the cigarette stink hanging in the air and Kelly's own, seventeen-year-old face staring down at her from the opposite wall: *Mona Lisa,* in all its glory.

"Haven't you done anything since 1992?" she said to the empty room. "Don't you have anything else you can be proud of?"

Kelly noticed something holstered onto the right side of the big wooden frame. When she moved closer, she saw that it was a remote. She yanked it away, pressed the button, heard her own voice, young and sad and pathetically hopeful. "*I miss you. Why won't you visit?*"

Kelly gritted her teeth. She winged the remote across the room. It smashed into a framed, black-and-white photo of Bellamy, breaking the glass.

Great, she thought. *Great.*

What was she doing here? What exactly did Kelly hope to accomplish now that Shane was off with his sister, now that his father was dead and covered in her fingerprints? How did she ever expect him to listen to her words without them being warped into something ugly by the living, breathing fun house mirror that was Bellamy Marshall, artist?

Kelly noticed a jacket hanging on the coatrack by the door—Shane's denim jacket. Same one he'd put on before leaving the house yesterday morning. *You'll come to the funeral, right? You'll hold my hand.* Kelly went to it. She held it up against her face and breathed in the clean smell of it, her eyes starting to tear up, her teenage voice still echoing out of the speakers. "*I miss you . . .*"

Shane and his squirreled-away bottles of pills, the conversations he would have with his father. Sunday nights, in his separate bedroom, his voice hushed so Kelly wouldn't hear. Shane, who slept apart from Kelly on her insistence, who never saw his own family except on Skype. Shane who had recently searched for Rocky Three on his computer . . .

It wasn't all Bellamy's fault that Shane had left Kelly. Maybe none of it was.

"*I miss you. Why won't you visit?*"

Kelly put the jacket down. She pressed the button on the remote until the room was quiet again. On the big, mission-style coffee table was a stack of cream-colored stationery sheets. She searched her bag for a pen but couldn't find one, so she opened the drawer of the coffee table and found a disarray of Post-its and pastels and discarded sketch pads. After all these years, Bellamy still couldn't keep her drawers straight . . .

Kelly found a pen and took a piece of stationery and wrote a letter to her husband. She told him the truth.

When she was finished, she folded up the letter into fourths and placed it in the inside pocket of Shane's jacket, same place he kept his extra lenses. He would find it there because he always checked that pocket—she knew that much about him, at least.

She got up, rehung Bellamy's photograph and tried her best to clean up the broken glass, dumping it all in the trash can under the kitchen sink, working quickly. After all, the real Realtor would be arriving any minute, showing up at the neighbors to pick up that key.

Last, she grabbed the remote and moved to replace it. She avoided *Mona Lisa* as best she could—her huge, pixilated, glitter and feather-festooned face—focusing only on the leather holster at the side of the frame, watching it so intently that when she started to slip the remote back in, she noticed something at the very bottom of the pouch. It glittered.

She pulled it out and stared at it—the golden heart at the end of the delicate chain. The two tiny diamonds, one slightly bigger than the other. For a long moment, she held the necklace in front of her eyes, unable to think, to move, to breathe.

CHAPTER 21

APRIL 16, 1980

aybe it fell off," Bellamy said over the phone.

"How could it have just fallen off?" Kelly said. "Clasps don't just come undone. Do they?"

"Sometimes."

"Oh no."

"Are you sure you didn't take it off at the party? We were pretty out of it."

"No," Kelly said. "I didn't take it off. I *would never take it off.*"

"Hey, relax. It's just a necklace."

"Not to me."

"Huh?"

"Nothing. I'm just . . ." She exhaled, breath shaky. "It was my sister's."

"Oh, Kelly, I'm sorry."

"She asked me to keep it. Right before she . . . I feel like I let her down."

"You didn't, okay? You were a great sister."

"You don't know that."

"Kelly?"

"Yeah?"

"You *are* a great sister. No matter what stupid jewelry you're wearing."

She swallowed hard. "Thank you."

"Listen. It'll probably turn up. And if not, I'll buy you a new one . . . Flora, keep your shirt on! I'm coming! Kelly, I've got to go to school, okay? The housekeeper's totally screaming at me. I'll call you when I get home."

Kelly hung up. She was standing in Jimmy's empty room. She stared at her reflection in the mirror—her tired eyes, the streak that Bellamy had put in her hair a week ago, now just a remnant, the platinum now just a slightly lighter shade of sand. Kelly touched the base of her throat, the spot where the diamonds used to be. "You're gone," she whispered. "I can't talk to you anymore."

Bellamy was wrong. She had to find the necklace.

Retracing her steps was hard to do without a car or any money, but there was a jar of quarters on Jimmy's nightstand. Kelly poured a bunch of them into her hand, ran out of the house, caught the bus to Sunset and Gower, and ran the five blocks to Vee's apartment building. The whole trip, she kept tapping her fingers against her bare neck, as though if she did that enough she might magically be able to bring them back, the two little diamonds. *Catherine and me.*

THE FRONT DOOR TO VEE'S CASTLE WAS LOCKED. KELLY HAD FORGOTTEN to call and tell him she was coming back and so she pounded on it, again and again with the side of her fist, hoping someone would hear. Finally, a little old lady came to the door. "You are a friend of the young actor's," she said.

"Yes," said Kelly. "How did you know?"

"I opened the door for you last night." She gave her a look—half amused/half disgusted. "You're wearing the same outfit."

"Oh. Um . . . Well . . . I uh . . . forgot something at the party . . ."

"That doesn't change facts. Or, for that matter, your clothes."

"Huh?" Kelly gave up. She headed up the stairs, fast as she could, rounding five, six, seven, eight flights. She knocked on the door. "Vee!" she called out. "I think I left something here!" Did it again, harder. "Vee!"

The door opened halfway. It took Kelly a few seconds to register that it wasn't Vee standing there—hair mussed, oxford shirt buttoned wrong, half his chest exposed. It was Vee's father. "Didn't I just give you a ride home?"

"Um . . ." She tried not to look at his chest, the thick patch of hair at the center.

"Let me guess. You're looking for Vincent."

"Yeah." She forced herself to smile. "I think I might have left something."

"You ran up one flight too many."

"Oh. I'm so sorry."

"It's fine, but Vincent's not at his place anyway. He had a breakfast meeting with some TV people." He smiled. "I know because I arranged it."

Kelly closed her eyes, opened them again, breathing through her nose, that panicky feeling returning. "Mr. McFadden?"

"Yes?"

"You didn't happen to find my necklace, did you? Last night or this morning? I . . . I think it might have fallen off at the party."

"I didn't see anything."

"Are you sure?"

His blue eyes narrowed. "Tell me what it looks like so Vincent and I can keep our eyes out for it."

She blinked at him. "It was the one I was wearing last night."

"I didn't notice."

"Yes you did."

"Excuse me?"

"*You were staring at it the whole time I was talking to you.*"

His smile dropped away. "What are you talking about?"

She cringed. Had she really said that out loud? "Sorry."

"Are you all right?"

"I'm just . . . I really liked that necklace. It was very special to me . . ."

"Obviously," he said.

"I guess . . . When we were talking . . . It seemed like you noticed it."

"Any reason why you aren't in school today?"

"I . . . uh . . . I'm on my way."

His jaw tightened. His eyes went hard, and for a second, his face looked familiar in a way she couldn't place. "Are you on drugs, Kelly?"

"No, sir." Her gaze dropped. On his neck, she saw a long scratch—angry and red. She heard movement in the apartment behind him. Light footsteps. A female sigh. "The . . . the necklace was gold," she said quickly. "A heart, with two little diamonds on it."

"Okay," he said.

"I just thought you might have . . ."

"I'll let Vincent know you were here."

"Thank you," she said. "Bye."

Kelly tore back down the stairs, face burning, footsteps landing hard. How could she have spoken to Vee's father like that? What was wrong with her? *It's just a necklace. It isn't Catherine. Catherine's dead and she always will be, whether you find it or not.*

Kelly made it down the final flight and through the lobby, apologizing in her head to John McFadden. As she pushed open the door, she tried not to think about the way he had looked at her, the coldness in his eyes. She thought of the fingernail scratch on his neck and the movement in his apartment and realized that on top of everything else, she'd interrupted him and a woman—probably that model, Cynthia Jones.

Great going.

She pushed open the front door and stepped out into the bright day and fished around in her pocket for more quarters. At least she had bus fare home.

What a dumb idea, coming here. She ventured one last look up at John McFadden's apartment. Again she saw the female figure behind the sheer draperies, the arms stretching up like a dancer . . . Kelly kept watching. She pulled the draperies open, gazed out at the street below, and for a few seconds, Kelly got a clear look at her—John McFadden's apartment guest. Her stomach dropped. She squeezed her eyes shut, as though they'd stopped working properly, and when she opened them again, she hoped and half-expected to see someone else. But there she was, peering out the window, then letting the drapes fall closed. Had she seen Kelly watching her?

It hadn't been Cynthia Jones standing in John McFadden's window, wearing a big T-shirt, nothing else. It had been the startle-eyed girl from the Mounds commercial. She couldn't have been more than thirteen years old.

BACK AT HOME, KELLY CALLED VEE THREE TIMES BUT HUNG UP BEFORE the phone started ringing. She couldn't talk to him, couldn't talk to Bellamy either. She didn't know what to say. Maybe she'd seen the girl wrong. Maybe it had been some kind of optical illusion created by reflections and the angle of the sun at that hour of day and her own panicky thoughts and it hadn't been the Mounds girl at all in John McFadden's window—just some skinny red-haired model who looked young but was actually grown up.

Maybe.

That had to be it. It would be too weird otherwise, and Kelly's life was so very weird already. She thought of the promise Mom had asked her to make. "*I don't want you spending time with that girl,*" she had said.

Would that have been such a bad thing? Without Bellamy she'd be friendless, yes. But she wouldn't have an arrest record, wouldn't have gotten suspended. She wouldn't have ever done cocaine or pot or mushrooms or speed or downers or acid. She wouldn't have learned how to shoot a gun and she wouldn't be flunking out of school, she'd still be getting Cs. She wouldn't have ever met Vee—perfect Vee, who had been weeping in her arms last night, Kelly couldn't remember the reason, though she did know it had made her profoundly, immeasurably sad . . .

She heard the door opening, Jimmy coming in. "Kelly?" he said. "You awake?"

His voice was like a punch to her gut. She caught a glimpse of herself in her mirror—her bare neck—and she fell apart.

"Kelly? Are you crying?"

Jimmy knocked softly on her door. She answered it, tears rolling down her cheeks. She looked up into her dad's tired, kind eyes. She hated herself for ever thinking John McFadden was a better father.

"What's wrong?" Jimmy said.

She hugged him, crying into his chest for a long time before she was able to speak. "I'm so sorry, Dad," she said.

"For what?"

"I . . . I . . ." *I didn't go to a girlfriend's house last night. I went to a party and I got drunk and did drugs and met some horrible people and . . .* She couldn't say any of that—not because it would get her in trouble. Jimmy had no idea how to punish Kelly. Both of them knew that. She couldn't say it because it would hurt him too much. "I lost the necklace," she said.

Jimmy pulled away. He watched Kelly's face. "That's why you're crying?"

"Yes." She swatted at her eyes. He pulled a cloth handkerchief out of his pocket, handed it to her—her dad giving her a handkerchief—which made her cry more.

"Honey, it's okay."

"It's not."

"It is."

"Get mad at me," she said, her throat clenching up. "Please get mad at me. I need you to."

"Listen," he said. "You want the truth? I'm not the one who gave Catherine that necklace."

She caught her breath, looked at him. "What?"

"I told you that whole story because I promised her I would. She made me swear that if anybody ever asked, the necklace was from me."

"But . . . why?"

"It was from . . . a friend," he said. "She didn't want your mother to know. She didn't want you to know either."

"What friend?"

Jimmy shoved his hands in his pockets. "Please don't ask me that." Kelly watched Jimmy, his slumped shoulders, his fried-egg eyes, starting to well. "I'm no good at keeping secrets," he said. "The few I have sometimes hurt worse than all my injuries put together."

"Me too," Kelly said.

"You're too young to have secrets, honey," he said. "By the time you're my age, you'll forget 'em anyway."

Kelly thought about the girl in John McFadden's window—a girl even younger than Catherine had been two years ago. She touched the spot on her neck where the diamonds should be, hoping what Jimmy said was true.

"Don't worry about it," he said. "You lose things. You survive. It's what life's about."

He patted her on the shoulder, said good night, and headed off for his own room. Kelly kept looking in the mirror, thinking about lost things—necklaces and people and also those little parts of yourself you lose when you see things you shouldn't—some of them more lost than others.

CHAPTER 22

MAY 30, 1980

K elly tossed the birdy into the air. It hung there for a few seconds, sparkling in the sunlight before she whacked it with the badminton racket. She loved this game. She'd never played it before—never even seen anyone play it, except for maybe on a TV show. But then a few weeks ago Bellamy's dad had set up the net in their yard "to get Shane and me out of the house," Bellamy had explained. She'd handed Kelly a racket and Kelly had taken to it instantly. She loved how the birdy lingered, holding still for her like nothing else in life seemed to be doing.

Today had been the last day of school. She had no idea what senior year would feel like, let alone next month or next week or even tomorrow.

"Good one!" Bellamy smacked the birdy back over the net. Kelly returned it easily and the birdy nose-dived into the soft grass on the other side before Bellamy could get anywhere near it. "You've got super-good aim," Bellamy said.

"Thanks." Kelly said. *Now's the time. Tell her now.*

For the past month, before and after her two-week suspension, Kelly had been wanting to tell Bellamy about the girl she'd seen in John McFadden's window—something easier said than done. Bellamy had other friends besides Kelly, and during Kelly's suspension she began relying more on their company, shopping after school with them, going to their parties—tanned, grinning groups of shimmering stars' kids who wanted nothing to do with a nobody like Kelly.

Vee's party, the Jailbird Party, was probably old news to Bellamy and the morning after even more so. But it haunted Kelly's thoughts— and she was spending so much time alone with those thoughts . . .

Once she started going back to school, Kelly had been making plans to get together with Bellamy every chance she could. She'd call and invite herself over or pass Bellamy a note, asking if she wanted to go to McDonald's in the afternoon. Once or twice, she'd even invited Bellamy over to Jimmy's place, embarrassing as it was with the plastic flowers in the window box, the old lady next door gaping from around her draperies. She needed, so badly, to talk to her about the girl.

Bellamy said yes every time, which was encouraging. But much as she rehearsed speeches in her mind, Kelly just couldn't get herself to bring up the subject of the girl in John McFadden's window—especially when she was stoned, which she was most of the time when she was with Bellamy. Kelly would smoke a little pot and wind up staring too hard at her own memories. She'd start to doubt them, the image of the Mounds girl going hazy and dreamlike in her mind, her features rearranging themselves. Kelly would start to question the way her brain had been working the morning she'd gone to the castle, hungover as she'd been, upset over the missing necklace. *Maybe it had been Cynthia Jones in the window after all,* she would think. *Maybe it had been no one—just a shadow.* Paranoid, she'd wind up keeping quiet. "*Penny for your thoughts,*" Bellamy would say, and Kelly would just laugh and take another hit or ask if she wanted to go outside, play a game of badminton.

But the thought continued to nag at her—John McFadden, standing in his barely opened doorway, the hard look in his eyes, the scratch on his neck. Sometimes, she would even see him in dreams, smiling at her with snake's teeth, opening his door wider, rearing back and ready to bite.

"Your serve," Bellamy said.

She dropped the racket, sat down on the grass. "Hey. Can I talk to you about something?"

"Sure." Bellamy slipped under the net and collapsed next to her.

"Remember at the party, how you said John McFadden is weird?"

Bellamy plucked at one of her silver bracelets, looked down at the bright green grass. "Yeah."

"What did you mean by that?"

"That's what you wanted to talk about? Really?" She laughed a little. Kelly didn't.

Bellamy sighed. "Just . . . he's one of those obsessive director types, you know? And he isn't very nice to Vee." She cleared her throat. "Don't worry, though. Your screen test will go fine."

"This isn't really about the screen test."

"It's not? Well . . . wait a second." Her gaze drifted past Kelly's shoulder. "*Get out of here!*" She shouted it at the big magnolia tree next to her house, then jumped to her feet and waited, glaring at the tree until two skinny legs emerged from the tallest branch, followed by the rest of Kelly's little brother. "Unbelievable," she said, Shane shimmying down the side of the tree with Bellamy watching him, hands on her hips. "I swear to God, he's like a monkey," she said. "An *incredibly annoying, ugly little monkey who never leaves me the hell alone!*"

With both hands, Shane grabbed onto a lower branch and hung there, swinging back and forth like a chimpanzee. "Ooo oooh aaa aaa!" he shrieked.

"Go away!"

He dropped to the ground. *"You're not the boss of me!"* he shouted in his squeaky little voice, so much smaller than he thought he was.

Bellamy started toward him, but he scurried away, took off around the side of the house. "Seven whole years, I got to be an only child," Bellamy said. "It isn't fair."

Kelly stared at the tree, thinking about Shane, still a tree-climbing little boy, a little monkey, not even half grown up yet. And Shane was just two years younger than the Mounds girl.

"Bellamy."

"Yeah?"

"About a month ago . . . I saw something."

"What do you mean?"

"John McFadden . . ."

"We're still talking about him?" She sighed heavily. "Can we play and talk at the same time?"

"No." Kelly felt as though she were standing at the edge of a cliff, but there was a raging fire barreling toward her. She had to jump and she had only seconds to do it.

"Oookay, weirdo," said Bellamy. "What did you see?"

Kelly jumped. She told Bellamy about going back to the castle to look for her necklace, about knocking on Vee's father's door by mistake. She told her how strange John McFadden had seemed, so secretive and angry, told her about his unbuttoned shirt and the scratch on his neck and the sound she'd heard—a girl's sigh. The whole time, Bellamy kept picking at one piece of grass, ripping it to shreds. "There was a girl in there," Kelly said, "in John McFadden's apartment. I saw her."

Finally Bellamy looked at her. "I saw her too. Remember? In the window? He's been screwing that model Cynthia Jones."

"It wasn't Cynthia Jones."

"No, it totally was. It's been all over the gossip magazines."

"Bellamy. It was the Mounds girl."

"Who?"

"That girl from Vee's party. The *kid*. She's like an eighth grader at the most."

Bellamy stared at her for a long time. She plucked at her bangle bracelets, wiped her nose. "Did you ever find your necklace?"

"No. But . . . Are you serious, Bellamy? *Did you hear what I said?*"

She nodded. "I heard you."

"So . . . What do we do?"

Bellamy pushed a lock of hair out of her eyes. "We go up to my room," she said, very quietly. "We get super-stoned. You forget you ever saw what you did. I forget you ever told me about it."

"But—"

"Kelly."

"What?"

"Stop."

Kelly blinked at her. Bellamy pulled herself to standing, brushed the grass off her shorts. "Just be glad," she said quietly, "that you're too old for him."

She gave Kelly a hand up. The two of them picked up their rackets, started heading toward the house.

Kelly followed her into the house, into the kitchen where Bellamy grabbed a bag of Doritos off the counter, then up the stairs, into her room. Bellamy locked the door, opened her window wide. The magnolia tree had just started to bloom, and the sweet, buttery scent swept into the room as Kelly tore at the bag, Bellamy sliding open her vanity drawer, sneaking out her Baggie full of weed and rolling papers—same drawer where, a month earlier, Kelly had found the other Baggie, the blood-crusted razor. She thought about that razor and her mother's years-old box of chocolates and how, a few nights ago, she'd gotten up to get a glass of water and heard Jimmy crying in his sleep, saying Mom's name.

So many things better left unsaid and she'd heard them all. She knew too many things she didn't want to know.

Bellamy couldn't finish rolling the joint fast enough. Once she was done, the two of them smoked the whole thing, taking long, gulping drags, exhaling out the open window, neither one of them saying a word until only ashes were left and they were both numb, floating.

Bellamy unlocked her bedroom door, shoved a tape in her VCR. The screen lit up, and before long, they were looking at the mouth of a saxophone and then, the cute boys of Madness in their fedoras and mod clothes, bouncing and weaving to "One Step Beyond."

"Our song," said Bellamy. She grabbed a fistful of Doritos, handed Kelly the bag, and she turned the volume up, full blast. Kelly forced her mind back to that first day of meeting Vee, to the three of them racing round and round Bellamy's Rabbit. She remembered how Vee had laughed, how thrilling that was to see, the first time she'd ever seen someone that perfect-looking laugh that hard and with all those angry drivers blasting their horns around them, that saxophone wailing . . .

A whole other world. Kelly had barely known Bellamy and Vee that day. She'd never heard of his father.

Kelly shoved a few Doritos in her mouth and put her head on Bellamy's shoulder.

Bellamy threw an arm around her, kissed her forehead. She smelled of pot and herbal shampoo. "My sister," she said.

There was a knock on the door. Sterling Marshall stuck his head in. His hair was glossy and his dark eyes twinkled and he wore a blue-and-white-striped Oxford that picked up his movie star tan.

"Please turn the music down, girls."

"Okay, Dad." Kelly hoped she didn't have orange Dorito dust all over her face. She scooted over to the TV, turned the volume down.

"Oh, before I forget, Kelly," he said. "John's girl didn't know how to get hold of you, but he's got a break from shooting *Resistance* at the end of next week. He can see you on June seventh, at two P.M. in his Century City office."

"Um . . ."

"You should write this down."

"Huh?"

He frowned at her. "Your screen test," he said. "With John McFadden."

She swallowed hard. "Oh," she said. "Okay."

"All right then. I'll let him know I told you." He closed the door.

Kelly turned to Bellamy, confused, a little scared. "Bellamy," she said. "I don't really want to be an actress. I just said I'd do the screen test so you guys would like me."

But all Bellamy did was grin. "Did you just call my father Dad?" she said. "Oh my God, that's so cute!"

"I HAVE A BOYFRIEND!" BELLAMY SAID RIGHT AFTER KELLY PICKED UP the phone, first thing the next morning. Not even a "Guess what?" Not even a "Hello." Kelly was still half asleep. She'd gone into the kitchen to answer the phone with her eyes still closed, stubbing her toes twice on the way. She glanced at the kitchen clock. 7:00 A.M. Parts of her dream still swirled around in her head—Vee smiling up at her, his head in her lap . . .

A sound escaped from Jimmy's room, a type of half breathing/half snoring, so loud she figured Bellamy could probably hear it. Kelly once watched a TV movie—Robby Benson dying on a respirator. That's what the sound reminded her of. It worried her a little, though for Jimmy it was probably normal. Last night, when she'd come home, he'd been in bed already, door closed, snoring and moaning. It had been only 8:00 P.M. What if he just started sleeping forever? He hadn't worked for two weeks, and since school was out, he didn't have to get up and make Kelly's lunches, so it was possible.

Bellamy said, "Did you hear me?"

"You have a boyfriend?"

"I was going to tell you yesterday, but you got me all distracted."

Jimmy let out a long, pained groan. Kelly winced.

"What's going on over there?"

"My dad's sleeping."

"Huh? Okay. Anyway, he's an actor in Vee's new movie *Resistance*."

Kelly swallowed hard. Vee had been cast in a small part in his dad's latest. "Your boyfriend is in the John McFadden movie."

"Uh-huh." Not even a pause. Not one minute of knowing, of understanding. *You forget you ever saw it. I forget you ever told me.* Bellamy Marshall, girl of her word . . .

Kelly said, "What's your boyfriend's name?"

"Steven Stevens. Isn't that cute?"

"That's his real name?"

"He goes by Steve."

"Wow."

"Anyway, Steve plays the best friend of the male lead and he's older and totally mint. Like, he makes Vee look like a dog."

"How old is he?"

"Not *that* old." She said it with a bite. *Guess she does remember.* "He's nineteen."

"Oh," Kelly said. "Okay."

"And you know what, Kelly? John McFadden isn't that bad. He's been really nice to Vee on set."

Kelly rolled her eyes. "That's great."

"He treats him like a real actor, not just his kid. I bet your screen test goes great."

Kelly wanted to tell her that not everybody is able to forget things just like that, that it might take her a few days before she joined the John McFadden fan club. "You know . . ." she started. But then she stopped. "I don't hear anything," she said.

"Huh?"

Once, one of Kelly's movie magazines had run an interview with a soap opera actor who had survived a plane crash. The actor had described how quiet the airplane had been right before the flight crew made the announcement. "*You could hear a pin drop,*" he had said. "*And let me tell you. That absolute silence, in an airborne jet, was more terrifying than an explosion would have been.*" The silence, the actor explained, had meant that both the plane's engines had died.

"Are you still there?" Bellamy said.

"Hold on a second."

Kelly put the phone down, ran to Jimmy's room, pushed open the door. Blackout curtains shaded the window, the room washed in darkness. Even with the door open, it took her eyes a few minutes to adjust in this room, this thoroughly quiet room. She went for his bed, kicking an empty bottle, the clink the only sound. "Dad!" She clicked on the light on his nightstand, took hold of his shoulders, shook him hard. He didn't move, didn't speak. His face stayed still, his eyes shut. There was a bluish tint to the skin around his mouth. Kelly fell to her knees. Put her ear up to his nose, his mouth. "Dad!" she screamed again.

He wasn't breathing.

"DO YOU HAVE ANYBODY YOU CAN CALL, HONEY?" SAID THE EMER-
gency room doctor. "How about your mom?"

Kelly looked up—not at the doctor. At the clock on the wall. It was almost noon. She'd been here, in the waiting room at Hollywood Presbyterian, for four hours. "I want to see my dad," she said.

"I know, sweetie," said the doctor—a female doctor with big pitying eyes behind thick glasses. "But that's not gonna be possible for a while."

"How long is a while?"

"Forty-eight hours."

Across from her, a Mexican woman who couldn't speak any English held a baby that wouldn't stop screaming. The woman and the baby were the only two other people waiting right now, but since she'd been here, Kelly had seen an older man complaining of heart attack symptoms, a panicky mom whose little girl had swallowed bleach, and a boy a few years older than she was rushed in on a stretcher, his leg mangled in a motorcycle accident. Two out of three of them had been treated and left. Even the boy with the mangled leg was seeing visitors. Kelly tried again. "I want to see my dad. Please."

"I know it's a long time," the doctor said. "But that'll be how long it takes to detox."

"Detox?"

"You seem like a smart girl so I'm not going to sugarcoat it. Your dad overdosed on Percocet. You know what that is?"

She nodded.

"So your dad took around ten times the prescribed amount, mixed with a significant amount of alcohol."

Kelly stared at her, awful thoughts running through her mind—Elvis and Keith Moon and Sid Vicious and all those other celebrities she'd read about in her gossip magazines, lifeless on hotel room floors or curled up around toilets, choking on their own vomit, dead on arrival. The screaming headlines: TRAGIC OD, DRUG CASUALTY, GONE TOO SOON . . . She thought about all the times she'd given Jimmy his pills, his glass of Jack on the rocks, and wished she could punch herself, pound her head into the wall. Wished she could take all the pills Jimmy had taken, so she could feel nothing like him.

"He'll be fine," the doctor said. "He didn't stop breathing long enough to incur much brain damage."

"Much?"

"We just need to clean him out, dust him off, he'll be good as new." She looked at her. "But I am going to make a pitch for the Betty Ford Center."

Kelly tried to smile. "That's a good idea," she said, thinking, *Not much brain damage.*

"So," the doctor said. "Your mom? Should I call her?"

Kelly shook her head. She heard herself say, "I don't have a mom."

"Your dad said . . ."

"He's wrong."

"Well, do you have a family friend? You are a minor, and if there's no one to take care of you, I will have to contact foster services . . ."

"I have a family friend," Kelly said quickly.

The doctor introduced her to a nurse, who brought her to the front desk, let her use the phone. She called Bellamy first, but Flora the housekeeper said she'd gone out. Weird. Bellamy had said "Call me if you need me" this morning, right before Kelly had hung up with her to call the hospital. Had she shut Kelly and Jimmy out of her mind, just like she'd shut out the girl in John McFadden's window?

Next, she called Vee's apartment. He picked up fast. "You're lucky you caught me here," he said. "I was just getting a few things." It wasn't until she heard his voice that she realized how much she'd missed him these past few weeks while he'd been away shooting *Resistance*. "Kelly?" he said. "You sound like you've been crying. Are you okay?"

"My dad stopped breathing this morning."

"What?"

She told him everything—from waking up to Bellamy's phone call on, her voice cracking, breaking over the details. When she got to telling him how she'd pounded on her dad's chest, how she'd shaken him and driven her fists into him, she felt it again, that blind, awful panic. "I love him so much," she said. "Why couldn't I make him stay?"

Vee said, "Oh my God, if that ever happened to my dad . . ."

Kelly started to cry.

"We'll be right there," said Vee. "You can stay with us. Long as you need to."

She could barely speak. "Thank you."

After she hung up and sat back down in the waiting room again, Kelly let Vee's words sink in. She ran them over in her mind. "*We'll* be right there," he had said. "You can stay with *us*."

And sure enough, when he arrived at the waiting room forty-five minutes later, Vee wasn't alone. His father was there, standing right behind him, his hands crossed over his chest. "Your dad is one of the strongest men I've ever worked with," he said to Kelly. "I know he'll pull through this."

Vee rushed over to her, hugged her hard. She put her arms around him but her gaze stayed fixed on John McFadden, her whole body tensed, a feeling coursing through her . . . a growing, tearing rage.

"It's okay," Vee said. "It's okay."

Kelly couldn't reply. She stared at John McFadden and the world turned in on itself, crushing her, taking bits away . . . *Why didn't I see it before? How could I not have known?* But she couldn't say a word about it, not to Vee. How could she? A dim, drunken memory unfolded in her brain. Vee at the Jailbird Party, crying into her neck . . . "I loved her," he had said. "I loved Catherine."

Kelly hugged Vee tighter, tears springing into her eyes.

"It's okay," he said. "I'm here."

"I want my dad," she whispered, crying for Jimmy and for Vee. Poor Vee, who believed he had a father worth wanting.

John McFadden was dressed all in black. He was wearing the same mirrored aviator glasses, so there was no mistaking it, no lying to herself, no looking away. John McFadden was the man in the Porsche. He was the older man who had taken Catherine home.

CHAPTER 23

*Guess who was spotted in a corner table at the Polo Lounge, sharing a bottle of Cristale—and what looked like a whole lot more? None other than stunning model **Cynthia Jones** and Oscar-nominated director **John McFadden**! Seems Cynthia's got a part in the lensman's latest, which has made for some steamy hanky-panky away from the cameras! Sipping champagne with leggy beauties isn't the usual for McFadden, 40—a teetotaler who's known for making movies, not moves. But it seems gorgeous Cynthia, 25, has stolen his heart—and changed his stick-in-the-mud ways. "This is a big deal for John," reveals a pal. "The last lady he romanced like this was his ex-wife, [model **Leilani Valle**]."*

John McFadden has a type—and it sure is pretty!

EXCERPTED FROM
a column in
Rona Barrett's Hollywood
magazine
May 17, 1980

CHAPTER 24

APRIL 23, 2010

arry called Kelly Lund's cell two more times from Sterling Marshall's burner. It went straight to voice mail both times. Obviously her phone was turned off or the battery was dead. But he'd have been lying if he said it didn't make him smile, just a little, to know that when she charged up her phone again, she would be greeted, *Twilight Zone*–style, by three missed calls in a row from the man she killed.

May have killed. Innocent until proven guilty.

What Barry wished—what he'd trade in his house and his car and possibly every sexual experience he'd ever had in his life for—was a recording of the 11:49 P.M. phone conversation between Kelly and her father-in-law. Because, while the call had drawn a distinct line between Kelly and Sterling Marshall on the night of his death, the dead man had been the one to draw it.

Marshall had called Lund, not the other way around—which, in Barry's book, raised more whys than anything else. The call had been close to midnight—the last call he would ever make, according to the records they had. And they weren't exactly prone to late-night confidences, Kelly and Sterling. In fact, everyone in the family claimed they never spoke at all—including Kelly herself.

"Why do you suppose he called her?" Barry said to Louise as they headed upstairs to the scene of the crime.

"I've been thinking about that."

"Maybe he wanted to tell her about his cancer like he did with Shane. Bury the hatchet or whatever?"

"Seems like a weird reason to buy a burner."

Barry nodded. "Yep. Agree." He still couldn't figure it out, and he'd been running scenarios through his head ever since he'd pressed redial and heard Kelly Lund's voice mail recording. Making things even more puzzling, the call to Kelly was the only one that had been made from the burner. When they checked the phone's call record, there had been no other numbers listed before or after it.

"I do have a theory," Louise said as they climbed the last of the pink marble stairs, Barry focusing on them more than he should have been. *Where do you find pink marble, anyway?* They reminded him of the Barbie Dreamhouse his niece, Kaitlyn, used to have. Such a cute kid, but Chris's first wife had gotten full custody and moved across the country and Barry hadn't seen her in a dozen years. Jesus, she'd be graduating high school in June . . .

"You listening?" Louise said.

"Yeah. What's your theory?"

"I don't think Kelly Lund killed him."

"Why not?"

"Well, for one thing, he's dying anyway—his cancer had progressed a lot more than he let on to his wife and kids, and I think she knew that. I think he may have told her."

Barry shook his head, thinking again of Kaitlyn, his only niece. Chris's only child. Did his dickhead brother ever think of Kaitlyn when he was bleaching teeth or collecting wives? Late at night in his mini-manse, did he ever fill a bowl and take a hit and think of that cute little girl with the Barbie Dreamhouse, now a complete stranger and the same age Kelly Lund had been when he'd tormented Barry with her picture? "We're all dying, Louise," he said.

"Wow. Okay, Mr. Nietzsche."

As they reached the study, Barry pulled out his phone and put in a quick call to Kelly Lund. "Hi, Mrs. Marshall," he said, making sure to use the name she preferred. "This is Detective Dupree. Please call me back as soon as possible." He ended the call, put the phone back in his pocket.

Louise tried again. "Okay," she said, "first of all, Sterling Marshall was basically supporting her."

"Huh?" Barry said, but then it dawned on him what she was talking about. Last night, outside the Hollywood station, that writer Sebastian Todd had told them how Kelly Lund had managed to find a good paying job right out of prison.

"Remember? That cheaters' Web site she writes the profiles for. Sterling Marshall was a silent partner. He got her that job."

"Kelly Lund doesn't know that, though."

"Maybe she does, maybe she doesn't."

"Sebastian Todd says she doesn't."

"Regardless, he bought her and Shane their house. She's got to know *that*. He paid for it outright."

"So?"

"So maybe he didn't hate her as much as everyone thought he did." She gave him a meaningful look. "Maybe there are other burners that no one knows about. Other conversations that were just between the two of them . . ."

"What are you getting at?"

"He's very good at keeping secrets. Would you have guessed, in a million years, that husband and father-of-the-year Sterling Marshall was part owner of a hookup site for philanderers?"

"I don't know." He thought about what Hank Grayson had told him, how twenty-odd years ago, Sterling had managed to keep Shane out of jail, his violent freak-out away from the press, with only immediate family, arresting officers (and, of course, that poor chef) the wiser. He didn't say it, though . . .

"What if he had something going on with Kelly?" Louise said. "What if Shane found out?"

He winced. "Sterling Marshall wasn't that kind of guy."

"He's an *actor*."

"He never visited her in prison. Never wrote a letter to the parole board."

"He didn't need to write letters," she said. "Sterling Marshall was a string-puller."

Barry sighed. A group of uniforms passed them, nodding and smiling. *If they only knew what we've been talking about.*

Once they were out of earshot, Louise said, "You ever wonder why Bellamy Marshall despises Kelly Lund?"

"Because of what she did to her father."

"Exactly."

"I meant killing his best friend."

"I didn't."

"Louise," he said. "She's married to his son."

"It's Hollywood."

Barry said, "Okay, fine. Sterling Marshall and Kelly Lund have been having a steamy and incredibly disgusting affair for years. That doesn't mean she didn't kill him. If we go with your story, she's got a motive. He could have called her on that burner. Broken things off.

He's dying, like you said. Maybe he wanted to make things right and told her so and she couldn't handle that."

"True," she said. "But we still don't know who that is on the surveillance video."

Inside the study, the crime scene techs were still bagging evidence, taking pictures. Barry had been in here briefly before, but it had been yesterday, just after his interview with Kelly Lund, when he was still getting acclimated. He paid more attention now—he saw the blood, so much of it, pooling on the floor, spattered across the bookshelves, thick, dark gobs of it, hanging from the draperies. The opposite of a clean kill, which could support Louise's theory, if you bent it that way. Somebody had obviously been very angry. "Footprints," Barry said, pointing to the floor. He could make out several sets of them in the cordoned-off area, which made sense—Mary and Bellamy had both been in the room with the body before calling the police. Both women, they had told them, took a size six shoe.

"Did you see this one?" Louise crouched down and pointed to a sneaker imprint—the logo visible at the center.

"Adidas?"

"Size eight," she said. "Men's. There was another one in the kitchen."

BACK IN THE DEN, MARY MARSHALL LOOKED A GOOD DEAL WORSE than she had half an hour ago—pale and drawn, her head lolling back in a way that made Barry pretty sure she'd gotten into the pills again.

But when Louise asked if they could "shoot her a few questions" about Kelly Lund, she didn't fall asleep or tell Barry and her to go screw themselves, as Barry imagined she would. She even managed to lift her head and look at them. "Sure," she said, the word hissing out of her, her eyes working to be alert.

"We could always come back at another time, ma'am," Barry said.

But she shook her head. "No, no, no," she said. "I want to help."

"You happen to know what shoe size your son takes?" Louise asked.

"Not sure," she said. "Eight or nine, maybe?"

Louise wrote it down in her notebook.

"I thought you wanted to ask me about Kelly Lund."

"We do, ma'am," said Barry.

Mary leaned back, energy seeping back out of her. "She was such a sweet girl when she was young," Mary said. "Always said hello to me. None of Bellamy's other friends would give me the time of day."

Barry looked at her. "So you guys liked Kelly, when she was a kid?"

She shook her head. "I liked Kelly," she said. "Sterling didn't. He never said why . . ." Her eyelids fluttered closed for a few moments. "What were we talking about?"

Louise said, "Kelly Lund."

"You know what's strange?" Mary said.

"Yes?"

"I've been married to Sterling for fifty-one years, and there are still so many things I never knew about him." She pulled the handkerchief from her sleeve, swatted away at a tear. "I didn't know how close he and John McFadden were until John was shot. I didn't know that John McFadden had given Sterling his gun—or even that Sterling had any desire to own a gun—until I found him dead in his study."

"You didn't know he had a gun?" Louise said. "Really?"

"I know it sounds strange," she said. "But at this point in my life, I know for a fact that the reason why Sterling and I stayed married—the only reason at all as to why we were so compatible, so happy . . ."

"Yes?"

"We were never honest with each other. About anything." She smiled—a sad, vacant smile.

Louise gave Barry a look.

"Stop it," he said, very quietly.

"Oh you're here!" Mary said, her face lighting up as Bellamy Marshall walked into the room, trailing expensive perfume. She wore a deep red blouse with three buttons undone, tight jeans, black hair washed and shiny—a 100 percent improvement over yesterday. Barry made a point of not gawking at her, though she really did clean up well.

"I'm sorry we're late," Bellamy said. She gave her mother a quick hug and then made way for her brother, who held on longer, tighter. She smiled at Barry. "We hit a lot of traffic," she said.

Barry's gaze traveled to the mother, looking at her daughter as though she was drowning, Bellamy the last lifeboat.

What did that mean: *We were never honest with each other. About anything.*

Shane Marshall cleaned up well too—although to be fair, Barry had only seen him passed out in a holding cell, and there were very few sentient beings who couldn't clean up better than the way he'd looked then. When he pulled away and sat down, Barry noticed how sallow Shane's skin was, the dark circles and that look in his eyes . . . It was something beyond grief. Something tired and defeated and drained of hope. Instinctively, Barry looked down at Shane Marshall's shoes—hiking boots. Probably more of a size ten. "Detective Braddock?"

"Yes?"

"I'd like to change my previous statement," he said. "What I told you yesterday."

Louise tapped on her notebook, flipped the page. "Which one?" she said.

He tried to smile, then gave up. He shoved his hands into his pockets, but not before Barry noticed that they were shaking. "I want to change what I told you about my wife," he said. "About my wife being home last night."

"HE'S BEEN IN A GOOD MOOD TODAY," AN OVERLY CHEERFUL NURSE named Dahlia said when Kelly first showed up at the rest home where her father lived—a place called Hollywood Haven that reminded her of an efficiency motel, but with a heavy smell in the air—ammonia and air freshener and something else underneath, something cloying and stale and sad. The place hadn't changed much in five years—same beige and gold color scheme, same bright lights and impressionist prints on the walls of the common room, same TV flickering probably the same daytime game show, same number of men and women parked in front of it, some hooked up to IVs, no one speaking.

"I think it's because we gave him a shave," Dahlia said.

"Huh?"

"Your father," she said, a slight sting beneath the sugar. "A good shave always makes him happy. You might not know that?"

"I didn't."

She peered at Kelly. "When was the last time you were here?"

"Five years ago."

"Oh. Well . . . nice you're here now."

Kelly felt a tinge of guilt—Dahlia's intention, no doubt. Of course Dahlia was new here—too young to be anything but new here, really— and so she had no way of knowing that Kelly's father hadn't raised her from birth, that the sum total of her memories of Jimmy Lund consisted of four months thirty years ago, two or three prison visits, and one hazy, soft-focus trip to Disneyland, back when she and Catherine were too small for any of the E-ticket rides. A memory flitted into her mind— the visiting room at Betty Ford, Jimmy smiling and clear-eyed. *"We'll show 'em all, kiddo. You and me. We're stronger than anybody knows."*

"Your daughter is here, Mr. Lund." The nurse ushered Kelly into her father's room, a sparse, dimly lit space with a single chair, a night-stand, a tiny closet, and a hospital bed. The only personal touch was the bedspread—the same maroon plaid comforter Jimmy used to keep folded on the couch at his old house. More than once, Kelly had draped that comforter over him when she'd found him passed out in front of the TV, and now, here it still was, covering her barely conscious father—the only person in the room. The second bed and the shouting man in it had both vanished since her previous visit; Kelly didn't want to ask where. A lot can happen in five years, and in places like this, it usually does.

Jimmy was propped up to sitting, an uncertain smile on his face. Kelly tried to smile back. "Hi, Dahlia," he said to the nurse.

"I'm going to leave you two alone." Dahlia gave Kelly a pointed look. "You probably have a lot of catching up to do."

Kelly wasn't sure what to do. She wasn't much of a hugger these days, especially with strangers—and from the way he was looking at her, she was pretty sure that's what she was to him.

"They gave me a shave," Jimmy said.

"Dahlia told me you like that. Getting a shave."

"I just say that because it makes her smile at me."

Kelly pulled a chair next to his bed and sat down. "You look very nice," she said. He did. His steel gray hair was neatly brushed and he had on a crisp army-green sweatshirt, a white T-shirt underneath that brought out the whites of his eyes and made him look more alert.

She thought back to the first day she'd knocked on his door, kicked out of her apartment, alone and terrified, nowhere else to go. Kelly hadn't really known Jimmy—only heard about him from her mother. She'd expected a crazed, angry drug addict. But she'd gotten the oppo-site. Kelly could still remember the door flying open, the way those watery eyes had lit up. "*Kiddo!*" he'd said, hugging her as though he'd been waiting for her forever. "*I just wish your sister could visit me too.*"

So many times, when she was locked up, Kelly would think about what her life would have been like if Jimmy had never OD'd. She'd had a lot of time to think about those "what ifs" at Carpentia, and this was such a huge one. If Jimmy hadn't OD'd, Kelly's life wouldn't have changed in the same way it had. She never would have found out about John McFadden and Catherine when she did because she wouldn't have asked Vee to pick her up at the hospital. If she hadn't seen John McFadden in his aviator glasses on that day—one week before her screen test—Kelly probably wouldn't have looked further. She wouldn't have made that awful discovery days before the *Resistance* wrap party. McFadden would probably be alive. Kelly wouldn't have been charged with his murder. Vee might have stuck around . . .

But there was more to it than that—something she couldn't help but think of now. If he hadn't OD'd and she hadn't gone to prison, Kelly might still be living with Jimmy. She might be the one taking care of him. That's how much she'd loved him back then. That's how much she'd loved having a real father.

"Do you know me?" she asked.

Jimmy gave her that uncertain smile again—a smile with nothing behind it other than basic decency, politeness, which was in Jimmy's fabric, as much a part of him as his scars. Interesting, most people had to work at being good, but for Jimmy it was a genetic trait. And judging from Kelly and Catherine, a recessive one.

"Sondra?" he tried.

"I'm not Sondra Locke, Dad." Kelly pulled her chair a little closer so he could see the necklace she was wearing—the necklace she'd taken from Bellamy's house. "See?" she said, lifting the delicate gold heart away from her throat to show him. "It's me."

Jimmy stared at the necklace. The smile fell away. Tears welled in his eyes.

"You remember me?"

He nodded quickly. He grasped her hand. "Catherine," he said.

"Kelly, Dad," she said. "I'm Kelly."

"Kelly . . . Kelly never called me Dad," he said. "She called me Jimmy."

She closed her eyes. "You're right. I'm sorry. I'm sorry, Jimmy."

"I should be sorry. I'm the one who let you down. I let everybody down."

"Jimmy."

"I was a bad father."

Kelly put a hand on the side of his face, brushed away a tear. "You weren't."

"I couldn't keep you out of jail. You shouldn't have gone to jail."

She shook her head. "I should have gone and I did," she said. "It's okay. I survived."

"That bastard deserved to die."

"McFadden."

"Yes. McFadden. I tried to tell them I killed him myself."

She thought back to her talk with Sebastian Todd. "You told Mom."

"She didn't believe me. The police didn't believe me either."

"Because it wasn't true, Jimmy." She plucked a Kleenex out of the box on the nightstand. "You didn't kill him."

"*He deserved to die*."

"Dad."

"He ruined my life."

"Because of *Demon Pit*? Your injuries? Why didn't you ever tell me about that? You said you got hurt on a horror film but you never . . ."

Her voice trailed off. He was shaking his head, again and again. "You okay?"

"It wasn't because of my damn injuries."

He closed his eyes. Kelly took his hand in hers. "It's okay," she said softly. "It's okay, Dad." She looked at his hands—the skin so dry it was cracked in places—scars over scars over years of battered muscle, the long, deep red blotches, burn marks that would never heal. She wanted answers. Needed them. But she didn't want to hurt him any more. Poor Jimmy, so much of his life spent hurting. "Maybe we should talk about something else."

"I'm okay," he said. He opened his eyes again, looked at her. His breathing settled, and it was as though he'd just landed after a long, rough flight. "Can you get me a cup of water? There's a stack of cups in the bathroom. It's right next door."

Kelly nodded. She left the room and went into the bathroom, filled one of the plastic cups with water from the sink. A nurse passed her in the hallway—same bright, fake smile on her face as Dahlia's. This place was a madhouse, really. No wonder Jimmy could hardly keep it together.

When she returned to her father's room and handed him the cup, she half-expected him not to recognize her, but he thanked her by name. He drank the whole cup before speaking.

"Why do you have that necklace, Kelly?"

"Catherine told me to keep it for her," she said, watching his face.

"Didn't you lose it though? A long time ago?"

"I found it," she said. "I found it today."

"Wow . . ." He swallowed hard. "Some things won't stay lost, I guess."

"Jimmy," she said. "Where did Catherine get this necklace? You told me that it was from a friend."

"Yes."

"Was it John McFadden? The friend? Is that why you hate him?"

"Let's talk about something else, honey."

"I need to know, Dad. It's important."

"I can't tell."

"Why not? John McFadden is dead."

"I know."

"Catherine is dead."

"I know that too."

"So who is this going to hurt?"

He began to tremble. A tear rolled down his cheek. "Me."

"You?"

"Secrets," he said. "They can kill you."

"What do you mean?"

His eyes started to cloud and shift, his gaze drifting over her head. Taking off again. "Secrets gnaw at your insides, and you try and kill 'em with booze . . ."

"Jimmy . . ."

"They kill you. They kill you every time." He started to cry. She tried to put her arms around him, but he pushed her away. "Can't cry in front of you, Sondra," he said. "You always were a pal."

Kelly let out a long, trembling breath. Bad idea. Cruel. *You try to get answers and you just make things worse. You always make things worse.* So often when she was young, Kelly wished she understood people better, wished she knew how to make them happy, calm them down, draw them in. The shrink at Carpentia had said she didn't care enough about others—that her mother had failed to teach her empathy during her toddler years and so she needed to learn late. But that had never been the problem. She cared about other people a lot. Maybe too much. She just didn't understand how most of them worked. "Shall I get the nurse?" she said.

Jimmy shook his head, the tears subsiding. He blew his nose. "Sondra?"

"Yes."

"Where did you get that necklace?"

She didn't reply.

"My daughter used to have one just like it." His gaze drifted back to her. *Landing*. He knew who she was.

The same look had been in Jimmy's eyes when he was on the witness stand, offering timid yeses and nos to the prosecutor's questions. From time to time he'd meet Kelly's gaze and try to smile and that's when she'd see it. Fear. Not a fear *of* Kelly—which everyone else seemed to have, including Bellamy and even Mom. It was a fear *for* her.

"Dad," Kelly said.

He shook his head. "No," he said. "No, Kelly. I can't tell you."

She exhaled.

He said, "I want to talk to Sondra."

Kelly nodded slowly. She placed her hand on his. "Jimmy," she said. "It's your pal Sondra."

"Hey, how's it going?"

"Not bad," she said. "Get to missing Clint sometimes."

"You were always too good for him, kiddo."

She smiled.

"I think you were going to ask me a question?"

"Yes, Jimmy, I was," she said. "Who was it that gave your daughter Catherine this lovely necklace?"

"No one."

She looked at him. "I don't understand."

"No one gave it to her. She took it. It belonged to her mother."

Kelly's eyes widened. "Her mother?" she said.

"Rainy Daye."

"Rainy Daye," she whispered, thinking back, way back, to Catherine's discovery—the box of zed cards in their mother's closet.

"You know what, Kelly? I don't think anybody really knows each other."

"Except you and me, right?"

"Except you and me."

"Rainy wore it to work on *The Demon Pit*. She was wearing it when I met her and when she and I got married, she threw it out. I swiped it. Figured the girls might want it someday, but that's before I knew who it was from. After I knew, I still kept it. Out of spite, I guess."

"Who was it from, Jimmy?"

"Catherine came to visit me once, and she found the necklace. She was always going through closets and drawers, that one. Always looking where she wasn't supposed to look . . ."

"She stole it?"

"Just started wearing it. I shouldn't have told her who it was from, but she caught me a few glasses of Jack in, caught me feeling sorry for myself . . ."

"Who was it from?"

"Catherine wore it around. That awful secret. Around her neck. I made her promise not to tell Kelly. I told Kelly the necklace was from me."

"I remember," Kelly said. "Who gave it to Rainy, Jimmy? Tell me. Please."

He took her hand in both of his, squeezed so tight it hurt. "I'm sorry," he said, and that sad fear took over his eyes, his face. "The necklace came from their father, Sondra. From Kelly and Catherine's real father."

OUTSIDE HOLLYWOOD HAVEN, KELLY FOUND IT HARD TO STAND UP— knees weak, head floating, a strange feeling coming over her, as though she were coming apart, atom by atom. She'd felt this way before, thirty years ago, the world pulled out from under her, up turning to down, black becoming red, friends disappearing.

Everything a lie.

It should only happen to a person once, yet there it was, the same ugly shock, lightning striking twice, burning everything to ashes. It all fell into place now, and in a different way than it had back then—Catherine's taunting of their mother, Rose's growing rage. "*Where did you get that necklace? Answer me!*" Rose had shrieked. And oh, how Catherine had delighted in not answering, the necklace her loaded weapon, reveling in that type of freedom that comes from leverage. Catherine could do anything back then—drop out of school, do drugs, screw her way through Hollywood, *live life up to its bendy edge* at just fourteen, fifteen years old.

She could steal her mother's car and run off to see John McFadden, a black-hearted Hollywood narcissist who had been older than Rose. Catherine could wind up dead in a canyon and Rose couldn't fight back. She had to stay silent, because keeping the secret had been that important. She had given up everything for it—including her own child.

Kelly's birth father had been that powerful.

She couldn't think too hard about him. Couldn't ask herself who her biological father was because she all but knew the answer for sure, and that answer was too ugly, too sad. The answer was in that necklace, stolen off her while she slept by a knowing Bellamy thirty years ago. It was in Bellamy's feelings toward Kelly, that sister-love turned to hatred, in her creation of a piece of art designed to keep her in prison—and away from her family—forever. It was in Kelly's mother's desperate attempt to keep her away from "Hollywood Royalty," Bellamy in particular and in the one letter Sterling Marshall had ever sent her, demanding she terminate her pregnancy, that she never have any children with his son.

Saddest of all, it was in the feeling she got when she looked at Shane—a pang in her heart that had nothing to do with really knowing him. She felt the same way about Bellamy. Bellamy who had once kissed her and said, "*We're sisters.*" Bellamy, with her slender, slashed wrists, forever hinting at her "secrets." Bellamy, who must have known the truth, even back then.

Call me Dad . . . My girl . . .

Credits scrolled through Kelly's mind. Sterling Marshall, executive producer on *The Demon Pit*—a film that had come out the same year Kelly and Catherine were born. Sterling Marshall, employing his best friend as director, his pregnant mistress as makeup artist. Poor Jimmy, falling in love with Rainy on that set, walking into that web . . .

"*I knew it . . . maybe a few months after you guys were born,*" Jimmy had told her, back in his room. "*I found a heart-shaped box of chocolates in her drawer with a note: 'For my three beauties,' it said. Unsigned. I threw out the note. Left the box. She didn't say a word about it and I didn't bring it up.*"

"*Why not?*"

"*I was scared.*"

"*Of what, Jimmy?*"

"*The truth.*"

Kelly could still see his face, his eyes misting over. "*As long as Rosie didn't say anything, I was still your dad.*"

All those years of living a lie, of keeping Rose's secret—a stand-in his whole life, even as a father. When Jimmy had moved out of the house, it had been because she'd kicked him out—Kelly remembered.

She remembered the fights, but she hadn't been able to hear what they were saying. Catherine had heard a little. Later, it seemed, she'd found out more, learning something even Jimmy didn't know: her birth father's name.

"*Why did you put up with all that?*"

"*Because I loved you. I loved all three of you. I always will.*"

Kelly started to choke up again. "*You deserved a better father,*" Jimmy had said, when the opposite was true. They didn't deserve him. Not a single one of them did.

She swatted a tear from her face, looked at her watch. Sebastian Todd should have been here by now. What was taking him so long? Her phone's battery dead as usual, her charger left behind in Joshua Tree, Kelly had called him from the front desk at the nursing home and asked him to take her to her mother's cult. Two hours away, Todd had said. In the middle of the desert. "I'd be glad to take you there," he'd told her, claiming to be "just around the corner." That had been more than half an hour ago.

Kelly was about to go back inside and call Todd again when he finally pulled up, behind the wheel of a gleaming white Mercedes that matched his white suit, the white frames on his sunglasses. He rolled down the window.

"You're late," she said.

He removed the sunglasses. "I'm sorry."

"Don't worry about it." She moved to open his passenger-side door, but he kept it locked. "Could you unlock the door please?"

"Kelly."

"Yeah?"

"I still don't believe you're a murderer."

"Huh?" She stepped back from the car just as she heard the sirens, two police cars pulling into the parking lot.

"I didn't have any other choice," he said. "Detective Dupree called me seconds after you did. I didn't know you were in trouble. I shouldn't have—"

"Can you get me a lawyer?"

He nodded.

She took off the necklace, dropped it on the front seat. "Give this to my mother," she told him as Dupree and his partner made for Kelly fast as sharks, all business. "It's hers."

CHAPTER 25

KELLY LUND'S SURPRISING FAN

As controversy continues to swirl around the shooting death of movie legend Sterling Marshall, his daughter-in-law Kelly Lund has been taken in for questioning. But while many believe her to be guilty, convicted murderer Lund has gained an unlikely ally.

Pulitzer Prize–nominated author Sebastian Todd—who detailed Lund's 1981 murder conviction in both the Los Angeles Times *and in the acclaimed true-crime opus,* Mona Lisa—*has now launched an attempt to prove Kelly Lund is not a killer after all. Claiming that Lund is innocent of both the Marshall murder and the 1980 shooting death of director John McFadden, for which she was found guilty and served twenty-five years in prison, Todd says his change of heart was inspired by a surprising conversation. "I've spoken to Kelly's mother," says Todd, who refuses to reveal the whereabouts of Rose Lund, said to have joined a commune after disappearing from her L.A. home in 1984, three years after Kelly Lund's incarceration. "Rose has convinced me of her daughter's innocence."*

Todd recently conducted a full-length interview with Mrs. Lund at an undisclosed location, in which he questioned her extensively on the McFadden murder in particular, the details of which will be forthcoming in the July issue of Vanity Fair. *"Like Kelly, Rose got a bad rap," says Todd of Mrs. Lund, who was said to have abandoned her daughter four months before the crime, leaving the troubled young girl in the care of her father, James Lund, a drug-addicted movie stuntman with questionable parenting skills. "She had already lost a daughter [Kelly's twin sister Catherine] to suicide and was going through a rough time in her life, but Rose never stopped caring," Todd says. "And she never stopped believing in her daughter's innocence."*

But will anyone else believe? Already, law enforcement officials are accusing Todd, a notorious publicity seeker, of stirring up controversy for the sake of future book sales. (He's rumored to be speaking to publishers about a Mona Lisa *sequel.) "There is no doubt in anyone's mind that we put the right person behind bars," says former U.S. attorney Lawrence Schwartz, who prosecuted the case and is now in private practice. "With all due respect, Mr. Todd should know better than to try to tip the scales of justice."*

And those old enough to remember the chilling photograph of a teenage Kelly Michelle Lund, smiling on the day of her sentencing, would no doubt agree. "The poor girl never had a chance," remarks clinical psychologist and talk show host Dr. Bob O'Neil. "It was almost as though she was raised to be a killer. Sterling Marshall's strikingly similar murder is proof enough to me that some folks are best off behind bars for good."

Yet whether his main interest is human rights or movie rights, Todd isn't going away anytime soon. "We're always quick to blame the girl," says the flamboyant journalist. "Especially the girl who can't cry on cue."

ABC News Online
April 24, 2010

CHAPTER 26

JUNE 7, 1980

I n Kelly's dream, all the windows exploded. She found herself lying on Vee's mattress in a pile of broken glass, both wrists gushing blood. She called out for Vee, but she knew he was at his father's house—that's where he'd been staying all week, Kelly alone at his apartment at her insistence, despite Vee's protests. "It's convenient" and "I like it there" her only excuses. And so, in her dream Kelly was all by herself and she bled and bled, paralyzed, unable to call for help. A shadow fell over her—a person, standing in the room. But it wasn't Vee in the dream. It was John McFadden standing over her, shirt unbuttoned to reveal his pale chest, the patch of hair, Catherine's heart-shaped necklace glittering at his throat.

Kelly wrenched her eyes open, woke herself up. Was it normal to have such horrible, violent dreams, or did that make her a psycho? She'd had so many in her life, most of them after Catherine's death, but it had been much worse since she started staying at Vee's apartment. At least two of these dreams a night, all starring John McFadden, all ending in bloodshed.

She glanced at the clock on the floor—2:00 A.M. She stood up, shaking. This couldn't go on—keeping the secret of who John McFadden really was, waking up to that knowledge, more awful than the dreams.

Worse still, Kelly couldn't shake the feeling that she didn't know the half of it, that the rough kiss outside the Porsche was just a few pages in a long, ugly book. She needed to know the rest. She couldn't sleep until she did.

Kelly moved into the kitchen. She turned on the light and got down on the floor, peering under the refrigerator, hoping for those diamonds . . . The necklace wasn't there. Of course it wasn't. She'd searched Vee's apartment up and down for Catherine's necklace, made it a part of her routine ever since she'd started staying here: wake up from a bad dream, look for the necklace, eat breakfast, take the bus to Betty Ford to visit Jimmy, bus back to this apartment, eat more, hang out with Vee and sometimes Bellamy, wait for them to leave, look for the necklace, go to bed. Dream again. It was a vicious circle and it was pointless.

Kelly was nearly certain of it now: John McFadden had given the necklace to Catherine. John McFadden had taken it away.

She pulled herself up to the kitchen counter and picked up the phone. Without thinking, she called the one person she didn't mind hurting with her knowledge—the one person who might be able to tell her more. *She'll be awake. She'll be up cleaning.*

Sure enough, Rose picked up after one ring.

"I need to talk to you."

"Kelly?"

"Tell me about Catherine's Valentine."

"What?"

"On the last night of Catherine's life, she told you she was going to see her Valentine."

"Are you on drugs, Kelly?"

"No," she said. "But Jimmy OD'd."

"What?"

God, Kelly needed a cigarette. She spotted a hard pack of Marlboro Reds next to the kitchen sink. She picked it up. Shook it. Empty.

"Kelly?"

"Jimmy overdosed a week ago."

"Oh my God. Why didn't you tell me?"

"He's in rehab," Kelly said. "He'll be okay."

"Do you . . . would you like to come home?"

Kelly plucked a good-size butt out of the ashtray on the kitchen counter. *Home. What a joke.* "No," she said, grabbing the pack of kitchen matches off the stove. "I'm fine."

"I'm sorry, Kelly," she said. "I'm sorry I kicked you out. I was just . . . I was at my wit's end and your father kept calling. He kept wanting to see you."

She lit the butt, exhaled a billowy cloud. "Was Catherine's Valentine John McFadden?"

"I . . . I don't know what you're talking about."

"Is he the one she left to see that night she went away? Is he the reason why you didn't want me to spend time with Bellamy Marshall or the rich, famous kids?"

"Kelly . . ."

"Why didn't you tell me it was him?" Kelly said. "I would have understood. She was . . . we were just fifteen years old."

"I didn't know who your sister was spending her time with," Rose said slowly. "That's what I wanted to know, but ever since . . . Your sister never told me anything she didn't feel like telling me."

"Ever since what?"

"Nothing."

"Why were you so angry with her that night?"

"It was very late. She was drunk."

Kelly took another drag, inhaled right down to the filter. "She was always coming back late," she said, coughing. "She was always drunk."

"I wasn't angry."

"I can't do this anymore, Mom. I need the truth."

Kelly heard her mother take a deep, pained breath. She let it out slowly. "I wasn't angry," she said again. "I was scared."

"Why?"

"For your sister." Through the phone, Kelly heard a match strike, her mother, lighting a cigarette. "You were at school that day. I found the positive test."

Kelly's whole body went numb, her heart pounded up into her ears so that she heard it louder than Mom's voice—the pumping of her blood, the steady, sad thud of it.

"We fought about it all day. She told me he loved her. He would run off with her. He was a grown man and he was rich and they would go somewhere where they could be . . . I don't know. Accepted."

"A rich man," Kelly whispered.

"She never told me his name," she said softly. "Your sister only told me what she wanted me to know."

Kelly wanted another cigarette. Craved it. "That night . . ."

"What?"

"She was so upset."

"Yes." She exhaled. "Who could blame her? She'd thought she was running off with him on Valentine's Day. She thought she'd never see you or me again, but there she was, dropped home at four in the morning by her rich man, her Prince Charming."

Kelly remembered Mom slapping Catherine that night, begging her to tell her the Valentine's name. She remembered Mom crumpled on the floor, a lock of goldfish-colored hair stuck to the tears on her face. "*I'm sorry, baby. We can fix this.*"

But Catherine had left anyway. She'd stolen Mom's car and wound up in Pasadena, at a lovers' lane she'd never talked about during any of their late-night conversations. She'd driven there pregnant and wound up dead in the canyon, her skull crushed, every bone in her body broken to bits.

"She never told me about it," Mom was saying now. "I'm her mother and she never told me. I had to find the test . . ."

The cops had ruled it a suicide. But why would Catherine have killed herself over being pregnant if Mom had known about it, if she'd wanted to "fix" it? And now, Kelly was remembering something else Catherine had said that night, just before she'd left. Something she'd pushed out of her mind until now. "*I don't deserve this.*" At the time, Kelly had thought her sister was talking about the slap, about Mom's anger . . .

"Do you think she went back to him? Do you think she threatened to tell?"

"It was a suicide," Mom said. "That's what the police told us."

"They could be wrong."

"It doesn't matter. She's gone either way. It was two years ago. She never said his name. There's nothing we can do."

"But . . ."

"He's a rich, powerful man." Mom's voice was like ice, like stone. "There's nothing we can do."

KELLY DIDN'T WANT TO FREAK OUT BELLAMY'S PARENTS OR WAKE UP her little brother at two in the morning, so she waited. She paced around the apartment, made herself a peanut butter and jelly sandwich she couldn't eat any of, paced around some more, and smoked three more butts out of the ashtray and looked for the necklace and drank a glass of milk and took a shower and smoked one more butt and turned the TV on to the morning news and paced some more until finally it was 8:00 A.M. Then she called Bellamy.

The housekeeper picked up. Kelly asked for Bellamy. "One moment," she said. And Kelly waited, her heart beating so hard she could barely breathe.

She heard heavy footsteps, Bellamy arguing with her little brother about something—a waffle?—and then finally the footsteps neared, her friend saying her name into the phone. "Sorry about that. Shane is so annoying—"

"John McFadden got my sister pregnant," Kelly said. "And I think he may have killed her."

"*Holy shit. What?* Hold on." Bellamy closed her bedroom door, came back again. "Tell me everything," she said.

And Kelly did, the whole story tumbling out of her from the moment she saw the beautiful black Porsche pull up outside her old house, up through Catherine's death, John McFadden's aviator glasses, the conversation with her mother just six hours ago . . . She said it without taking a breath, only barely aware that Bellamy asked no questions, didn't interrupt once. Throughout the entire story, Kelly's best friend was as quiet as dead engines on a plane.

When Kelly was done, the line remained silent. She worried that Bellamy had hung up on her, that she hadn't even listened.

"Bellamy?" she said.

"I'm here."

Kelly sighed, expecting excuses or denials or "*Are you sure? Maybe it was a different guy in aviator glasses.*" She even thought Bellamy might accuse Mom of lying about the pregnancy, closing ranks, defending

Vee's dad, her own father's best friend, *a rich, powerful man* . . . But Bellamy didn't deny or defend or make excuses. What she said was, "John McFadden has a big garage full of cars."

"Huh?"

"He like . . . collects them . . . He's got to have at least two dozen, all different kinds, all really expensive."

"So . . ."

"So," she said. "Let's find that black Porsche. Now."

GETTING INVITED TO VEE'S HOUSE WAS EASY ENOUGH. KELLY SIMPLY called him, told him she was lonely at the apartment and wanted to practice with him for her screen test, which was at his father's office in Century City, later today.

Bellamy, she told him, was bored. "You guys can practice with me, and give me a ride to your dad's office?" she said. "I'm kind of nervous. I could really use the company."

"I thought you'd never ask," Vee said, which made Kelly feel relieved, but also guilty. She suspected Bellamy felt the same. When she picked Kelly up at Vee's apartment in her VW Rabbit, she made no mention of their plan. They spent most of the ride there barely speaking, listening to Bellamy's British bootleg tape, smoking Marlboro Reds and singing along.

When "She's Lost Control" came on, Kelly smiled a little. "Remember when you played me this song?" she said. "It was the day you introduced me to Vee. You were so excited about it."

Bellamy said nothing. She reached for her dark glasses, but as she was putting them on, Kelly noticed a tear, sliding down her cheek.

"Are you okay?" Kelly asked.

"He died."

"Huh?"

"Ian Curtis from Joy Division. He killed himself a week ago."

"Um . . . That's sad." Kelly didn't know what else to say. As she reached Mulholland, Bellamy lit another cigarette with shaky hands, holding the bangle bracelets against her wrist as she did. Even so, Kelly caught a glimpse of the scratches. They looked fresh.

"She's Lost Control" played on, those few driving piano notes and dead Ian Curtis's sad singing voice filling the car, haunting it. *And she gave away the secrets of her past . . .*

Kelly saw the gate up ahead. "We're here," she said. Bellamy pulled up to it and hit the button on the intercom, said her name. Vee answered fast, a smile in his voice. "Dad's at his office, you guys. We've got the whole place to ourselves."

Bellamy cleared her throat, adjusted her dark glasses, turned off the song. "I hate losing people," she said.

"I'M BORED." BELLAMY SAID IT AFTER KELLY'S THIRD READ-THROUGH of the script pages McFadden had left for her—a high school girl telling her best friend that she saw a space alien in her yard. Said it while sitting on overstuffed, velvet couches in jewel tones, bright bolts of silk cascading from the ceiling and shielding the windows in those same jewel tones, silk pillows scattered everywhere, a real hookah in the middle of the floor, alongside exotic-looking musical instruments that had never been played.

They were in the den of Vee's dad's sprawling house. It was a cozy room compared to many of the others, but so otherworldly, so magical. It reminded her of Jeannie's bottle from *I Dream of Jeannie,* even though it had been designed, according to Vee, to look like the harem quarters in the palace of a Moroccan sheikh. She'd wondered if Catherine had ever been in here, *Catherine the harem girl . . .* then forced the thought out of her mind. She could never imagine anyone feeling bored in this room, but Bellamy said it so convincingly, Kelly wondered why she wasn't the one reading for the movie part.

"Well, what are we supposed to do?" Vee said. "It's not like we can get wasted. Kelly's got an audition in two hours. And we have to drive her there."

"I want to look at your dad's cars."

"Seriously?"

"Yeah." She gave Kelly a prompting look.

She picked it up. "Bellamy was telling me about them," Kelly said, quickly. "I was talking about how much I loved the Jag and she said your dad has like two dozen other cars that are even more amazing."

Vee shrugged. "My dear guests. I am your host." He said it in his best Mr. Roarke from *Fantasy Island* accent and led them out of the Moroccan room, through a blue, Dutch-themed sunroom filled with fresh tulips onto a deck and across an expansive green lawn, to a garage that was about five times the size of Jimmy's house and the old lady's combined. This place was more impressive than Fantasy Island. It made Bellamy's house look humble and small.

Vee pushed a button and the garage door raised—the entire side of the structure. Kelly gasped. It was a showroom—a vintage Mustang alongside two brand-new Ferraris, one red, one electric blue, three Jags, a Bentley, a silver, convertible Rolls-Royce covered in crazy detailing—black and golden swirls, a butterfly at the back.

"That used to belong to Jimmy Page," Vee said to Kelly. "You want to go inside?"

"You guys can check that one out, I'm gonna explore," said Bellamy, who was weaving around a line of motorcycles, making her way to the far end of the garage. Bellamy glanced at her—a meaningful glance. Kelly saw the car she was headed for: a black Porsche with tinted windows and mirrored hubcaps. Kelly nodded.

"I love Jimmy Page," she said to Vee, though she wasn't quite sure if Jimmy Page was Led Zeppelin's guitarist or their bassist.

"Try the driver's seat." He opened the door for her, stepped aside. Kelly slipped in. The car smelled of leather and oil. She rested her hands on the wheel and leaned her head back, trying to get lost in it. But her thoughts were on Bellamy in the Porsche.

Vee smiled at her. "Someday, you can take it for a spin."

"I don't know how to drive," she said.

"Oh," he said. "I figured you could . . ."

"Why?" She looked at him. He winced a little. "Oh."

Out of the corner of her eye, she saw Bellamy making for the black Porsche. It wasn't lost on her, the weirdness of this situation, Catherine's ghost, looming over everything, a passenger in every luxury car.

"Do you know who taught Catherine how to drive?" she said. "Mom and I never knew."

He shook his head. Kelly had a flash-memory of him, crying in her arms at the Jailbird Party, shoulders shaking, her shirt wet with his tears. *Poor Vee. Poor both of us.*

"I'd give a million dollars to know what's on your mind right now," he said.

She swallowed hard, wishing for a cigarette. "I'm . . . I'm just a little nervous about the screen test," she said.

She made herself look up, into those warm blue eyes. "You shouldn't be," he said. "You're going to be amazing."

Her heart crumbled. *You are such a good person,* she thought. *And you don't know a thing about your father.*

"I've seen so many actresses in my dad's films, at clubs . . . Practically every girl I know wants to be in movies, and none of them is like you . . ."

Kelly stared out the windshield at the black Porsche, passenger door yawning open, Bellamy inside. She stared at the rear tire. Its mir-rored hubcap sneered at her.

"You're what my dad would call a 'natural,' Kelly."

Catherine's tire tracks weren't the only ones up at Chantry Flats when they'd found her body. Mom had asked the police detective about it. *If it was suicide*, Mom had said, *who was in the other car?*

"If he doesn't go nuts over you, then he's an idiot."

It's a lovers' lane, ma'am. That means lots of tire tracks, lots of cars . . .

"Kelly?"

"Yeah?"

"You okay?"

She closed her eyes, nodded slowly. "I'm so happy you're my friend," she said.

He knelt down and kissed her on the cheek. "Me too," he said.

Kelly was aware of footsteps, the passenger-side door opening. Bel-lamy's loud voice. "I'm bored again." She grabbed Kelly's hand and dropped something in it—something small and cold. "Found this in the trunk," she whispered as Vee stepped away. "Don't you think Kelly will do great at the screen test?" he said.

"I think your dad will love her," said Bellamy as Kelly glanced down at the cool object in her hand. A tube of lipstick, elegant, silver. She read the name. *Rouge de la Bohème*. Her blood went cold.

CHAPTER 27

WATCH! ARCHIVAL FOOTAGE OF
A MURDERER'S SCREEN TEST—
HER VICTIM IS BEHIND THE CAMERA!

In 1980, a shy teenager named Kelly Michelle Lund shot and killed director John McFadden in the midst of his own wrap party. Stoned and confused, Lund never gave a reason for shooting the respected lensman—nor did she seem to show any remorse for the deed. But because of her age, degree of intoxication, and other mitigating factors (many wrote letters to the parole board on her behalf, including several A-list celebrities and McFadden's ex-wife Leilani Valle) Kelly Lund was released from prison in 2006.

Still, this chilling footage may give those letter writers reason to reconsider. In a screen test taken just two weeks before Lund murdered McFadden, the 17-year-old appears openly hostile, refusing to take any direction from the Oscar nominee, whose voice can be heard offscreen, becoming increasingly frustrated. ("You're wasting both our time, Kelly," and *"You don't seem to be taking this seriously,"* he says throughout the latter half of the audition.) *The most disturbing exchange comes at 2:24, when Lund refers to the script's fictional town, Chatsworth, by the wrong name: Chantry Flats. When McFadden attempts to correct her, she snaps, asking him if Chantry Flats "makes [him] think of dead girls." Yikes!*

Comments:

Guest1: Wow, what a psycho bitch. She obviously wants that director's azz and he is not into her and so she's pissed. How is this freak not in jail for life?! Or better yet, fried!!! Not spending my taxpayer dollars supporting her sorry, psycho azz.

Guest 2: Run, John McFadden, run!

FlimFlam: Um, he can't run. He's dead. Another liberal Hollywood casualty. If he had a gun of his own, he could have defended himself.

Laney23: Pretty sure she shot him with his own gun. :)

BuzzFeed
May 1, 2009

CHAPTER 28

APRIL 23, 2010

hen was the last time you visited your in-laws at their house?" said the female detective, Louise Braddock.

Third time she and her ginger-pink partner Dupree had asked Kelly that question, phrasing it a different way each time. Kelly said nothing. She'd been here before. Literally *been here before,* in this same interview room. Different building or not, it felt like it. Same hard-backed chair as the one she'd sat in thirty years ago, same conference table between them, the announcement of the date and the presence of the tape recorder, police phrasing and rephrasing questions, Kelly saying nothing. Same routine. She'd known her rights back in 1980. She knew them now.

Kelly turned to her lawyer—Ilene Cutler. More déjà vu. She'd asked Sebastian Todd to find her a lawyer, and this, out of every criminal defense attorney in the greater Los Angeles area, was the one he'd found. Cutler had changed a lot in the past thirty years, just like Kelly had. But while Kelly had gone harder, grayer, and more angular, Ilene had smoothed out, her frizzy hair tamed and highlighted, wire-rimmed glasses abandoned for sky blue contacts, pasty skin spray-tanned and Botoxed to face the unforgiving cameras of the cable TV station where she'd been a regular commentator for more than a decade. Cutler was fifteen years older than Kelly, but age no longer divided them so much as experience. *The effects of prison versus the effects of TV. A study should be done.*

Ilene said, "Why should she answer that question?"

"You'd think she'd be interested in finding her father-in-law's killer," said Dupree.

"Don't see how asking her about socializing with her in-laws accomplishes much of anything, other than . . . you know . . . TMZ fodder." She smiled sweetly. "You guys on Harvey's payroll?"

"No," Braddock said between her teeth. "We're not on Harvey's payroll."

"Well then, how about something a little more relevant?"

"Their relationship isn't relevant?"

"Hey, Louise. I've known you for quite a while, and to be honest, I'd rather get a grapefruit juice enema than socialize with you. Does that mean I'm going to murder you? Not in the slightest."

Braddock shook her head. Kelly could have sworn Dupree stifled a smile.

She's good, Kelly thought. Strange—she'd done a triple take when Ilene had first shown up here, telling herself how dumb she'd been to have trusted ST. Yet still she had to admit that it was comforting, Ilene Cutler striding toward her, saying her name with the same intonation she'd said it thirty years ago.

"Kelly Michelle Lund. I've been a defense attorney for thirty-seven years. And in all that time, there's only one thing I feel guilty about."

"Repping those skinheads?"

"Treating you like a piece of crap. How about a do-over?" And the more time she spent with Ilene, the more she wanted to thank ST. A

familiar face—bronzed and Botoxed though it may have been—was something to cling to, with everything else in her life shifting, changing, falling apart . . .

Kelly wondered if Shane had read the letter she'd left him or if he'd just seen her handwriting and thrown it away. She didn't even know whether it mattered anymore. The truth was now a different thing than it had been when she'd written it. She was a different person.

I'm Sterling Marshall's daughter.

"Kelly, are you the only one who drives your car?" Dupree said. "Or does your husband sometimes drive it too?"

She glanced at Ilene. Ilene nodded.

"Just me."

"Okay, good. Can you tell me where you were in that car at"—he glanced down at the notebook on his lap—"two-eighteen A.M. on April twenty-first?"

"Excuse me?" said Ilene.

Kelly stared at him. "I . . . I don't . . ."

"There's a charge on your credit card at that time—Amoco station on Hollywood and Fairfax."

"Long way from Joshua Tree," Braddock said.

Ilene stared at Kelly. "You don't know anything about this, do you?"

"How did you get my credit records?"

"Also," Louise said. "And this is the part we're having trouble with, Kelly. We found blood in your car."

"*What?*" said Ilene.

"I . . . I was going to . . ."

"We'll talk later." Ilene swung around with her jaw set, and aimed her sky blue eyes at Braddock. Attack mode. "My client's rights are being violated."

"How so?" she said.

"Are you kidding me? You searched her car without a warrant and without permission. That's what's known as a violation, Louise."

"Oh we did get permission."

Ilene turned to Kelly. "*You gave them permission?*"

"No," Kelly said as Ilene turned back to the detectives, everything around her dropping away, Kelly knowing the answer before they said it.

"We got permission from the car's owner—her husband," Dupree said, Kelly staring at the two-way mirror, numb. Lost. "He also gave us his extra key."

"YOU DID THE RIGHT THING," SAID BELLAMY.

Shane looked at her. "I don't feel like I did."

"You protected your family. Our family. It's what Dad would have wanted."

"You're serious?"

"Do you want a drink?"

Shane shook his head. He collapsed on Bellamy's Navajo print couch, and as she went into the kitchen to mix cocktails for Mom and herself, he rolled it over in his mind, what his sister had just said to him. *It's what Dad would have wanted.* He couldn't even respond to that—the level of delusion.

But that was what Bellamy was about. It was what she'd always been about—believing the lines she said, the roles she played—Daddy's girl, party girl, respected artist . . . A natural actor just like Dad had been, Living the Part. She'd only taught at Irvine for one year, yet here she still was, six years later, in the condo the university had found for her, playing "artist-in-residence" because she couldn't find another character. She booked speaking gigs, invited local press into her home, brewed herbal tea for them in her Spanish kitchen, chatted them up in her southwestern-style living room, her one successful piece glaring down at them from the wall. She invited them into her studio out back, no doubt, just as she'd taken Shane there this morning, showed them her glitter and her paints and her fancy tape-recording equipment, these fresh young reporters who probably had no idea that she was just saying lines, wearing a costume, discussing "pieces in progress" that she would never complete or even begin. It was getting stale. Bellamy had to know that. "Artist-in-residence" had a short shelf life when you took no joy in making art, only in talking about it.

But now, Dad had given her a new role to play.

Bellamy returned from the kitchen with Mom's martini and a glass of red wine for herself. "Just the way you like it, Mom," she said, handing her the drink. "Cold and dry as an agent's heart." She gave her a brave smile befitting her new role: Brave Daughter.

Mom didn't look at her. She took the drink, downed half of it, then set it on the coffee table, staring straight ahead the whole time. "I miss my house," she said quietly.

Bellamy took a pull off her wine. She glanced at Mom, then at Shane and smiled again, her teeth stained bloodred from the wine. "When was the last time," she said, "when we were all together like this, as a family?"

Mona Lisa watched Shane from its spot over the fireplace, Kelly's teenage smile angry and accusing. The real Kelly, the grown-up one, was probably being questioned by police right now because of Shane, because of the credit card record he had printed out and shown the detectives—a gas station at 2:00 A.M. on the night of Dad's murder, ten minutes away from his parents' home—and also because of the things he'd told them about Kelly, all true, but damningly so when arranged a certain way.

He had to do it, he knew. As Bellamy had pointed out, he had no other choice—they were family after all. The family had to protect each other. But he'd taken no joy in it. And Bellamy, being Bellamy, so desperately wanted him to.

"Mommy," she said. "Remember when you and Dad had them shut down Disneyland for my eighth birthday party?"

Mom stared at her, that lost look in her eyes. "Yes. I remember."

Bellamy smiled again. Her bloody wine-smile directly under Kelly on the wall. One of those moments when positioning shows you something you could never put into words. Shane wished he had his camera, which made him think of his room, his home, his marriage. "I miss my house too," he said.

Shane. Your whole life has been built on a lie. Mom had said that to him yesterday morning at the house she now missed, a house caked in Dad's blood, strewn with yellow police tape. She'd said it, just before letting him know that fifteen years ago, he'd married his half sister.

"*I would have told you long ago*," she had said. "*I would have stopped the wedding. But you see, Shane. I just found out myself.*"

"You made the most wonderful cake for that party, Mom, remember? It was Cinderella, and her dress was the cake—vanilla with buttercream filling and blue fondant frosting."

"I do," Mary said, warming a little. "Flora and I made that together. It was her idea to use those edible crystals on the gown . . ."

Shane still couldn't get over it. Dad had never said a word when Shane announced his plans to marry Kelly. Dad, movie star, and war hero letting two of his children get married to each other without saying a word. How had he rationalized it? Had he told himself that he was protecting his family from getting hurt? That he could keep a secret forever if he had to, that this was *his* mess, why should Shane's love life have to suffer? *Family means everything.* He used to say that all the time.

"That birthday party was the best day of my life," Bellamy was saying. "You guys were wonderful parents."

Right after his mother had told him everything, Shane had gone into her bathroom and taken half her bottle of Ambien. Washing down the pills, he'd thought of all the times he'd tried to make love to Kelly, during arranged conjugal visits and then after her release. She never wanted to. She kept apologizing. It was prison, she'd say. It wasn't him, she'd say. She just had these barriers, she couldn't help it, be patient and things would change. But it *was* him. It had been him all along, and it had been the two of them together, and he had felt it too, much as he'd tried to ignore it . . .

Some families must have meant more to Dad than others.

Shane had taken the Ambien intending to off himself. Mom hadn't followed him into the bathroom. She hadn't even asked what he was doing in there for so long, and when he'd left her room, left the house . . . when he'd gotten behind the wheel of his car . . .

He couldn't remember the strip club, couldn't remember the fight or the arrest, or Bellamy picking him up at the station. The only thing he could remember from that entire night was Bellamy, putting him to bed in her guest room, kissing his forehead, telling him, "*You can't kill yourself. You have a purpose. And that purpose is to help your family.*"

He had drifted off to sleep again, longing for more Ambien, wishing himself back to a week ago, when the worst secret he had to struggle with was Kelly's affair with Rocky Three.

"I think I'm going to hit the sack," Bellamy said. She emptied her wineglass and put her arms around Mom, who made a weak show of hugging back. "I hope I dream of that birthday party tonight," she said, and for a few seconds Shane flashed on Bellamy in her prom dress, walking down the marble staircase to meet her date, her gaze focused not on the guy at all, but on Mom and Dad. It was 1981. Kelly had just gone to prison, he realized now. He hadn't thought of it then. That night, Kelly Lund had been the last person on anyone's mind. "Doesn't she look beautiful, Mary?" Dad had said. And Bellamy, his only daughter, had basked in his praise.

SHANE AND HIS MOTHER SAT IN SILENCE, MOM SIPPING HER MARTINI with the truth thick in the air, Bellamy no longer in the room to drown it out. Shane tried to think of something to say, but he couldn't. Everything had changed, including him. Especially him. Nothing made sense anymore.

His gaze traveled around the room—all this tasteful, sunbaked, West Coast college professor furniture, photographs strategically placed among bookshelves with color-coordinated books, most of them moody-looking black-and-whites of Bellamy—publicity promos from the '90s, when she was art's "It" Girl and took great pains to look the part. One of the frames was broken—a big chunk of glass missing from the front. He hadn't noticed it before, this one thing out of place in this orderly world, and he wondered why. Usually, his photographer's eye worked in his favor when it came to spotting things like that.

"That house on Blue Jay Way was a wedding present to me from Dad," Mom said. "Did you know that, Shane?"

He looked at her, the blue-veined hands delicate on the glass. "No, I didn't," he said.

"After we came back from our honeymoon, the driver took us up that hill and then he carried me over the threshold. I almost fainted from the shock."

"It was a surprise?"

"Completely. I'd never seen the house. I had no idea he was even thinking of buying. I looked at that marble staircase, that enormous window overlooking the canyon, and I just started to sob."

"Tears of joy."

"Yes, of course. But also . . . something else." She took another sip, set the glass down on the table. "The idea that he could have bought that house and kept it such a secret that I never had the slightest clue until we drove through the gate . . ."

"Yeah?"

"It was fear, Shane. That's what I was feeling and the real reason why I cried. I feared that part of your father . . . that ability to, to hide things . . . It terrified me."

"But, Mom, he was an actor." Shane winced. He bit back tears. Despite everything, it hurt to use the past tense with Dad, and he couldn't hide it. He didn't have that ability.

But Mom didn't seem to notice. "Your father called Kelly that night," she said. "I heard him on the phone with her."

"I know, Mom. You told me."

"He thought I was asleep. I never would have known about it if I hadn't overheard him calling."

"Mom . . ."

"He said he'd wronged the girls. He wanted to make things right with the one surviving one before he died. He was changing his will. So he could take care of Kelly in a way he never had in life. I thought, *What about me?* Our whole life together was a lie. How was he ever going to make up for that?" Tears started to run down her cheeks.

"He took care of you, though."

"That isn't the point," she said. "I married a man who abandoned two of his three daughters. He let one of them go to prison, and the other one . . . she died, Shane. He didn't go to her funeral. He never once shed a tear. Kelly would come over and he would treat her as though she was any other friend of Bellamy's. I married a man who was capable of that, and if I had known—if I had known what type of person he really was . . ." Shane put his arms around Mom and hugged her to him, her body so weak and frail and thin. "I didn't mean to shoot him. I was so angry and it was right there on his desk. I pulled the trigger. I don't even remember doing it. I didn't know it would go off . . ."

Shane didn't ask her about the last shot—the one that landed square in the middle of Dad's forehead. It didn't matter. None of it really did, now.

When her breathing finally calmed and she pulled away, Mom dabbed at her eyes with her handkerchief. Within moments, she was herself again—serene, elegant, slightly drugged. She stood up, steadying herself on the back of the mission chair. "I worry about your sister, Shane," she said. "She isn't as strong as she looks. I want you to promise me you'll be there for her."

Shane sighed. *Just like Dad.* "Trust me," he said carefully. "Bellamy has been doing fine without me for years."

She gave him a sad smile and headed for the room she was sleeping in—a fully equipped sewing room, with two spotless machines that hadn't been used once. "I wasn't talking about Bellamy," she said.

SHANE WOKE UP ON THE COUCH, SUNLIGHT POURING IN ON HIM, assaulting his eyes. His head felt heavy and he couldn't figure out why, until he remembered the four vodka rocks he'd consumed last night after his mother had gone to bed. He didn't drink usually, but he'd poured and poured to shut out his thoughts. To take the edge off the pain, he'd told himself. What a dumb idea.

Shane threw an arm over his eyes and groaned. Vodka was a crappy replacement for Ambien. His eyes were too big for their sockets. His stomach gaped. He was so thirsty and achy, he felt as though his entire body had been wrung out like a sponge.

He plodded into the kitchen and ran himself a glass of water, chugged all of it without taking a breath. He sliced off a piece of the crusty bread Bellamy kept on the counter, wolfed it down. ARTISINAL BREAD, the label said. He hated that, hated reading the words. Made him want to throw the loaf under a truck.

Shane gulped water from the faucet until he felt slightly human, then headed back into the living room again. He looked at the antique grandfather clock in the corner. Seven A.M. and so bright already. He hated this place—the big windows, the piney smell, the arduous, overbearing sunlight. Bellamy said she found it stimulating here. He would never understand her . . .

He started to lie down again when he spotted his denim jacket on the couch. He hadn't remembered leaving it there—he was sure, in fact, that he'd hung it on the coat tree, yet it had apparently been there with him all night, on the edge of the couch, next to his feet. He picked it up, his hand slipping into the inside pocket, fingers searching for his extra camera lenses, their reassuring feel. He wasn't sure why he always did this. It was almost as though touching them reminded him of who he was. Even now the cool feel of the glass lifted the hangover, just a little.

There was something in the pocket with the lenses—a thick piece of paper. He pulled it out and saw the writing.

He sat down on the couch and stared at it—Kelly's round, loopy script. Shane choked up. "You were here," he whispered. "You came to see me."

> *Dear Shane,*
>
> *I realize I never thanked you, all those years ago, for the letters you wrote me in prison. I've always felt that the best gift you can give another human being is to truthfully answer all their questions, and that's what you did for me.*

You are the only person who ever has. But I never answered yours. You've never asked, I know. But not asking questions doesn't mean you don't deserve answers—it just means you're kind.

From somewhere outside Bellamy's house, Shane heard a faint *wow, wow, wow* . . . Gambel's Quail. Kelly had told him about that bird, a desert bird. "*They like running better than flying,*" she had said. "*So they don't go very far.*" He closed his eyes for a moment and felt that heat under his lids—not tears so much as the threat of them.

To be honest with you, I wish I had answers for half the things I've done. They seem to make sense at the time, but shine a good, strong light on my reasoning, it all falls apart. Here are my answers: Why do I visit Rocky? I believe he may be someone I used to know. I can't bring myself to ask him, but I keep hoping he'll tell me on his own. That's why I keep going back to see him—I like the feeling of hoping for something. Why did I kill John McFadden? I learned that shortly before she died, he got my sister pregnant. I believed (and still do) that he killed her because she wouldn't get rid of the baby. 3) Why do I believe he killed my sister? Bellamy found a tube of Catherine's lipstick in the trunk of McFadden's car. It's very rare. At the time, you could only get it in Europe. It was called Rouge de la Bohème.

Shane's breath caught in his throat.

I never discussed my reasons in court because my lawyer said they weren't relevant—and no one would believe me anyway. I never discussed them with you because I promised Bellamy I wouldn't tell anyone, ever . . .

He dropped the letter. He couldn't read any more, couldn't breathe, couldn't move for the memory flooding his mind: the waxy leaves of the magnolia tree, his special perch in the crook of the thick, high branch, the place he always spied on Bellamy, watching his sister through her window, watching her opening her drawer, thinking she might do that scary thing with the razor again . . .

But she hadn't. He'd seen her take something shiny and silver from her jacket pocket, saw her put it in that drawer, pushing it all the way to the back. He'd thought, *Something important. Something she wants to hide.*

Later, when Bellamy was out with her friends, he'd sneaked into her room. He'd gone through her vanity drawer, looking for that shiny thing, thinking that it had to be very valuable. *I bet it's a silver bullet for killing werewolves* . . . God, he still remembered having that thought. He'd felt around her drawer for it, pulled it out. A fancy tube of lipstick. He still remembered the brand name, the strange words he didn't understand: *Rouge de la Bohème* . . . Shane had been eight years old. Bellamy, fifteen. It had been early in the morning on a weekend, just after Valentine's Day. Right around the time when Kelly's sister must have died . . .

Shane put the letter down. He walked down the hall to his sister's tastefully appointed master bedroom with its pillow-strewn sleigh bed and flat-screen TV and heavy silk curtains. For a few moments, he stood in the doorway, watching Bellamy the way he used to as a kid. Bellamy always thought it was creepy, the way he'd spy on her. She'd shut doors in his face and complain to their parents and set her friends on him, calling him names. But Shane had had a reason—the same reason he watched her now. He was trying to figure out who Bellamy was.

And still, all these years later, Bellamy slept the way Shane had always known her to sleep—on her back, her body still, breath soft, face placid: Snow White in her glass coffin. Bellamy Marshall, still posing, even in her sleep.

He backed out into the hallway, softly closed Bellamy's door. For a few moments, he stood outside the silent sewing room, thinking about what Mom had said last night. *If I had known what type of person your father really was . . .* But hadn't she? That pale memory worked into his head again, Mom clutching his hand on the *Defiance* set, the heaviness of her step as she went for his trailer. "*You wait here, Shane. Mommy's going to see Daddy for a few minutes.*" She had known what kind of person he was. She'd just chosen to be ignorant.

Did you kill Dad for keeping secrets all those years—or was it because he was finally ready to start telling the truth?

When Shane was sixteen years old, he'd overheard his family's personal chef on the phone with someone from the *National Enquirer,* talking about Mom. He hadn't heard the whole conversation, but he had heard "junkie" and "pathetic" and "life-threatening pill habit." And being sixteen and drunk, he'd gone ape shit. The police were called, lawsuits were threatened—that's how brutally Shane had attacked the chef, who had dared to try and tell the truth about his mother. Dad had made a big show with the cops, assuring them Shane had been out of his mind from booze and crystal meth and had lashed out against their trusted employee for no reason at all—ultimately shipping him off to Betty Ford for six weeks in order to fully satisfy the officers that Shane (who in reality had simply raided his father's liquor cabinet for the first and only time) was the drug addict in the family. In the car on the way to the clinic, the two of them alone, Dad had offered up the only words he ever would about the incident: "*You did the right thing, son. Your mother and I are grateful.*"

Shane went for his cell phone, called a cab. He waited for it in silence, staring up at *Mona Lisa,* looking into teenage Kelly's eyes, an emotion inside them he'd never noticed and didn't know the name for. *What would you call it—that feeling of being the only person left in the world?*

"I can't do this to you," he said to the picture—to seventeen-year-old Kelly, whom he had loved at first sight, the only friend of Bellamy's ever to say hi to him. Kelly, his dream girl. His pen pal. His soul mate. His sister. Shane couldn't let her take the fall for Sterling's murder. She didn't deserve that. More than anyone else in their messed-up family, she deserved the truth.

He got his phone out of the pocket of his denim jacket, typed in Kelly's number, and texted her everything he now knew to be true. It took a long time. Then he headed for the sewing room, knocked on the door. He listened for his mother's heavy, pill-fed sleep-breathing but heard nothing.

Shane tried the door. It hadn't been locked. And sure enough, when he pushed it open, the bed was empty and neatly made, everything in its place. His mother was gone.

CHAPTER 29

Kelly's rental car was much smaller than her Camry. It felt lighter too, as though it was skating over the road and a good strong wind could set it airborne. The car had an odd name—the Plymouth Breeze Expresso, which sounded like something more easily drunk than driven—but still she was glad to have it. Glad to be out of Parker Center and out of Hollywood and on her way back home to the desert at last.

On Ilene's advice, she had told the two detectives what had happened the night before in as few words as possible: She had been out on one of her night drives. Sterling Marshall had called and asked her to come over. She had rushed to his house and found him dead. No, she hadn't run into anyone there. She'd left the house so quickly because she was panicked. She hadn't woken her husband when she got home because she was in shock and exhausted and didn't know how to tell him. She hadn't phoned the police because she was Kelly Michelle Lund.

"*The one part I don't understand,*" Braddock had said, "*is why you rushed to Sterling Marshall's house in the first place. By all accounts, you and he weren't close at all.*"

Kelly had looked at her, flat-eyed and still. "*I guess I'm a little star-struck*," she'd said.

Braddock and Dupree hadn't seemed to like the answer much, but still they couldn't hold her. She hadn't been formally charged, though her car had been impounded. So Ilene Cutler had left with her, waving off press and ushering her into her shiny silver Escalade, chatting Kelly up, keeping her calm, making sure she knew her rights regarding the inevitable phalanx of reporters outside her house in Joshua Tree. ("*A press card is not a get-out-of-jail-free card. If they're on your property, call the cops!*") They'd exchanged information, Ilene urging Kelly to charge up her cell phone as soon as possible, asking her if she had any questions or concerns—and generally not acting like the Ilene Culter Kelly used to know. "*You're taking this whole do-over thing very seriously*," Kelly had said at one point.

"*I've learned a hell of a lot since 1980*," she had replied. "*You're my one and only chance to prove it.*"

There had been a lot of traffic, so by the time they finally escaped downtown, it had been quite late and Kelly was starving and exhausted. Ilene had dropped her off at a Holiday Inn near the airport, where she'd devoured a club sandwich and fries, caught a few hours of sleep, poured coffee down her throat, and shuttled to the car rental in the morning, craving the desert, the birds, the comparable silence.

Driving now on the 10, an open stretch of road ahead of her along with the still-rising sun, Kelly thought again about Ilene—the one strange thing she'd said after she'd pulled into the Holiday Inn drop-off, just as Kelly was about to leave the car: "*So were your ears burning about three weeks ago?*"

Ilene had explained that it had been particularly kismet-like, Sebastian calling her about Kelly when he did, because her name had come up in conversation at a cancer awareness fund-raiser at the Beverly

Wilshire—raised by Mary Marshall of all people. "She said something very nice about you," Ilene had said. "I assumed it was because she'd had several too many appletinis."

"Thanks a lot."

"No," she'd said quickly. "That's not what I mean. What she said was, 'Far as I'm concerned, that girl deserves a medal.'"

"For what?"

"Killing John McFadden."

Bizarre, Kelly thought as she exited the freeway and headed down the long local road to her home. Far as she knew, Mary Marshall had never felt anything but love for McFadden and pity for her—the poor misguided teen who never had a chance. *Has she found out yet that I'm her husband's daughter?*

Kelly needed some noise. She flipped on the Breeze Expresso's radio. Country music filled the car, something she had a lot more tolerance for now than in her youth, but still she had to be in the right mood for those sighing guitars, those vocals so thick with emotion they sounded as though they could burst from it.

She flipped the dial past NPR news and some top-forty song she'd heard countless times but had never bothered to learn the title, past a 1-800-Mattress ad and more country music to an oldies station, where she let the dial rest: Elvis's "Burning Love," one of Kelly's favorites from childhood, was playing, making her think of simpler times, happy times—dancing in the kitchen to Mom's transistor radio, Catherine using the broom handle as a microphone . . .

The song was fading, but on its heels, the blare of a saxophone. "You ready for a little Madness?" said the deejay. Kelly sighed completely, breath tumbling out of her. This station was lethal. "One Step Beyond."

Strange the way memories worked. How they could hide between the lines of an old song and jump out at you, ambush your thoughts, leave you wrecked and weakened. God, Kelly missed Vee and Bellamy. She missed her young self too. She missed standing on Vee's property in the middle of the desert, sun at her back, gun in her hands, drugs in her veins that made her powerful as a movie hero. She missed the way Bellamy made her laugh and the way Vee made her feel—as though her life was just beginning and the future was limitless. As though she could change the world, rather than the other way around.

Kelly could see her house ahead of her, the festival-like crowd lining the opposite street—TV news vans and paparazzi with their elaborate camera setups, her arrival home a red carpet event. *How did I get here from that day in the desert?* Kelly slowed down, staring at this group, this circus. She flashed back to the cameras outside the courthouse after her sentencing and her face twitched into the same strange smile, history nearly repeating itself. *Nothing like a mob scene to make you feel utterly, hopelessly alone*, Kelly thought. Until she realized she wasn't.

She lurched the Breeze Expresso into the left lane and careened up Hummingbird Springs, making the turn up the hill, holding her breath until she saw the army of prickly pears and then the broad, tattooed back, sinewy arms clutching the chainsaw, clouds of sawdust billowing around him as he worked. Just like the first day she saw him. That same thrill.

Without hesitating she turned up his long driveway, stopping once she was a few feet away from where he was working. She stayed in the car, watching him sawing away, waiting for him to feel her watching him.

Finally Rocky stopped, turned. He peered into the car. "Kelly," he said. He dropped the chainsaw. She got out and moved toward him.

"What happened to your car?" he said. "What happened to you? You look exhausted."

"The police have my car," she said. "They questioned me. I'm officially a suspect, I suppose."

"What can we do?"

"Nothing." Kelly took a step closer, ran a hand down the length of his smooth, sculpted arm, so much like one of his own creations. She'd never done this before, touching him outdoors, in broad daylight. But it didn't matter anymore. Her father-in-law was her father. Soon she'd be arrested for his murder, her husband/brother testifying against her. Getting seen with the neighbor was the least of her worries. "There's freedom in that, isn't there?" she said. "Knowing there's nothing we can do?"

"We can do something. We can run away."

She shook her head. "Aren't you tired of running?"

"What do you mean?"

She stared into his eyes, took both his hands. "Rocky," she said. "Remember how you told me to only ask about your past if I'm sure?"

"Yes. I remember."

"I'm sure."

"You are?"

"Life is so short and so misleading," Kelly said. "More than half of mine is over and it's been pretty much a lie. I'm tired of hoping for things. I'd rather just know them." She brought one of his strong hands to her lips and kissed it—a gesture she knew he wasn't comfortable with, but she didn't care. "So tell me, Rocky Three . . ." She cleared her throat. "Have I seen you somewhere before?"

He swallowed, the bottle green eye at his throat rippling. "Yes."

She touched his face, wishing she could brush the vines away, see beneath his tattoos to his skin, his lips . . . "Who are you? Where did you come from?"

The blue eyes clouded. "I don't want to say."

"Why?"

"Because," he said. "I was terrible to you."

"You weren't."

"I was."

"I know who you are," she said. "I just need you to say it."

"I read about your trial, Kelly. I remember getting the newspaper and just . . . staring at those courtroom sketches, trying to figure out how you were feeling. Wondering if you were okay. I saw that picture of you after your sentencing. That smile—you were in pain. I knew it because you smiled at me that way once, a long time ago."

"I did?"

He nodded. "You smiled like that when I hurt you."

Kelly had a flash, a dim memory of Vee late at night in his apartment, lying on his mattress, both of them stoned. "*I think I loved her,*" he had said. Talking about Catherine. A stab in the heart back then, but now . . . Now that she knew better . . . "That didn't hurt me," she said. "We both loved her. We both missed her."

Rocky's blue eyes narrowed. "Missed who?"

"It's okay," she said. "I understand."

He glanced over her shoulder, at the road behind her. "Should we go inside? Your husband—"

"It doesn't matter anymore. I told you. Nothing does."

He took a breath. "Kelly . . ."

"Yes?"

"Who do you think I am?"

"Vee," she said. "I know you're Vee."

He shook his head slowly, sunlight sparking the sad blue eyes. "I'm not even sure who that is."

"What?"

"Look at me, Kelly. I was blond when you used to know me. Shorter than you. I've grown since then."

"You aren't—"

"Look at me and think," he said. "Not about who you want me to be, but who I am."

Kelly looked at him, the blue eyes a shade or two lighter than Vee's had been, the jawline smoother, the forehead slightly broader. "You're . . . you're not . . ."

"My voice," he was saying. "Imagine it behind you. One row. I watched you all the time. You didn't know that but maybe you felt it sometimes."

"One *row*?"

"I liked your face, your voice. I liked how, when Hansen would drone on and on, you used to get lost in thoughts I probably would never be able to understand."

"*Mr. Hansen's science class . . .*"

"I was scared of you. The way you made me feel. I threw spitballs to get you to turn around, to notice me."

"Mr. Hansen's science class," she said again, Rocky's face coming into focus, the whole of it behind the twisting vines, the blond eyebrows shining like silk. She gazed at the body, lean and slight beneath the sea creatures and red roses, beneath the leathery skin and layers of sinew. She pictured him with hair—floppy yellow hair falling into his blue eyes, a child's eyes, a spoiled child. She pictured his thin lips twisting into a sneer, calling her a lezzie, a freak. "Evan Mueller," she whispered.

"Yes."

"Jesus . . . I . . . I hated you."

"If it's any consolation, I hated me too." He took her hand, the first time he'd ever done that. He led her past his creations and stopped in front of the skull-faced angel, the one he'd named Kelly. "Can I give this one to you?" He said it like a shy boy asking a girl to dance.

She swallowed hard. Nodded.

"Good."

They stood there, in front of his trailer, former convicted teen murderer and former high school bully, the world falling in on itself like color chips in a kaleidoscope, changing into something different, yet still somehow the same.

"You sent me that postcard," she said—a statement, not a question. "The one with the cactus."

Rocky smiled—a shy smile for such a strong, strange man. "Guess 'someday' is finally here," he said.

YOU GUYS HAVE NO IDEA HOW MUCH OF THIS STORY YOU'RE MISSING, Kelly thought to herself as she arrived home after seeing Rocky, passing the press carnival across the street and pulling into her driveway. Still holding her breath, she got out of her car. The shouts came fast and furious.

"Kelly, how are you feeling?"

"Kelly, did you kill Sterling?"

She kept her head down, a hand covering her face. Rocky had wanted to come with her but she'd said no. Smart of her.

"Do you have a statement?"

"What would you like to say to Sterling Marshall's family?"

If you only knew.

"Kelly, give us a smile!"

She glanced up, then back down at the walkway. *Not falling for that one again . . .* She slid her key into the door

"Kelly, are you glad Shane is home?"

She whirled around. "What?" she said as the door opened in, Shane standing there, exhausted-looking and pale, her letter in his hands. His eyes glistened. Tears. Her husband. Her brother. "You," she said quietly.

"Yes."

"You turned me in to the police."

Kelly heard one of the press people say, "Are you getting this?" She closed the door behind her.

"I'm sorry," Shane said. "I'm sorry I went to the police."

"I didn't kill him."

"I know."

He moved toward her. She stepped back. "He was my father too."

"I know."

"You do?"

"My mother told me."

Kelly gazed into Shane's eyes, black eyes, so very much like Bellamy's and their father's in color, yet shaped exactly like her own. "We have a lot of figuring out to do," she said.

"I'm going to make this right with the cops. I promise."

She didn't think it would be this hard, looking him in the eye. "I think it's a good idea," she said, "for you to leave right now."

"Okay," he said.

"You should probably leave out the back—avoid that scene out there."

He nodded. "After I leave, Kelly. Please charge up your phone and read your texts."

"Why?"

"There's a long one from me."

She glanced at the letter in his hand, barely remembering what it said. So much had happened since she'd written it in Bellamy's empty house, telling him her truths, asking him for his. "Is it a reply?"

"In a way," he said quietly. "It's about Bellamy. And Catherine."

BARRY DUPREE HAD NEVER LIKED GIVING PRESS CONFERENCES. THERE was something so hostile about the whole situation—standing out in front of the police building as though you're defending your home against marauders, reporters hurling questions at you, taping your every move, dying for you to screw up like the marauders they are.

The "dying for you to screw up" part was most pronounced when the press conference centered on a celebrity. Barry's ex-wife had been a supermarket tabloid reporter, so he knew for a fact that the possible crash-and-burn was the only reason they came.

You couldn't blame them, these celebrity journos. Police press conferences were carefully scripted. Any deviation from that script could hurt an ongoing investigation, so by nature they were brief and boring. These guys from the tabs and the gossip Web sites spent 90 percent of their time waiting for some Real Housewife to get out of a limo with no panties on—why should they give a crap about an ongoing investigation? They wanted to knock you off your game, get you to say more than you were supposed to. They wanted to turn you into the law enforcement equivalent of *Stars without Makeup*—and they knew all kinds of tricks to make it happen.

So when the lieutenant told Louise and him they'd be facing reporters this morning at eight, Barry tried to get his partner to take the reins. "*You're better at these things than me,*" he'd tried. "*You're more personable.*" Which had even made Louise laugh. "You know damn well I'm not personable at all."

Barry couldn't argue with that. So he bit the bullet, read the statement, telling TMZ and *US Weekly* and the rest that while Kelly Lund had not been formally arrested and charged with the murder of Sterling Marshall, she remained "under the umbrella of suspicion."

Man, Barry hated that phrase. Saying it out loud made him feel like a jerk. It reminded him of a song from those old MGM musicals his parents were always watching on TV when he was a kid. Every time he had to say it, he'd picture Gene Kelly and Debbie Reynolds in matching raincoats, twirling their umbrellas of suspicion and tap-tap-tapping away . . . "Thank you for coming," he said, making sure not to smile, because, unless you are a victim's family member who has finally gotten justice, smiling during any part of a murder investigation makes you look like a psychopath. *Just ask Kelly Lund.*

"Is an arrest forthcoming?" shouted one reporter.

"Was her husband the one who turned her in?" said another.

"Can you answer to the rumors that Kelly Lund had been having an affair with her father-in-law?"

Louise picked up the torch on the "no comments" and Barry said "thank you very much," and the two of them kept their funeral faces on as they headed back into Parker Center, their chorus of uniforms behind them, twirling their umbrellas of suspicion, tap-tap-tapping away.

"I THINK THAT WENT VERY WELL," LOUISE SAID AS THEY TOOK THE elevator back up to their floor.

"I'm just glad it's over."

As the elevator doors opened, Barry thought about Kelly Lund—a tough nut to crack, especially with Ilene Cutler for an attorney. But that wasn't what had struck him most during questioning. The whole time she was answering their questions about driving to Sterling Marshall's house the night of the murder, she'd looked directly into their eyes, paused an appropriate time to think, and showed no unusual signs of anxiety, and here she'd been taken in for questioning, no time to prepare. Whereas when Shane Marshall confided his suspicions about his wife back at his parents' house, his eyes kept seeking out his mother and sister, as though he were expecting them to give him cues.

Louise was saying, "I think the TMZ guys seemed pretty respectful, considering."

"I guess, but you're setting the bar pretty low," Barry said. He flashed on all those cameras, aimed at him firing squad–style. "Meet you back there."

He stopped in the men's room, checked himself in the mirror—no cowlick, nothing in the teeth, tie on straight, fly zipped. *Whew*. Probably should have done that before the press conference, though.

He splashed some water in his face, took a deep breath, then headed out the door and made for his pristine desk, ready to face the day— only to find Louise and Hank Grayson standing there. The rest of the squad was clustered around, all of them staring at him expectantly, like this was a surprise party and he still hadn't figured out that he was supposed to be surprised. "Um . . . Anything I should know?"

"Game changer," Louise said. Her face was flushed, her eyes wide. Barry had never seen her anywhere near close to this animated.

"Game changer?"

Grayson said, "We have a confession for the Sterling Marshall murder. She came in early this morning."

"What?"

"She's been booked, fingerprinted. But she says she wants to give her confession directly to you." He smiled. "Guess you made a nice impression on her . . ." He gave Louise a look. "Or a better one than your partner."

"Whatever, Hank."

Barry stared at him. "What? Wait. Did Kelly Lund confess?"

Louise said, "Wait. You honestly think you made a good impression on *Kelly Lund*?"

"Well, then . . ."

"The wife says she did it, Barry," Grayson said.

"*What?*"

"That's right," said Louise. "Mary Marshall with her urgent funeral plans. Next time you feel like giving me shit for being unsympathetic to victim's families, Mr. Bleeding Heart, you might want to chew on that one for a while."

IT WASN'T LOST ON BARRY, HOW DIFFERENT MARY MARSHALL LOOKED from the shattered woman he'd spoken to just one day earlier. Her face devoid of tears and tastefully made up, Mary was pulled together, relaxed in a clean white silk blouse and gray linen suit, manicured hands folded in her lap, her eyes surprisingly clear—which only pointed to what a mess she'd been back at her house with her two children.

As he slid into his seat across the table from her, he nearly expected it to be a joke—some sick practical joke of Louise's and somehow she'd convinced a grieving widow to play along. But no, she was serious. She was ready. "Let's get this over with," she said. "I've been waiting for hours."

Barry turned the tape recorder on. He stated the date and time and let Mary know she was being taped, asking her to state and spell her name, asking why she was at the police station, lingering on the technicalities a little too long.

"Fine," she said. "That's all fine. Let's cut to the chase. I have two confessions to make, and if you don't mind, I'd like to take care of the most painful one first."

He cleared his throat. "Okay."

"Thirty-five years ago, I visited the set of the film *Defiance*. My husband starred in it and it was directed by John McFadden."

"Yes," said Barry. He'd heard of the film, but only after McFadden's shooting. He'd been just two years old when it had come out after all. "Let me just get this straight: this is your most painful confession?"

She ignored him. "My daughter Bellamy was spending a lot of time on set," she said. "She'd become friendly with . . . the director's son. I was glad because it was summer and she didn't have many friends her own age, and frankly, it was nice to have her out of the house."

"Sure."

"Anyway, that day, I hadn't been planning on going to the set, but Shane begged and pleaded with me. He wanted to see his daddy . . ." Mary's voice trailed off, her gaze resting on the one-way mirror in a way that must have been unsettling for everyone watching, even to Louise. It was a gaze that could burn through glass.

Barry said, "I'm listening, ma'am."

"We got to the set, most everybody was around the craft services table. My husband wasn't there, but that was no surprise. He always took meals and breaks in his trailer."

Barry nodded. "Did you go looking for your husband?" He knew he shouldn't have said that. This was Mary's confession. He wasn't supposed to prompt her. But Barry desperately wanted her to get to the point of this story, which, from what he gathered, had to do with an affair of her husband's that was nearly as old as he was. He wanted that over with, so he could hear the murder confession.

"I didn't go looking for my husband. Like I said, he takes his meals alone." She closed her eyes for a moment, shut them tight, as though she was shaking away a bad thought. "I went looking for Bellamy."

Barry frowned. "Your daughter."

"Yes," she said. "McFadden's son was at the craft services table. But Bellamy was not. I . . . I got this awful feeling. An intuition. I went to John McFadden's trailer. I opened the door . . ."

"Yes."

"Bellamy was there . . . Her shirt was ripped. McFadden gave me this big smile, as though this were a perfectly normal thing for a mother to see. He asked if I'd like to stay for lunch. Bellamy ran out of that trailer so fast. I saw the tears on her face, the shame . . . She was twelve years old."

Barry swallowed hard, nodded, tried to keep his expression neutral. "What did you do next?"

"I went directly to my husband's trailer. Shane tried to go in with me, but I wouldn't let him. I told Sterling everything that had happened, demanded he pull out of *Defiance* for his family's sake. For his daughter. Prove to her he cared."

Barry thought of Marshall's face on the *Defiance* poster—the good-hearted sheriff, the man in the white hat. He thought of Bellamy Marshall, what a troubled piece of work she must be, her father giving interviews to the *Los Angeles Times* three decades after her rapist's death, calling him a "dear friend and one of the great directors of our time . . ."

So many thoughts running through his head. But he decided to go with the obvious. "Your husband didn't pull out of the movie."

Mary nodded. "He told me I must be seeing things," she said. "He called me delusional. He said *I* was sick. Made me promise never to mention it again."

"Wow," Barry said.

"When I got outside, there was McFadden, chatting up my son like it was any other day on set."

"What about Bellamy?"

"She didn't say a word about it. But she changed." She gave him a sad smile. "We all did."

She twisted her wedding band—a thick, white gold conversation piece, crusted with diamonds. "Sterling never stopped acting," she said quietly. "He played a role his whole life. Lied to the world, to all of us, time and time again."

"Mary?" Barry said.

"Yes."

"You want to tell me what happened three nights ago?"

"I killed him," she said. "Shot him three times, twice in the chest, once in the head."

"Do you feel bad about it?"

She glanced at the tape recorder, then returned to Barry's face. "What I feel bad about," she said, "is waiting thirty-five years."

CHAPTER 30

JUNE 7, 1980

ow did it go?" said Vee, after the screen test.

"Fine." Kelly couldn't say any more than that. The receptionist's lounge in his dad's Century City office was all white, with white leather couches, one wall lined with white-framed movie posters, the other made entirely of smoky glass bricks. It felt kind of like a spaceship to her, one from some old movie she'd seen on TV once but whose title she couldn't remember. She thought about that. The movie on TV. The whiteness of the room. She still couldn't look at Vee's face. Before the screen test, she'd been able to plead nerves when he asked her why she was so quiet. What could she say now?

"You okay?" Kelly felt Vee's hand at the small of her back, light, tentative. She wanted to scream.

"Uh-huh."

Bellamy had been reading a *People* magazine. She put it down. "Let's get the fook outta here," she said, her gaze moving from Kelly's face to the framed poster, just behind her, for the movie *Defiance*: Bellamy's dad in silhouette, eleven-year-old Vee in the foreground—a scared young boy in a cowboy hat. *A John McFadden Western* under the title in blazing red letters. Her eyes narrowed, as though she was angry at it.

The receptionist was a model-skinny woman in a white halter dress, with pale blond hair that looked as though it had been dyed to match the office. She was strikingly beautiful—one of those people of a different species than Kelly. Vee turned to her. "Isn't my dad going to come out and talk to us?"

"One sec, hon." She picked up the phone and buzzed him, speaking in hushed, concerned tones. "He's got a conference call, Vincent. He says he'll see you back at the house."

Vee frowned. "Okay." He headed for the door, and Bellamy and Kelly followed, Kelly watching the receptionist, who glanced up, meeting her gaze. Kelly held it. *Lucky for you, you're too old for him.*

Bellamy grabbed her hand, yanked her toward the door. She put her lips up to Kelly's ear. "Keep it together," she whispered.

IN THE CAR, BELLAMY SAID, "YOU WANT TO HEAR SOME MUSIC?"

Kelly shook her head. She was in the backseat, Vee in the front. They pulled out of the enclosed lot, Vee watching her, sea blue gaze on her face in the rearview.

"You okay, Kelly?"

Bellamy shot her a look.

"Yeah," she said quickly. "I'm just . . ." She cleared her throat. "I didn't get to visit my dad today."

"Sorry, sweetie, but I can't take you to Betty Ford," Bellamy said. "I have a date with Steve Stevens. He hates it when I'm late."

Vee said, "Do you always have to call him by his first and last name?"

And Bellamy picked up her cue, waxing on about Steve Stevens for the whole ride back to Gower, saving Kelly from the pain of trying to talk. When they got to the front of the castle, Kelly opened the door fast and flew out.

"I'll walk you up," said Vee.

"That's okay."

She tore for the front door and shoved the key in. Catherine's lipstick was in her front pocket. It pressed against her hip bone, burning. She took the stairs instead of the elevator, took them two at a time, her feet slamming into the stairs, forcing herself winded, just so she could breathe.

When she got to her floor, she bent over, hands on her knees, breath coming in gasps. *I can't. I can't. I can't do this . . .*

Soon, Kelly became aware of a pounding on the wall, just above her. McFadden's second apartment. She moved back on the landing, moved halfway up the next flight. She saw red hair, skinny legs in Dolphin shorts, little fists slamming into the door. She said, "He's at his office," and the girl turned. The Mounds girl.

Her eyes were wide, panicky. She swallowed hard, her face relaxing. Acting. "Thanks."

The girl started down the stairs. She was tiny up close, a spray of freckles across her nose. The Mounds commercial had taken place on a playground. She'd sprouted wings and flown off the jungle gym to get to the candy. Kelly said, "You should stay away from him."

She passed her without replying, without looking at her. Kelly pulled the lipstick out of her pocket and stared at it, flashing on Catherine, who could apply her lipstick without looking in a mirror. "*It's only available in Europe,*" she'd told her once. "*A special friend gave it to me . . .*"

Tears sprung into Kelly's eyes. She heard more footsteps on the stairs and soon Vee was rounding the flight, winded and smiling. "Bellamy ditched me for her date so I'll have to call a cab," he said. "But I'm walking you to the door whether you like it or not."

She looked at him.

"What's wrong?"

She gripped the silver lipstick tube, her throat clenching. He moved toward her. She felt the weight of his hand on her shoulder, the warmth of it, and she couldn't hold it in. She couldn't keep it together. Kelly grabbed Vee's hand, dropped the silver tube into it. "Your father," she said. "That's what's wrong." She slipped to the floor and he slipped down with her. He put his arms around her. "Talk to me," he said.

She told him everything.

After she was finished, he stood up. Kelly gazed up at him. She had expected tears to match her own, but what she saw in his face was worse—something in his eyes that was beyond anger, beyond hurt. Some emotion she'd never seen before, one that made her feel as though she'd set off a bomb, the timer ticking, nothing she could do. "I'm sorry," she said. "I couldn't . . . I had to . . ."

"I know," he said quietly. "I know you had to."

He turned. Headed down the stairs, faster and faster, footsteps like firecrackers exploding.

Kelly didn't see Vee again for two weeks, when he showed up at his father's wrap party, on the hottest night of the year.

CHAPTER 31

APRIL 25, 2010

R uth stared at the face on the laptop screen—the elegant, ageless face of Sterling's wife.

MARY MARSHALL CONFESSES TO HER HUSBAND'S MURDER, the headline read. But really, all Ruth could do was marvel at the fact that in 2010, Mary looked just as good as she had in 1963, if not better. After reading the article, she returned once again to the smooth skin, the golden hair of her ex-lover's wife. *I could pass for her mother now,* Ruth thought, amazed at the advances made in plastic surgery over the last twenty-five years.

The more she looked at the Internet, the shallower, the more Rose Lund–like Ruth Freed became.

Ruth was in the canteen again. Since Sebastian Todd's visit, she'd been coming in every morning after clearing the breakfast dishes, then logging on once again every night, before bed.

It was interesting and a little frightening how quickly she had taken to the Internet. She clicked on every link provided in the stories, became a fan of lurid gossip Web sites—TMZ and Perez, her gaze hanging on old pictures of Sterling, Rose Lund's old desires creeping in with each keystroke. She needed to stop. She'd exiled herself for a reason after all. And now that Mary had confessed to killing her husband—an impulsive move "after years of listening to his lies"—there was no more need for Rose to keep up with the outside world. Her daughter was in the clear.

Well, as much as she could ever be.

TMZ had run a recent photograph of Kelly leaving the Hollywood police station after her husband's arrest. She held her back straight now. Her cheekbones had grown pronounced and her laugh lines suited her, and she had a strength to her as a grown woman that she'd never had as a girl, an electricity in her gaze. For the first time, Ruth was able to see Sterling's features in the face of her daughter, and it made her smile for a moment—until she saw the headline: PSYCHO KILLER KELLY LUND IS ALL GROWN UP!

She had created a gmail account for herself. Sebastian had given her Kelly's e-mail address and she'd made the account for the sole purpose of writing to her daughter—explaining why she had never told her who her birth father was. She'd wanted to talk to Kelly about men like John McFadden and Sterling Marshall, the power they wielded back then over "nobodies" like herself, and how as a nobody, you were left with no other choice than to keep their secrets, go along with their lies. You could get a little money that way, salvage a hint of what you could fool yourself into thinking was self-respect. It was what everyone believed back then: the Rules of the Game. She wanted to tell Kelly that if she had killed John McFadden, she understood. But either way, she wanted to apologize for the sad path she'd set both her daughters on by moving to Hollywood in the first place.

The screen name was SkipToMyLou—Kelly's favorite song when she was a very little girl, though Ruth doubted, at this point, that she would remember. She couldn't bring herself to use the gmail account, though. Getting out of Kelly's life was one thing, apologizing for everything was quite another. She wasn't even sure who the apology would be for, Kelly or herself. *Some things are better left unsaid.* She used to say that to Kelly all the time. God, Ruth had been a terrible mother.

Toward the bottom of the page, Ruth noticed a link to the *Los Angeles Times*—an interview with Sebastian about his upcoming *Vanity Fair* piece. She opened it, reread it briefly. There was a recent photo of Sebastian in yet another white suit as well as a picture of Ruth, taken thirty years ago when she was Rose—rail thin, bleached hair pulled back in a bun, wearing a dark blue Evan Picone suit she'd bought at a discount from I. Magnin. Ruth clicked away from it quickly—she hated old pictures of herself—but the click brought up another picture—Kelly, right after her sentencing. She stared at it—that sweet smile, those soft, child's eyes. *Poor Kelly. My poor baby.*

"Who is that?"

Ruth jumped a little. "Always sneaking up on me," she said.

Demetrius smiled. For such a big boy, he had the quietest footfall. Ruth wondered what career that might help him in—ballet dancer, maybe. Librarian. Ninja. "What's up, honey?"

"Zeke wants to talk to you," he said. "But he wants you to read this first." Demetrius handed her a book. Her eyes widened when she saw the picture on the cover—the same picture of Kelly she'd just been looking at. *Déjà vu,* only a literal translation. She read the title: *Mona Lisa: The True Story of Hollywood Killer Kelly Lund.* Sebastian Todd's book. She winced at the phrase: Hollywood Killer.

It was a stolen library book—they had more than a few of these here at the compound, residents going to town for supplies, returning days later with some swiped literature. But this book . . . "Did you take this, DeeDee?"

He shook his head. "Zeke says he did."

"When?"

"Like a year ago."

She frowned. Strange he hadn't mentioned it to her. Though, maybe it wasn't all that strange. She remembered her most recent conversation with Sebastian Todd: *"How did you track me down in the first place?"* *"Don't you remember the letter you sent me? You said I had it wrong. That John McFadden was the real villain."* "Jesus, Zeke sent the letter . . ."

"Huh?"

She looked at Demetrius. "Nothing, honey," she said. "But wait a minute. Your dad wants me to read this entire book?"

Demetrius shook his head. "Just page seventy-five."

She opened the book. Page seventy-five was in the middle of the pictures section—a black-and-white head shot of a handsome young boy with sharp cheekbones and penetrating eyes and the caption:

Missing since 1980.

She read: *John McFadden's troubled son, teen actor Vincent Vales, disappeared two weeks before Kelly Lund shot his father. Some in attendance at the ill-fated* Resistance *wrap party claimed to have seen the then-16-year-old boy, running from his father's property the night of the murder.*

"Why does he want me to read this?" she asked. But then she looked closer at the photo—the boy's jawline, the strong chin. She thought about Zeke as he lay dying in his room. Zeke whom she had met three years after this boy's disappearance—Zeke, who had the same eyes, the same bone structure, who had changed his name and fled the material world at the same time as Vincent Vales had disappeared . . .

"I don't get it either," Demetrius was saying. But Ruth did get it. She understood. She left the canteen quickly and hurried to the cabin of Ezekiel, a grown man who had named himself for a biblical exile whose father's name meant "contempt."

ZEKE'S ROOM WAS DARK. RUTH HEARD HIS BREATHING, FRAIL AND labored. She went to the window and pulled open his draperies, the morning light illuminating his delicate cheekbones, his clean-shaven face. His eyes fluttered open. "Ruth?"

"Vincent," she said.

And with the name, he fell apart, tears streaming, shoulders shaking, arms reaching out to her. She held him until he caught his breath and calmed—or maybe he had simply grown too tired to cry. "I'm sorry."

"For what?"

"Deceiving you, all these years," he said.

"You didn't deceive me," she said. "I never knew who you were before this place because I never asked who you were."

"But I knew who you were, Ruth. I came back into town and I sought you out . . . all because of Kelly."

She looked at him, the beads of sweat on his forehead, his chest, so fragile it could collapse any minute, his whole body caving in on itself, as though it were made out of sticks. "Kelly killed your father," she said.

He shook his head. His skin was flushed There was a towel next to the bed, and Ruth took it, dabbed at his forehead. "She didn't," he said.

And Ruth noticed what the towel had been covering—a clunky old tape recorder, no doubt stolen years ago from a school or local library. "Play" and "record" had been pressed. The cassette tape inside whirred.

"What is going on?" Ruth said.

"Kelly didn't kill my father."

She stared at Zeke, face flushed, his sheets damp from his sweat. "What?"

"I killed him." He said it loudly, clear enough for the tape recorder to catch it all. "I killed my father, John McFadden."

KELLY HEARD IT FIRST FROM A TMZ REPORTER, WHO ANNOUNCED, slasher movie–style, that he was calling from "*right outside your house*." He'd asked her to step outside and let him know how she felt about her mother-in-law's confession. Kelly, who had just finished reading the text from Shane, had been so out of sorts, she'd nearly done it—until Mary Marshall saved her from herself by calling on the other line, collect from the L.A. County Jail.

"I've spoken to my lawyers. And I've made sure that should you decide to divorce Shane in light of . . . recent information . . . you'll still be provided for always."

"Did you know?"

"No," she said. "Not until the other night."

"Oh."

She lowered her voice to a near whisper. "I didn't tell the police about it. It's your news to tell or keep to yourself."

"But . . . didn't you have to tell them why you shot him?"

She let out a low, mirthless laugh. "It may have been the final straw, but trust me, I had plenty of other reasons."

"You did?" Kelly said. She was genuinely shocked, but then again nothing was as it seemed, the kaleidoscope turning in on itself again, her eyes going back to Shane's text, rereading it yet again. *Bellamy* . . .

"Trust me, honey," her mother-in-law was saying. "A woman can only be lied to for so long."

"Mary?"

"Yes."

"Do you miss him?"

She said nothing for several seconds. On Mary's end of the line, Kelly heard noises at a distance—a loud clang, a woman's voice shouting. "I miss who I thought he was," she said.

For a moment, Kelly flashed on the Marshalls at the dinner table, the picture-perfect couple she remembered from her youth. Sterling slicing a roast, drugged, serene Mary ladling out peas for her beautiful children. *To have a house like this*, Kelly had thought. *To have parents like those*.

"Life is very strange," Mary said. "Though I have learned this, Kelly. Ultimately, everything comes out in the wash. We all get what we deserve."

"Including John McFadden?"

Again, Mary took a long pause, the prison sounds bringing back memories . . .

"Did Ilene Cutler tell you what I said?"

"Yes."

"About John McFadden. How you did the world a favor."

"Yes," she said. "But I'm not sure what you meant by that."

A man's voice shouted, "Two more minutes!"

"All I can say, Kelly, is that as Bellamy's mother, I wish you'd made it hurt more."

Kelly's breath caught.

"I have to go, dear," Mary said.

"Wait," said Kelly, recalling the way Bellamy would avert her eyes when John McFadden was in the room, how she'd taken rides from him, but only in groups, always insisting on being dropped off first.

"We'll talk again soon." Mary sighed. "You must give me advice on how to get used to prison life. Timed phone conversations at my age. Really."

There was a hummingbird outside Kelly's kitchen window, sitting on the edge of her feeder. She'd never seen one take the time to sit still before, and it was so beautiful at rest, its needlelike beak, tiny wings shining like jewels. *To be that perfect, that free. To have that short a life span.*

She didn't want to think about what McFadden had done to Bellamy, how much he must have hurt her, but she couldn't help it, couldn't get herself to look away. She remembered the blood-crusted razor in Bellamy's vanity drawer and the cuts beneath Bellamy's bangle bracelets and how she'd begged Kelly to keep them a secret, their secret. *Sisters.*

Kelly had. She'd never understood the red slashes, but she'd stayed quiet about them her whole life, not knowing until this moment that Bellamy's cutting wasn't a secret in and of itself; it was a symptom of a secret so much bigger and uglier.

Everything comes out in the wash.

Kelly read Shane's text again, making sure she understood it correctly. The morning after Catherine had fallen to her death, Shane had seen Bellamy stashing Catherine's prized lipstick in the back of her drawer. No tale of abuse could cover up that fact. It was written on Kelly's screen. Shane had seen it for himself. Bellamy had probably been the last person to see Catherine alive.

Was it warped jealousy over McFadden or over the father Catherine knew they shared that had brought them both to Chantry Flats on Valentine's night, 1978? Kelly needed to know. It had been thirty-two years. As Mary Marshall had so eloquently said, *A woman can only be lied to for so long.*

Kelly grabbed the butcher knife off the counter, stashed it in her purse, headed out the door to her rented Breeze Expresso, ignoring the shouts and camera flashes as she turned the ignition, set her GPS for Bellamy's address.

ZEKE TOLD RUTH EVERYTHING. HE SHARED EVERY DETAIL OF A NIGHT thirty years ago that resulted in a twenty-five-year prison sentence for her only daughter, who spent more than half her life behind bars. He was so frail it was hard, at first, for him to get the words out. But strangely, they seemed to give him strength, the story his life's purpose . . . or at least the tiny shred of life that remained.

"He had killed Cat," he said. "He'd pushed her in that canyon."

"Kelly told you this."

"Yes. She had proof."

She closed her eyes. Kelly had been living with her father at the time. The two of them weren't even speaking, Rose having thrown Kelly out of the house over her choice of friends, her seventeen-year-old daughter having to deal with this ugly truth on her own . . . *Why didn't she call me? I would have helped her* . . . But then she remembered. Kelly had called her. Three in the morning, she'd been up cleaning, Kelly had called to ask what her and Catherine's last fight had been about, and Ruth had told her about the pregnancy . . . How could Rose have just let Kelly hang up? How could she have been so awful?

"I was gone for weeks," Zeke said. "On a bender. That's the way I handled things back then. But I came back in time for my father's wrap party."

"Okay."

"I planned to kill him. And I did."

Ruth swallowed. "She wouldn't speak to police, other than to say she did it. She was definite about that. She told me too."

"Kelly didn't kill him. I showed up at the party and she was there. She only wanted to confront my dad . . . to ask him why he did it. She followed me into the Moroccan room. He was in there, rehearsing his speech. I'd swiped one of his guns out of his safe. She begged me not to do it. He started saying things to me. Terrible things." His voice quavered, the strength leaving him, fast as it had come.

Ruth took his hand in hers. "It's okay," she tried.

"It's not okay. I shot him. Twice in the chest, once in the head. There were screams in the hallway. Footsteps. People heard. Kelly opened the sliding door. She told me to run, so I did. I ran away like a coward. Hid for years. Let her take the rap."

She thought of Kelly, paralyzed in that mansion on that record-hot night, police cars arriving, sirens blaring, cuffs clamped on her wrists. "You're right," she whispered. "It isn't okay."

His head fell back on the pillow. "It's exhausting," he said.

"What is?"

"Telling the truth."

She nodded.

"I'm so thirsty," Zeke said. An empty glass stood on his nightstand, full pitcher next to it. He didn't have the energy to reach it, she knew that. But she couldn't get herself to pour it for him. She glanced at the old tape recorder, cassette whirring and chugging, holding on to their words. "Kelly isn't a killer," she said. "She never was."

"No, Ruth," he said, his voice nothing more than struggling breath. "You raised a very good person."

Ruth's eyes began to well. She picked up the pitcher, poured Zeke a glass. "Here," she said. "Drink this." He didn't take it. He didn't move.

CHAPTER 32

A DEATHBED CONFESSION
EXONERATES KELLY MICHELLE LUND

Special to the Los Angeles Times *by Sebastian Todd*

April 26, 2010, Mariposa, Calif.—She served 25 years in prison for the murder of Oscar-nominated director John McFadden. But five years after her release, Kelly Michelle Lund's name—and reputation—have been cleared at last.

With tears in her eyes, Kelly Lund's mother, Defiance commune member Ruth Freed, 67, delivered a taped confession to Mariposa County Police—made by the commune's founder Zeke Freed, 46, shortly before his death due to complications from stage 4 Hodgkin's disease. On the tape, Freed (real name Vincent Vales) reveals himself to be the long-missing son of McFadden and claims to have shot his father following a two-week-long drug bender. "She took the rap for him," explains Ms. Freed, formerly Rose Lund. "Zeke wanted me to know that my daughter was never a murderer."

For the past 27 years, Mr. Freed, Ms. Freed, and from a dozen to 20 other rotating residents, all using the same last name, have inhabited 40 acres of land just outside the tiny desert town of Mariposa, Calif. Known by locals as Defiance, it was the location of the 1976 John McFadden–directed western of the same name, which featured an 11-year-old Vincent Vales in a leading role.

The land—a self-sustaining farm on which milk, cheese, fresh eggs, vegetables, and homemade candles are produced and sometimes sold — formerly belonged to the director McFadden, but was quietly transferred to his son's name three years after his death. Vales, who went by a series of aliases, went about legally changing his name to Ezekiel Freed, tilling the previously barren land and recruiting "lost souls" for his "utopian community," as Ruth Freed puts it. "It was a place to start over. We all desperately needed that. And as the mother of Vincent Vales's most self-sacrificing friend, I was number one on his list. After all, he owed Kelly his life."

Indeed, before his own communal rebirth, Vincent Vales McFadden was quite a "lost soul" himself—a known drug user with a rap sheet that included three arrests for possession of illegal substances and one for discharging a firearm in a public space.

For years, conspiracy theories have abounded about the troubled teen, with some claiming to have seen him running from McFadden's Mulholland Drive mansion on June 28, 1980, shortly after the fatal shots were fired.

According to Ms. Lund, the dying Mr. Freed summoned her into his quarters when he knew the end was near. "For the first time, he told me his real name," she says. "All these years, I'd thought he was a stranger who had seen me on the news during Kelly's trial and somehow sensed I was a kindred spirit. His final gift to me was the most precious of all gifts—the truth."

In his will, Mr. Freed left the Defiance land to Ms. Freed—who intends to keep the commune going, at least for a while. "I have many dear friends here," she said. "I wouldn't have them thrown out on the street."

Kelly Lund was unavailable for comment at press time.

CHAPTER 33

As she headed up the 405, Kelly turned off her cell phone. Too many reporters calling, plus, she didn't want to be tracked.

The Breeze Expresso glided over the highway, with the radio off, avoiding the news. The drive went quickly—more like five minutes than twenty-five. She drove through Bellamy's complex, that hive of condos, each one exactly the same as the next. *How easy it would be to get lost in here,* she thought, her eyes tracking a way out. A getaway.

She reached Bellamy's house, the draperies open, showing a hint of her southwestern furniture and, once she reached the curb, the bottom half of *Mona Lisa*.

Kelly left her car and walked up to Bellamy's front door, her mind shifting, turning, aware of the butcher knife weighing down her purse as she rang the bell, blood running hot, angry.

"MY GOD," SAID BELLAMY WHEN SHE OPENED THE DOOR.
She hadn't changed much. Though she was thinner and a bit more tired and faded than she'd been as a teen, with years of cigarettes etching tiny lines around her lips, Bellamy still put the same amount of effort into her appearance. Kelly

noted the ebony dyed hair, the deep red lips and eyeliner, even though she wasn't yet dressed. She wore a thick, white terry cloth robe. She looked like an actress, shooting a soap opera scene that took place at a luxury spa.

"I need to talk to you," Kelly said.

Bellamy didn't put up a fight. How could she? Kelly hadn't killed her father. Her mother had—something she'd no doubt known all along. Bellamy let her in. "I guess I should say congratulations," she said.

"For not killing your father?"

"You didn't hear?"

Kelly frowned at her. "Hear what?"

Bellamy exhaled. "You were cleared of John McFadden's murder. Vee confessed to it."

"*Vee?*"

"Deathbed confession. All these years, he's been living with your mom in some cult."

Kelly stood there for several seconds. Unable to form words. "Can I get you some tea?" Bellamy said.

"You're lying."

She exhaled. "I don't lie, Kelly," she said. A lie in and of itself.

She's full of crap. Trying to distract you. Don't take the bait. "Bellamy, why did you say that to me on the phone about John McFadden?"

"Huh?"

"Why did you say that John McFadden was your father's best friend, nothing more? That was a lie if there ever was one."

"Shane was in the next room. I thought he might wake up."

Kelly closed her eyes. She didn't have time to dance around subjects, and even if she did, she'd never been very good at it. "I know what he did to you," Kelly said. "I know what John McFadden did to you."

"He didn't do anything to me."

"Your mother told me," she said quietly. "I'm sorry. If it was me, I would have wanted him dead too."

Bellamy let out a long, tired sigh. She collapsed onto the big mission chair. "Kelly, why are you always bringing up ancient history?"

"Twenty-five years in prison will do that to you," she said. "What I'm trying to say, Bellamy, is I know you planted the lipstick."

"What?"

"Catherine's fancy lipstick. The thing that made Vee and me go crazy."

"I found it in the trunk of John McFadden's Porsche."

"Yeah that's what you said and it was dumb. If he'd killed Catherine in that car, it would have been scrubbed within an inch of its life. And he certainly wouldn't have left a tube of her one-of-a-kind European lipstick in the trunk so you could find it there two years later."

She shrugged. "If it was so dumb, why did you believe it?"

"Because I was dumb too. I was seventeen and I loved you and I wanted to believe every word you said."

"Okay, Kelly." She sighed. "You win."

"What do I win? *Say it*."

"Fine. I planted that lipstick in John McFadden's trunk when I was seventeen freakin' years old. Yes, he abused me as a kid. Yes, I hated him, but I didn't think it would drive you so insane *you'd show up at that wrap party*. Jesus you were so wasted. And Vee—"

"Why did you kill Catherine?"

"*What?*"

"You killed my sister."

She stared at her, jaw gaping. "I . . . I . . . did *not* . . ."

"The lipstick. It was obvious you planted it. I knew that for years. But here's the big question, Bellamy. How did you get it? Catherine took that stupid tube of European lipstick with her everywhere, that silver tube, limited edition Rouge de la Bohème that nobody knew of in the States. She guarded it with her life, but when you wanted to make it clear that John McFadden killed her, you had that Rouge de la Bohème at the ready."

"It wasn't the only tube ever made."

"It was *hers*. Shane saw you hiding it right after she died. You killed her. And she wasn't just my sister. She was *your sister too*."

"Oh . . ."

"I found out yesterday. But you've known for longer. Another lie."

Bellamy's head tilted to the side and she got that look in her eye, that mean glint she used to get when things weren't going her way that would frighten Kelly when they were kids. It didn't now. "You wearing a wire, or what?"

Kelly looked at her. She thought of the knife in her purse and placed her hand on it. "What is this, some cop show? You want to frisk me?"

Bellamy folded her hands in the lap of her puffy spa robe. "No, I don't need to frisk you."

"Bellamy," Kelly said. "We're not getting any younger. Doesn't it get tiring, playing mind games all the time?"

Bellamy took a deep breath, in and out, pulled the belt of her robe tighter. "You know when I found out about my dad and your mom?"

Kelly shook her head.

"Thirty-three years ago. Catherine told me."

"She did?"

"She had this necklace . . . God, I hated that necklace. It was like she was taunting me with it. It was a 'love gift,' she told me. She said your mom bragged about it."

Kelly shook her head. "She didn't. My mom hated Catherine wearing it. She didn't want anyone to know."

"That's not what your sister said."

"If my mom wanted people to know, how come I thought Jimmy was my birth father until last Tuesday?"

She looked at her. "Well, your sister tortured me with it."

"How did you even meet her?"

"Through Vee. Jimmy had introduced her to Vee and his father, but I guess her plan all along was to get close to me. And it worked for a while. I liked her at first. Until she started calling herself Hollywood Royalty."

"When was that?"

"I don't remember. One night, we're all wasted at Vee's dad's mansion and Cat pulls me into the bathroom and drops the bomb. She and I are half sisters. She said your mom told her."

"She must have worn her down . . ."

"I didn't believe her. I thought my dad was a good guy. But then I asked him."

"What did he say?"

"He said no at first, but then he admitted it was true and he made me promise never to tell anyone, ever. He said it would kill my mother. Flash-forward to Valentine's Day, Cat was pregnant by McFadden." She winced. "I thought it was disgusting. But she had some kind of dream of raising her baby in luxury."

"She thought he'd support her, move in together . . . She went to see him that night."

"Yes. But then when he told her no way, she came to me."

"She stole my mother's car."

"Yes."

"Left at three in the morning."

"She drove it to my house. She got me to buzz her in through the gate. She was acting crazy. I'm pretty sure she was on something. She kept saying she was going to wake up my mom and tell her who her real father was. And how he was going to be a grandfather soon so he'd better pay up . . . She was making all this noise. I said, 'Cat. Let's talk about this.'" Bellamy's voice broke. A tear trickled down her cheek. "I . . . I . . . sneaked out of my house. I was always doing that. She took your mom's car and I followed her in one of my dad's all the way to Chantry Flats. The whole way there, I was getting angrier and angrier and when we both got out of our cars I couldn't . . . She swore she'd tell my mom . . . I lost control."

"So you pushed her."

"We were fighting. I'd never been in a physical fight before, but there we were on the edge of the canyon and I was . . . I was filled with this . . . I couldn't explain it . . ."

"Rage," Kelly said, because she knew, she understood. "Powerlessness."

"I punched her in the face. She fell and kind of . . . she tripped." Kelly nodded.

"She slipped over the edge of the canyon. She reached for me. I didn't get there in time."

"I understand," she said.

"You're different than her, Kelly. I made friends with you because I wanted to find out how much you knew. But you didn't know anything. You didn't play games. You were good." Bellamy stood up. A tear slipped down her cheek, then another, trailing mascara. "You were my sister," she said. "My real sister."

Kelly moved toward Bellamy, toward her outstretched arms. She looked into Bellamy's black sad eyes and wanted to hug her, to put the past in a box and lock it, gloss it all over and move on, the way family does. But something stopped her—a cold, nameless feeling. "I'm sorry, Bellamy," she said quietly. "I don't believe it was an accident."

Bellamy's lip trembled. "It wasn't," she said. Then she pushed Kelly onto the couch, pulled a gun out from her robe, and shot her.

CHAPTER 34

JUNE 28, 1980

You want some more?" Len said.

Kelly was sitting in his Trans Am, snorting cocaine off this crazy mirror of his—a big, pink plastic thing that looked like it belonged in a 1950s beauty parlor. "Where did you get this mirror anyway?" Kelly said.

"It's my mom's."

Kelly laughed. Len wasn't so bad. With Vee having run off somewhere, Jimmy still in rehab, and Bellamy spending close to 100 percent of her time with Steve Stevens, Kelly had been easing her loneliness with Len, whom she'd run into a week ago when she was eating a burger at Tommy's. "I know you, don't I?" said this skinny guy, still with the same pencilly mustache, the same rattlesnake belt buckle he'd been wearing the day she'd gone to Bellamy's house for the first time. He'd been her first kiss, her first everything, and he barely remembered her. That was okay. She'd never learned his last name.

Len had offered her a ride back to Jimmy's, where she had been staying alone these days. It had been so hot out lately, the air thick and pressing like bad breath. Kelly couldn't stop sweating whenever she went outside, and so they'd gone into Jimmy's bedroom, which was the only room in the house with air-conditioning. They'd shared a bottle of Jack Daniel's and then Len spent the night.

The rest was history, though it wasn't a boyfriend thing. The day of the screen test had done strange things to Kelly's head. She didn't want a boyfriend anymore. She was too angry for a boyfriend.

"So do you want to come as my date or what?" Kelly said, after snorting another line.

"To some movie wrap party?" He chuckled, showing long horsey teeth. "No way. Those things are bouge."

"Bellamy's going to be there," Kelly said. "And Steve Stevens."

"Steve who?"

"Some actor." Len didn't know who anybody was. She liked that. "Do you have any weed?"

THREE HOURS LATER, LEN AND KELLY WERE DRIVING THROUGH JOHN McFadden's open gate, parking the Trans Am behind Rollses and Bentleys and Jags, both of them tumbling out, smoke all around them. Kelly pressed up against him. His Black Sabbath T-shirt was wet with sweat. "I hate John McFadden," she whispered in Len's ear, licking his neck as she did it. "He killed my sister."

"He what? Wait. You don't have a sister."

She put her hands on his face, tried to make it stand still. "You are very cute," she said, words slurring. "But you are too dumb to live."

SHE WANDERED THROUGH THE HOUSE—LUXURIOUS, AIR-CONDITIONED rooms moving in and out of focus. *More high than I thought I was.* A familiar-looking actor walked by—an older man in a velvet suit. He looked Kelly up and down, but not in a complimentary way. She was aware of her denim shorts, the orange Hang Ten T-shirt she'd pulled out of Jimmy's closet, the sweat in her hair. *Probably should have dressed for this thing.*

She hoped she didn't stand out too much—she had purposely worn this outfit so she could run quickly, but she hadn't thought much about how it looked. The goal was to break things. That had always been the goal. If she couldn't sue John McFadden or get him arrested, Kelly was going to break every expensive thing in his house and run away before he saw who did it. Len would drive the getaway car. If she could find him. Where had he gone? She passed a group of mile-high models in vintage miniskirts, go-go boots sparkling on their long legs. Kelly couldn't figure out whether they were cast members or paid entertainment, but they had that look to them, like they were startled by their own beauty. In Kelly's state of mind, they looked otherworldly, spectacular.

At the other end of the room, she saw Bellamy, in a red silk dress that played up her black hair. She reminded Kelly of a princess. Snow White? No. Rose Red. A tall, blond guy stood next to her—Steve Stevens, probably. Kelly watched her for a while, the way she laughed, her head thrown back, as though the conversation was something delicious, something to be savored. How could she look so happy in John McFadden's house? How could she act as though she didn't care what he had done to Catherine? She raised a hand and waved. But Bellamy looked right through her. Did she not see her? Kelly started to head toward her when she felt a hand on her arm, grabbing. She figured it was Len, but when she turned around she saw Vee's face, dirty and wild-eyed. "Oh my God, Vee—"

"Ssssh." He put a finger over his lips. He kept his head down. She followed him through more rooms, past more beautiful people, everything shimmering around the edges, the two of them ghosts.

"Do you want to break things with me?" she whispered.

He shook his head. "Come with me." He took Kelly's hand and led her through the sunroom, through some other room with a tiger's head on the wall and a group of men with cigars, laughing, to the same place where they'd run lines together two weeks ago—the Moroccan room. He ushered her in quickly, locked the door behind her. She turned around. "Vee," she started to say again. But he shushed her. They weren't alone.

John McFadden stood in the corner with his back to them, rehearsing a speech. "All of you are more than family to me," he said to the curtains. "We share a bond that's thicker than blood—and that bond is creation. It is art. Thank you very much. Now enjoy the party!"

Vee clapped, loudly. For the first time, Kelly got a good look at him—dirt-caked jeans, greasy hair. There was a stale smell to him too, as though he hadn't showered in weeks. Where had he been staying? What had he been doing? And there was his father, in his black expensive suit, practicing what to say in front of a bunch of actors. His own father, who hadn't even bothered to look for him. "Bravo," Vee said.

McFadden whirled around. "Where the hell have you been?" He looked at Kelly. "What's she doing here?"

"You don't get to ask me those questions," Vee said. "I'm here because I need answers and you're going to give them to me."

"Don't you dare talk to me like that. My God, you reek."

"How could you do that to her? She . . . she was a living, breathing person."

"Who?"

"Cat," he said. "You took her away from me. From everyone. Why?"

McFadden exhaled. "I don't know what you're talking about, Vincent. Now I want you to go upstairs and shower and put on some clean clothes . . ."

Vee pulled something out of his jean jacket pocket—a gun. Same gun they'd taken to the desert all those weeks ago. He aimed it at his father. McFadden froze. Kelly's mouth went dry. "No," she said, as calmly as she could. "No, Vee. Don't."

Vee said, "You're not the man I thought you were." He held the gun straight out in front of him, his hands shaking. "You're not a man at all."

McFadden's face was perfectly still, his whole body motionless. Kelly's gaze went from Vee to his father, and for a moment, time stopped, the two of them locked like this—Vee with all the power, McFadden waiting to see what he did with it.

Until finally, McFadden shifted. His shoulders relaxed. "Listen, you little drug-addicted piece of shit," he said. "You put that gun down or I'm calling the police and having you thrown in jail for the rest of your life."

Vee's eyes went soft, scared.

"I'll do it. You know I will."

"You . . . You took Cat."

"You're a big disappointment to me, Vincent," McFadden said. "It's no wonder your mother wants nothing to do with you."

The gun shook in Vee's hands. "That isn't true."

"Ever wonder why we never hear from her anymore? Not even on Christmas?"

"Because . . . because she hates you."

"Guess again."

Vee winced, as though someone had slapped him.

"You're mean," Kelly whispered.

McFadden didn't even look at her. "Put that gun down and go to your room," he said to his son. "I don't want you around my guests."

Vee's arms dropped. He started to cry. McFadden turned around again and began reciting his speech to the ruby curtain, as though Vee and Kelly weren't in the room with him at all. "I'm sorry," Vee whispered. He put the gun down on the desk and looked at Kelly. "I'm sorry."

"I would like to welcome you, my true family," McFadden said as Vee crumpled up and wept. And within Kelly, something snapped. "The work you have all put in makes me feel like a proud parent . . ."

Kelly picked up the gun. She held it out in front of her, fingers on the trigger, power coursing up through her arms, into her heart. "John McFadden," she said.

He turned around.

"Are you sorry about Catherine?"

"Oh Jesus. You too?"

Kelly fired at him, twice in the chest.

"Oh my God," said Vee. "Oh my God, Kelly." His arm went around her back, the weight of his hand on her shoulder.

McFadden fell to the ground, gazing up at her. *What have I done,* Kelly thought. His mouth was still moving, trying to form words. "Thicker than blood," he said, and she realized he was still rehearsing his speech. Kelly raised the gun and shot him between the eyes.

CHAPTER 35

JUNE 2, 2010

It still felt strange to Kelly, sitting next to her mother, but she was getting used to it. Mom had visited her in the hospital several times when she was recovering from her bullet wound, accompanied by guards from Mariposa County Jail. The guards treated the two of them like A-list celebrities. Odd, one of them a farmer who used to work at I. Magnin, the other an ex-con who worked for a semi-illegal dating Web site. These guards couldn't get enough of them. One had even asked for Kelly's autograph.

Of course, people change. Wounds heal, some faster than others. Kelly's neck wound, for instance, was almost completely healed, flesh wound that it was, while her shoulder, still in a sling, would keep her in physical therapy for months. Good thing Bellamy wasn't a better shot, her southwestern couch having taken most of the bullets. *It's not personal,* she'd kept saying as she fired and fired, Bellamy who had once picked up Vee's gun and shot at a stream full of fish without checking to see if it was loaded. Bellamy had always been more about impulse than aim.

Strange, as Kelly lay bleeding on Bellamy's living room floor, Bellamy knelt down and said to her, "*I'm only protecting my family.*" But who had she meant? Her father was dead, mother had already confessed to the police, and her brother had left her house, vowing never to speak to her again. "*I'm* your family, you idiot," Kelly had whispered. And that's when Bellamy had finally called 911.

So the irony wasn't lost on Kelly—her mother and herself sitting across from Bellamy in the sun-drenched visitors' room of Malibu's Passages Mental Health Center, the closest thing to family that Bellamy Marshall now had. As usual, she wore full makeup, bright red lips, but the effect was strange with hospital scrubs, vacant eyes.

Her intense gaze was gone—Kelly knew it was probably the meds, but Bellamy looked as though she'd had the spirit sapped out of her, as though she had nothing to live for with her family gone and she was wandering through life aimlessly, a ghost looking for the next role to inhabit. Maybe that's why she'd asked them to come. It had been her doctor who called both Kelly and Ruth, saying it would be a great service, but she'd never explained why Bellamy wanted to see them, or even if she did.

"I'm writing a book," Bellamy said now for the third time, staring at the middle distance between Kelly and Ruth, so neither one of them knew to whom she was speaking. "A tell-all about growing up in Hollywood."

"Are we going to be in it?" Kelly said.

"Maybe." She lit a cigarette. Exhaled slowly. Looked at Ruth. "Can I ask you something?"

"Yes."

"Did my father love you?"

Ruth's gaze moved from Kelly to Bellamy. "It was a long time ago."

"I know that. But did he? Did he tell you he loved you?"

She cleared her throat. "Yes, Bellamy," she said carefully. "He did."

"What did that feel like?"

"Being in love?"

"No. How did it feel to hear my father say 'I love you'?"

Kelly looked at her. "He never said it to you?"

She shook her head. "Not once," she said, her voice small, lost. "I'd love to know how it sounds, my father saying those words."

KELLY AND RUTH LEFT THE FACILITY IN SILENCE, IMAGES ROLLING through Kelly's mind—Bellamy Marshall at seventeen passing her notes in science class, mascaraed eyes searching for her in the rearview mirror of the car, asking if she was having fun.

"You know what I liked most about Bellamy when we were kids?" she said.

Ruth turned to her. "Her glamorous lifestyle?"

She shook her head. "No," Kelly said. "I liked her because she paid so much attention to me. But now that I look back on it, I think maybe she was just sizing up the competition."

Ruth shook her head. "Don't be cynical about your memories, Kelly. Paint them in a golden light. Make them into beautiful fiction. They're all you've got."

"Okay," she said. "Bellamy adored me. She really did love me like a sister."

"That's the spirit." As she slipped into her pickup truck, ready to head back to Defiance, she touched Kelly's hand, gave her a smile. "You know, now that I think about it, I'm not entirely sure Sterling ever said he loved me. But it's still nice to remember it that way."

Kelly swallowed. "I miss Shane," she said.

"It's good to miss people. It reminds you you're not alone in the world."

"Did you miss me, Mother?"

"Every day."

Kelly kissed her mother on the cheek. She watched her drive away, thinking of Shane just one week ago, leaving for good to go to San Francisco, the latest person in her life to fall away. Their parting had been amicable but strange and sad. "*You're not losing a husband, you're gaining a brother,*" he had said as he'd gotten into the airport limo.

"*But I am losing a husband,*" she'd replied.

"Miss Lund!" An excited young voice shook her out of her thoughts. Kelly turned to see a nurse rushing across the parking lot toward her, waving a piece of notebook paper.

"Did I leave something?" she said.

"No." The nurse had shiny blond hair. Round, light eyes like a kitten's. "I just can't believe it's you. I'm a huge fan."

Kelly stared at her. "Of *me*?"

"Yes! Taking the rap for your friend like that. All those years in prison when you didn't kill anybody. You're a hero."

Kelly forced a smile, the night of June 28, 1980, coming at her in flashes before she shoved it into a drawer. "Thank you," she said.

The nurse handed her the piece of paper and a pen. "Can I have your autograph, please? I'm Jenna. With a *J*."

Kelly held the paper against the car and wrote.

To Jenna:
Don't stop believing!
Love, Kelly Michelle Lund

The girl nearly swooned. Kelly got in her car. "Thanks, Vee," she whispered, though really, she'd never needed any favors from Vee, never needed him in her life for any longer than he'd been in it.

In two hours, she'd be back at her home with her birds and her laptop computer, her skull-headed angel and her tattooed ex-bully—

Rocky Three, who for now was someone to believe in. She pulled out onto the Pacific Coast Highway and rolled down the windows, smelling the ocean air, gazing out at the road ahead, and, for the briefest of moments, recalling McFadden's last words, the feel of the gun discharging in her hands as he lay on that jewel-toned carpet, mouthing his speech. *A hero.* Kelly felt as though she could drive forever.

ACKNOWLEDGMENTS

Big thanks to detectives Tim Marcia and Mitzi Roberts of the LAPD's Robbery-Homicide division, who graciously allowed me into their workplace and answered many, many questions. Anything I got right in the Barry Dupree sections is due to their help. Anything I got wrong . . . well, that's on me.

As ever, thanks to the wonderful Deborah Schneider, my outstanding editor Lyssa Keusch, and the tireless Rebecca Lucash. I am so grateful to Liate Stehlik and the HarperCollins/William Morrow team for all their support.

Thanks to Stephanie Riggio for her Joshua Tree expertise, Marcia Clark for early-on legal expertise, Bill Ward for naming my strip club, and Linda Flyntz Rubin for her memory of defective '70s dolls. I'm grateful as well to my writer friends for their help and feedback—particularly Megan Abbott and Paul Leone at the beginning of this process and Abigail Thomas at the end. And to the FLs, who instigate and inspire me and make me laugh on a daily basis, even when I'm on deadline. Thanks to The Golden Notebook in Woodstock, NY, aka best bookstore EVER, for their support of local authors.

Chas Cerulli and James Conrad, Anthony Marcello and Paul, Jamie and Doug Barthel, thank you for listening to my whining and helping to keep me (reasonably) sane during the writing of this book. Thanks and love to my amazing in-laws, Sheldon and Marilyn Gaylin, and my wonderful mom, Beverly LeBov Sloane. And to Mike and Marissa, who I can't possibly hug enough.

Coming July 2017

The new novel from A L GAYLIN

Turn the page to read an extract . . .

PROLOGUE

From the Facebook page of Jacqueline Merrick Reed
October 29, 4:00 A.M.
By the time you read this, I'll be dead.

This isn't Jackie. It's her son Wade. She doesn't know where I am. She doesn't even know I can get on her FB page, so don't ask her. Stop asking her things. This isn't her fault. I am not her fault.

I am writing to tell my mom and Connor that I'm sorry. I never meant to hurt anyone. I wish I could tell you the truth of what happened, but it's not my truth to tell. And anyway, it doesn't matter. What matters, what I want you both to know is that I love you. Don't feel sad. Everything you did was the right thing to do. I'm sorry for those things I said to you, Connor. I didn't mean any of it.

Funny, I'm thinking about you right now, Connor. How you used to follow me around all the time when you were a little kid. How you used to copy everything I did. You probably don't remember this but when you were about four, I taught you the middle finger, and you did it to that mean babysitter we had. What was her name, Mom? Loretta? Lurleen? Anyway, whatever her name was had some crap reality show on the TV. Real Housewives of the Seventh Circle of Hell. She wouldn't let us watch the Mets game and called us nasty little brats and told us we had no business talking at all because children should be seen and not heard. Whatever that's supposed to mean.

So, Connor gets off the couch, walks up to Lurleen and flips her the bird. He was so little, he needed two hands to do it. He used the left hand to hold down the fingers on the right. Do you remember this, Mom? Because I'm pretty sure she ratted us out without explaining the context of forcing us to watch her crap TV show. You were so mad, we didn't get dessert for two weeks.

I remember thinking how unfair the whole thing was and how quick grown-ups were to believe the lies of other grown-ups, especially when it came to their own kids. But looking back on it now, all I can remember is how red Loretta's face got and how hard we both laughed, even with her shrieking at us. It was one of those moments. My English teacher Mrs. Crawford calls them "memory gifts". You keep them in a special part of your brain and you kind of wrap them up to preserve them and tie them with a ribbon, so when you need them, when you're feeling really bad, you can unwrap them and you remember all the details and feel the moment all over again. So thanks for that memory gift, Buddy. It's making me smile now.

I'm writing this just after taking the pills, but I won't post it until I start to really feel them. According to what I read, death comes pretty soon after that.

So I'm typing extra fast. Sorry about typos lol.

This will probably make a lot of you very happy. Good. For anybody who might be sad, sorry. But you know what? Stuff happens. Things go wrong. And the more you stick around, the wronger they get. I know I'm just 17. But I think of what life would be like if I wasn't here. I think of the way things could have gone without me in the picture, how much better it would be. And then I know. I'm sure of it. I've lived too long already.

ONE

TEN DAYS EARLIER

I n bed late at night with her laptop, Jackie Reed sometimes forgot there were others in the house. That's how
quiet it was here, with these hushed boys of hers,
always with their heads down, with their shuffling
footsteps and their padded sneakers, their muttered greet-
ings, closing doors behind them.

When did kids get to be so quiet? When she was
their age—well Wade's age anyway—Jackie clomped
around in her Doc Martens and slammed doors. She'd
blast her albums as loud as they'd go – Violent Femmes
and Siouxsie Sioux and Scraping Foetus Off the Wheel –
edging up the volume until her bones vibrated with the
bass, the drums, flailing around her room, dancing as
hard as she could while her parents pounded on the walls,
begging her to turn it down.

Please, Jacqueline, I can't hear myself think!

Looking back on it now, she saw it as a rite of pas-
sage, the same one her mother had gone through with her
Elvis and her Lesley Gore, and her grandmother too, no
doubt, cranking the Mario Lanza like she was the only

person who mattered in the cramped Brooklyn walk-up where she grew up.

There was such power in loud music, such teenage energy and rebellion and soaring possibility. Who'd have thought, back then, that it would all go extinct with just one generation? These days, teens plugged themselves into devices, headphone wires spooling out of their ears like antennae. They kept their music to themselves, kept everything to themselves and their devices and the friends they talked to on those devices, all of whom you couldn't hear, couldn't see unless you swiped their phones away mid-conversation to read the screen, and who wanted to do that? Who wanted to be *that mom*?

They shut you out. Your children shut you out of their heads, their lives. And that was a form of rebellion so much more chilling than blasting music or yelling. They made it so you couldn't know them anymore. They made it so you couldn't help.

Just yesterday, she'd been making breakfast when Wade's phone had gone off like a bomb on the kitchen counter. That incoming text tone of his, literally *like a bomb*, the sound of an explosion. *When and why did he download that?* Jackie had nearly jumped out of her skin, spattering bacon grease, hand pressed to her heart . . . She'd picked it up, more reflex than anything else, looked at the screen. The text had been from someone he'd nicknamed simply T:

LEAVE ME ALONE

The gut-punch of those words, the intimacy of the single initial. Who was this person? A girl? *How could she say that to Wade? What has he done?* All those questions swirling through her mind. And here, a day later, Jackie still didn't know the answer to a single one of them.

Once Wade had retrieved his phone and left for school, she'd checked his long-abandoned Facebook page for cryptic posts from friends with T-names, dusted his room for evidence of a girlfriend –

but not too deeply. She couldn't bear to hack his laptop or go through his drawers. She wasn't *that mom*.

Casually, in the car on the way to his piano lesson, she'd asked Connor, *"Do you know if Wade has been fighting with any of his friends?"*

Connor had shaken his head and replied quietly, said it to the car floor in his cracking, changing thirteen-year-old voice. *"I don't really know too many of Wade's friends, Mom."*

Jackie sighed. She and Wade needed to talk. But not now. It was past midnight and his third and final chance at the SATs was tomorrow and he needed his sleep. Wade was looking so tired lately, she wondered if he ever really slept at all.

Jackie felt a chill at her back, cold night air pressing against her bedroom window, against the thin walls, creeping through cracks in the plaster. Her house was so drafty, even now in mid-October. She hated thinking about what the winter would be like. Jackie pulled the comforter tighter around her and focused on her laptop screen—scrolling down her Facebook feed with its lurid shots of five-star dinners and lush gardens she'd never have the time to keep up, of vacations in St. Bart's, Miami, the Mexican Riviera, filtered pictures that made you feel warmer just to look at them.

So many selfies, too. One caught Jackie's eye: Helen Davies, who worked with her at the Potter Bloom real estate agency and had gone to high school with her close to thirty years ago in this very town. Blissful, forever-married Helen with her chunky gold earrings and her Mona Lisa smile, head tilted down, ducking the camera in the same way Jackie did, that middle-aged female way, hoping for low light. But Helen looked so much livelier than Jackie, so much more satisfied, her peachy-skinned, seventeen-year-old daughter Stacy thrust in front of her like the lovely feature she was.

Girls' day in the city, the caption read. *Shopping at Saks!*

Jackie looked at Stacy's bright smile and felt a stab of jealousy. Did they know their children better than she did, these mothers of daughters? Were they as happy as they looked?

Stupid question. Nobody was as happy as they looked on Facebook—even Jackie knew that. She reached for her glass of Chardonnay and took a long swallow, feeling the comforting tartness of it at the back of her tongue, the warmth as it slid down her throat. She glanced down at the corner of the screen. 1:00 A.M. Time to sleep. Or try to. Why did her brain do this to her every night? She'd wander through her whole day exhausted, and then as soon as it was time to go to bed, all of the worries and misgivings she'd successfully buried during the past fourteen hours would pop out of their shallow graves, one by one, and parade through her brain, keeping her awake. Memories, too. Like the time she was showing her very first house and the couple got the time wrong and she wound up half an hour late at Wade's preschool, showed up to find him sitting on the bench in the parking lot, his little face pinched red, teacher dabbing at his tears . . .

Mommy, where were you? Did you forget about me?

Jackie slid open her nightstand drawer, plucked out her bottle of Xanax. She took half a pill – just half, washed down with the rest of the Chardonnay. By the time she'd logged out of Facebook, closed the laptop screen and flicked off her light, her breathing had slowed and she felt calm again. Resigned, anyway. Jackie closed her eyes and drifted off, drowsy and warm with the knowledge that everything in life was temporary, life included. And really, when it all came down to it, nothing was worth the effort it took to worry.

A sound jolted Jackie awake, she wasn't sure what. She'd been dreaming she was in a rowboat in the middle of choppy waters and the oars wouldn't reach and when she woke, she felt queasy from something, either the dream or the Chardonnay. It took her several seconds to blink the cobwebs out of her brain and focus on the sound, which was coming from across the hall—a scuffling, the clink of metal. She reached for her phone. *911*, she thought. *Call 911. No. No, breathe first. Listen. Could be the wind. Could be anything.*

Jackie breathed. Three deep breaths, what Helen called cleansing breaths, Helen and her yoga classes: out with the bad energy, in with the good. She tried to focus on the scuffling, really hear it. She exhaled again, hard, air tumbling out of her. Listened.

Arnie. Connor's pet hamster, racing around his cage. But still . . . She couldn't quite rest.

From down the hall, near the front door, Jackie heard the creak of floorboards. A thump. She bolted up to sitting. Looked at the digital clock on her nightstand. 2:07 A.M.

Heart pounding up into her throat, Jackie grabbed her phone, crept toward the bedroom door, bare feet on the hardwood floor, heel to toe, heel to toe, breath soft and shallow, arms straight out like a tightrope walker . . . *Don't make a sound.*

She pressed 911 on her phone, her finger hovering over the send button. If she saw anything, anyone . . . She cracked the door. *Don't hurt my boys,* she thought. As though they were smaller than her. *You hurt my boys, I'll kill you.*

Jackie peered into the darkened hallway.

Behind Connor's closed door, Arnie squeaked and shuffled in his cage.

Jackie kept a baseball bat by her bedroom door, left over from Wade's long-forgotten Little League days. She took the bat in hand, the cool metal at her palm calming her.

She moved into the hallway. "Hello," she said. "Anyone there?"

Jackie flipped the hall light on. She glided across the hall to Connor's room, bat and phone in the same hand. With the other, she cracked the door. The room was warm, pitch dark, heavy with the sound of her son's sleep-breathing, Arnie's insistent squeaks. Her eyes adjusted. No one in here but the two of them.

She exhaled, her heartbeat slowing as the last shards of sleep fell away and everything grew clear. *Okay*, she thought. *This is what's going on.* She backed out of Connor's room. Softly closed his door.

Wade's door was ajar, and she knew without looking that the bed would be empty, that the thumps she'd heard earlier had been the sound of someone leaving the house, not breaking in. From where she was standing, she could see him through the long window next to the front door, the shadow of him in the porch light. A few steps closer and she saw him in full. Wade. His back to the house, the glow of his cigarette. Watching the stars. *When did he get so tall?*

Jackie should stop him, she knew. He needed to sleep. He shouldn't be smoking. She knew all of this. But she couldn't.

Let him have this.

Jackie slipped back into her own room, slid open her nightstand drawer and took the other half a Xanax, this time with nothing. She pulled the comforter up to her chin and closed her eyes, waiting for the calm. As she started to drift, she found herself thinking of Wade. How smiley and talkative he'd been when he was little, so eager to please. He was different now. A different boy, a sad boy . . .

No, sad was the wrong word. Sad was something she understood.

Pearl Maze was on the phone with the drunk's wife when the rain started.

"I'm sorry, Ma'am," Pearl was saying, eyes on the drunk, headache starting to blossom. "But we can't just hold him here indefinitely."

"Isn't that what they're for?" the wife said. "Holding cells? I mean, Jesus. It's three in the morning. Why should I have to suffer for his idiocy?"

"We don't have a holding cell, Ma'am," she said. "We're too small for a holding cell. We just have a holding bench."

The drunk was cuffed to the bench. His head lolled to one side and his eyes were half-closed and his mouth open, drool trickling out the side of his clean-shaven face and into the collar of his pink-and-white striped, Oxford cloth shirt. The drunk did have a name, though Pearl didn't see the point in remembering it, him losing consciousness and all. She'd typed it into the computer and fingerprinted him after Tally and Nadell had brought him in, kicking and screaming that he'd committed no crime, that he hadn't been driving, he'd been enjoying the evening for chrissakes and looking up at the stars and what the hell did they mean, disturbing the peace, disturbing the peace was his *God-given right as an American, you're all worse than my wife, you know that?*

The drunk wasn't from around here—he was visiting from New York City. A leaf peeper, staying at the Pine Gables B&B with his incredibly put-out-sounding wife. Pearl was over and done with the both of them. *Go back to New York City. I'll pay for your train tickets.* The whole booking room stunk of him now—whiskey and stale cigarettes and whatever else he'd rolled around in between consuming five Jamesons and a beer chaser at the Red Door Tavern and sitting cross-legged in the middle of Main Street, yelling obscenities at the flashing traffic light. The smell wasn't doing anything to relieve her headache. Pearl shut her eyes and squeezed the bridge of her nose. She needed a glass of water, two cups of coffee, three Advil.

"All right, fine," said the wife. "I'll be right over."

"Thank you." Pearl hung up. *Thank you, Jesus.*

The drunk said, "She coming?"

Pearl nodded.

He nodded back at her. Then he leaned over and threw up all over the booking-room floor.

"Beautiful." Pearl jumped up from the desk and hurried into the break room to get paper towels and water and away from the drunk. That's when the sky opened up. *Could this night get any better?*

"What happened in there?" Nadell said it as though he couldn't care less. He said everything as though he couldn't care less. Nadell was one of the younger officers, about Pearl's age. Nice enough, she guessed, but to her mind he was suspiciously mellow for a cop. He'd grown up in this town. Maybe that had something to do with it.

Pearl looked at him: those watery blue eyes, that weak, little boy's chin. Cradling a mug with a map of New York State on it in smooth cherubic hands. She felt old enough to be his mother. "You don't want to know."

He chuckled. "Jim Beam tossed his cookies, huh?"

Pearl found a bucket and started to fill it in the sink. "Jim Beam," she said. "That's a good one." She grabbed a glass out of one of the cupboards, held it under the running faucet and gulped it down. The rain drummed on the roof. It made her heart pound. *Any day now*, she thought. *Any day the roof will cave in . . .*

Pearl had known about the structural damage since she took this job. All the cops joked about it because what else are you going to do? In keeping with the rest of Sawkill, which was more often than not referred to as Historic Sawkill, it was a charming-looking building— bright blue shutters, brass door knocker. Window boxes even, as ridiculous as that may sound. But it was also condemned. A shell of a place, falling apart for years, though Hurricane Irene had pounded the final nail into its coffin. *The Death Trap*, the sergeant called the station. *The Busted Bunker.* The hardwood floors buckled and popped, wind whistled through gaps in the doorjambs. And on rainy nights like this, the ceilings bled out in dozens of places. Pearl could see a spot now, right at the center of the break room, dripping angrily, water spattering on the floor. Less than one week, and the Sawkill PD would break ground on a new station, Pearl and her fellow officers moving into a double wide in the new parking lot. Closer quarters, but much safer ones, especially considering the nasty winter the weather people kept predicting. *Keep it together, Busted Bunker . . . Just six and a half more days . . .*

A gust of wind knocked into the side of the building, the rain thudding now. Hammering. She ripped off a swath of paper towels, grabbed the full bucket, a bottle of Murphy's oil soap, a mop out of the janitor's closet. *The puke is fixable. Focus on that.*

"Need any help?" Nadell said in his half-hearted way. Pearl shook her head. As she headed down the hall on her way back into the booking room, she was certain she could hear the creak of shingles detaching.

In the booking room, the drunk was slumped on the bench, snoring. Holding her breath, Pearl poured some of the water from the bucket onto the mess he'd made, followed it up with a few squirts of cleaner. It roused him a little. "You don't know," he murmured at her.

"Huh?"

His eyes opened. "You're young," he said. "Just a kid. You don't know yet, how very pointless life can be."

She stared at him for a few seconds, remembering his name. "You're wrong about that, Mr. Fletcher. I do know."

"Shit," he said, not to Pearl but at the explosion of noise—a furious pounding on the front door and then the buzzer, someone leaning on it so hard it was as though they wanted to break it.

"That doesn't sound like your wife, does it?"

He shook his head.

Pearl rushed toward the door, Nadell, Tally and then the Sergeant leaving his office, moving in front of Pearl, pressing the intercom and trying to talk to her, the woman on the other side of the door, trying to calm her, half-screaming, half-crying like women never did on the quiet streets of this historic Hudson Valley town.

"Please, Ma'am," the sergeant said. "We are going to let you in."

But she didn't seem to hear. "An accident." That was all she kept saying, over and over again, even after he opened the door for her and she fell through it—make-up smeared, weeping, wet as something dredged up from the river. "There's been an accident."

"Mom?" Connor called out from the kitchen.

Jackie couldn't answer. She was in Wade's doorway, eyes fixed on his empty bed.

"Mom!"

Jackie swallowed hard, made her way into the kitchen. It smelled of the coffee she'd set to brew last night. "Can you take me to Noah's house?" Connor said it around a mouthful of cereal. He was sitting at the kitchen table, back turned to her, eating fast. "I'm gonna be late."

Jackie said, "I thought Wade was taking you."

"I . . . He said he didn't have time."

"He said that?"

"Yes."

"This morning?"

"Yes, Mom . . ."

"It's ten." She said it slowly, staring at the back of his head. "Why didn't he have time? The SATs don't start till eleven-thirty."

Connor shrugged elaborately. "How do I know? I just need a ride." The word *ride* pitched up an octave. The back of his neck flushed red. Poor kid, voice constantly betraying him. Puberty was cruel and, for Connor, it often proved a lie detector, his voice cracking more than usual during those still-rare attempts to be deceitful.

"Connor."

"Yeah?"

"Did Wade come home last night?"

"What?" A thin squeak.

"It's a simple question."

"Mom, if I don't leave for Noah's like now, we won't have enough time to work on our science project."

"Did you see him?" Jackie said. "Did you see your brother this morning?"

"Yeah, of course I did." He said it quietly, carefully. "He was leaving when I got up. Said he was late."

"Look at me."

Connor turned around. He blinked those sad blue eyes at her, his father's eyes. "Mom," he said. "Are you okay?"

Jackie swallowed. *No*, she wanted to say. *I'm not okay. I used to know you guys so well I could read your thoughts, and now, it's as though every day, every minute even, I know you less. You're turning into strangers.*

You're turning into men.

She looked at the half-empty coffee pot, the demolished bowl of cereal placed next to the sink, unemptied, unwashed, a few stray Cheerios swimming in puddled milk. Wade never washed out his cereal bowls. Connor did. Wade drank coffee. Connor did not. Wade had been here this morning, she decided. Last night, he'd had his moment on the front step with his cigarette and the stars, and then he'd come back inside. He'd gone back to bed, gotten up this morning and left early, for whatever reason. Connor wasn't lying. Connor didn't lie. Not about anything big, anyway. *You still know them that much.*

"Mom?"

"I'm fine."

"You sure?"

She cleared her throat. "Maybe after I get home from work, you and Wade and I can do something."

Connor looked at her as though she'd just sprouted a third eye. "Umm."

"Maybe go out to dinner. See a movie? Talk?"

He blinked at her again. "Sure," he managed after a drawn-out pause during which they both locked eyes, a type of stand-off.

Jackie smiled. It was natural, she knew, this aching feeling, this growing divide between the boys she raised and herself. All those books she used to read, the shrink she used to go to, all of them told her that as a single mother of sons she needed to maintain distance, to teach them to stand on their own early, lest they grow up too dependent on her, too possessive. Nobody liked a mama's boy. But still, that didn't make it any easier, your baby wincing at the thought of spending time with you.

"Go get your stuff, and I'll take you to Noah's."

Connor propelled himself out of the room.

Jackie went to the sink, spilled the milk and cereal out of Wade's bowl and rinsed it, thinking about all the times she'd yelled at him to rinse his bowl, how carefully she'd explained to him that if he didn't wash it out right away, the cereal would crust on and never come off, no matter how many times she put it through the washer. She'd shown him the evidence—the scarred, ruined bowls, cereal remnants clinging to the sides like cement. Wade would nod at her, that dyed black hair of his flopping into his eyes, but it never sunk in. Or maybe he ignored her on purpose, the same way, without warning, he'd blackened the sandy blond hair that used to match her own. The way he'd taken his phone yesterday morning, checking his texts without looking at her. And how he'd said, *See you later, Mom* in that calm, unreadable voice, without making eye contact, without looking at her at all.

It was normal, the way the boys treated her, the way they made her feel. Growing up was hard and parents bore the brunt of it, mothers especially. Mothers of teenage sons.

It is normal, she thought. *Isn't it?* And then the doorbell rang. The police.